Between
Tungsten
& Gold

by Taryn Skipper

◊SPLINTER PRESS

© 2025 **Taryn Skipper**
All rights reserved.

No part of this publication may be reproduced, distributed, or transmitted in any form or by any means, including photocopying, recording, or other electronic or mechanical methods, without the prior written permission of the publisher, except as permitted by U.S. copyright law. For permission requests, contact info@splinterpress.com.

This book is a work of fiction. Names, characters, places and incidents are the product of the author's imagination and are used fictitiously. Any resemblance to actual events, locales, or persons, living or dead, is coincidental.

Cover art by Taryn Skipper
Chapter art by Taryn Skipper
Cover design by Elesa Hagberg

Published by:
Splinter Press,
Spanish Fork, Utah
splinterpress.com

ISBN-13: 978-1-960108-17-3

To C. A., A. C., and R. S.—I love you more. So, hah.

CHAPTER ONE

Desperate Times Call for Cheese

Teleportation was the ultimate life hack no one could shut up about. An avalanche of praise for my parents' invention buried any other headlines when they unveiled the teleportation booth network. From painful morning commutes to life-threatening delays in disaster relief, all our problems were solved, they said. A decade later, the severed hand dominating my news feed told a different story.

I lifted my dad's antique cell phone from my shoebox of assorted components and set it gently onto our pitted linoleum counter, then propped up my phone. In the shaky video, the bodiless hand leaked all over the bottom of a teleportation booth. A delicate, gold chain sparkled against dark blood. Fashionable, probably, but you can't buy twenty-four-karat gold these days without signing a mountain of waivers. Anyone who passed the booth license exam and got a card knew gold was too dense to teleport. An official-looking person in an Emergency Teleportation Commission windbreaker picked up the bracelet with a white-gloved hand and turned away from the purple booth, angling the charm into the morning light. The other two booths in our block's row of three stood immediately to the right, and I spotted our beigey-gray apartment building in the background.

I stopped the video and rubbed my jaw, sore from clenching. The sun had set hours ago, and the sky outside my kitchen window finally matched my stabby mood. Every port booth accident made me want to break something, and the news reels hadn't failed to point out that this one hit less than fifty meters outside the door of the late scientists whose invention it was. My apartment, where my parents spent sleepless nights running calculations and formulas. My home, where I'd pretend to be asleep in the mornings so Dad would roll me up like a breakfast burrito and carry me downstairs. Where they'd tinker with prototypes at the kitchen table until my big sister Nadia ported us home from school. I'd never forgive them for getting themselves killed in the name of science, but they'd devoted their lives to building a better world. It wasn't fair for the world to remember them only when something tragic happened.

I yanked open the silverware drawer and dug until I found the paring knife with the broken tip. It might have snapped when I'd pried the housing off our toaster, but who could tell, really? And now it was the perfect size for the screws on my latest project.

I popped open the old phone's casing and hurried to remove the screws holding the guts together. Everything would go dark in half an hour, when the Emergency Teleportation Commission throttled overnight power to charge the teleportation booths' emergency backup batteries. I had enough time to desolder the obsolete pairing chip and make room for a faster one with more range.

I understood the need to regulate power, but the lack of nighttime electricity ranked high on my list of ways the ETC managed to annoy me, right up there with their stingy tech policies. Someday, I would submit the application with the ETC to purchase an actual soldering iron. For now, I plugged in Nadia's curling wand. It would do until she caught me.

My gaze drifted out the window to our leaf-strewn street while I waited for the wand to heat. Our row of teleportation booths stood a few meters down in muted colors I'd named day-old-bruise purple, gaslight blue, and pustule mustard. Bright safety lights reflected off the glossy plastic walls, and a scrap of leftover police tape still fluttered against the light post, tainting my parents' legacy. The glow from the next row of booths shone between apartment buildings, about halfway down the block.

Blinking red light flashed around the edges of the middle booth's door, indicating an incoming user. Seconds later, a delivery person balancing a stack of four pizzas exited the booth, pushing the gray-blue door open with his elbow and then letting it glide shut behind him. The design firm behind the booths' aesthetic called it a "tonal postmodern minimalist" look. To me, they looked like a cell phone from the 1990s and a fridge from the 1950s had a sad, beige baby.

The light on Nadia's curling wand changed from red to green. I pulled a silicone oven mitt out of the drawer and used it to grasp the wand close to the end. I held a paper clip against the metal to create a smaller soldering tip and focused on reworking only the solder holding the chip in place, and not destroying anything else. It would take more patience than I could usually scrounge up, but I had to get this right. I couldn't work in FutureMove's teleportation labs until I finished school, which cost money I didn't have. So if I wanted to make progress improving booth safety, I had to get creative.

My parents founded FutureMove with their buddy from grad school, Dr. Shane Clarke, almost twenty years ago. They enjoyed ten years running headlong into research and development of better and faster tech, plus another five free years after they opened the teleportation booth network, before the ETC took regulatory control over the company and implemented safety measures. My parents pushed back against the restrictions for another year until their luck ran out and they died in their lab. I was thirteen when they sliced my heart to shreds, and for the past four years, every report of an avoidable injury twisted the knife a little deeper. The device I was building would be a massive step toward ending these stupid accidents for good.

One of my hearing aids chimed. Low battery. I didn't have a free hand for that; one held the wand and the other steadied the wand's end, ready to pull the chip away. The solder points started to give. *Almost there... Got it!* I set the curling wand down, and the paper clip stuck to it. I'd melted it to the wand's plastic cap. *Oops.* Nadia would flip when she saw it, but she'd forgive me once I made this remote work.

The old phone, my dad's ancient Gooseberry, had lain abandoned in his nightstand drawer well past its prime. But it ran the Goose operating system, same as the port booths. Since it was an older phone, it didn't have as much dense metal to replace as a slightly newer model would, and the touch screen and physical buttons made it the perfect vessel for my DIY booth remote. Once I installed a longer-ranged pairing chip, I'd be able to communicate with the port booth from a distance, changing settings and destinations without having to stand inside. I'd risk only whatever dense metal I used for testing, and keep my extremities attached while I foolproofed port booth safety.

If I could demonstrate successful safety upgrades, the ETC overlords would release their clutches on FutureMove, my parents would finally receive the caveat-free respect they deserved, and I'd have a job at the company. My own headlines would roll in: "Alyona Zolotova, Genius Daughter of Teleportation's Inventors, Perfects What They Started." Nadia and I would both gain access to the best tools on the market, whether for soldering circuits or curling ringlets.

But I wouldn't make my debut in anyone's news feed—at least not for anything good—until I made a lot more progress, and my next move required a second body. I preferred to work solo, like an angsty lone-bat action hero, with no one around to hear me mumbling half-formed thoughts out loud. But when my work required the help of an eager sidekick, I was lucky to have the best one ever close at hand. I squatted at the kitchen vent by my feet, which carried anything I shouted straight into my downstairs neighbor's living room.

"Hey! Jax! Get up here for a minute!" I picked up my laptop and a clipboard and patted my back pocket to make sure my trusty set of lock picks were there, ready to assist with the next step of my plan.

Jaxon Jeong's familiar knock sounded, and I tugged open my sticky front door. My bestie's navy sweats, Boba Fett t-shirt, and dark, tousled hair worked together to remind me why Nadia didn't allow boys in the apartment while she wasn't home.

Too bad I'd friend-zoned myself two years ago. He'd ported us to a quiet park on the south side of town and asked me to his senior prom. The shock of Jaxon acting out a scene I'd fantasized sent me into vocal arrest. I stared at him, silent and unblinking, slowly stepping backward into the booth. I punched in some random numbers and ended up fifteen miles away at a cheese festival where I sampled brie until I felt like it was safe to go home. I'd avoided the subject—and soft cheeses—ever since.

I pointed at his ocean-blue socks with swirling yellow

jellyfish. "You should have worn shoes, Baby Shark. We're going on a field trip."

Jaxon smiled and leaned against the door frame. "So nice to see you, too, Alyona. No, I wasn't doing anything important."

"This is way more important than whatever textbook you were probably reading down there. It's my second-to-last step." My Gooseberry remote would provide a quick and efficient path to my last step: to fix whatever fault my parents didn't eliminate in their quest to teleport denser materials.

"Is this a walking excursion, or should I grab my bike?" Jaxon lifted his left pant leg, revealing a dull metal bracelet locked around his ankle. He'd been growing his ridiculous sock collection as long as I'd known him, but the disciplinary accessory was only added to his wardrobe about a month ago. The dense, tungsten core made it impossible for him to port, keeping him close to the ETC's parental presence.

"We're walking to the booths, but not going in. You know those maintenance devices the tech guys connect to install updates?"

"Yeah?"

"I made my own. Almost." It currently sat nested among various parts and tools on the counter, a baby booth fix, nearly ready to hatch. "I can pick up a pairing chip tomorrow morning, so I want to get the booth end set up to receive a signal in the meantime." My other hearing aid chimed. They'd both run out of batteries by the end of the night, and I couldn't get new ones until the swaps opened up the next day.

"Wow, Aly, that's legit!"

A smile sneaked across my face. I loved that nickname. Nadia dropped the *a* sometimes and called me Alyon, or she'd call me the cutesiest version of my name, Alyonushka, to annoy me. Only Jaxon called me Aly.

I polished my uneven fingernails on my shirt. "Yeah, I'm awesome."

Jaxon gestured for me to lead the way with a flourish and a bow. I tucked my laptop and clipboard under my arm, curtsied, and headed outside toward the booths. Jaxon followed, shoeless and ready for shenanigans. For him, my tinkering was an excuse to hang out. While I was always glad to have Jaxon time, for me, taking things apart and finding new ways to put them back together helped me feel in control when so much around me was broken.

"So you'll be able to talk to booths with this thing? Make them obey your every command like a cyberpunk supervillain?"

I turned, walking backward to face him, and tapped my fingers together. "Mwa-haha! My evil plan is nearly complete. I need to plug in directly because the ETC is actually smart enough not to allow remote account creation." They at least tried to keep FutureMove data secure, which made my experiment more complicated. Another thing to add to my list of good but annoying ETC moves.

A breeze sent a chill through the October air, and the hairs on my arms stood up. I should have grabbed my jacket, but I'd been too excited to consider bodily comfort. Or maybe the goosebumps were due to the fact that we'd be messing with the booths out in the open, where it was much easier to be caught. I'd planned the operation for the quiet time before the power cut out and nighttime security made rounds, but I couldn't guarantee no one would come by.

I aimed for the circuit breaker first. "Hold these," I said, extending the clipboard and laptop to Jaxon.

Jaxon took them and waved the clipboard in the air. "There's nothing on this."

"Well, don't show the whole block."

Jaxon pulled the clipboard down and hid his face behind it. "Sorry."

"It doesn't need to have anything on it. It's risk mitigation. Hold it up and smile at anybody coming to or from a booth, and they'll assume we're official." It would work fine for the general public, but I'd get in and out as fast as my fingers could go. An empty clipboard wouldn't do us any good if an ETC patrol came by.

I pulled my lockpick set from my back pocket and opened the thin wallet-style holder. The padlock hanging from the breaker box was a popular and easily bypassed brand. It wouldn't take any finesse, so I chose the rake pick. I placed a narrow tension wrench just inside the keyway and pressed gently in the direction the lock would turn. Then I scraped the thin, bumpy rake pick quickly across the lock's internal pins a few times, knocking them above the sheer line. I popped the lock in four seconds flat, opened the breaker door, and swapped the padlock for my laptop with Jaxon.

"Okay, look." I pointed to the second breaker down on the left. "When I say so, flip this switch off and then on again."

"I can handle that." Jaxon made a flicking motion in the air.

"But not too fast, it has to power down, and then back up again. But not too slowly, because—"

"Aly, I know how to flip a breaker."

"And only that second left one, not the—"

Jaxon tilted his head and gave me his "I'm not an idiot" look. I felt terrible when he did that. I didn't mean to hurt his feelings, I only wanted to make sure everything went smoothly. This was the most important project I'd ever nearly completed.

"Alright, hold on." I pried open the rubbery cover on the booth's USB port and plugged in a cable connecting my laptop to the base of the far-left booth, the day-old-bruise-purple one. Locals only used the right two, even before this morning's hand incident. A couple years ago, neighborhood kids found a platinum skull ring on the floor of the left one, still attached to an oozing finger. Rumor had it someone who used to work at FutureMove lost it going on the lam after claiming on social media that my parents' experiment was tampered with. The post was debunked, but the kids named the booth Slaughterbox, and it retained a reputation no one on the block wanted to test.

I crouched and plugged my laptop into the other end of the cable. "Ready?"

Jaxon nodded.

"Now!"

Jaxon flipped the switch off and then back on. "Uh oh." He turned his head away from the breaker box and peered down the street.

"You did great. I'm hijacking the boot sequence now. I just have to—"

"No, the sirens. Are they coming closer?"

I scratched the back of my hearing aids. No static feedback meant the batteries had reached the end of their usefulness. It was like putting on earmuffs. Without my hearing aids, I couldn't distinguish consonants, and background noise became nonexistent. "You tell me. My ears are dead."

Jaxon craned his neck toward the street outside our neighborhood. Few people drove anymore, including the police. But the new tungsten-coated handcuffs couldn't teleport, so they kept it old-school and took arrestees downtown by car.

I finally heard the wail of the slow siren as it reached a lower frequency. It was coming closer, all right. The police had no reason to be looking for us, but we didn't need to give them one standing here plugged in, clipboard or no. My fingers shook as they raced across the keyboard, giving myself admin access and creating a backdoor listener for my future pairing chip.

```
> add user system_patch42--password
'k4r4t3Pr13$tbh'
> add user system_patch42--group
admin
[+] Admin account created
>
> pchip_listen--mode pair
[+] Awaiting pairing request . . .
```

"Done! Lock it up. Let's go." I jumped up and ran homeward.

Jaxon clicked the padlock into place and jogged after me on his toes. "You owe me new socks for this. The ground is still dirty from the snow last week."

I turned and stepped backwards to answer him. "You got it, Jax. I'll find you the most random, outrageous socks ever made."

Jax waggled his eyebrows. "Now you're speaking my love language."

I faced forward again so he wouldn't see the color blooming in my cheeks.

If I'd gone to the booths alone, I would have simply teleported anywhere the police weren't. Despite the dangers of porting, the thrill of knowing I could move through space at incomprehensible speeds hadn't dulled since my first trip. My mom was first to port across state lines, and I'd been second when we picked up the design firm's representatives in San Francisco. Looking back, I was naive to trust her with my life on a semi-inaugural long-distance port like that. But that's how kids are. I'd grown up since the accident.

I wrenched my front door open, set the laptop on the table, and pumped my arms into the air as I spun around to face Jaxon. "Yes! Jax, we did it!"

Jaxon held up his watch hand. "And we did it in . . . perfect . . . wait for it . . . time!"

The lights in the apartment blinked out, which meant we had about an hour before Nadia got home from her date.

"What's the last step, now?" Jaxon said.

My mind produced several ideas for steps to take in the dark with Jaxon, but he moved to the fridge. He opened the dark refrigerator a crack, slipped his arm in, pulled out a crinkly package, and slammed the door. Nadia had drilled into both of us how dangerous it was to open the fridge while the power was out. According to her, everything would rot, and we'd die of food poisoning. Our neighbors had upgraded to models with power reserves to keep food cold at night, but they cost more than Nadia made in several paychecks.

The rechargeable light I'd rigged above the kitchen table clicked on, illuminating the half-empty bag of shredded cheddar Jaxon held like a bucket of popcorn.

"Now," I said, "you hand me some cheese, and we find the tech swap location for tomorrow so I can get my pairing chip. Everything else is ready to roll, thanks to your breaker-flipping prowess."

"I'm a flippin' boss, yo."

"Once I add that chip, I'll be able to shoot whatever I put in that booth to any other booth, all from the outside." I flicked a piece of pocket lint toward Jaxon and made a *pew* noise to illustrate.

Jaxon dodged. "I assume that's not a part they carry at the government swaps?"

I let out a sarcastic laugh, shaking my head as I sat at my laptop and logged in to the underground message boards.

The ETC had legal tech swap locations all over the city. But at the right—or wrong—places, you could find less-legal, highly regulated tech by trading in other interesting parts. Those hidden gems showed up at different locations every Saturday, and every Friday I had to hack my way through a series of clues to the hidden port booth code and directions.

Jaxon took the chair next to me. I reached for the cheese, and he slapped my hand. "No celebratory snack for you until you dig up that location code. And hustle. Your battery is low."

He reached across my screen and pointed at the power indicator in the lower right corner. I slapped his hand back.

"*Did'ko*," I said, borrowing my mom's favorite Ukrainian curse. I'd had the laptop on since I called Jaxon through the vent, and It seemed to be draining faster every day. The power would be out for another seven hours.

For normal people.

"No problem, I'll take a quick detour through the grid and turn our electricity back on for a while." A few weeks ago, I'd left a couple of USB drives in FutureMove bathrooms loaded with a spreadsheet titled "next fiscal year raises and layoffs" and waited for someone to open them. The spreadsheet contained macros that, when enabled, would install a keylogger. From there, I had an AI chat bot parse through everything the unsuspecting employees typed into their keyboards. I'd found one employee's fall down a rabbit hole about time zones on the moon, and another who liked to write out email responses to his superiors with colorful descriptions of where they could shove their requests, and then delete them. *Whatever gets you through your day, I guess*. More importantly, I'd found a few functional passwords.

"Stay on target!" Jaxon said, waving cheese in my face. "Just find the location code quickly. The ETC will never let you work at FutureMove if they catch you breaking in. Or you can wait for next week's swap."

I shook my head. "That's where you're wrong." I grabbed him by the shoulders "I can't wait another minute, let alone a week. I'm too close!" I gave him a playful shake.

Jaxon let his head flop around. "Okay, okay."

The power grid software wasn't accessible from the internet, but some numbskull had connected a FutureMove printer to the internet for updates. From the printer port, I took control of a FutureMove computer terminal on the internal network. Whatever I did on the terminal would appear on its monitor, visible to anyone passing by. But it was well after hours, and this wasn't my first digital rodeo. I opened the power grid software with one of my stolen passwords and entered the non-gendered version of our last name, Zolotov, into the customer lookup field and pulled up my account. I hovered the mouse over the slider to override power restrictions and—a big red no battery symbol flashed onto my screen, and it went black.

Oh no.

My chest squeezed inward, and I grabbed the edge of the table. This was bad. I'd left my account wide open on an unmanned FutureMove terminal, with a cursor arrow pointing out my plan, like a big sign saying "Alyona was here." I wouldn't be able to fix *anything* if I got myself banned from my parents' company.

Jaxon slapped his forehead. "Oh, no." His hand slid down to his cheek, and he passed me what was left of the cheese.

I stuffed a pinch of shreds into my mouth and wrangled my reeling brain. "We need power, quick."

Jaxon and I scoured the kitchen for a power source. My stomach dropped lower every second. The longer my name sat up there on the terminal, the better chance some ETC overnight grunt with no life would see it and ruin mine.

I made myself breathe so my brain wouldn't go as blank as

my monitor. "Check the junk drawer. Power banks, batteries, any size—"

"How about your phone?"

"Not a chance. My phone holds all my hopes and dreams. I can't risk it." And by hopes and dreams I meant notes and schemes, and some of the last pictures I'd taken with my parents. It was long overdue for an upgrade, but I couldn't risk hurting it. They'd surprised me with it, told me I was old enough, and that they trusted me with technology. I literally slept with it under my pillow.

Jaxon reached for his back pocket. "Then, my phone?"

"No way." I pointed to his ankle. He'd already been arrested for phone-related charges. "In fact, you should head home. I don't want you guilty by association if they come for me." My heart pounded in my ears.

Jaxon shook his head and pointed at the light above the table. "That's still got a charge!"

"Yes!" I climbed up on the table and pulled the batteries out of the light, casting the kitchen into uneven shadows. I lost my balance and Jaxon shot out of his seat to steady me. *Alright, stop panicking and think.* The batteries would work to keep my laptop running for a while once it started, but I didn't want to drain them during the more power-intensive boot phase. I needed something else to give it an initial boost.

I scanned the room from my elevated vantage point and my eyes rested on the microwave.

"The capacitor!" If it could start a microwave older than Nadia, it could boot a laptop. "We need to remove the cover. Jax, go to my room and find the screwdriver. It's under the bed, inside my left softball shoe. If you find bolts, check the right shoe."

"Aly, breathe. You've got batteries. The light's cover comes off without—"

"No, the microwave, for the quick burst . . . just, screwdriver, please!"

Jaxon turned on his phone's flashlight and jogged up the stairs, shaking his head. Red and blue lights caught my eye from the kitchen window. The flashing crept between buildings at the end of my street. Safety patrols by car? There was nothing illegal about taking a microwave apart, but my heartbeat surged anyway. I ducked my head down and hopped off the table.

Jax came back downstairs and started removing a screw at the back of the microwave.

I pulled the screwdriver out of his hand. "I've got this. You go watch for Nadia. She'll be back soon, and she'll be in a bad mood." She'd reached the point in her relationship when she usually came up with a reason to dump the dude. Finding me taking apart another appliance with a boy in the apartment would put her over the edge.

"You don't trust me with a screwdriver?" Jaxon pouted.

I forced my focus away from his lips and back to the task at hand. "It's not that I don't trust you." I struck a pose with the back of my hand to my forehead and put on my therapist's British accent. "I have deep-seated control issues stemming from childhood trauma, and I'll never let anyone close enough to trust them with even the most mundane of tasks." I joked, but the Social Services-mandated counselor wasn't far off. Just one of many flaws helping kill off any chance of ever leaving the friend zone with Jax.

"No, you're just a control freak," Jaxon said with a smirk. Also true.

"I'll take Nadia watch," he said.

"Thanks, Jax. And see if you can tell what the police are slow-rolling around in cars for." When my hearing aids were working, I could hear Nadia coming. Sort of. I'd connected my hearing aids to her phone's location data with an applet that announced her proximity into my ears. But they'd run out of juice, and I was glad to help Jaxon feel useful.

I held my breath as I removed the microwave's capacitor and tried to avoid shocking myself—a task complicated by the lack of light. I pictured my name still on the FutureMove terminal, glowing brightly on the power override screen without authorization. My heartbeat pounded in my temples.

After much finagling and a few curse words, I'd beaten the batteries and capacitor into submission and hovered my finger over my laptop's power button. "Moment of truth!"

"You have this. No way anyone had time to see anything."

"Well, there's no way to know, barring a knock at the door. But I can at least stop advertising my own ineptitude."

"Oh, good," Jaxon said. "We'll keep your ineptitude between us."

I looked up to glare at him and caught him standing with his back to the window, holding my baby album up to the scant light and smiling like a buffoon.

"Jax! You're supposed to be the lookout!"

"But you're so cute!"

As a baby, he meant. Everybody's cute as a baby. The fluttering in my chest was probably my worry over whether I was about to blow up my computer, or Nadia's impending arrival. I may avoid ETC discipline, but my sister's disappointment would be equally awful.

Jaxon shifted his focus to the street and immediately dropped to his hands and knees. "So, don't panic, but there's an ETC guy walking straight for your front door. Like, ten seconds away."

Panic choked out my next breath, despite Jaxon's instructions. I dived over the back of the couch. My foot knocked the decor on the side table—a defunct computer laid on its side and filled with marbles and trinkets. I pushed the decoration back into place to avoid a loud spill, and then grabbed Jax by the arm. I would not let him be seen here with my tech project and give the ETC an excuse to extend his probation. He fast-crawled as I dragged him across the living room and pushed him against the wall on the far side of the bookshelf. I willed time to stop so that I could freeze there with him for a few seconds.

Harsh pounding on the front door made me jump into the shelf. Someone must have seen my unauthorized meddling on the terminal. I'd taken too much time.

The pounding came again, five fist-slams into the door. "ETC. Open up."

I didn't have a chance to hide my new tech or pretend I wasn't home before the door swung wide and a tall figure in an ETC windbreaker barged into my kitchen.

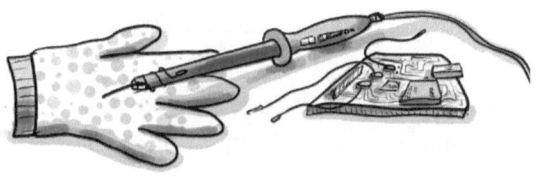

CHAPTER TWO

The Dread Pirate ManBun

THE ETC SECURITY GOON clicked on a flashlight and swept the beam around the main floor of the apartment. He seemed overdressed for night patrol in dark jeans, pointed leather shoes, and a blazer peeking out from under his black windbreaker. Great. I'd gone and ticked off their leader.

"Alyona Zolotova?"

I flinched into the shelf and managed to catch a textbook before it fell onto my foot. "Can I help you?"

The flashlight's beam landed on my face. "You can save us both a little time. I have to get back to HQ. So, if I were to perform a search of these premises, would I find any unauthorized files or tech configurations?"

I did my best to take a slow, even breath. "Um, no, sir." Definitely nothing to find in my desk, in my backpack, or sitting on the kitchen counter. Or a few centimeters from my knee in the hollowed-out book where Mom kept thumb drives with backups of their research. Or in the bottom of the giant can of dried lentils in the cabinet above the fridge, where she kept her backups of the backups. I hoped this would be the only question, and he'd be gone before Nadia came home. But that seemed far too easy.

The executive-looking agent tilted his head, his high bun bouncing against his shaved undercut. He was missing the ball cap with ETC on the front that usually completed the uniform, probably because it wouldn't have fit over his bun. He moved the beam slowly along the rows of books on the shelf. "We've heard reports of tomfoolery in these parts. Care to explain?"

Tom-what now? "Sir?"

"Malarkey. Hijinks. Skullduggery." He pulled a fist up to his chest as he said the last word in a poorly executed pirate voice.

Just when I thought the situation couldn't get any more confusing, Nadia pushed past Captain ManBun and kissed him on the cheek. "Well, now you've ruined it," she said.

ManBun laughed. "I felt bad, Nad. The look on her face . . ."

"You're such a softy, *lapochka moya*." She placed her pale hand onto his olive cheek and followed the term of endearment with another peck to the lips.

Yuck. The tension in my chest melted into a puddle of annoyance.

"Oh, no," I said, using the book in my hand to point to my sister and her kiss buddy. "Tell me this isn't some kind of scared-straight gag."

Nadia giggled. "I was telling him tonight how I could almost guarantee you'd have another appliance completely disassembled before I got home. We thought it would be funny."

"Oh, did we?" I said, frowning.

ManBun pulled Nadia into a loose hug. "I do have to run though, babe. The on-call engineer pinged me about some red flag on the network. I have to go in."

My ears tingled. Some red flag named Alyona Zolotova? Maybe. But if Nadia's new pirate-talking boy toy was the one in charge of catching me, maybe I didn't have anything to worry about.

Nadia pouted and ManBun brushed her cheek with the back of his hand. "Freaking mandatory sweeps for every digital bump in the night. I wish I could stay. I'd love to get to know Alyona and her friend." ManBun turned his smirking face to the dark half of the room by the bookshelf and pegged a spotlight on Jaxon squatting against the wall. "Find what you need over there, pal?"

Jaxon stood too quickly and hit his shoulder on the TV stand. "Ouch. Yeah, no, I guess you don't have that book, Alyona."

Nadia broke from the hug to nail me down with her eye daggers. "Alyona! No boys when I'm gone. You know that."

I shot an eye knife of my own toward ManBun. *Way to go tipping off my sister, you eagle-eyed rat.* "We were just—"

"Studying," Jaxon said.

Nadia repositioned ManBun's arm to point the light at the book in my hand. "You're studying *Human Anatomy and Physiology* together? In the dark?"

My ears burned and my fingers longed to throttle the extraneous man in our apartment for complicating my life. I hefted the book. "No, Nadia, not this one. Anyway, you'd better let this guy go." Forever.

ManBun winked at me. "Unfortunately, yes. But I think it's great you're playing with electronics. Best way to learn. I remember giving myself a good shock with a battery and some copper wire about your age. Great to finally meet you."

My ears burned hotter, embarrassment shifting to rage. He was ten years older than me, tops, the condescending jerk. I was seventeen, not a child goofing around with a circuitry kit.

ManBun and his snitching flashlight finally left, and Jaxon followed him out the door with a quick salute.

I took control of the conversation before Nadia could lay into me. She was already upset, and she hadn't seen what we'd done to the kitchen. "So, how was Monte Cristo?"

Nadia tried and failed to keep her glare in place. Her eyebrows relaxed into rainbow shapes as she hugged her purse. "Perfect. The trip was perfect, he's perfect . . . but Monte Cristo is a sandwich."

"Oh, yeah." With swiss. "Monte . . ."

"Carlo." She closed her eyes. "Like a fairy tale. Oh!" Nadia reached into her jacket pocket. "Look what the ocean pushed right up to our feet on our walk! It's perfect." She held up a smooth, beige, heart-shaped pebble and placed it on top of the marbles in the computer decoration.

I snatched it back out on impulse. The yellowed, boxy computer had been Dad's first. He'd refused to throw it out. Too full of memories, he'd said, even if the hard drive didn't have enough memory to run a modern program. Mom filled it halfway with blue and green marbles, topped them with a shell she'd found on their honeymoon, and called the piece "Memory Marbles." No way I could let Nadia put some dude's rock next to the tiny umbrella from Dad's coconut drink and the clay bead I found on a hike with Mom.

"Hey!" she protested.

I took a breath and reminded myself to choose my battles, just for tonight. "Sorry, I wanted a better look." I pushed it into a corner until it was half-concealed by marbles. "How does he get to port across the world like that?" Dad had insisted the port grid remain cost-free for Denver's users, and Mom had convinced the city to keep the clause in their contract by arguing that the Regional Transportation Department would save over a billion dollars annually by switching from bus and light rail to porting. But international porting was not cheap.

"As head of security, his booth card has priority clearance. He's amazing." She squinted at me. "What do you have in your hair?"

I raked my fingers through my dark-brown mane. It was cheese, but she didn't need to know that. "So, you're not at the breakup stage yet?"

The typical maternal edge seeped back into Nadia's voice. "Of course not. We should set up a double date. He might be the one, and I think he and Jaxon would get along."

My cheeks turned pink, and I hoped Nadia's voice wasn't carrying down the vent. "Jaxon isn't . . ." I said in a low voice. Jaxon wasn't into me like that anymore. I'd blown my chance, and he'd dated a couple of randos in the interim. I was grateful our friendship reverted to normal. I needed him too much to risk making things awkward again.

Nadia plucked another piece of cheese out of my hair and grimaced. "Well?"

I appreciated the gist of her suggestion. She didn't tell me much about the guys she liked anymore, or anything overly personal since our relationship status changed from "sisters" to "it's complicated." Mama Nadia was great, but Team Siblings got pretty lonely when she'd taken the promotion to parent. She must really like this joker.

"Maybe," I said. "I'm booked for a while. I've got some copper wire to wrap around a battery."

"Oh, lighten up. He was only trying to connect with the electronics talk."

"I'm good, thanks."

"Speaking of lightening up, why is it so dark in here?" Nadia reached for the kitchen light switch.

I pulled her into a side hug and veered left before she

realized I'd taken the light apart. "You must be exhausted, right?"

"I suppose I could sleep. We walked half the city. They don't allow porting anywhere near the tourist areas over there. I'd almost forgotten how nice it was to stroll, hand-in-hand, under the stars . . ."

"That sounds, like, so amazing," I deadpanned. What did sound amazing was the prospect of getting upstairs to finally get my search off that ETC screen. Then maybe cloning Manbun's booth card sometime, and making it look like he was going about his business while Jax and I found our own non-heart-shaped beach rocks. "I want to hear all about it over breakfast."

"No, you don't." Nadia laughed. "Good night, love you, Alyonushka."

"'Night, *babe*."

Nadia growled at my kissy face and left up the stairs. I'd spared myself her wrath, but only for the night.

She'd most likely kill me in the morning.

CHAPTER THREE

Trouble Afoot

Natural light trickled into my windowless bedroom from the hallway. I pulled my phone out from under my pillow, turned off my alarm, and opened the news feed before heading down to whatever breakfast Nadia made.

Nadia started in on me before I even made it into her line of sight. "*Chto za yerunda,* Alyona! What did you do?"

I backed up a step.

"I heard you. I know you're there." Curse that squeaky step and curse my dead hearing aid batteries for not warning me I'd hit it.

I plodded down the rest of the stairs. Nadia held her melty curling wand like an injured kitten, pulling at the paperclip I'd accidentally attached.

"It was maimed for a good cause, I promise. I'm about to eradicate booth accidents." Getting closer to eradicating them, anyway.

Nadia raised an eyebrow, and I tilted my phone toward her so she could watch the replay of the hand incident. She paled and turned away.

Just as I shoved an entire slice of bread into my mouth,

my phone vibrated in my hand. I recognized the special buzzing pattern I used only for Jaxon. Chewing furiously, I checked my reflection in the microwave door. Mornings were not kind.

Nadia smirked. "You'd better answer. I'm not sure how long you two can go without talking before you implode."

I glared at her and raked my fingers through my hair.

Nadia tucked a flyaway lock behind my ears, and then patted my curls. "There's no helping this hair without my wand. But he's seen you looking way worse and hasn't run yet."

I turned abruptly from my reflection. "I'm checking for crumbs. I don't care how I look." My face flushed. I angled toward the window and hoped the light would wash out my ruddy skin tone.

Jaxon's winking picture floated above the words *Accept video chat?*

I swiped *yes*.

Jaxon leaned against a wrought-iron park bench, his road bike visible behind him.

"What's up, biker boy?" I said. "You forget it's the weekend?"

"Biker *man,* thank you. I had to get out before my upstairs neighbor started stomping around in search of Crunch Munchies cereal."

"Shut up, you and your kale smoothies are so jealous. Sweet helmet, by the way."

Jaxon knocked the side of a neon pink bike helmet and flashed me his exaggerated fashion model smile. He had no idea how gorgeous he was, the giant dork. Meanwhile, the light from the window had only managed to highlight my halo of frizzy, unbrushed hair.

"Safety first. I'm glad I'm biking instead of porting. Yesterday's accident is still all over the feed."

"What are you watching the news feed for? Aren't you supposed to be preparing for your interview? Procrastination scrolling is *my* thing."

"I got a decent amount of prep in before I was so rudely interrupted last night."

Nadia squished into the chair with me and pushed her head into view of the video call. "Jaxon, are you getting a new job?"

"Hi, Nadia." He waved at the phone. "Tutoring for pay on campus. They've got a sister university in San Diego, where I'm hoping I'll work at least some days once my probation is over."

I squeezed Nadia's arm. "Work-study jobs get a guaranteed interstate port pass. We're hitting the beach!"

"*If* you convince me to let you in the booth with me. Better be nice." Jaxon's curved lips distracted me from whatever else he might have said.

I hip-checked my sister off my chair. "Plus he'll get free elective credit. His parents will only pay for college if he chooses a business major. But he wants, what, Anthropology-something, right?"

"Social Anthropology, yeah," Jaxon said. "But the interview isn't until Monday and the news reels are making me nervous about interstate porting. I am somewhat partial to my limbs."

Nadia walked to the sink, jerked the handle on the dripping faucet, and filled her mug. "The booths aren't supposed to allow anything to teleport when they detect heavy metals. FutureMove had a company-wide meeting about it when we completed the density sensors."

"And you'd trust your life to that? Even after the sensor install, people lost body parts and mutilated a cemetery's worth of cell phones."

I pulled the last two slices of bread out of the bag on the table. "If I wore jewelry, I'd play it safe and give up gold altogether. Maybe switch to a nice string of pearls."

"It's those anarchist hackers we can't trust," Nadia said, taking a drink from her mug. My boyfriend says the ETC is tracking down their leadership." She pulled her fuchsia lips into an angry pout. "What kind of person hurts others for fun?"

Jaxon snickered. "My dentist."

I sighed at his dad joke and set the phone face-down.

"Hey!" Jaxon said.

I leaned back in my chair. "The ETC probably wants a scapegoat for when their safety measures don't work. Either way, porting is perfectly safe when people take responsibility for what they're porting with instead of relying on the ETC. Why put your life in their hands?"

"Or put your hands in their hands, as the case may be. You'll lose them faster than a medieval thief," Jaxon wheezed in his *I'm-so-hilarious* voice.

I propped up the phone and made a face like the laugh-crying emoji. "So funny." Jaxon swore his nerdy humor helped the kids he tutored remember the facts, but I wasn't sure how they hadn't strangled him.

"*Voobshe*, Alyona." We'd unleashed Nadia's inner babushka. "That was a real person, you know. With people who love her. *Uzhasno*. Not funny."

I shook my head at Jaxon. "Seriously, dude, have some decorum." I sneaked him a grin, but Nadia was right, as usual. I put up a good front most of the time and tried to avoid investing emotion into every tragedy on the news—I had my own to manage. But I couldn't ignore this accident, right in our own row of booths. I had to get that pairing chip today.

My sister punched some non-responsive buttons on the

microwave and whirled around. "Alyona." Cold tea water splashed onto the counter as Nadia banged her mug down.

The noise was muffled with my hearing aids dead, but I still winced.

"I thought I said no more tampering with kitchen appliances. Now you've ruined the microwave *and* the stove. I can't even make tea. I'd have some toast instead but . . ." She picked up what was once the toaster lever and dropped it back into the pile of assorted metal parts.

I held up the empty bread bag. "We're out of bread, anyway."

Nadia glared at me under her long lashes.

"And you shouldn't microwave your tea, Nadia. I don't trust those things."

"Alyona!"

"I'll fix it," I said. "The microwave is easy. I needed to borrow the capacitor last night."

Jaxon clicked his tongue at me from the phone. "For shame," he said as if he hadn't helped me take the thing apart himself.

"Whatever, just put it back," said Nadia.

I couldn't put it back; the capacitor was blackened and smelled like the fresh excrement of a sickly robot. "It'll be working by tomorrow. Jaxon and I are going on a parts swap."

"That's what you said last week about the stove." Nadia wrapped her ridiculous fuzzy pink scarf around her bleached, flat-ironed hair. She normally curled it after she straightened it—which struck me as maddeningly inefficient given our natural curls—but I'd made that impossible. I added the curling wand to my mental list of transgressions to make right. Oven, toaster, microwave, kitchen light, curling iron. Maybe she'd relax if I fixed everything in one go.

"It will, I promise," I said. "And don't forget the bread on your way home." I shoved the last morsel of pumpernickel into my mouth.

Nadia sneered on her way out the door, as intimidating as an angry baby bunny. "Can you at least resist the urge to destroy anything else today?"

"I prefer the term reverse-engineer." I blew her an exaggerated kiss and a few dark crumbs. "Love you. Have a good day."

"Love you too," Jaxon said from my phone, mimicking my sing-song tone.

Nadia rolled her eyes at me but winked toward my phone at Jaxon. "Don't let Alyona get you into any more trouble." She slammed the door on her way out so it would close properly. We couldn't afford to heat the whole neighborhood, as she put it.

"She's still working Saturdays?" Jaxon's face zipped out of view as he turned his phone around, probably strapping it onto his arm. After a few seconds of jostling, the intricate gold-leafed patterns of the Capitol walls glittered in the rising sunlight as Jaxon pedaled past.

"Somebody's got to answer FutureMove's phones."

FutureMove allowed us to stay in the apartment rent-free—something our parents had set up in case anything were to happen to them. But we still had to pay for everything else: essentials like bread, online college courses, and Nadia's cosmetics subscription boxes. Dr. Clarke helped us further by employing Nadia as the head receptionist, even though she was barely eighteen at the time.

I balanced my phone on top of the toaster's heating element, the capacitor, and the stove's fuse as I carried them upstairs. Jaxon and I spent half our days on video chats, so we were used to long silences. I fished my backpack out from where it had fallen down the crack between my bed and the wall and stuffed the pile of components inside. I added the fried kitchen light rechargeables to the rattly tin of used batteries I kept in the front pouch, then retrieved my earbuds to help hear Jaxon while he wasn't holding the phone to his face.

I propped up the phone on my desk in time to watch Jaxon's view pass under Bonita Boulivard on the Biino Creek bike trail, almost an hour's ride away. "You *did* leave early."

"Working off interview jitters." The phone's view tilted sideways—he was probably taking a swig from the flask he wore on a silly belt for long rides. He passed the Denver Performing Arts Complex, where dull construction fabric still covered the largest buildings, making the whole area appear drab and claustrophobic.

"I hope the city manages to gild those buildings eventually. I know tungsten is just as port-proof as gold, but that view is depressing."

"Funding issues," Jaxon huffed. "With unemployment stuck in the double digits, voters won't approve a ballot measure to—"

"Gross, you know I hate politics."

"You hate plain water, too, but I'm going to keep dosing you with both."

Denver port-proofed city buildings as soon as a couple of FutureMove scientists achieved a proof-of-concept for porting without a receiver booth. Mostly only mice had ported without a receiver, and they usually ended up dead, landing halfway through walls or underground. The ETC made porting without a destination booth highly illegal, but it was enough of a security risk that the city applied gold leaf along the outside walls in artistic patterns tight enough to prevent anything human-sized from porting through. When the money got low, they did what they could with tungsten, which could be pretty all polished up, but the cheap tungsten-weave construction fabric wasn't made for looks.

I reached into the keyboard drawer at my desk until I felt my small stack of envelopes. I pulled them out and tucked them into the laptop slot in my backpack to try to keep them somewhat flat. Technically, I worked Saturdays too. I served court summonses, and it was the best day to find people at home. Only instead of greeting them with a "How may I be of service?" like Nadia did for her job, I told them they'd been served and then took off like a foul ball. The pay was decent, and every summons I served got me a little closer to the tools and components I needed to finish my parent's research, fix the booths, and earn a place at the company I was born to work for.

Jaxon grunted as he propelled his bike uphill. "So, where are we meeting for the swap? You got the location with your computer witchery, right?"

"Of course I did. I'll text you the port booth code." To find the code, I'd had to reverse-engineer a binary and scour a terrible website written entirely in Comic Sans. The final clue was hidden in the metadata of a GIF of a stick figure with a shovel and hard hat captioned, "This website is under construction." He looked like he'd been digging there since 1998.

"Call me when you get there. You keep forgetting I can't port." Jaxon twisted his upper arm so the phone's front camera faced his feet in what must have been a hilarious display of balance and flexibility to any passersby. He'd tucked his pant leg into a bright green sock speckled with tiny retro sunglasses. As his pedaling foot came up I caught the dull glint of the battered metal ankle bracelet.

"Oh yeah, ya hooligan." I appreciated the ETC taking safety seriously after a rocky beginning, but the punishment seemed a little harsh for getting caught with an unregistered cell phone. I'd let him use one of my burners while I installed an upgrade to make his battery last longer for our marathon video chats. He'd taken the blame, and now he was stuck riding everywhere.

I cleared an itch in my throat. Allergies, not guilt. "Head toward the Mall. The port code looks like it's over that way again this week." I switched to my sister's scolding voice and added, "And take some time to consider your actions during your ride."

I swiped *end call* and opened the false bottom in my lower desk drawer. I grabbed a couple of my more questionable items to trade at the underground-market swaps: a port-proof unlocked SIM card and a port booth activation card registered to the social security number of someone recently deceased. Normally, free government SIMs came with port-proof copper connections instead of gold, and booth cards were issued to everyone statewide, as long as they passed the booth license exam. But those of us who didn't want the ETC's grabby hands pawing at our data through the government SIMs' backdoor or tracking our every move with the booth card would pay a pretty penny for these puppies. I stuck them both in my shoe and jogged down the stairs and out the door to my street's three port booths.

I bent down in front of the pustule-mustard booth on the right and pretended to tie my shoe, pulling out the scrap of paper with the numbers I'd jotted down last night. I stepped into the sleek plastic housing. The ETC's cheesy informational video played in every booth—an attempt to calm public fears about porting. Few people had more than a surface-level understanding of how teleportation worked. Some might mention the phrase, "predictive quantum mapping" from the videos, but apparently, even my parents got it wrong about the density barriers.

I let the video play on the port code screen while I studied the coded instructions. On the screen, a cool cartoon dude dressed like a vintage surfer stepped into a blue booth, which transformed into a blue surfboard. He and his booth board wobbled in a gentle wave pattern through tiki huts and palm trees.

A friendly voiceover bounced around the small space: "... The subject remains intact for the whole journey, and every molecule stays right where it belongs." The huts and trees shimmered apart to let the surfer dude pass directly through them. He landed in a booth on a beach, ran out through the sand, and hit the waves. "Remember," said the voiceover, "walk or drive your old electronics to the nearest ETC exchange center for booth-proofing, and trade in or store your gold and platinum accessories. Now, hang loose, and—."

I cut the video short by punching in the eight-character port code. The screen prompted me to tap my booth card or transfer the ridiculous five-dollar fare for anyone without a card. I'd programmed card data registered to one of the unused social security numbers into the RFID ring Jaxon had given me for my birthday last year. I tapped my ring to the card reader and did a mental safety check. I had DIY booth-proofed my phone ages ago, and my silver earrings were the densest material on me at ten grams. Teleporting *was* considerably safer than traveling by car, according to the stats. As with cars, people generally didn't care how it worked as long as it got them where they were going. But I'd seen enough of the horrifying ways it could go wrong to make me squeeze my eyes shut and hold my breath every time I hit the *go* button.

After a bright flash and a floating feeling, I felt the floor back under my feet. I took a few seconds to shake off the intense pins and needles sensation. Even with dead hearing aid batteries, I could faintly hear the whine of an electric shuttle and the low murmur of tourists through the booth door. I'd correctly assumed the Sixteenth Street Mall was the general area of this week's secret swap location.

The tech swaps were next on my list of the ETC's well-intentioned annoyances.

From homeowners associations to nation states, teleportation threw presidents of anything with a border into full panic-mode. No one knew how the technology would affect the way we kept our spaces safe, or whether some other status-quo-destroying invention lurked just around the corner. In their rush to appear proactive, the politicians decided it best to save us from the possibility that any additional innovations might take them by surprise. Homeland Security hooked up with the Travel Security Agency, and their unholy union spawned the Emergency Teleportation Commission.

The ETC published a hefty tome of tech regulations and monitored hardware like a syndicate of stingy librarians. They couldn't risk people attempting home-brew modifications to port units or masterminding any other secret experiments, so you could only buy new components after turning in broken ones at an official swap location. If you didn't have anything to trade, they made you register for the new parts and tools or submit an application with an explanation of their intended use. So stupid!

The outdoor pedestrian shopping district bustled with tourists, who were easy to spot in autumn. The out-of-towners were bundled in new coats and snow boots against the fortyish-degree chill, while Denver natives sported shorts and sandals. I landed somewhere in between with my olive hooded jacket, tan cargo pants, and broken-in gray sneakers.

I "tied my shoe" again and tucked away my scrap of paper after a final look. *10062082R4L3FLUX*. The first part was the code I entered to get here. The rest hinted at the exact location of today's underground market. R4L3FLUX was either some kind of sci-fi soldering droid or a code. Rale Flux? Did I need to get to the light rail station? Maybe flux meant flux capacitor, like in the old classic film, *Spaceman From Pluto*. There was a historic clock tower down the block.

I glanced over the row of white vendor tents. The first three tents on the right displayed jewelry and scarves and Colorado souvenirs. The fourth tent on the corner was a licensed electronics swap. This could be R4, R meaning the right side. I rounded the corner to the right and continued down the side street, lined with more tents all the way to the next block. I counted down three on the left side and pulled out my phone so it would look like I was busy texting while I considered the options.

Unlike the licensed trade tents, these underground guys had the swoon-worthy wares: CPUs, GPUs, motherboards with the gold connectors already replaced with less-dense metal, and so on. But if I were to ask for the wrong thing at the wrong tent, I could not only land myself some sweet new ankle bling and be twinsies with Jax, but I could compromise the whole underground tech swap and lose access to the tools I needed.

I'd apparently spent too long in one place, and some clipboard-wielding polo shirt locked on to my position. Not just any polo shirt; I recognized the bun bouncing toward me. ManBun homed in with his friendly eyebrows on. I decided a fake phone call would be more effective than fake texts at this point.

"Hey," I said into the phone, and then pointed at my earbuds and shrugged at ManBun.

What was he doing here? Weekend volunteer work? His lanyard had little trees and globes on it, and his clipboard seemed too full of actual signatures to be a prop.

"Yeah, I'm here, Sixteenth and Welton," I said to no one.

ManBun hovered. Didn't Mr. Head of Security have more important things to do? I held up my pointer finger to him and stepped away. Crap, why did I do just-a-minute when I wanted to talk to him approximately never? I didn't have time for anyone else's cause right now.

"Oh, yes, sure, I'll head your way." I jogged to the left side of the cross street and ManBun meandered along behind me. My phone buzzed several times with incoming texts. So glad I had it on vibrate or my jig would be up. "Uh-huh. Yeah. Mm-hmm." I hurried up the row of vendors until he was out of sight, hoping ManBun found someone else to trick into saving the whales or whatever.

I had passed L3 a few tents ago and ended up at the bike racks, where a bike that looked a lot like Jaxon's stood locked up. Good; I wouldn't have to wait forever for him to get here. The third tent on the left was another licensed electronics swap. They had name-brand batteries and the appliance parts I needed, so I traded in my "reverse-engineered" parts on Nadia's fix-it list and sent the payment for the balance on the new parts through my phone. I couldn't wait to switch out my hearing aid batteries; the Mall was a barrage of jumbled noise, and my ears were ringing.

"Got it, thanks," the ETC lackey at the swap tent said when the payment came through.

I pulled out my earbuds, leaned in and lowered my voice. "So, you have any flux?" If he did, I'd have to pretend to change my mind about wanting some. If he recognized it as a code word, I'd have to make up my mind whether to let him know that I did, too.

"Like, for soldering?" He turned and shouted to someone loading non-port-proof goods into a truck. "Hey Steve, where would we keep the soldering flux?"

My ears tingled and I did a visual sweep for ManBun. Shut up, I wanted to yell at the swap attendant. Anyone on the entire block with the same instructions could know what I was up to now. Maybe I should have turned left—

"You needed flux?" A one-woman anime convention perusing the wares at the next tent raised her pink eyebrows at me from under a sparkly purple hat with cat ears.

I darted my eyes from side to side like a cartoon spy and nodded.

"I can show you where they have some." She could be for real, but her outfit was over the top for someone looking nearly thirty. She could have been an ETC spy trying too hard.

She stared at me during my internal debate. Her neon yellow nails, bright against her deep ochre fingers, clicked an impatient rhythm against the tent's leg.

My phone buzzed again. *Oops.* I hadn't called Jax to tell him where I was yet, only pretended to. "Hold on, I have to make a phone call."

She sighed and beckoned with her bobbly head. "It's just up here."

I nodded and started walking again. Another text popped up as I was typing in his name.

"Away from three," it said. Autocorrect? I scrolled up to check his other messages.

```
Jax: Stay home. They know whoops you
ate.
Jax: Whoops you are
Jax: Who you ate
Jax: WHO U R. THEY KNOW. GO HOME NOW.
Jax: I'm serious don't go it snot
safe.
Jax: OMG I HATE THIS PHONE just get
Jax: Away from three
```

A sort of dying chipmunk noise escaped my throat. They who? The underground-market people? The police? The ETC? Who could possibly know I was looking for under-the-table trades?

I took a deep breath and tapped Jaxon's name and hit call. The phone thought for a half-second and gave me a "call failed" error.

I kept the phone pressed to my ear, in case I'd heard wrong. Silence, except for my runaway heartbeat.

Maybe a rolling blackout was affecting a cell tower. Jaxon was *fine*. I rested my phone-free hand on my hip and tried again. It rang once and hung up. He was probably mad I took so long to call, trying to freak me out or something. My heart pounded as I mentally retraced last night's steps. Was my power hack the reason ManBun had been called into work last night? Was he here now because of me?

"This way." The flux girl urged me toward the bike racks.

The bike that looked like Jaxon's now hung awkwardly, its pedal stuck in the next bike's spokes. The untoasted pumpernickel squirmed in my stomach, and the smell of stale urine wafted in from the alley ahead.

Flux Girl started toward me, reaching for my arm with her neon yellow fingernails. I took a step back from her invasion of my personal space.

"STEP BACK, PLEASE," an official voice blared through a megaphone over on the Mall. Something must have happened. I kept moving backward away from Flux Girl.

"PLEASE, CLEAR THE AREA."

"Look," said Flux Girl. "I really just need you to come with me."

I turned and ran toward the booths past a few tourists scurrying away from the sound of the megaphone. I tried Jax again on the way. Nothing. The increasing pressure in the front of my head and the ringing in my ears made it hard to think. I had to get home and figure this out. The pairing chip would have to wait, but I could fix the microwave, and Jax would call, and everything would be fine. I rounded the corner at Sixteenth and came to an abrupt halt. Police wrapped their favorite yellow tape around my ride home, and ETC officials helped divert foot traffic to give them a wide berth. Somebody must have left another involuntary tissue sample in the port booth.

"Wait!" Flux Girl called, running up behind me. Her persistence freaked me out. I had to lose her and get to another booth before the line got long. After two accidents in two days, they might even shut the booths down for diagnostics.

I pushed into the gathering crowd of unnecessary snow boots, ducking to hide my height and keep my unruly head of hair from view. I caught a glimpse of the taped-off booths, red lights flashing around their doors. An investigator in white gloves kneeled in front of the pustule-mustard booth and reached in to collect whichever appendage had been left behind.

One of the tourists spun around and threw up right in front of me. I jumped away, stomach reeling from the smell of vomit and the churning dread I was desperately repressing. I turned back to the investigator who held a large athletic shoe with soggy, limp laces over an evidence bag.

She slowly pulled a battered metal security bracelet up over the bloody remains of a sunglass-spangled green sock.

CHAPTER FOUR

To Think That I Saw it on Sixteenth Street

Cold shot from my toes to my throat, and my breakfast made a partially digested debut in the gutter. I remained hunched over, my hands on my knees, and watched the dark-brown gloop mix with the trickle of water and stretch thin toward the drain. I fought my brain for any kind of sign that this wasn't Jaxon's foot. Maybe there was a sale on offensively distasteful socks last week and all the cool kids were wearing them.

But Jaxon Jeong wasn't a cool kid. He might have the face of a dreamy K-Pop star, but he was as big a nerd as I was, and I never let him forget it.

He was also too smart to port with his ankle monitor on. He'd said as much less than an hour ago. So what could have compelled him to get inside that booth? I straightened, done hiding. I had to call the hospitals or the police. Maybe Nadia could find out something from Dr. Clarke.

"Alyona!"

I spun.

Flux Girl pulled her phone away from her ear and hissed something at it before shoving it into her pocket and heading my way.

What did she want with me? She knew my name, knew who I was, like Jax had tried to say in his texts. My fight-or-flight instincts had a quick argument amongst themselves while I scanned the scene for any friends Flux Girl might have stationed nearby, but I saw only shoppers in new coats. She would know something, and without backup, Flux Girl was small enough to fight off if it came to that.

Her infantile sparkly cat ears glinted in the autumn sun like a bouncing disco ball as she jogged over. Yep, I could take her down in a scrap. I stepped onto the curb when she got close, so she was a full head shorter than me. Her face was shining as well. Cheek glitter? Or was she *crying*?

"It wasn't me," she said, panting. "This wasn't the plan."

"Where is he?" I asked. "He'd better be in a hospital, and not bleeding out in some basement . . ." I folded my arms to hide my trembling hands.

"He's safe, he's being cared for, I heard from—"

"Where is he!" I yelled.

Her cat ears flopped as she startled. "I—I'm not sure, exactly," she replied, shoving a dark twist of hair back under her knit cap. "I'm so sorry, it wasn't my call . . . I can't believe . . ." She swatted at her cheek in a poor attempt to hide a tear. "But I know he's safe—"

Some primal instinct had urged both of my hands forward, palms down and ready to shake some answers out of her by her stupid choker-clad neck.

Flux Girl's neon-taloned hand came up to shield her face.

"Where. Is. Jaxon," I growled.

"I . . ." Flux Girl grabbed her upper arm and took a step back.

"Listen, Flux Girl," I said.

"Kendall," she squeaked out with an inflection that sounded like she was asking me. "You can call me Kendi."

Facing me up close, I could see the faint worry lines between her eyebrows. She was older than she dressed. "Whatever, I don't care. Who sent you, how do you know my name, and what happened to my friend?" I flicked my head toward the alley. "Get over here and talk."

Flux Girl—Kendi—followed me to the shade in the alleyway. She ran her eyes along the edges of the surrounding buildings, hand up to shield her face. Probably hiding her features while she checked for cameras.

"I'm with the ASF. You know the ASF?"

I nodded. Of course I knew them. They did good work, if you asked anyone outside the government. When the ETC first cracked down, the most affronted fans of open source advancements and free-range technology formed a group called And So Forth, their name a play on how the ETC's initials looked like *et cetera*. As a circuit connoisseur, I preferred something in between the unfettered future the ASF promoted and the ETC's suffocating control.

"Lots of people claim to be the ASF, and last I checked, they didn't amputate innocent people's feet."

"I didn't want to take him," Kendi insisted. "We didn't want him, we wanted *you*. He's easier to track than you are, and he's come to every market with you. We knew when he showed up that you'd be here."

I stood to my full five-foot-nine-and-a-half height and dug my chipped fingernails into my palms. "I *am* here! You didn't have to take Jaxon!"

Kendi's palms shot up, revealing a smudged R4L3FLUX in purple ink. "No, I didn't . . . I don't . . . listen, we need you for something important. You've got skills. You've been to every single secret market—we can't hide the port code well enough for you not to find it."

I felt my eyebrows butt up against each other. "Isn't the point of putting the location out there so that people *will* find it? I mean, it was hard, but not impossible. Wait, have you been *tracking* me?"

"The locations were hidden as a game, Alyona, a test. We needed to know you had what it takes to help us, and you passed with flying colors." Kendi glanced up the alley and stiffened. "We've been here long enough. I'll tell you everything if you decide to help us, but not now."

"But Jax—"

"He's . . . he'll be fine," Kendi said as she whipped a pen out from somewhere on her vivid person. She grabbed my hand and was writing on my palm with a thin marker before I could protest. "Go home and stay there until I can explain, please. Or do whatever you do on a normal day. Don't draw attention, and meet me at this booth, 2:00 a.m. tomorrow."

I pulled my hand away and looked at the writing, clearly an eight-digit port code. "As in tonight, or like, tomorrow night? Where is this? You think I'm going to—" I looked up and let my sentence die. Kendi had already made it to the other end of the alley like a ninja kitten. I thought about pursuing her but collapsed against the cold, brick wall behind me and pulled out my phone. I tried Jaxon again. Straight to voicemail.

My throat itched and I couldn't quite fill my lungs. The Jaxon-shaped black hole in the air next to me was sucking my oxygen away. I sank to the dirty cement, dizzy.

Jaxon had hardly left my side since the funeral. Nadia had sat bawling on the pew next to me, and I'd stared straight ahead, unable to absorb whatever was going on around us. Fifteen-year-old Jaxon walked right over and sat next to me on the hard chapel pew, put his arm around me, and didn't say a word. He didn't ask if I was okay, or why I wasn't crying. He was simply there, a warm, steady presence to lean on. He'd been that ever since. I would do whatever it took to get him back.

I needed to breathe. I dialed my sister's work phone. "When's your lunch?" I said when she answered.

"Um, whenever, I guess, why?" Nadia sounded bored, as if the world as I knew it weren't dangling by a bloody green thread.

"Can you meet me in twenty minutes?"

"For lunch? No way. That'll be like, ten in the morning. Besides, I'm meeting Manny."

"His name is Manny? Manny ManBun? Really?" I might remember this one's name, but that wasn't important at the moment. "Never mind. Your ManBun can back off for today. I need—"

"His name is Manuel Ourives, Alyona, and if you gave him a chance—"

Jaxon's severed foot took priority over her flavor of the month, and stupid Manuel had been at the Mall. I wasn't sure what was safe to say over Nadia's desk phone. Time to invoke the sister code. "Come on, sissy, we haven't done lunch in forever."

Nadia didn't answer right away. She knew I hated pet names of all kinds and would never call her something so ridiculous. Plus, I don't "do" lunch. I'm not that fancy. I just eat it.

"Sure, okay Alyonushka," she answered. Code accepted and returned. "I won't have long, but I can take a quick break, Moondollars Coffee?"

"Isn't that where your work friends go? I don't want you distracted if I only get ten minutes of break time."

"Yeah, I'm pretty sure we keep that place and The Pie Plant in business. Manuel loves this place called Kim's Corner. He likes to support local businesses. He's so—"

"Okay, Kim's in twenty," I said. "Just you."

⋯▶

Kim's was already busy when I got there about five minutes after I hung up. It smelled of chai and omelets, and my now-empty stomach let me know it would take anything on the menu. I looked for a quiet place away from the students and a chattering crochet group. Some guy in dark jeans and a maroon beanie packed up his laptop and left the broken-in couch in the corner free. I dived for it before someone else could, brushing his side as I passed.

"Sorry," I said.

He waved me away without turning back around.

From the couch, I could see all exits, and no one could see what I was up to on my phone. I spread my jacket next to me and tilted the ordering device on the coffee table toward me, hoping the girl behind the counter would recognize that I was waiting for someone and not kick me out before Nadia ordered me a drink. Nadia made more money than I did, which was nonsense if you compared our skill sets. I hacked us free after-hours electricity, and she used it to watch makeup tutorials.

I should have told her to meet me in ten minutes, not twenty. My blood felt like it was trying to beat the land speed record as it pulsed through my body, and Jaxon's name whirled through my head on an endless spiral.

I picked up the boxy ordering device and ran my eyes over the screen-saver news article in an attempt to calm my mind. "Third Major Airline Merger Announced," the headline read. Still no Nadia. I read on, desperate for distraction. "The aftershocks of teleportation's advent persist, wreaking havoc on industries still struggling with nearly overnight obsolescence. Massive layoffs in the shipping, hospitality, transportation, automobile manufacturing, and road maintenance sectors, to name a few, continue to terraform the economic landscape. This week, representatives from Epsilon Airlines announced their sale to Northeast . . . Full Story: $1.99. Up Next: Oil, Gas and Stagnating Stock . . ."

Bleh. Still no Nadia, and I didn't exactly have a stock portfolio to worry about. I swiped across the lock screen to get to the games. They cost money, but I tapped a pattern in the top corners of the screen to gain access to the back end, where I could play for free. If only I could concentrate on anything other than my mounting anxiety. The games themselves were crap, but the small victory of cracking the paywall staved off my meltdown for long enough to notice Nadia coming to my rescue.

My napkin fluttered in the cool air as she walked in and ordered a hibiscus tea and a hot chocolate. She was taller and thinner than I was, and despite the panic building in my chest, I realized she bore a striking resemblance to the Truffula trees from Dr. Suess's *The Lorax* with her pale-yellow sweater and fuzzy pink scarf.

She planted herself next to me and wrapped an arm around my back, rooted to the spot as I bombarded her with the account of my morning. She held me and listened, and I felt my pulse slow to a regular rhythm. I made a decision to keep the part about the foot to myself. She could be my support without having to hear the gory bits. I'd spare both of us the retelling, and she'd find out in due time.

"I have to go meet this girl tonight, Nad, right? I mean, it's Jax, and they took him to get to me."

"*Da nyet*, Alyona, no way. You know I love Jaxon, but you cannot go to some random booth by yourself in the middle of the night. These *hooligany* are willing to kidnap a grown man. She shuddered. "Who knows what they might want with you."

"They already did the worst they could do to me." I grabbed her scarf off the table where she'd piled it in a neat circle and ran my hands through the folds. The scarf was silly, but also amazingly soft and cozy. I was still scared out of my mind for Jaxon, but Nadia's familiar warmth was the anchor I needed to think clearly. "You know Jaxon would come for me."

Jaxon had come for me before, and he was the reason I got to stay with Nadia at all. When I'd heard the Child and Family Services people were coming to evaluate our apartment a few weeks after the funeral, I'd packed my lockpicking set, a USB full of files, my phone, and a blue marble, and snuck to the bus station. When Nadia couldn't find me, she'd begged Jaxon to bring me home before the social worker showed up. He'd caught me before I spent the last allowance my parents would ever give me on a ticket to San Diego.

"Jaxon has saved us both. I can't argue with that." Nadia sipped her tea. "We absolutely have to find a way to help him, but this is unhinged. He wouldn't want you to do anything rash." She took another swig, and I could almost see her mind bouncing back and forth between her desire to help Jaxon and her need to keep me safe.

I swallowed some hot chocolate and let her think. We both knew I'd go in the end.

"I've got to get back to my desk, but we'll talk about it at home," she said, snatching up her scarf. "And don't get hot chocolate on my things."

"Everybody needs a Thneed." I quoted *The Lorax* as she

carefully covered her head with the pink fluff and wrapped it in place around her neck. My voice cracked, betraying my desperate attempt at humor as a coping mechanism.

She pulled me into a hug and then leaned away and met my eyes. "We will find another way to help our Jaxon, Alyon. I will start asking around and making phone calls as soon as I get back to work. I'll have Manny talk to his law enforcement friends. He'll be able to get the word out and point us in the right direction. But you need to let yourself process this and avoid making anything worse. Do you have your hearing aids in?"

"Oh, I need to replace the batteries." She knew from experience that I lost my patience faster without my hearing aids in. When my brain had to work so much harder to understand the sound coming at me, my energy level and ability to manage stressful situations plummeted.

"Do it now. I will see you after work, and I'll call you if I find anything out."

I pulled the aids off my ears and swapped out the batteries. The low murmur of the cafe sharpened and intensified. I heard a spoon clink against a glass. Something in the kitchen was beeping, and I could understand the conversation between the two moms at the table in front of me—an anecdote about potty training I'd rather not have pictured. The door chimed as Nadia backed out of it, waving a pinky finger goodbye.

I focused on the rhythm of the cafe and breathed, slow and steady, even though my head still throbbed with worry. Nadia was my home base, somewhere to anchor my flailing thoughts. Ever since our parents died, she was my motherboard, and without her to ground me, I was a pile of worthless components. She'd held me together and helped me to function since our parents died. I knew she'd tell me to stay home tonight, and she knew I'd go anyway, but I needed the routine, the predictability of the program. I took a deep breath for the first time since breakfast.

I pulled out my phone and took a picture of my palm. I could not lose that code, and the purple ink had already begun to smudge in my cold sweat. Public port codes came up in a map search, but a growing list of unpublished codes appeared online in user-generated databases. I pulled up a browser and typed in *boothpwn.com*.

An error message flashed across my screen:

```
This site's security certificate is
not trusted.
```

Crap.

In my freaked-out state, I'd forgotten to turn on my VPN, and I was using the cafe's public Wi-Fi, like a derp. So someone hijacked my connection, sending my web traffic somewhere with an outdated security certificate—not the website I'd typed in. It was the man-in-the-middle attack. Intercepting my communication with the router meant they could gather data about where I'd been recently, calls I'd made, even my AppyBucks login.

I powered down my phone and looked for anyone suspicious. We hacker types don't always fit into the black-hoodie-and-sunglasses stereotype, and no one was wearing a Guy Fawkes mask. It could have been someone scanning for anyone on the open network, but it was possible someone had targeted me, specifically. I'd received countless texts and grammatically incorrect email manifestos over the years inviting me to join one cause or another. Everything from pleas to help ban teleportation, to campaigns to prove porting was a human right. Someone obviously wanted my attention enough to kidnap Jaxon, so they very well could have tried to steal my data, too.

I powered my phone back on, turned off Wi-Fi and

enabled the encrypted VPN. I couldn't slip up again if I planned on meeting with Kendi and the ASF later tonight. 2:00 a.m. was hours from now. What was I supposed to do until then? I would lose my ever-loving mind if I tried to sit still. I had a few summonses with me. I could scout out the meeting location and search for signs of Jaxon's whereabouts under the guise of combing the city to serve the delinquent debtors called to court. Kendi and Nadia had both suggested staying home, but it would make more sense to act as if everything were normal. Besides, I'd need money for incidentals and, I don't know, gauze?

I pulled my battered gray backpack onto my lap. My dad had given it to me after he got it for free at a technology conference. It had some doomed tech startup's logo all over it, the company now a casualty of the ETC's tech lockdown. I carried it in remembrance of my dad, and of a time when people could innovate without a government stiff's stale coffee breath fogging down their neck.

The backpack's main compartment was already halfway open. My pulse quickened and I sorted through the contents, but nothing appeared to be taken. The zipper must have slipped.

I pulled some rumpled envelopes from the laptop compartment. Each envelope displayed the name of some poor schmoe about to have a damper slapped onto their day. Legally, you had to be over eighteen to serve court summonses, but the lawyer I worked for didn't ask about my age or methods as long as I got the job done. They were never for anything interesting, anyway. Mostly just unpaid dental bills. She sent me summonses to serve, and I put my particular set of skills to work tracking down people who thought they could ditch their bills like they ditched their oral hygiene.

My now-encrypted boothpwn.com search for Kendi's

code came up empty. It was either a new unlisted booth or a new duplicate code for an existing booth. I flipped through the envelopes for an address that might take me to the more industrial parts of the city—places the ASF might hold hostages—so I could snoop around with a reason for being there. It was a long shot that I might happen upon a hint about Jaxon's location, but I had to do *something*. Today's lucky winners were David Lukas, Doris Boon, a Michael Wells without an address, and the last envelope in my stack, Atty McNair. Her envelope was smooth, and the address was printed in a different font from the rest of them. *Odd.*

I set the envelope down on top of my backpack, picked up my phone, and found Atty's unlocked social media profile. Knowing something about the target greatly increased my odds of social-engineering them into taking my not-so-fun delivery. Atty's profile picture featured short salt-and-pepper finger waves with a streak of teal framing her warm ochre face. She mainly posted GIFs of glittering flowers and videos of pets reuniting with military members. Also lots of images of fingernails. Nail artist, maybe? Probably the type that would accept a hand-delivered envelope if I brought it with a bouquet.

I scrolled to the section listing her workplace, where she'd likely be at this hour. She'd posted a picture of a client's nails—hearts in fall colors—an hour ago, so she did nails for sure, and she was definitely working today. I was about to check the map when another of her client photos caught my eye. Purple cat ears.

I enlarged the photo to full screen. Pointy yellow nails.

Kendi had been to see Atty last week. Denver was famous for being a "big small town," but this was looking less like a coincidence and more like a web I wasn't keen to step into. Kendi's face wasn't visible, and she hadn't been tagged, but if there was a connection here, I might be able to use it to my advantage.

I packed up the court summonses and pocketed my phone. Spots darkened my vision, and I steadied myself against the arm of the couch. I'd risen too quickly, I told myself. I definitely wasn't panicking. But the relative calm from my sister's visit vanished at the prospect of a lead on Jax. I hurried out of the cafe, flipped up my jacket's hood, and jogged toward the nearest booth. Frayed nerves or not, I would find my Jaxon.

CHAPTER FIVE

Server Upgrade

I DIDN'T BOTHER LOOKING up a place to get flowers for Atty. Most of the early port booths were assigned an easy code, like the numerical equivalent of 2AIRPORT or COLOAPEX for the baseball stadium. I was sure the new Lariatt Suites paid a pretty penny to have the code GO2HOTEL send people directly to their establishment. I punched in 2FLOWERS for the flower market, tapped my ring, and hit *go*.

I took a few minutes to walk the perimeter of the market, peeking around tents and into the backs of cargo vans the vendors still used to transport large or heavy loads. No sign of Kendi or Jaxon, but the cheapest flowers among all the vendors were perfect: neon carnations. I picked up a half dozen, and then put down three. No need to decrease my profit margin any further than I had to. I scrawled a note on the back of the receipt and pulled up AppyTrip to look up the salon.

The app gave me a choice of two port booth codes and walking directions from each. I ported to the further one from the salon, located in the lower downtown area. No industrial warehouses, but plenty of empty storefronts to check for clues. I scanned the street and searched the alleyways. My phone's flashlight revealed nothing as I peered into the gated front window of an empty gas station. I carefully set the flowers down and pulled myself up the fire escape of a boarded-up boutique hotel to peek into a few windows. Not even a footprint in the dust.

My mind was so mired in worries over Jaxon that I passed the salon and had to double back. A customer left *Exhibit A Beauty* as I approached, pushing the door open with the backs of her hands like a germaphobe in a public restroom. A whiff of acetone and a hint of conversation followed her out the door. A jovial, "Oh no he did not!" in a thick Southern accent.

A younger nail tech dried her hands and came to the front counter from a few chairs back. "Oh, cute flowers! What can I do for you?"

"I have a delivery for an Atty McNair?"

"Well, that's me darlin'!" Atty's voice carried from the back of the room. "Bring them here—who could they be from?" She shuffled up the row of chairs without waiting, shimmying her shoulders. When she met my eye, she jumped, clearly startled. Her expression flickered for a heartbeat before she arranged the smile back into position, but her eyes stayed locked on mine.

Rude, lady. I knew my hair was bedraggled-orphan-level messy, but I had much bigger problems to worry about than my appearance. I handed her the flowers, the envelope of doom, and a note in my terrible handwriting on the back of the receipt. "The sender asks that you read this note silently," I said.

Atty snatched the note out of my hand and glared at the technician next to her who had craned her neck around. She pulled a pair of reading glasses out of her apron and set them low on her nose. There was something familiar about her like this that I couldn't quite place. She probably resembled one of my elementary school librarians.

I could tell exactly what part of my note Atty was reading by the shape of her watermelon-colored lips. A shocked circle, then a tight line, then a slow one-sided grin.

"You've been served," I'd written. "I'm so sorry to have to do this but I hope the flower brightens your day a little. Feel free to invent a secret admirer."

Atty held the crooked grin as she shoved the receipt deep into her apron pocket and pulled the summons from the envelope, reading it close against her chest like a paranoid poker player.

The nosy nail tech shook Atty's arm. "Well? Come on, who are they from?"

"Oh, wouldn't y'all love to know," Atty shouted with dramatic emphasis on every other word. She loud-whispered, "But I am sworn to secrecy."

The salon echoed with a chorus of "ooh," "aw," "what," and "girl, go on now."

One of the other techs shouted, "I bet it's Rusty. Why else does he keep coming in with his mom? She can walk on her own." The tech broke into hoots of laughter, and her client kicked, splashing the foot bath water as she added her giggles to the cacophony.

I took a step closer to Atty. "Sorry, but I think one of my friends might come here, and I really love her nails. Do by chance know a Kendall?"

Atty frowned. "I do *not* know anyone named Kendall."

If that were true, I wouldn't think the question should annoy her so much.

"Okay, but—"

"Why don't you come on back with me. I need to ask you something."

I pointed at myself and raised my eyebrows.

Atty nodded and waved the summons in the air.

I followed her into an office at the back of the salon, eager to hear anything that might get me closer to Jaxon.

Atty moved to the in-charge side of a lime-green chalk-painted desk and sat in the pink velour desk chair. I stood halfway inside the door as she opened the summons and quickly scanned the contents. She pulled a pen out of a pink mug with the words, "I'm an esthetician, not a magician" in swirly gold letters. Then she looked up at me again, her eyes searching mine like she had her own admin password to my soul. What was she looking for?

"Listen, sugar. I don't owe money to any dentist. The only crown I ever had was back when I slayed at Miss Corn Fest Days in high school."

"Oh, if it's a mistake, you can talk to the dentist—"

"Where did you get this?"

"It was in my packet, from the lawyer I work with?" I wasn't really asking, but she'd made me nervous.

"You didn't see who gave you this one, in particular? Maybe it was dropped off by a courier you've never seen before, or left somewhere they might have been caught on a doorbell camera?"

She must have really thought someone was messing with her. Judging by her face, whoever it was better hope she never caught them. "I'm sorry, I just found it in my backpack where I put the stack this morning."

Atty's thin, shapely eyebrows pulled together. "You need to exercise more caution. Someone slipped this summons in with the others without your knowledge or consent." Her Southern accent was still present, but she spoke with an authority that felt like I was sitting in the principal's office. There was more to this lady than glitter GIFs. I looked beyond the brightly colored furnishings and noticed a large calendar filled with small, tidy handwriting. I made out the words *interview*, *supplier presentation*, and *meet with payroll*. She wasn't just a nail tech; she ran the place.

"I will be more careful," I said, and added, "Ma'am," because it felt right. I smoothed my frizzy curls, which were certainly sticking out at odd angles. "You're sure you haven't helped a Kendall? Maybe you know her as Kendi. She had neon yellow done last week—"

"Young lady, I see a plethora of nails of every color variety around here, and I've got to get back to them now. You've been ever so kind to speak with me. I will let you get on your way now."

That was a refusal to share if I'd ever heard one. "Yes, ma'am. Thank you."

Atty softened her gaze. "Thank you, sweet child. And listen, now, if you ever need anything, if you're looking for a manicure, or, you know, if you're ever in trouble, you're welcome here."

Trouble? She must know more than she was letting on, but I wasn't sure what to ask, or whether she was working with Kendi or against her. "Okay, thank you, I'll just . . ." I pointed back toward the door with my thumb.

Atty walked me back out the front where one of the ladies was propping the carnations up in a little pink vase. "You look after yourself, now."

I backed out the front door and waved to Atty, then snapped a picture with my phone to text to the dentist for payment. Atty turned back to the salon as I left, shouting to the ladies. "Nah, Rusty's just a good son. But I'll tell you who I *wish* it were."

The door swung closed. After all that noise, the street sounded muffled and dull. I tapped my hearing aids to make sure they were still working; the name-brand batteries should last me at least four days. I checked the time on my phone. That had been the weirdest sales pitch for salon services I'd ever experienced. How could she know I was in trouble, unless she knew Kendi? Maybe she mistook my current distress for the pains of a hard-knock life. Or maybe she wanted to give me a makeover, like Nadia was always begging me to do.

One small mission accomplished, but still impossibly many hours before I'd force some answers out of Kendi. I wouldn't let her ninja-frolic away so easily this time. I knew I'd have to stay busy if I had any chance of keeping myself together. Jaxon's stupid winking face from my phone kept popping up in my brain, every time sending a shot of cold straight to my fingertips. I wanted to find his contact in my phone and tap his face to call him and hear his voice. But even more, I wanted to warm my frigid fingers on the soft skin of his actual face and know he was alive.

I had to keep moving. Serve another summons, keep my eyes and ears peeled, get the money I'd need to take care of my friend, and breathe. I walked a little further outside the salon, ducked around the corner and pulled out the next envelope. David Lukas at 833 Pickery Lane. was the next victim caught in the crossfire between the ASF and my Jaxon.

Nobody answered the carved mahogany door at Pickery Lane, and thick, embroidered drapes obscured the front window. Most summons servers might get a caffeinated drink and a bag full of tacos and wait at the closest bench until the target got home. But I wasn't most summons servers, and I had neither the patience nor the taco money.

SERVER UPGRADE

I paced the wide porch, trying to keep the knot in my stomach from rising into my throat. I had to keep my mind glued to the task in front of me. The doorbell didn't bring anyone to the door, but I could still get it to help me. It was equipped with a video camera, and there was a chance I could log in to it. I stepped back down the clean, broad steps, past the stone lions on pedestals at the end of the driveway, and toward the evergreen to the left, out of view of the doorbell.

Mom had hated how nearly ubiquitous the cameras had become, knowing she was surveilled at every turn. Dad had taught me that this popular brand of video doorbell, the Chime, used the first initial and last name of the user as the oh-so-clever default username. I pulled up a publicly accessible database on my phone, which stored known usernames tied to passwords from various corporate breaches. DLUKAS wasn't listed. But that probably wasn't the username I needed anyway, since anyone who could afford this place wasn't likely to let their dental bill go to collections.

I opened up a creepy public records site masquerading as a living genealogy website that had way too much personal info on display. David Lukas came up right away, along with a list of possible relatives and their ages, addresses, and phone numbers. Like most single adults these days, David lived with his parents. One Mr. Robert Lukas seemed the likeliest candidate for David's father. RLUKAS returned two results in the password vault, one with the password "Ilovep1ckle$" and the other with the password "072090Kt!" I took an educated guess, and voila, I was in Mr. Lukas's video doorbell account.

The video doorbell's motion sensors had caught a woman—probably nicknamed Katie and born on 07/20/90 if I was interpreting Robert's password right—leaving in a suit around 6:00 a.m. The motion at 6:25 was a man leaving with a leather bag over his shoulder. Probably Mr. Lukas.

At 7:24, a squirrel zoomed across the screen. At 7:26, a fluffy cat crept into the field of vision, wiggling his tensed haunches back and forth. The front door opened, and the startled cat performed an impressive aerial twist and then shot away. Out walked a twenty-something in a purple Moondollars Coffee polo shirt.

So he worked at one of the eleventy billion Moondollars locations in the greater Denver metro area. Awesome. I couldn't even narrow it down by distance, as they were all one port away.

I could start calling each location and asking for David until someone answered, "David? One minute." Or I could save myself some time with my newly acquired password. David's Facebook account was private, but I could likely get into his father's with everyone using the same passwords for everything. 072090Kt! and the phone number from the public records site got me into Mr. Lukas's Facebook account, and from there I could see David and his check-in to the Moondollars by the theater. *Gotcha.*

···➜

I jogged away from the long row of port booths on the second floor of what used to be the parking garage for the Denver Performing Arts Complex and into the nearest Moondollars. The smell of warm cinnamon and mocha lattes reminded my knotted stomach that I hadn't had anything since that hot chocolate with Nadia, and that my breakfast was out on a sewer adventure, hopefully creating some kind of mutant ninja gutter raccoons. There was only one person in line between me and the sweet, glazed cinnamon roll I was about to free from its glass cage, and I could see by his name tag that David was serving her. I caught the last of his conversation with the girl and it broke my laser focus on the baked goods.

"I'd give you your change, but I think you're perfect the way you are." He handed the girl ahead of me a few coins.

Ick. I guess it could have been cute in some context, but the way David leaned in and winked made the slapping side of my hand tingle.

The poor girl eyed her coffee, which had already shown up at the end of the counter, and tilted the coins in her palm. "Well, I think it should have been eighty-seven cents, right?"

David frowned at the coins in her hand and found a manager to open the cash drawer. *Come on, people. Who even uses cash anymore? I want my pastry.* I pulled his envelope out of my backpack and stepped forward.

David waited until his eyes made it back up to mine to speak. "And what can I do for you?" He gave a little smug smile like he thought he was adorable.

"Cinnamon roll, stat."

"You sure know what you want. I like that."

"Give me my pastry, please."

David bent over and grabbed the gooey golden goodness with a napkin. *Don't smoosh it, creep.*

"Would you like whipped cream with that, or can I bring it to your place later?"

Seriously? That line didn't even make sense. I could not wait for him to open the little present I had for him. I wished the court summons was for more than two hundred and fifty dollars. I should have filled the envelope with glitter. Who didn't love a good glitter bomb?

"My boyfriend doesn't like whipped cream—I'll take it to him as is." My cheeks warmed when I heard myself say the word boyfriend, which was weird. Jax and I had pretended to be together before to get couples' discounts at restaurants, or to prank my sister. It had never been a big deal. But then, I'd never faced the prospect of losing him. The cafe's air thickened as I stood. I had to keep moving, or I would suffocate.

David handed me my pastry, and I paid with my AppyBucks digital wallet. No change, and no tip. I shifted my face into an innocent smile and wide, blinkey eyes. "I do have something for you, though. You served me so well; I'm serving you back." I shoved the envelope at him, took a picture, and power-walked out the door, pausing momentarily to turn and watch the long arm of the law smack that stupid grin away.

I was almost to the port booth down the street when none other than David himself called out to me. An elderly man waited in front of me for the booth to open. I should have run back to the row of booths by the theater.

"Come back here, you—" A line of city goers stretched out toward the Moondollars like a caffeine-powered inchworm and cut off his charge toward me. The old man in front of me stepped into the booth, and I ran up, ready to yank the door open as soon as the red lights around the door stopped flashing and the lock released. I wasn't sure what David had in mind other than assaulting me with terrible pickup lines, but I had no desire to find out. I pounded on the door of the booth. *Let's go already!* David was five steps away. My flight wasn't fast enough, so I attempted the fight reaction to buy a few seconds. I stomped toward David, angry pointer finger locked and loaded, and stood as tall as I could, which was an inch or so over him.

"You think you're having a bad day?" I called. "Woke up on the wrong side of your parents' designer foam mattress?"

I'd caught David off-guard, and he stopped long enough for me to hear the beautiful clicking sound that meant the booth was open.

I backed up, whipped open the door and stepped inside. I spun round and yelled at him, "Try losing a foot."

His confusion manifested in his eyebrows as I forced the door closed and engaged the lock by starting to punch in numbers. I didn't even care which eight digits they were, I wanted out of there. I tapped my ring and hit *go*. Nothing happened. Someone else must have been porting in or out, and my request was queued. I screamed in frustration for three seconds before, finally, the whole world floated, my cares suspended in bright, tingly light.

When I came back to the cold floor of a heavily scuffed booth spray-painted with a crude yet unmistakable anatomical diagram, I realized that my left hand was clenched. I'd smooshed my cinnamon roll, and left half of it somewhere in the street. My eyes burned and started to leak tear water and I collapsed right there in the booth and sobbed. I wanted to go to Jaxon's apartment and try out the terrible pickup lines I'd learned and hear an overly enthusiastic explanation of the first recorded historical courting initiation attempts. I wanted Nadia to tell me how she knew someone who dated David and that he had a disgusting growth somewhere on his body.

I wanted a hug from my mom.

Why did she have to make such a stupid mistake? A wave of choking despair threatened to push its way through my weakened defenses. I shoved it down, rolled it into a dense ball, and spat it out in a furious roar. "Why wasn't she more careful?" I yelled aloud, slamming my fist into the booth's wall. "Didn't she care?"

Some girl in chunky boots opened the booth door and nearly stepped on me. "Give me a minute!" I shouted at her from the floor, bursting a snot bubble coming out of my nose. She jumped and stumbled backward, and the door closed itself again. It would only lock if I started typing in another port code. I wiped my eyes and nose on the back of my jacket sleeve and shoved the remains of the pastry into my mouth. I took a second to melt some sweet cinnamon glaze on my tongue, and then I stood and entered the code for home.

CHAPTER SIX

The Stuff of Stress Dreams

I PUSHED THE PORT booth door open and stepped into a chilly gust of wind that made my eyes water. Colorado could be warm and sunny one day and get three feet of snow the next. I wasn't ready for a cold front in my worn canvas jacket, and I was glad we had a booth so close to home. I hurried down the familiar sidewalk to my building, my hair flying in my face. I wished I could port to some tropical beach and float away for the next four hours, but I didn't have the money or clearance for long-distance porting.

    I tugged open the door to my building with both hands and trudged over to the stairs. I'd never been so relieved that we didn't live any higher than the second level, since I wasn't sure my legs would make it even that far. I somehow got our sticky front door open and tossed my backpack toward the couch. My aim was off, so my pack bumped the Memory Marbles on the end table. Luckily, I hadn't knocked it over; I was too tired to pick up that kind of mess. I repositioned Mom's seashell and righted a tiny Apatosaurus, then dropped my exhausted body onto our faded blue couch. If I could slow my pounding heart and relax for a minute, maybe I could get through the three hours before Nadia got home from work by fixing a couple of appliances.

Once I had my breathing under control, I heaved myself off the couch, dragged my backpack into the kitchen and tackled the repairs on the toaster. I couldn't get the lever to pop when the timer stopped, but at least it made toast. The microwave should have been an easy fix—I just had to replace the conductors I'd commandeered. But I'd wiggled something loose in my haste the night before and had to trace connections until I found and secured the faulty wire. I checked my phone to set the microwave's clock. 3:55. *Ugh.* Could time move any slower? At least Nadia would be home soon, and while I'd calmed down enough about the summons situation not to have to dump more drama on her, I always felt better with her nearby.

I grabbed her curling wand and oven mitt from the counter and brought it upstairs to work on later in my bedroom. I lay the wand on my desk and checked a text.

```
Nadia: Following up with Manny about
Jaxon plan, then stopping for grocer-
ies. Home later. Love u.
```

I figured I had another hour before she got home, maybe two with Manny time in there. The wand fix was basically cosmetic. I reheated the paperclip and pulled it away from the plastic, and then pushed some of the melty plastic into the groove it left behind and sanded it smooth. I used up another hour coming up with ways I could still use the wand as a soldering iron without doing any more damage.

"Home," Nadia called from the kitchen. "Alyon?"

I glanced at the time. 6:02. "Up here," I shouted. "Check out the microwave."

"It's working! Good girl! That'll make it easier for me to make us some dinner, and then we can talk."

If she'd heard anything useful from Manny, she would have led with that. So I had no leads and another eight hours before I'd learn anything. My heart rate picked up again. I had to stay busy if I didn't want to completely lose it before my meeting at 2:00 a.m. Maybe I could look for leads on the summons without an address on the envelope: Michael Wells.

I pushed the curling wand, paperclips, sandpaper, and oven mitt to one side of my desk, pulled out my laptop, and ran my fingers along the smooth, familiar keyboard, which served both to calm my nerves and to unlock the screen. My laptop had a built-in RFID reader, so I programmed it to unlock with the port booth card data already stored in my ring.

I turned the ring around my finger and scraped off a stubborn bit of pastry frosting. Nadia made fun of me for wearing it on the left, like an American wedding ring. But Russians and Ukrainians like Dad and Mom wore their wedding rings on the right hand, so she would have made fun of me either way.

Wearing the ring on the left was a matter of convenience; my laptop's RFID reader sat to the left of the track pad. The hand I wore it on didn't matter as much as the fact that Jaxon had given it to me. I'd never take it off, even if the tech became outdated or stopped functioning, though I'd probably keep sabotaging any attempts to progress beyond friendship. I wouldn't risk losing him to my trust issues by complicating things, even if he could ever forgive me for getting him caught in the crossfire of whatever this kidnapping situation was.

I straightened the ring and focused back on my computer screen. Michael Wells's envelope was thicker than the others, so I'd steamed it open to see what he was on the hook for. He'd had gold fillings removed from three molars and replaced with an updated, port-friendly composite. He was put under general anesthesia and had a couple other fillings and a root canal done in one visit. His unpaid bill was monstrous. I wouldn't have been surprised if he'd faked his name in order to avoid the bill. That would explain why there wasn't an address on the envelope. But he used the same local dentist Nadia and I did, and he couldn't port while he had his gold fillings, so it was possible he lived nearby. And if he lived in this neighborhood, he could be one of several FutureMove employees keeping that dentist in business. Dr. Clarke helped most of the early FutureMove people negotiate rental contracts in our complex.

I used Nadia's login to access the FutureMove directory. I typed Michael Wells into the search bar and watched the spinning arrow as the search processed. It occurred to me that if Michael worked for FutureMove, he probably would have switched out any gold fillings a decade ago, when porting went public. As I suspected, the search came back with no results for Michael Wells. Fake name, then, or not an employee. But several blinking red bell icons underneath the empty results section diverted my attention down to the company-wide alerts related to former FutureMove employees.

I scanned the list of names and recognized two near the top, though I barely remembered them—Carleson, B., and Kolodetski, M., assistants to my parents. Dr. Clarke placed them on leave after the accident while everyone tried to figure out exactly what had gone wrong. They'd vanished back when the investigations were ramping up again, the cowards. If the rumors were true about the skull ring finger found in Slaughterbox having belonged to one of them, it served them right. The company directory's notes accused them of everything from moonlighting to threatening national security.

"Dinner," Nadia called out.

I checked the time on my phone—6:42. Still over seven hours to kill. I could smell one of my favorite dishes on my way down the stairs. "Mac and cheese and hot dogs? Yay!"

"Um, no. This is Mom's three-cheese elbow noodles and sausage. Don't disrespect our culinary tradition."

I wasn't hard to please food-wise, but Nadia had a knack for cuisine. She'd spent as much time cooking Ukrainian recipes with our Kyiv-born mother as I had tinkering with Dad's Russian physics kits.

Nadia scooped a pile of noodles into a bowl and chopped up a hot dog for me. "Tell me about your day. What have you decided?"

She was smart to attempt reaching my heart through my stomach. It wouldn't be the first time she'd used a delicious meal as prepayment for siding with her. I almost told her I was too nervous to eat, but my growling gut paid no mind to socially acceptable grieving cliches and insisted I was ravenous. "I found a new beauty salon," I said through a mouthful of noodles.

Nadia's shoulders slumped. "You know what I mean. I know you're scared, but let me help you."

I wasn't scared, I was pissed off, and I didn't want to drag Nadia into the churning depths of my wrath against anyone who would harm Jaxon to get to me. "This lady Atty is super friendly, you should check it out. It's called *Exhibit A Beauty*. I'm not sure if they mean 'exhibit a beauty,' which is kind of weird, or 'Exhibit A,' as in a diagram or something."

Nadia let her breath out like a unicorn pool float with a slow leak. She wrote down the name of the salon on her phone's note-taking app. She'd never go. She'd consumed enough tutorials to do her own nails fifty different ways and couldn't justify spending the money.

"I called friends all over town, and Manuel set up alerts at the hospitals," Nadia said. "He's got his buddies on the police force helping out. I'm worried sick over Jaxon, but it's best you stay here, safe and out of the way of the professionals." Her phone buzzed. "Hang on, that's Manny."

She swiped to answer the call. "Hey, anything?"

I watched her expression.

She listened, then looked and me and shook her head.

The thin veil of nonchalance disguising my panic wouldn't hold if she kept reminding rather than distracting me. I took a second helping of elbow noodles and two intact hot dogs, grabbed my backpack, and hiked up the stairs to my room. I sat at my desk and checked the clock. Bile rose in my throat as I calculated the ages-long minutes separating me from Jaxon. Even my selfish stomach couldn't pretend for long.

I set my bowl of noodles on the oven mitt and then searched the internet for B. Carleson, the first assistant from the FutureMove directory alerts. I clicked on a transcript of an interview the two assistants took before they disappeared and started reading partway through.

". . . denied ever having seen the full scope of the experiment's programming. Carleson said, 'The Zolotovs had us helping with equations and theories, but they understood the potential dangers of the experiment, not only if it were to fail, but if it were to succeed. The formulas were closely guarded, and the research was destroyed after it failed.'

"Kolodetski made an even wilder claim, saying that he, like FutureMove's founding partner Dr. Shane Clarke, had opposed the line of research pushing density boundaries. Kolodetski, an integral physicist for the project, told our reporters, 'I have never used the teleportation booths myself. The science is incredible and has its uses, but the current project was threat [sic] to boundaries as we know them. No prisons, no NORAD, no Fort Knox. No Hermitage, no Louvre, no place safe or private. We shouldn't have persisted without first coming up with plan [sic] to mitigate the threat.'"

Heat spiked in my chest. Everyone claimed to think it was a bad idea, but nobody had the fortitude to stop my parents from proceeding with the test. Maybe the assistants had been just as enthralled by my parents' enthusiasm as I had. The government didn't give top-secret clearances to thirteen-year-olds, but my dad couldn't help sharing his excitement. "It's the next technological singularity," he'd told me. "A world without borders, walls, or fences." To him, it was utopia. To my introvert mom, it was hell. But both of them loved the science too much to stop when there were barriers to break. They argued that breaking through the density restrictions would save lives and make the booths safer, and that they'd never release the upgrade until they had a way to keep it under control.

My parents had unflinching faith in their own abilities and the team around them, and that faith failed them. The team might not have been as capable as they thought if one of them had worn a platinum ring into a port booth on his way out of town. Kolodetski said he never teleported at all, but something about this whole thing itched my brain. Maybe I was making connections where there were none, but seeing the alert while searching for my elusive summons guy sparked a thought. I pictured this Kolodetski panicking when the investigation intensified. He could have replaced all those gold fillings at once so he could port for the first time and get out of there, only to forget his skull ring in the scramble.

Latin dance vibes floated up from the living room and carried me back to the present. Nadia must have finished the dishes and turned on her "kickboxing" class, which was a series of free videos where already-fit people danced around, punching and kicking the air to a beat. She seemed to think it was teaching her life skills, but so far she'd only kicked over a lamp and dented the drywall with her elbow. Both by accident.

I checked the date of the dental work on the summons, then pushed away from my desk and headed for the stairs. My foot slipped down a step as I searched the date of the finger incident. The finger was lost one day after the gold fillings had been replaced. The scenario was plausible, if Kolodetski had used a fake name, Michael Wells, for his dental work. I ran down the rest of the stairs to the living room. Dodging a backfist and a rhythmic roundhouse kick, I crawled to where Nadia's phone sat on the bookshelf, casting the class to the TV screen, and pulled off the shimmery rose gold case.

"Hey, what are you doing? Don't mess up my class."

"Checking something." I slid out the photo she kept tucked inside. The same photo hung on the storage room door in the old lab. Dad kissing Mom, their faces glowing with the elation of having completed their first successful booth test. The photo was too big for the case, so Nadia had folded back both sides. I unfolded the right side and saw the prototype booth in the background. I slowly folded out the left side, finding the assistants. The woman was soldering something, and the man stood watching. I held my fingers over the photo intending to zoom in on his hand, which rested on the table at the edge of the photo. My tired brain caught up before I tried to pinch and zoom on a physical photo. It was hard to see, but there definitely could have been a lump on his third finger under the glove. Too bad I couldn't see his molars.

"How do you say 'well' *po-russki*?"

"Um," Nadia breathed out between punches. "I guess you'd say *nu* or *tak*?"

"No, not the 'well, well, well, what do we have here' kind. Like, the one you drink out of."

"Oh, *istochnik*. Or no, maybe, *kolodets*?"

Bingo. "And what was that assistant's first name, the one who rode bikes everywhere like Jaxon?"

"Misha. Why?"

Misha, short for Mikhail, the Russian version of Michael. *Tak, Tak, Tak.* Misha Kolodetski was Michael Wells.

Thought you were clever, but I got you.

I set the phone and the photo on the shelf and ran back upstairs. An actual name might help me track this dude down better.

"Excuse me," Nadia called up. "You're not going to put my phone back together?"

I yelled down to her. "Just be glad I only took the case off. I could disassemble it much more, you know."

Nadia grunted through an aggressive kick. I'd better fix the oven I'd disassembled too if I didn't want to find myself on the receiving end of her cardio training. I brought the heating element for the oven down to the kitchen and installed it while she was in the shower, then sat back at my desk and looked up the quantity and purity of gold in a filling, and then calculated the value of Misha's three fillings using the day's gold prices. Not much, since so many industries had dropped the use of gold completely. Not nearly enough to cover his bill.

"Hey, sis." Nadia startled me on her way past my room after her shower. "What's with the questions about Misha? Does this have anything to do with Jaxon?"

"Just trying to keep my mind busy. I hate not knowing anything."

"Manny said the police will let him know any developments. He said to give it the night, and if nothing turns up, we'll take next steps tomorrow morning, okay?"

I nodded. "Tell him thanks for taking care of that."

She tugged at the sleeve of her bathrobe. "I get the anxiety over not knowing what to do, though. I keep my routines for that very reason. There's a lot I've had to figure out over the past few years, but even if I can't control everything, I can still make dinner at six and work out before bed. Try to focus on what you can control, and have faith that the things you can't will work out."

"I'll try." I'd tried to serve summons like I usually did, but it hadn't gone well. And I couldn't pretend everything would be fine when I had no idea.

"And please don't do anything too stupid." She knew I would likely be doing something at least a little stupid. And I knew she wasn't going to bed. She might take a nap, but she'd be waiting up later to make sure I got home all right.

"Stupid like punch-dancing by myself in the living room?" I said, wiggling my butt in my chair.

"It's self-defense," she said, and shook her damp hair at me, spraying me with rose-scented water as she left.

I wiped down my laptop screen and checked the time. Still five excruciating hours before I'd get any answers.

The interview with the assistants and Nadia's mention of routines reminded me of one of my own calming rituals. I pulled out my phone and tapped on a shortcut to an old news video. After my parents' death, I'd watched the video every night before bed until I'd processed my new reality, no longer forgetting overnight that my parents were gone only to be punched in the gut with that fact again every morning. I still watched it sometimes to help me sleep. Maybe it would keep me from spiraling now.

The slick news channel graphic spun around and flew off the screen, the music fading as Special Guest Dr. Shane Clarke, my parents' business partner, entered and greeted the anchor with a hearty handshake.

"Dr. Clarke, so grateful you could join us this morning."

"My pleasure, Rick," said Dr. Clarke with a billboard smile shining out from his unnaturally tanned face.

"What a tragic reason for our meeting today."

Dr. Clarke let his smile drop with the corners of his mouth. "It truly is, Rick."

"You've known the Zolotovs for several years, is that right?"

"That's right. We shared a wall in grad student housing when I was working toward my Doctorate of Business Administration and they were eyes-deep in post-doctorate physics research. I'd had some success in commercial realty . . ."

They showed still images of my beautiful mother and young father. Them standing with Dr. Clarke and two others in hiking gear, holding an elevation sign at the top of Quandary Peak. Dr. Clarke in graduation robes flanked by my parents. Mom holding a pair of oversized scissors while Dad and Dr. Clarke stretched a red ribbon in front of the pillars outside a stately building he'd secured for FutureMove.

". . . but I knew what they were on to was bigger than any real estate deal. I helped them set up a state-of-the-art lab and . . ." Dr. Clarke droned on about his part in their success and the contract he brokered with the newly formed ETC. "We secured government funding and collaborated on safety protocols . . ."

Another image faded in. Dad shaking hands with the Mayor of Denver, Mom by his side, and Dr. Clarke standing with his arm over her shoulder.

Anchorman Rick was talking now. ". . . incredibly difficult time for you. What can you tell us about exactly what happened to these brilliant scientists, your dear friends, a week ago today?"

Dr. Clarke sat back in his seat and folded his hands in his lap. "Listen, their research should be celebrated, not scrutinized, and the details aren't public. They were courageous to a fault, willing to proceed with testing even after I'd urged them to postpone. I begged them to wait until the ETC's safety protocols had been implemented."

Well pin a rose on your freaking nose. A lot of good that did.

Maybe it wasn't fair of me to channel my feelings about what they had done toward Dr. Clarke. Their assistants had been there, too. We'd all believed in them, and we'd all lost. But Dr. Clarke was still around, so he became a nightly surrogate—a target for the tempest in my heart so I'd have a shot at sleep. I'd have to work on that.

Dr. Clarke leaned forward on his elbows. "I loved them like family. They were driven by science and discovery." He paused, and then sat up straight. "The Zolotovs' fearlessness revolutionized our understanding of physics. They changed the world, and after knowing them, I'll never be the same." His confident voice cracked on the last word, and his shoulders fell.

Anchorman Rick shook his head. "None of us will."

Some of you will, Rick. Some of you won't wake up to find yourself suffocating under the ruins of the world collapsed around you.

"Now, we'd like to play a clip we've secured of an expert in the field, to reassure our viewers they won't meet a similar fate on their morning commute."

The camera cut to a recording of a woman identified by the title across the bottom as Melanie Moreno, Theoretical Physicist at FutureMove. She appeared to be talking to someone across from her to the left of the camera. "Yes, sir, we're still analyzing data, but that's the hypothesis. I've got a strict NDA, and this is all hypothetical.

A gentle voice encouraged the lab tech. "Please proceed, Ms. Moreno. We're here to help."

Dr. Clarke's voice broke in from the news studio over the recording. "This is a witness statement from an active investigation. You can't air this. Where did you—"

The studio must have cut his mic, and the clip played on. "... theorize that if there were an experiment testing the teleportation of denser materials, and a glitch were to cause the density settings to decrease instead of increase, the subject would not survive." A tear rolled down Melanie's cheek, and she took a breath.

A hot mic somewhere in the studio picked up Dr. Clarke's echoing protests, and I could make out a few words throughout the lab tech's explanation. "... obstruction of justice ... our lawyers ..."

Melanie continued in a flat, professional tone. "The less-dense materials such as fabrics or lung tissue would travel, while the denser materials such as bone or muscle—"

The recording cut back to the studio, where a red-faced Dr. Clarke stood and gestured animatedly toward the back of the studio.

Anchorman Rick held both hands up in submission. "Now, Dr. Clarke, let's have a seat, and please pardon the difficult subject, but in service to our viewers, we must ask, how can we know that the port network is safe?"

Dr. Clarke didn't sit. He faced the camera, and his mic turned on a couple of words into his reply. "... assure your viewers that FutureMove's port grid technology is perfectly safe for daily use. We've wiped the experimental data from the affected unit as a precaution and have terminated and destroyed all research and development along those lines. We've placed any involved parties on paid leave until we can pinpoint the source of the glitch, because FutureMove will make difficult calls and put the interest of the greater public above our own. It's called integrity, something this station clearly knows nothing about." Dr. Clarke tore off his mic pack and walked out of the studio.

Rick's words finally failed him, and the camera cut a final time to a video overlaid with the words "In Loving Memory." My parents held one another, Dad guiding Mom in a quick waltz through the main lab, dodging carts and workstations. Dad grinned in his dark sweater, and Mom laughed and twirled, her long lab coat fanning out like a white gown. I used to imagine the scene as their perfect physicist wedding. Dad led Mom toward a supply shelf and let her go long enough to grab two conical beakers. He handed her one, and they clinked them together, linked arms and pretended to take sips. The video faded out and my eyelids drooped.

I found myself on a crowded beach in a bikini made of smooshed pastries. Too hot. Sticky. Exposed. The sunscreen was locked in a tungsten cage, and my picks became brittle sticks of driftwood. I pulled out a keyboard, I'm not sure from where, and typed a message telling Jaxon they had his favorite milky grape soda here, but I couldn't afford to buy him one. Guilt, despair. I was the worst possible friend. Useless. I sank to the sand to rest with only rocks for pillows—

I awoke with a jolt when a coconut crashed down next to me. I snapped my head up and saw I'd knocked the bowl of noodles to the floor. I checked the time—1:48. My chest tightened, and my fingers went cold, despite my small burn from fixing the curling wand. Suddenly I needed more time. I'd set the alarm for 1:50—plenty of time to walk to the port booth and get to the secret location with a few minutes to spare. But no time to rethink. I reminded myself that I wasn't scared, only angry.

In honor of Jaxon, I found my ugliest socks—red and

orange softball socks from pitching a couple of summers ago—and pulled them up my calves under my pants for luck. I stuffed my phone and my lock picks into my pocket. I had no idea what waited for me, but I would open any mystery door that might lead to finding and helping my best friend.

The chilly night air made my stomach contract as I made my way to the port booth.

Hold on, Jax.

CHAPTER SEVEN

Pinball Witch

THE PART OF ME drowning in desperation wanted to burst out of the booth and run around screaming until I found Kendi. But the smarter part of me took over, and I opened the booth door a tiny crack. I had the disoriented feeling I got when waking in a strange hotel, having forgotten I'd been traveling. No one waited outside the booth—not surprising at that hour. I took a few seconds to get my bearings, then pulled up my AppyTrip and shared a location pin with Nadia. Hopefully she wouldn't need it.

Colorful, flashing lights shone from a storefront across the street. The windows flickered with reflections from games inside like an eight-bit fireworks show, and that nasty, delicious nacho cheese smell lured me out of my hidey-hole. I checked the map again to find out what else the building might house. I'd expected a remote, deserted location—some kind of seedy dock with henchmen hiding behind rusty cargo containers. Sure, Colorado's a landlocked state, but it would have seemed a more appropriate setting for a clandestine meeting with kidnappers than a sweet vintage twenty-four-hour arcade.

I tugged open the glass front door and stepped into the cacophonous venue. If this meeting didn't taint my opinion of the place, I'd take Jaxon here. He'd love the nostalgic vibe, and most of the games still cost only a quarter. They must exchange digital wallet payments for quarters at the food counter or something, because who carries change anymore?

A pair of purple glitter cat ears sparkled in the flashing lights of the claw machine.

I walked up and leaned against the game's plexiglass enclosure. "Time to tell me where my friend is."

"One second." Kendi made some miniscule adjustments with the joystick, as if she were soldering a circuit board and not playing a rigged game. Impressive, considering her two-inch, bright yellow fingernails. The claw hovered over a pink unicorn with stupidly huge eyes.

"You know these are a total scam, right?"

She didn't respond.

"Some friends of mine rented one once and we dug into the programming," I said. "There are settings where you can set the percentage of wins you want the machine to allow."

Kendi looked over at me, frowned, and pushed the release button without even looking back at the claw. She studied my face as I watched the claw lower over the unicorn's oversized head and clamp down milliseconds before it lifted off again. The laden claw made its way to the shute and dropped the unicorn into it. Kendi didn't have to squat down to retrieve it, she was so short. Short, and more clever than I'd assumed.

She squeezed the unicorn in my face, and it squeaked.

She's freaking playing with stuffed animals while Jaxon's who-knows-where without a foot.

I swatted her arm away and stepped closer. "Jaxon," I said. "Tell me where he is, right now."

"He's safe—"

"Where is he, you evil pixie? I'm about to—"

"I'll tell you, just listen," Kendi said, lowering her voice as some kid up way past his bedtime got too close. She headed toward an empty table.

I sat across from her and folded my arms to keep from shaking her like a can of glitter spray paint and then raised a you'd-better-start-talking eyebrow at her.

"It wasn't my idea. Well, *you* were, I knew we needed you. Using Nadia would have caught the ETC's attention. I thought we could use Jaxon to get to you, but . . . his foot . . . that was not part of the plan. Maybe Jaxon resisted, or they were about to get caught and had to leave suddenly—"

I pounded the table and yelled at her. "You could have asked!"

Kendi flinched and smiled at a passing arcade employee to show him everything was cool. It was not, but she continued. "We've tried to recruit you in the past, but you've always ignored our requests. We needed something you couldn't ignore, but wouldn't compromise the mission, and they—we—thought using your friend as leverage would work. I'm so sorry, I didn't know we were going to take him that way."

Kendi blinked, and her brown eyes glimmered in the incessant flashing of the pinball machine behind me. She did look sorry. But Jaxon lost his foot. Sorry didn't begin to make it right.

"Who is 'we' and where did you take Jax? And what requests? Start making some sense, Kendi."

"I don't know how much I can—" she began, and then jumped in her chair when I growled at her. "Right," she said, "Jaxon is being held by the ETC. We needed to get him taken, but not by us; we're not kidnappers. Our inside man is holding him at FutureMove on suspicion of ASF involvement."

"So, kidnapping is a no-go but dismemberment, that's

fine? And the ASF and ETC are one big jolly partnership now? They can only hold him for twenty-four hours—"

"Without charging him. We'll give them whatever evidence they want. They'll wait until the last minute to charge him, and then they'll draw out the whole process as long as it takes you to get what we need." She avoided eye contact, twirling her phone around in her hands. She looked up at me and I noticed heavy bags under her eyes, and a raw patch under her nose. She'd had it rough, for whatever reason. Not as rough as Jaxon, but she looked more exhausted than I felt, which was saying something.

I narrowed my glare and made it look like I was waiting for her to continue instead of staring and trying to figure her out.

She sighed. "We're not working with the ETC. We've got someone on the inside who can make Jaxon's charges go away, but you have to cooperate. You only replied to one of our messages. You wrote, 'not interested, move on.'"

My arms unfolded and my hand drifted to the phone in my pocket. I probably sent that same reply to a hundred messages. The invitations came often. Requests to team up with some other hackers for a good cause, take down the monopoly, stick it to the man, all that hippie nonsense. The problem was, as much as I complained about the ETC, I knew it had its place. It could have saved my parents lives, if they'd followed its safety protocols. I hadn't realized any of the emails had been from the actual ASF, but my answer wouldn't have changed. When it came to the ETC, I wanted more than subterfuge. I wanted the company my parents built back, and every summons I served, every component I acquired got me closer to the booth fix that would get me hired. These people were nothing but a distraction.

"I'm not the hacking queen you seem to think I am. I only

ever dabble for fun. I don't have whatever skills you're looking for. You guys messed up, and I want my friend back."

"But you passed every test we threw at you, Alyona. You found the market every single time. Do you know who else did that?

"I—"

"No one. Only you. You're *exactly* what we think you are, and you're closer to this than you think."

What was that supposed to mean? "Of course I'm close to it—you have my best friend."

She leaned forward, chin hovering over the sticky tabletop. "Alyona, we need you to take down the ETC."

Now I *knew* she was playing me. The ASF wanted me to *take down the ETC*? Were they nuts? Besides, the underground-market locations were only tricky for about five minutes. They were presented as ARG games, Alternate Reality challenges to find the location, earn some street cred, and swap for illegal parts to level up your hardware game. I found them hidden in source code, behind locked utility doors in random businesses, or scribbled onto alleyway walls. The clues pointed right at them in the forum, and from there it was a bit of creative keyboarding. The ASF were clearly amateurs who couldn't attract any legit skilled professionals to their cause and resorted to extortion to recruit a seventeen-year-old girl.

Plus, I hated that she used my name twice in a row. She didn't know me. She needed to stop acting like we're some kind of friends.

"Well, *Kendi*," I said, pocketing my phone and standing up. "I'm not going to *take down* anything until I know Jaxon's safe."

"Of course," she said, standing with me. She tapped at her phone. "We don't need much—we need you to extricate some files. At least for the first step. I can probably at least let you hear Jaxon's voice." Kendi looked up at me with wide eyes and a hopeful smile.

"So call already," I said, putting up a tough front. I turned and a racing game caught my eye. The cars kept spinning out over cliffs and then magically appearing whole back on the road and pointing in the right direction. I was still skidding toward the edge, praying I ended up knowing which way to go at the end of this long and wholly unmagical day.

Kendi stepped away and dialed a contact on her phone. I couldn't hear what she was saying over the *ding dings* and *pew pews* of the games; the higher tones amplified by my hearing aids. She rushed over to me and handed me her phone.

I snatched it up and sealed it to my ear as best I could. "Jaxon?" I yelled. No answer at first, and then I could hear a conversation, as if I were on mute and someone had their phone on speaker.

A man's voice, not Jaxon's, in an echoey room. "I'm just saying, I wouldn't eat rodents. Squirrels are rodents. Would you eat a cute little squirrel? Or a fluffy bunny?" I listened for any sign of the beeping of medical equipment, or the creaking of a bed.

"Well, actually," said Jaxon. My heart ached and soared at the same time. I'd recognize that obnoxious tone anywhere, even with one ear on a bad phone connection in a noisy arcade. Jaxon was alive, and well enough to be correcting someone. "Rabbits aren't rodents, and they're not so innocent either. Napoleon was once taken down by a horde of hungry bunnies—"

"Jaxon!" I yelled. The phone call cut off, and my chest burned as much as my tear ducts. He hadn't known I was there, but he had to know I was coming for him. I shoved the phone back at Kendi. "Tell me what you need."

Kendi spoke to the floor as she tucked her phone away and rubbed her thumb over a charm on one of her bracelets. "We need code files—port booth software source code, and any information you can find on the glitch that occurred during your parents' test." She kept her head low but met my eyes. "The ETC's got a stranglehold on the port network. But what if we could break free of their control? What if we could make our own booths?"

Kendi sat back down on the bench, and I sat next to her, only because I couldn't hear her from a standing and scowling position.

"They sell the booths to cities and other governments around the world," she continued as if giving a rehearsed speech, "but the actual porting programs and the physics behind them are so encrypted and guarded that someone would have to independently rediscover teleportation to build their own. We'll make it open source, available to all, and we'll study the glitch so that nothing like it ever happens again. No more stranglehold. FutureMove sold us on convenience: no more delays for disaster relief, no more children without a ride to school, whatever. But the ETC decides who gets to go where, and they track our every move. The government phones everyone swaps for now makes monitoring our every word effortless. Concentrated power has never led anywhere but oppression."

Pretty words, but I wasn't buying it. "Why you, Kendi? You're not losing it over some abstract utopian free-for-all. Maybe the ASF wants that, but what do they have on *you*?" If I could find out what she *actually* wanted, I might be able to use it against her to find Jax.

Kendi met my gaze, a fresh tear pooling. "I—" The tear spilled down her cheek as she blinked. "I can't tell you, except that you're right, there's more to it. We need the source code, but please, get everything you can surrounding the accident. And be careful." She sniffed and rubbed the tear away from her chin. "The woman on the news, the... the hand... she's a friend of mine. She attempted the data theft we're asking you to do, and it's my fault she was hurt." Kendi's shoulders came up in a silent sob, and I almost wanted to put an arm around her. "No one has seen her since, so if you happen to see anything in there about where she might be, or any other company secrets..."

There'd always been forces opposing FutureMove's tech in general: the arguments that society wasn't prepared for such a giant shift, or the massive impact on jobs and the economy. One side was accused of hating sick children in need of quick transportation, and the other accused of reckless endangerment of life as we knew it. They were both wrong and they were both right, but the potential for those in power to gain more made the winning side obvious. But the ETC weren't the ones taking hostages like this woman Kendi had lost. Why would they know where she'd run off to?

"You're not responsible for her wearing a bracelet that can't port. She knew better. But whatever you're feeling, you deserve it for taking Jaxon," I said, reminding myself that she was the enemy here. I was a means to an end for her. I didn't want to dismantle the parts of the ETC that could have kept my parents safe, then throw what's left of their company to these hacktivist revolutionary wannabes. But I wanted Jaxon safe, so I'd have to balance their needs with mine.

Kendi's face hardened. She took a steadying breath and stood. She stuffed a quarter into a nearby pinball machine, pulled the ball shooter back as far as it would go and let it fly. The ball escaped the shute like a crazed baboon from an experimental lab, and Kendi made the paddles flap like she was trying to fly the whole machine out of there. She kept hammering them at hummingbird speed and the ball bounced in every direction with unfettered abandon.

"What are you doing?"

"This isn't a game, Alyona. It's simple. If you do this, we let Jaxon go and we don't come after him again. Win-win."

There it was. The extortion. The pinball drained into the machine and big flashy letters spelled *game over* on the back box.

"Move," I said. I picked up one of the quarters she'd lined up on the glass and pushed it into the machine with my thumb like I was squishing a bug. The lights blazed again. "If I do this, I'm doing it myself. No micromanaging, no manipulation. There is always more than one way to win." I sent the ball into the machine, and it bounced lazily against the bumpers, racking up points and then landing in a free ball zone.

"So you'll help us?" Kendi pulled her phone out, fingers poised to pass on my answer to whatever boss tasked her with recruiting me.

I tracked the ball carefully and hit the buttons on the side every few seconds. My flippers looked less like a hummingbird and more like a stoned penguin, but I had already beaten Kendi's score. "I'll get the files, but I'm not helping you, I'm helping Jaxon. Screw all of you."

Kendi whispered, "Thank you." I never would have heard it without my hearing aids. Her thumbs zipped around her phone's screen.

I let the ball slide down the sleepy penguin's flipper arm and fall into the dark cavity below.

Kendi's phone dinged with an incoming text, and she read it out. "'Let her know the specifics are on a USB drive which has already been delivered to the purple booth nearest her home.' Thank you, Alyona. You don't know how much this means to me. To us."

The last ball sat in the shute waiting to be played. I'd find whatever they needed to get Jaxon back, and then they could all go to disorganized amateur rebel hell.

CHAPTER EIGHT

Pancakes, Eggs, and Hashes

I STOMPED ACROSS THE street to the port booths and punched in the code to the booths near my house, adding the letter "a" to the end of the code to designate that I'd end up in the purple booth. The security lock clicked into port mode. I squeezed my fists closed, tapped my ring to the control panel, and felt gravity loosen its grip, and then my weight gently pressed down into my feet until I felt normal again. In the quiet of night, I heard the lock disengage, and the musty smell made it clear I'd made it to Slaughterbox.

Dust wafted into my nose like the fart of a forgotten statue, mingled with a hint of rotten digit. I coughed and checked around the floor for the drive. Nothing. I stepped outside. The safety lights were bright enough for me to search around the front and sides, and I used my phone's flashlight to look around the back of the booth. Nope. I went back inside and searched the floor and ceiling for cracks or hidden doors. Nothing but a peanut-sized nest of silky webbing in the top left corner—a spider's egg sac shining in the white glow of the ceiling's LEDs. No way I was touching that, spiders were the absolute worst. They wouldn't hide the drive in there . . . would they? All those legs and eyes and fangs . . . not a chance. They'd have to be sick freaks to hide something in a revolting hive of nightmares. Sick freaks, like the kind who take people's feet to get my attention.

Well, crap.

I opened the flap on my pants cargo pocket, pulled out my lockpick wallet and found my longest pick—a flat metal piece with a gentle hook on the end. I pinched it between my fingers at the back of the pick to give myself as much distance as possible and raised my arm into the back corner of the booth. I gave the hairy little yuck ball a quick poke and retreated, stretching my arm back up again when nothing disgusting scampered out. I raked the hook over the nest to pull it down and it fell to the floor with a muffled thump. I slid another lockpick out of my set and used both to open the nest. Up close, it looked more like a stretched-out cotton ball, with a clump of glue on one end. But I wasn't taking any chances. I held up the nest with both picks and shook it until a tiny square USB drive clattered to the plastic floor.

Yes! The frenetic pinball from earlier ricocheted inside my chest. I could do this. *Game on.*

I sprinted to my apartment and held the knob as I nudged the door closed so I wouldn't wake Nadia. Three-in-the-morning Nadia had the croaky voice and scary glare of Baba Yaga, the forest witch my parents said might eat me if I didn't stay in bed.

My hand flipped on the kitchen light switch out of habit, and when nothing happened, I remembered it was just shy of three in the morning. The streetlight outside our dark apartment glinted off the bag of fresh bread on the counter. Sourdough this time. My stomach encouraged me to take the loaf with us upstairs. I picked it up, only to nearly drop it again when I noticed the subtle shape of my sister, curled up with a blanket on the couch.

She'd fallen asleep waiting for me, so I had to decide whether she'd be more mad at me for waking her up, or for not letting her know when I'd arrived home. I had the best sister in the universe, even if she did have a little forest witch in her.

I decided to let her sleep and took the steps two at a time, bread under my arm, and kept to the left side away from the creaky parts.

Tiptoeing through a minefield of three-cheese elbow noodles and two fancy hot dogs, I collapsed at my half-charged laptop, and logged in to my VPN so no one could trace my IP to my physical location. And I couldn't have my laptop dying in the middle of getting what I needed for Jaxon's freedom, so I logged in to the power grid, pulled up our user account, and then toggled the button labeled "override electricity timer." As long as I turned it back off before five a.m., the power would switch on automatically. All I had to do was delete the entry in the usage log for the night, and no one would be the wiser. I clicked *confirm* and held up the bag of sourdough. Before I could pull out a single slice, the lights in the kitchen blazed up the stairs like an ETC security patrol flashlight in my face, asking what I'm doing out so late.

The bread bag went flying as I heaved my body toward my bedroom door and down the stairs, catching myself before I tumbled into the living room. With one hand on the railing, I swatted the light switch and prayed to the gods of nighttime mischief that none of the neighbors saw electricity happening at the Zolotov family's apartment after hours. Nadia squirmed on the couch, and I froze until she stilled again, then I crept back up the stairs.

I plugged the USB drive into my laptop and ran a

malware scan. No viruses. Just one file, and it was password protected. I could have searched the usual forum for the password, or clues to find it, but I hated the thought of doing what they'd expect.

Luckily for me, they used a document type that stores the password hash within the actual file. I ran the document through a program that pulled out the hash—a string of characters representing the password used to verify credentials while keeping them hidden—and then used another tool that converted hashes of common passwords into clear text. If it were the season followed by the year, or any version of Pa$$w0rd1!, this program would crack it fast.

I wiggled my mouse around, downed a couple slices of bread I recovered from across the room, and took a few spins in my chair while I waited. I typed out a ghostly "hurry up" several times on the blank space below the keypad, and I watched the scrolling characters on my screen. The password must have been at least somewhat tricky—no results in the century-long five minutes I forced myself to wait.

More processing power would speed things up. Luckily, I knew a guy—a friend I'd made in the ARG forum with a mutual love of virtual puzzles.

Knew *of*, at least. I couldn't quite say I knew him—I didn't even know if it was a him, for sure, but it was a statistically likely assumption in a tech forum. His handle didn't make sense to me either. I typed it into a private chat window. N031fn8r. Was it "No Elven Ate Her?" "Noel Fin Hater?" I pronounced the first part *Noel*, which sounded French, but I knew the person was Russian speaking. He'd typed *blin* once in the chat, which I recognized as Russian slang. It literally meant pancake, but he used it where I might say "crap" in English. I'd called him out, and he asked me not to tell anyone his native language.

I couldn't pinpoint where he lived—it could have been any of the fifteen or so countries where Russian is an official or popular unofficial language. But based on the hours he was usually online, I figured he probably lived somewhere near the real Baba Yaga, in some Siberian forest, and would be awake now.

"*Dobroye vecher*," I typed under my handle, AuGurl. *Good evening*. "*Dobroye utro*," he replied, *good morning*. I couldn't tell whether he was correcting me or trying to tell me he knew it was morning where I was, and I didn't dare ask. If he sensed I was snooping, I could scare him away. I'd tried before to scrounge up clues on his whereabouts by making jokes about us being the harmless neighborhood Russian hackers. He hadn't given anything away, but he had warmed up to me. We both hated the whole Russian hacker stereotype. There were benevolent and malicious hackers across the world, and if people thought all Russians were born knowing their way around network security, it made me less cool.

```
AuGurl: Hey, I need your mad skillz.
Can you crack a password hash for me?

N031: Of course. Send me.

AuGurl: OK sent, you get it?

N031: Yes, scanning now . . .

AuGurl: Sweet. Anything new w/you?
```

I squished a slice of bread into a ball and popped it into my mouth while I read his reply.

```
N031: Nothing, everything is nor-
mal. I thought government finally
shut down my satellite yesterday
morning, but I checked wires, it
was only small squirrel. He chewed
wires. I see too many squirrels this
autumn, I suspect they train squir-
rels to report my location and chew
```

> my wires. So I trapped squirrel, and
> now I have squirrel pet)) He chewed
> my shoes also. I don't like this(((
> But I train him now. He will watch
> for intruders to my area.

Autumn. So he was at least in the northern hemisphere, but most Russian speakers were.

> AuGurl: You're so weird.
>
> N031: You are not usual.
>
> AuGurl: So true.
>
> N031: I don't like usual people.
>
> AuGurl: Me neither, friend. Thanks again. LMK if I can help you back!
>
> N031: OK I will LYK.
>
> AuGurl: LYK is not a thing. And BTW, ")" by itself is not a smiley for English speakers. You need the eyes or it's confusing. Like, you have a squirrel pet :). You don't like it :(See? Eyes.
>
> N031: Look, you helped me back, thank you. :) Wait please . . .
>
> AuGurl: Waiting.
>
> N031: I got it! «RoX+R0LZ» What do you break into this time? Something you can share, or it is secretly?
>
> AuGurl: Yes!! Thanks, you saved me so much hassle. You're better off not knowing what's in there, plausible deniability you know? You're the total bestest!!
>
> N031: Yes, I am the total bestest. Sending it now. Poka.
>
> AuGurl: poka poka!

I switched back to the folder on the USB and tried N031's password. *Success!* I resolved to send him a thank you via messenger squirrel as soon as I found out where he lived.

The unlocked file from the ASF instructed me to get the booth source code and everything else I could access, "for the good of the nation and the world, so we might all enjoy free movement outside the ETC's power-hungry . . ." blah blah blah. I scanned down through a mission statement and more propaganda before I got to the good stuff.

The files they needed were air-gapped, meaning I couldn't hack into FutureMove's networks from the comfort of my own hovel to get them. No sneaking in through open printer ports this time, like when I stole power. I had to *physically* access FutureMove's internal closed network. The ASF gave me a blueprint of the building indicating the server and data storage areas, and said they had an ETC insider at FutureMove who would lend as much assistance as possible without breaking cover. A lot of the files they needed were probably backed up in the hidden places around my home, but they didn't need to know that. In any case, I didn't have anything at home about the glitch, which they mentioned specifically, so I'd have to get to the server room regardless.

Then I read the next line about three times in a row.

"Jaxon is safe and in excellent condition." Our definitions of *excellent* differed greatly, but I read on. "Copy any/all secret or hidden files you are able to access. Do not remit these to the insider. We will indicate a drop site, and we can process Jaxon's release as soon as the files are in our hands. Your help to take down this dangerous monopoly of power—"

Whatever.

I switched off the electricity to our apartment and deleted the log entry. My foot itched, and I reached into my shoe to scratch it, my face hovering a half inch above my keyboard.

Couldn't hurt to rest a second.

"Alyona!" Nadia slapped me awake with the bread bag. There were only a few slices left, but combined with Nadia's tone, the limp plastic bag had the scare power of a tube sock full of batteries. "You seriously ate a whole loaf of bread in one night? I bought it yesterday."

"Only like, three-fourths a loaf."

She sighed. "Well I'm glad you're alive, anyway. You should have woken me up." She took the bread with her as she stormed back out of my room.

The keyboard left imprints in my cheek when I peeled it away, and my ear was sore from the weight of my head against my hearing aid. I flopped my tingling hand onto my phone. Squinting my eyes in the glare of the screen, I checked the time. 7:15. *What is wrong with that woman, making such a racket at this hour?* My face wasn't awake enough to form any expressions, but I grimaced on the inside.

"You actually fixed something, I see!" Nadia shouted from downstairs. Or maybe she said it at her regular volume, but it was too early for that nonsense.

I tried to tell her I fixed *four* things, to be exact, but it came out like "Foorfing" due to the aforementioned state of my face. I must have been destroying my keyboard with drool for about three hours.

My bed called out a siren song, but the heavenly smell wafting upstairs from the kitchen won out. I swiveled in my chair to face my door and shouted toward the stairs. "You made *syrniki*."

"But still no toast, since you stole the bread."

She'd rewarded me for making good on my word to

complete the repairs with the heavenly cottage cheese pancakes our mom used to make, and which Nadia conjures from the magic of the motherland when she's exceptionally happy with me. The smell of a perfect golden-brown outer layer summoned my heavy legs down to the kitchen.

"You're like a black hole for baked goods. What do you do with all those carbs?" Nadia sounded as perturbed as ever with my wanton grocery consumption, but syrniki spoke louder than words. Her tea was hot, her oven was still warm, and her hair was perfectly curled—she'd noticed my foorfings.

I ignored her, grabbed a plate, and piled on fried potatoes and about a thousand syrniki. Nadia appeared at my side and promptly stole all but three back from me.

"Thanks for putting everything together."

"Mm-hmm." I picked up my phone and scrolled through my news feed while I chewed. "Thanks for the best breakfast ever, from the best sister ever, who will totally help me break into FutureMove's secure networks today, because you love me so much."

Nadia almost dropped the only whole mug we had left. "What? *Why*? Is that what these ASF people want from you? They do know you're welcome there any time, right? Have they heard of asking?"

I kept my eyes on my feed, trying to stay calm and keep my breathing steady. If Nadia didn't think I had this under control, she'd jump in and try to control it for me.

"They don't want any one company to have all the power, and they apparently hate the ETC enough to kidnap and maim to take them down. If I give them the files they're asking for, they give me Jaxon and we can be done with them." As irritating as the ETC was, they at least tried to keep people safe. They were just extra bad at it.

Nadia pulled her eyebrows together and frowned, but not

in her confused kitty way. She looked mature, like she knew something I didn't. Ironic, considering the ugly fact about Jaxon's foot that I was keeping from her. "Are you going to get it for them?"

"I'm going to see what I can find, and give them as much as they asked for, but nothing more. I'm not opposed to spreading out the power, but I prefer not to give it all to some dangerous group of zealots."

Nadia looked up at me with that knowing look. "You sound like Papa." I supposed I did. He believed in free access to the technology he helped create, but he and Mom accomplished that in Denver with logic and negotiation, not violence.

I turned back to my news feed and a headline caught my eye. "FutureMove's Q4 Prospects Bright Despite These Five Insane Whistleblower Concerns."

Nadia put her fork down. "Wait, did you say maim?"

Oops. "I'm just worried. You know how I get. The ASF girl I spoke with said they have an inside source at the ETC. The source is using ETC charges as an excuse to hold Jaxon until the ASF gets what they want. So I'm going to FutureMove today. I'm coming in shortly after you, so try to not notice when I come in or leave. Don't make a scene."

"I don't know, Alyon. I think we should go to Dr. Clarke. Manny didn't mention Jaxon coming into custody, but if he's there—"

"I don't want anything messing this up. He's got to know the ETC is holding Jaxon, and he didn't tell us. I don't know who's in on this whole thing—whatever it is—and who isn't."

"Maybe he didn't say anything because the ASF is lying."

"And maybe everyone is lying, or no one. I shouldn't have told *you* anything, either, if you're going to complicate the situation."

Nadia huffed and stood, her downy sweater snagging on a split in the wooden chair.

"Sorry. I didn't mean to snap at you," I said. I was too tired and angry to contain myself much longer.

"I know." She sat back down and tugged at the snag, trying to pull the thread back through and make everything look like it had before it was yanked apart. But it wouldn't ever look the same. It would be functional, but never whole. Like our family. Like our sisterhood, now that she was a parent. And now, like Jaxon.

Enough was enough. I wouldn't wait around for the ASF or the ETC to fix things. Both sides had points, pros and cons, and I wouldn't be surprised if the ASF was right about the ETC hiding valuable files at FutureMove. They'd moved right in as soon as they took regulatory control of the company, like a clingy, overbearing boyfriend, taking up office space in the building for their field office. If they were going to hide something, they would do it there. *Get everything*, they'd said. I'd get into the networks, and I'd hand over enough to see Jaxon released. But if I found anything at all that pointed to ulterior motives or shady dealings in either organization, I'd keep that intel for myself until I could take them all down.

The manipulation ended today.

CHAPTER NINE

ManBun Strikes

NADIA AND I STEPPED out of the port booths facing the FutureMove building. The gold leaf adorning the east-facing front gleamed in the morning sun. I couldn't help but admire the artistry in the flowing patterns of art-nouveau-style circuitry curving across the wall, like a giant Elven-made motherboard blazing with molten circuits. I pulled my gaze away. I was here to steal data, hand it over to the ASF, and get Jaxon out of there.

I focused on the revolving doors, and Nadia pushed into the building ahead of me. She'd switched her schedule around to take Sundays when she'd found out her boy toy worked the whole weekend. *Gagtastic.* I stepped onto the polished gray quartzite floor to Nadia's reception area.

The interior decor felt minimalist compared to the embellishments outside, except for a large, obnoxious painting of Galileo prominently displayed behind the tall counter where Nadia answered calls and registered visitors and whatever else she did. One of those old Italian artists had painted ol' Gali staring straight out of the canvas, so his eyes seemed to follow me around.

I'd passed the painting a million times while visiting my parents' lab, and his glare always seemed to say something starting with "Pitiful mortal." I felt more comfortable with the three cameras on that level watching me than his disdainful face, which today said, "Darest thou not try anything stupid, or I shall bash thine pitiful mortal skull in with this telescope." *Sorry Gali, I tend to do stupid things when I'm desperate.*

Nadia's squeal seized my attention. "Alyon! Come say hi! I'm so happy you guys finally met."

ManBun took Nadia's hand and twirled her into his arms. He still wore a polo shirt underneath a black windbreaker with SECURITY across the back.

I gave them an upward bro nod. "Yeah, I ran into him hawking his Save the Insert-Trending-Endangered-Species-Here campaign on Sixteenth Street, too."

Nadia frowned. "He's not volunteering for likes and shares, Alyona. He actually cares."

"I would say you ran *away* from me, more than ran *into* me." ManBun chuckled at his own attempted humor. "They're called Boreal Toads, and their habitat is—"

"Whatever, I have places to be."

Nadia's jaw shot open. "Rude, Alyona! What is your problem? You'd like him if you gave him a chance for five seconds."

I heaved an admittedly dramatic sigh. "I'm sorry, Nad, I just . . ." I lowered my voice and reminded myself not to give away my purpose here. "I'm worried about Jaxon, and while you're both so smitten you've forgotten he exists, I'm ready to, you know, ponder what to do in the best place I know of for thinking."

Both of them annoyed me further with their faces melting into pitying frowns, so I added the rest of my thoughts. "Plus, with that goatee . . . he looks like a hipster magician I mean, right?"

Nadia glared at me but couldn't help turning up the corner of her little pink lips.

I didn't have any serious complaints against him. I simply didn't have energy to filter which of my thoughts made it out into the open right now. I wanted to get this file and get Jax and be done with this whole mess.

The elevator chimed, and Dr. Shane Clarke strode into reception. He raised his arms, the lights catching the slight sheen of his doubtlessly expensive suit coat. A coat which, unlike everything my parents had been wearing the day they died, wasn't shredded to bloody bits. I tried to focus on his warm smile, to disassociate his presence from my parents' absence.

"Both Zolotova sisters here in the building! I almost didn't believe the front door feed when it popped up on my screen. To what do I owe the pleasure, Miss Alyona?"

I smiled enough to mask my incoming frown. I'd hoped Dr. Clark had taken the rare day off. Sometimes I wondered if the guy slept in his office. "Good morning, Dr. Clarke, just missing my parents today. Thinking I might spend a little time in the old lab."

Dr. Clarke leaned his elbow on Nadia's counter-height reception desk and handed her a small parcel, probably office supplies he'd ordered. "Of course. You do tend to show up more often this time of year. It's hard to believe it's been four years already."

I didn't reply. It certainly wasn't hard for me to believe they were gone when their room remained excruciatingly unoccupied at the end of our short upstairs hallway. It wasn't hard for me to believe it when it stabbed me in the chest every day. Sure, the pain was duller than it used to be. But it hadn't gone anywhere.

Dr. Clarke straightened. "Manuel, why don't you escort

Alyona to the old Special Projects lab. I've got some schedule changes to go over with Nadia."

Like he couldn't send her an email.

"That's not necessary, I know my way around." I glanced up and frowned at Galileo.

"Can't be too careful lately," Dr. Clarke said from behind me. "I've had to call security frequently as of late, both physical and digital. There have been power anomalies—usage overages that are yet unaccounted for. Employees have found suspicious drives lying around, and we even had to have a chipmunk removed from one of the labs."

He paused, and I was dying to know whether he'd given me any kind of knowing look when he mentioned the anomalies, but I had to play it cool. I turned back his way and inspected my nails, channeling "bored."

Dr. Clarke continued. "So don't you go sneaking off anywhere little miss, or I might have to chain you in the basement for your own protection." He chuckled and saluted at Manuel like a silly sergeant.

Whether all of Dr. Clarke's speech was a threat, or just the part about staying out of trouble, I'd have to cool down the power piracy after this was over.

I strode past ManBun to the elevator, resisting the urge to turn and glare back at him. I couldn't risk eye contact with that smug nerd in the painting, who'd now be looking at me like, "Canst thou lay upon him blame for being suspicious? Thou art indeed here to rob the joint . . . eth."

Still, Dr. Clarke didn't have to "jk but seriously" threaten me and send me with a guard. I'd told myself to work on my unfair linking of him with the accident, but he wasn't helping at the moment. I mashed at the elevator's up button until it finally chimed, and the door slid open. ManBun followed hot on my heels as I stepped inside. Awesome. How was I supposed to get anywhere with this mustachioed chaperone on my tail? I pushed the button for level three, where my parents' old lab lingered, frozen in time. Their team was dissolved, and their project developments abandoned, but no one wanted to pack up their stuff or repurpose the lab. As far as I could tell from my few visits a year, it was mostly used for temporary storage or quiet study.

"Nice to see you again. Sorry again for the scare," said ManBun.

"Mm-hmm."

"Nadia's told me how amazing you are. I've been looking forward to getting to know you."

"Yeah? She hasn't said much about you."

Awkward silence.

I didn't have a good excuse for being a jerk to him—nothing about this was his fault. I tried to think of something kind, or at least neutral, to say.

But then he leaned over to me and smiled with half his mouth. "I can help you."

During another short but equally awkward pause, I wondered whether he always smiled like that or if he'd been to the dentist and couldn't move the other half of his face. I didn't see any drool or other signs of numbness.

I had to escape this guy for the second morning in a row.

"Oh, no thank you. I'm fine. In fact, here we are, I can take it from here. Down and to the right. Thanks for the elevator company." The doors began to open. He stepped in front of me and pushed the close doors button. *What the—*

"No, Alyona, I'm your man." He gave me one of those exaggerated old-timey movie winks that showed up on a debonair face before a proper lady slapped it.

"Well, I never!" I said. It seemed right for the moment, and I was becoming somewhat nervous.

He shook his head. "No, no, I'm the inside man. I work with the ASF. I can help you get what you need."

Sure he was. He looked more like Dr. Clarke's right-hand man to me. But then, how did he know I was here looking for anything, and also expecting help from an insider? He could be involved. In fact, ManBun had been there on the Sixteenth Street Mall at the time of Jaxon's abduction, and now the ASF's insider was holding him here. ManBun was ETC security. Was he the one who took Jaxon and left his foot? Could this actually all be his fault?

And suddenly, I was past slapping. My uneven fingernails dug into my palms and my face burned hotter than an overclocked gaming PC.

My left fist flew into the air. "What have you done to Jaxon, you steaming pile of bantha poodoo. I'm going to—"

ManBun's hands shot up and he ducked his head behind his arm.

"Wait! Stop, you don't understand, it's not what it seems." He wiggled the fingers on the hand he was hiding under like a jazzy magic man.

He straightened and reached for the elevator buttons again. "You can trust me, I'll show you." He hit the door-close button, then the door-open button twice and the close button again three times in rapid succession. The elevator made a beeping sound, and ManBun punched in a three-digit code using the floor numbers. He tried to block my view, but I watched him press 682 in the polished metal wall's reflection. A bright flash, floating, and second later we were back on our feet in the elevator.

Only, it was a different elevator. There were no mirrored walls in this one, no Muzak, and no buttons. Just a badge reader and a touch screen retrofitted to the side of an old-fashioned accordion gate. We had to be inside the building still.

Otherwise we'd have been shredded by the gold gilding outside the walls and the tungsten mesh within them.

This was a private port booth inside the FutureMove building.

The gate clattered on its hinges as ManBun pulled it open. "Voila!" he said and lifted a jaunty arm as if he'd abra-cadabraed us here. "After you."

I stepped into the dim basement and made out shapes—metal boxes. No, cages. A box of screws and a weird wrench sat atop a wooden crate to my right. Dust-covered desks and chairs were littered among the cages and other unused fixtures to my left. *Great, I'm about to be disappeared in a secret basement by ManBun the Magnificent.*

As my eyes adjusted, I noticed that the cages held shelves of bags and boxes sealed shut with red or yellow tape. This was the ETC Security's evidence room. The dusty smell was reminiscent of Slaughterbox, and the room's walls and floors were cement. The small, high window would make a difficult escape route. If my hips fit through, it might do, but it would be super tight. The door at the back right corner was a better option—it likely opened to stairs up to the ground level out back. I tried to remember whether the grounds behind the building were fully fenced or guarded. I sucked in a sharp breath as something moved in the back of the room.

"Holy freak show, Bunman! Do you have something living down here?"

"Don't worry, we feed it. This way."

"Oh, hold on, I got a text." I said, and by that I meant I had to send one to Kendi. I had to know if this was the inside man. I did have an unread text, so I flashed him the screen to show the notification. He didn't have to know it was a spam text offering to hook me up with hot lonely singles in my area. I typed out a text to Kendi.

> Me: Hey, is your contact here named Manuel? I don't want to give him anything I shouldn't.

I considered clicking the link in the previous text while I waited for Kendi to respond. Nadia would need a new beau after today.

> Kendi: Can I call you?
> Me: Sure I gue—

My phone rang as I was typing. "Yeah?"

"Alyona, yes that's him. Is he there?"

I couldn't let ManBun know I was talking about him or with whom. But other than Nadia and Jaxon, I couldn't think of anyone who might be calling me. What did normal human friends even call one another about? The news? Shopping? Plans? This had to sound natural.

"Yes, of course. I would be happy to see a movie at the theater soon for fun."

Too many words.

Luckily, Kendi caught on fast. "Alright, I get that he's with you. I don't want to scare you, but I don't trust him. He was hand-picked by some government contact to take his position with the ETC. And Dr. Clarke trusts him. I don't know what he's after."

"I don't know how it ends, either, because I haven't seen that one. But I don't scare easily," I said.

ManBun leaned over and I smashed the phone to my ear. My hearing aid squealed with high-pitched feedback.

ManBun straightened and folded his arms. "How do you get a signal down here?"

"Wouldn't you like to know," I mouthed. I had a signal booster in my phone case.

He frowned. He probably hadn't thought I'd be able to call for help when he lured me down here.

"Can your social life wait a few minutes? It's not much further."

Kendi's soft voice was hard to catch. "Be careful."

"Well, if you can handle it, then I can too. I'll meet you there at the indicated showing time."

Kendi snorted. "'Indicated showing time?' Did you learn your social skills from an AI chatbot?"

I actually had asked a chatbot once about how to hang up when I was finished talking to someone on the phone. "Kind of."

"Right. Just don't give Manuel the files. Let him help you get to them, but don't let him have them. Who knows where he'd send them."

"Don't worry. I'll smuggle the candy in myself."

"Listen, he was there when Jaxon was taken. Jaxon's, well . . . circumstances . . . that could have been Manuel's idea. Watch your back."

My stomach clenched. I'd had the same thought. "I think that covers everything for today. Thanks for your time."

I hung up. There was no way ManBun bought the charade, but I didn't care. Maybe Kendi was wrong or lying, but that didn't temper the rage building in my gut toward this person who may have seriously hurt my best friend.

I screamed on the inside. Whether or not he was the cause, Manuel had to know what happened to Jaxon. My sister was dating a sociopath. This two-faced monster was using my beautiful, naive, amazing sister, probably to get closer to me or to use her against me.

I would destroy him. I'd find my blackest black hat on the wrong side of the internet and hack him to virtual pieces. Credit cards, bank accounts, social media—I'd make his life online such a tangled web that he'd have to form a new identity just to send an email. Messing with me, that's one thing.

But you mess with Nadia, and you'd better move somewhere without a data connection.

    This wouldn't be the first time I'd tried to run off one of her suitors. Nadia would believe me if I told her what he'd done, and that would be the end of that. But I'd need to be sure, and convincing. I had to get him to admit to working for the ASF and taking Jaxon. I'd get whatever I could out of him to help me access the files, find Jaxon, and get out of there.

CHAPTER TEN

A Trick Up My Pant Leg

I SLAMMED THE SIDE of my fist into the nearest cage. Like an echo, the living thing in the cage at the back of the room skittered around its enclosure. *What else have they disappeared down here?*

ManBun cocked an eyebrow. "Try not to break anything."

I took a full stride toward him, fists balled. "I'm going to break everything if you don't take me to Jaxon right now. I know it was you. How could you? How dare you date my sister—"

"Whoa, whoa, calm down, it's not like that at all. I have something to show you." He jogged away toward the back of the room, pulled a box off the shelf, and placed it on a metal table. He whipped a knife off of his belt, which made my pulse skyrocket until he used it to slice open the evidence tape, then closed the blade.

"I don't want to see anything from you unless it's Jaxon or the files I need to set him free. I will not calm down until—"

A strange gurgle replaced my next word as ManBun

pulled out a big plastic bag containing a red-soaked shoe, still full of severed foot.

My hands flew to my face to block the gory view. "You sick *freak*. Why would you—are you *laughing*?"

"Alyona, it's not real. Look."

I peeked under my hands.

ManBun opened the bag, poked his finger inside and pulled it out, licking off the blood, and then immediately spitting it out again. "I suppose I should have kept it refrigerated. But it's jelly and silicone. It's his shoe and sock, but that's all he's missing. That, and his ankle monitor. I didn't think he'd miss that."

Not real?

My hands dropped to my sides.

They faked his amputation? "But why? Why do this? Why take him? Why not just ask me?"

"The ASF needed you, and we *did* ask you, several times. But you refused. We couldn't . . . we *can't* tell you everything because you tend to act before you think. You're too close to this. So the ASF found another way to get your full attention."

Manuel kept making words with his mouth, but I stopped processing. The cement floor felt like the surfboard from the FutureMove promo video, and my legs wobbled. *Fake. Jaxon was okay other than being detained.* My vision darkened around the edges as a strange combination of relief, distrust, and anxiety flooded my head. I needed a moment to recalibrate. I looked up at the corner cage and walked briskly away from the talking. Something scampered around the three-foot square cage. I blinked to clear my vision and attempt a minute's distraction from the matter at hand.

"Alyona, wait!"

I leaned my face close to the cage and jumped back as something pressed its front paws against the little hinged door.

I took another step backward. Was this the chipmunk Dr. Clarke had mentioned? I stepped closer again and it ran to huddle in the far corner, wrapping its tail around its body like a blanket. It wasn't a chipmunk, just a scared squirrel.

"Poor thing! Why would you keep it in the dark like this? Do you only care about toads or what?"

"It's down here *because* I care. It was much too comfortable with humans. I'm trying to rehabilitate it and keep it away from people as much as possible. Best practices. But I think we have something more pressing to focus on."

I took a deep breath and waded back into the mess of a situation he'd helped create. "Yes. First, how long have you been a spy for the ASF?"

"Not a spy. You could call me a sympathizer. I like to think of myself as checks and balances. I don't want an ETC dictatorship, and I don't want ASF-sponsored anarchy."

He tucked his knife back into his utility belt, the slimy evidence bag flopping in his other hand. "There are a lot of moving parts here, including parties in much higher places. Some serve the people, and others serve self-interest. I represent the former, as long as they are moral. There is an incomprehensible amount of power up for grabs with your parents' tech and its potential, so lots of opportunity for corruption."

"Does Dr. Clarke know you're holding Jaxon here?"

"Yes. I told him I intercepted Jaxon's kidnapping and planted the foot to put the ASF off long enough to get you here. Dr. Clarke thinks he's keeping Jaxon safe."

I scoffed and turned back to watch the lonely, captive squirrel.

I heard ManBun take a step closer.

I put up a hand behind me so he'd keep his distance. "I want to see Jaxon for myself."

"I can't take you to him right now. Dr. Clarke is keeping the truth about the foot being fake out of the news and blaming the ASF so that he can keep public opinion on his side. But he also suspects you know something, and wants information from you, anything you know about the ASF or their leadership. He won't ask you point blank, because he's not sure you'd give him a straight answer."

I spun to face him and folded my arms. "So he's using Jaxon to manipulate me as well? I guess I can't be straight with any of you."

He shrugged, and a drop of rotten jam fell from the evidence bag. "You can blame me for that, too. I suggested he stay aloof from the nitty-gritty and let me handle keeping FutureMove safe."

"So how does the ASF trust you? How does *anyone* trust you?" How could I trust him with my sister?

"I don't think they do, but I'm in too good a position for them to resist using me."

I shook my head and turned my back to him again. It would take more than a couple of minutes to adjust to the fact that ManBun—Manuel—didn't mutilate my best friend. I covered my face with my hands to cool my skin and hide how he'd affected me.

Manuel turned and headed toward the elevator, giving me some blessed space. He must have noticed my agitation despite my incredible talent for staying calm and collected.

I still hated that he'd included Jaxon in his calculations, but he'd given me more information about both sides than either party had, and I didn't see any obvious inconsistencies in his story.

"I know this is a lot to think about, but I'm doing my best to help a complicated situation work out as smoothly as possible for you. I believe some of the ASF have good intentions, but

I wouldn't show them all your cards, only the files that might help them build an alternate port grid. Nothing about any new research or development. This is a hostage negotiation, and you want to keep whatever upper hand you can get."

I didn't need the upper hand. All I wanted was the lower foot and the rest of Jaxon, safe. He'd said the same thing Kendi had, though. Neither of them trusted their own organizations, or whomever was calling the shots. And neither of them knew Mom's backups of the research existed, or they'd have demanded I hand them over—they might have even scrapped the kidnapping idea and gone with burglary.

I leaned against the table next to me. "This wouldn't be a hostage situation if you'd just release the hostage. You're Head of Security. Get the files yourself."

"I can't, I'm security, not IT. I wouldn't know what to look for. Satisfy the ASF, I'll get him out legally, and neither organization will need him anymore. I'll assist with file access where I can."

"Sure. Just trust the computer-illiterate double agent, and it's smooth sailing."

"Hey, I can email with the best of them." He checked his watch. "We've been down here too long. I have one other trick to show you down here, and then I need to get upstairs. I hate to leave the security cameras unmonitored, but I promised Nadia a brunch break."

I hoisted my weight away from the table and walked toward the elevator. "Nadia might not want brunch or anything else from you once she hears you okayed a plan to use my best friend as bait. Of course, she's probably part of your grand scheme. Must come in handy to be close with the reception—"

"Don't you dare imply that my feelings for your sister are less than genuine." Manuel stabbed his index finger at me, and then let it drop. His eyebrows fell apart, and his eyes took on a dreamy sheen while he looked up to the ceiling, as if he could admire Nadia at her desk through several feet of concrete and rebar and whatever else separated us. "Your sister is the most amazing person I've ever met. I've been in love with her since the day I saw her with your parents during my first tour of the building." He hugged the evidence bag in his hand—still dripping with sticky jam—and lost himself in memory. "Her smile, at first, and then getting to know her and everything she's gone through . . . it might dim down some people, make them bitter. But she's only bloomed brighter." He swung the foot-filled bag out to the side, and I jumped back to avoid the bits of flying ooze. "I can't believe she is even going out with me. She's my dream come true. The more I get to know her, the deeper I fall. The more intimately—"

"Gross, stop." I didn't need any more slime or sentiment flung my way.

"I don't want you ever thinking my love for her isn't all-encompassing—"

"So you *like* like her, for realzies. Got it." For her sake, I hoped he *was* the stalwart romantic he played so well. But he had kidnapped my friend and coerced my involvement, and I wouldn't forget that so easily.

The cage in the corner gave another small shake.

Manuel came back to Earth and turned to put the nasty packet back into the box. "Now, as far as I understand it, there are two ways to get onto the closed network where they keep the most important research. One is to use a computer in the active research lab, which always has people in it, even Sundays. The second is to access it directly from the server room." He hefted the box back onto the shelf and turned back to me. "Does that sound right?"

"Correct."

Manuel nodded. "I'm one of the only people with access. Our IT director can come in to do whatever regular maintenance or troubleshooting they need to run in here. But the most sensitive files are stored on servers locked behind metal doors, and the keys are stored in Dr. Clarke's vault."

"Server storage cages have pathetic locks; I'll be fine there. But aren't you worried about using your badge to get into the server room?"

"I'm not going to use my badge. This building is American Disability Act compliant, and we've got a closet full of these." He opened the closet door.

I leaned forward to see what was in there. "A bullet-proof vest? What does that have to do with ADA? We're not shooting our way—"

"No," he chuckled. "May I?"

I stepped back to allow him to reach into the closet.

He pulled the vest off and chucked it to the floor. "ADA compliance means that the doors in the building have lever-type knobs." He held up the wire hanger. "So this, with . . ."—he felt along the high closet shelf and produced a small roll of twine, "—this is all we need."

I cocked my head to the side.

"I'll show you. Hang on." Manuel untwisted and bent the heavy-duty hanger into a long bow shape with his bare hands and tied the twine to one end. I followed him to the door to the outside stairwell, and he locked himself outside with the bow. I thought about ditching him then, but I was intrigued, and he obviously trusted me. I could still use him.

His muffled voice came through the door. "Watch."

I stepped out of the way as the hanger slid under the door and hit my shoe. When most of the length had pushed under the weather stripping and into the building, he turned the bow upright and, after a few attempts, hooked it over the door handle. He pulled the twine, bending the bow down and pulling the handle down with it. The door latch clicked, and I pulled the door open, revealing a kneeling Manuel and his triumphant grin. It was still lop-sided, but the smile came with a dimple, and I saw, for one brief second, how someone like Nadia could think that he wasn't terrible looking.

"See? Did you see what I did?"

"Got it." It was impressive, actually. And terrifyingly easy. I already knew digital security was usually a sham. Apparently everyday physical security was just as impotent.

"So that's how you'll get into the server room," He held out the three-foot tool.

"Sure. And where do you propose I hide this? My back pocket?"

"Oh. Uh, would it fit down your pant leg?"

I didn't answer him with words, but if looks could maim, I would have etched my annoyance into his forehead. I motioned for him to turn around as I stuffed the stupid thing down the back of my left leg. It was cold on my skin, and the twine itched my ankle where I tucked the end into my shoe. Good thing I wasn't wearing any of Nadia's jeggings today. Relaxed fit for the win.

"You can turn back around now. It kind of works."

"You sure? Everything's decent?"

"Yep." Especially decent of him to be so careful with my privacy. Point to him for that.

"All right." He turned around. "Get to the old lab. Stay there a minute in case anyone checks. Then get into the server room, then go home."

"Got it."

Manuel held the elevator door open and then latched it closed after me. I tried to watch the code he entered to access the upper floor, but he effectively blocked my view with his not-scrawny body. I heard the pleasant chime and button prodding, then floated in bright light and landed.

Manuel stepped up to the main elevator doors as they opened into the lobby. "Don't let your guard down. Security is an illusion. And get this done while Nadia and I are out, okay?"

"Yep."

He walked out and I smashed the door-close button, then floor three, to the lab that used to belong to my parents.

CHAPTER ELEVEN

Selfie Stick It to the Man

I PULLED A PIECE of paper out of a printer and left a note on the desk saying that I'd gone to the bathroom, in case anyone came to check on me. Hurrying to avoid being pulled into any of the countless memories the room held, I half-jogged, half-dragged my leg over to the stairwell. The server room was one floor up.

I heaved the solid fire door open. The metal bow poked out of my waistband as I climbed the fourteen steps, but I finally made it. The fourth floor was quiet, but I tucked the bow under my shirt after easing the door closed behind me.

A bubble camera affixed to the ceiling about halfway down captured the entire corridor. I hoped Manuel really was the only one monitoring cameras for the day. Not only was I hobbling down the hallway with one stiff leg like a drunken flamingo, but when I tried to get the bow out from my pants it lifted up the back of my shirt. I twisted around and tugged my shirt free, preferring not to add poorly executed striptease to my list of today's offenses.

I turned up my hearing aids and paused to listen for

anyone coming from an office or an elevator, and then squatted down and fed the bow under the door. Manuel had made it look relatively easy: push it through, flip it up, hook the handle, pull it down. My hands must have been more sweaty and gross than his, even with his being coated in expired preserves, because it took me about three times as many tries to catch the handle. I yanked down on the twine and pushed on the door, only to have it slip off the handle before the door opened. After wiping my hands on my roomy jeans I tried again, this time hooking the handle faster and pulling the twine down slowly. The latch clicked and I pushed the door open.

Soothing lights blinking on the stacked servers, beckoned me inside, and I nudged the door closed. The room was chilly and dark, perfect for a room full of electronics and a heisty atmosphere. Stacks of servers on racks about six feet high lined three walls, glowing with flickering LEDs and sprouting cables which wound around the equipment, branching off and joining back together like techno ivy snaking through a cyberpunk jungle. It wasn't like some server rooms I'd seen—masses of jumbled cables like the bottom half of a plant pulled from too-small pot. It was as orderly as Mom's alphabetized spice rack, which Nadia could still keep precise because I never cooked and wouldn't know what to do with spices. But I did know my way around here.

One of the racks was closed off with a metal mesh door, alerting me to exactly which server stacks contained the juicy stuff. I tucked the metal hanger bowl between two racks at the back of the room and retrieved my small lockpick set from my pocket. The pitiful wafer lock was no match for my jiggler—a small, lumpy pick. It took about four seconds for me to insert the pick and turning tool, rake the pins, and turn the lock. Inside the door, I located the KVM drawer: a small slide-out keyboard, monitor, and mouse connected to the servers.

```
> Login: admin
> Password: Sumer2031!
[-] Authentication    failed.    [2]
attempts remaining
```

The password from my most recent phishing attack had worked a couple days ago. It was the middle of October, so I'd figured they must not make their employees change passwords quarterly, like many companies do. It must have been changed soon after my power-stealing kerfuffle when I flagged the system and Manuel got called in.

Or maybe they had entirely different logins for the air-gapped servers. I should have made better plans for how I'd actually log in once I broke in physically. My pulse quickened, but I wouldn't allow panic to set in. I could figure this out.

```
> Login: admin
> Password: admin
```

This worked when no one bothered to set up an actual login.

```
[-] Authentication    failed.    [1]
attempts remaining
```

My hands became slippery again, and I thought I heard footsteps outside the door. I sucked some saliva down the wrong tube and coughed on my own spit as quietly as I could, stepping out of direct line of sight to the door. When I didn't hear anything besides the low humming of CPU fans, I took a controlled breath in, held it for four counts, and then let it out and held it for four counts before breathing in again—something I'd learned on my meditation app. Okay, so it was something I learned from an ad for a meditation app which interrupted a mindless game I was playing, because I won't pay for ad-free games on my phone. It was helpful, nonetheless.

Maybe the forced password changes didn't coincide exactly with the season.

```
> Login: admin
> Password: Fall2031!
```

I didn't push enter. If this third attempt didn't work, I might be locked out and flag an urgent notification to some on-call tech that someone was messing around in the server room.

I took a second to think. FutureMove employees were intelligent people, so they wouldn't have misspelled Summer in Sumer2031! accidentally. Although, who knows with abnormally smart people. They can be amazing in one field and complete buffoons in another. But I was overthinking. Maybe they weren't allowed to repeat consecutive characters in their passwords. So Fall2031! wouldn't work. They clearly needed to have an uppercase and lowercase letter, a number, and a special character. What about length? Was Fal2031! long enough?

I recalled other passwords I'd captured during the phishing attack, including iH8temybos$, 14thP@sw3rd, and Rememberthis!20. They seemed a little longer. I guessed they had to be at least ten characters.

```
> Login: admin
> Password: Autumn2031!
```

Like a sniper timing her heartbeat, I breathed in sync with the flashing lights and hit enter. I peeked at the screen with one eye.

```
[+] Welcome, admin.
```

Bam!

I hoped that, given the immaculate state of the room, the files inside would be orderly. I was not disappointed. Everything was in its proper place, but the folders and files had such technical naming standards that it blended together. To someone like Manuel, it would have looked like a smorgasbord of random letters and numbers with a healthy serving of underscores sprinkled throughout. But I'd pored through the port unit code enough to recognize the folders I needed.

Tucked a few layers deep inside a folder called sysdev-qres_live, I recognized file names like coeff_qtunn_final.bin and pthsolv_seq-M19.yaml. This was it. I transferred the whole folder onto the massive thumb drive the ASF left for me in Slaughterbox—massive in storage capacity, not in physical size. I still had to sneak the thing out of the building.

I half-heartedly scanned the servers for anything about my parents' failed demonstration. The ASF wanted to study information about the glitch in order to stop it from happening, they'd said. It was the one objective I fully supported, since I'd been working on making the booths safe as well. All I could get anyone to tell me about the accident was that my parents thought they'd be able to teleport with dense metals. Mom had worn gold jewelry into the test, and Dad had held a tungsten light bulb above his head, as if to represent their big idea. But instead of porting everything to the second booth in the test lab, the demonstration's density settings glitched to an even lower threshold than usual. The tungsten and gold, along with some of the denser structures of the human body, stayed in the first booth while the rest of them . . . Anyway, it hadn't worked.

I found a folder in the Research and Development directory called Density-Thresholds, but it was empty. The ETC truly *had* deleted any FutureMove data related to the research leading to the accident, as they'd claimed. The idea of people porting anywhere they wanted with no way to keep them out must have really disturbed the higher-ups. I searched for anything surrounding the investigations afterwards, but no luck there, either. Apparently, the server room backup drives weren't where FutureMove spilled its hottest tea. In here, it was all clean code and cold engineering.

I hated that my parents' latest research had died with them. The density breakthrough would have been a big deal, but in the information security world, at least, new exploits never lasted long before someone invented a patch for them. People could have found a way to control this tech, too. I'd done a search for it here and there from the old lab when I thought I could get away with it, and I'd scoured every drive in both of Mom's secret hiding places. Nothing. She probably hadn't had time to make a backup, or she was planning on doing so after the first big demonstration.

I likely should have left the server room at that point. I had no idea whether they had alerts set up to flag activity on the server or how often techs visited, but I had a personal objective I couldn't resist. I found the folder for the security feeds and double-clicked with the speed of a hummingbird's heartbeat, accidentally opening two windows, which took a few agonizing seconds to populate. I searched the folders for Jaxon's last name, Jeong, and it came up right away in a list of arrests. He had two entries. "Jaxon Jeong, possession of unregistered mobile device," and "Jaxon Jeong, suspected ASF affiliation." This entry had a booking date and holding cell number, *A3*.

I knew I was pushing my luck, but I had to check one last folder—Surveillance. I would have hidden the sensitive files in folders labeled "spreadsheets" or "boring tax documents" but, luckily for me, I wasn't in charge here.

I digitally waltzed right up to the backup footage for holding cell A3, and grainy black-and-white images of Jaxon slapped me in the feels. If I were one of the servers in the stacks, my fan would have gone out, and a couple of cables would've popped loose.

There he was, pushing broccoli around a plastic tray with a plastic fork. *Those bastards.* He hated broccoli. He'd eat the stems if they were drenched in ginger sauce, the way his mom made them, but he couldn't abide the texture of the tops. And speaking of, his parents would be freaking out if they weren't off working in Seoul, totally ignorant of this whole mess.

Sure enough, both feet were attached and healthy. My knees buckled, but I caught my balance before I smacked my chin on the pull-out tray. I also caught a drip of escaped tear liquid before it short-circuited the keyboard. Manny had him in plain white socks like a common criminal, but my Jaxon was okay! I had to wrap this up and get to him. The server lights blinked with joy, and the warmth of the beautiful cable jungle helped me believe the world could be right again.

I tried copying the security folder to explore later, but it was too enormous with all the video. I ejected my thumb drive. "I'm getting you out of there," I said out loud, and touched my finger to his hair on the monitor. Today. I'd turn over some of the teleportation files to the ASF, and they'd give me Jax back, and I'd buy him new socks and a giant cheeseburger with my summons money.

A sudden beep of the building's PA system blared into my brain, and I startled, bumping the tray. I shoved it back in and closed the cage door.

The calm, pleasant voice announced my doom like a flight attendant kindly letting me know that they were out of pretzels and also the plane was plummeting uncontrollably toward Earth.

"All visitors, please report to the lobby immediately. Personnel, remain in place."

I'd been flagged after all, and the on-call tech hadn't been asleep at the wheel. My ears tingled. They knew. I ran to the server room door, hoping to get to the hallway before anyone else did. The announcement repeated. "All visitors, please report to the lobby immediately."

Please, the recording said, as if it were optional. As if I wouldn't be thrown into the nearest open cell if they caught me anywhere but the lobby. I inched the door open, raced to the elevator, and pounded the down button before my brain kicked in. Anyone, like Security, could be on that elevator. I'd be better off ignoring the announcement from my parents' lab than complying on the elevator coming down from a floor I wasn't supposed to have visited.

I ran to the stairwell door. I yanked it open, but my fingers slipped, and I smacked my forehead on the edge of the thick, solid door. I let out a suppressed yelp of pain and hefted it open again. I hurtled inside, regained my balance, and scrambled down two half-flights of stairs to the fourth floor. Then I cracked the door open with my shoulder. I saw no one in the hallway, but I heard squeaking shoes and voices from around the corner. The lab door was across the hall and three doors down. But the utility room door was right across from me, and it had a door leading into the next room, which also connected to the lab.

I positioned my legs like a sprinting champion and braced my shoulder against the door. I counted in my head, *one, two,* and then burst through the fire door and into the storage room. I dodged a stack of boxes and slowed, momentarily distracted by the translucent jewel-tone of a vintage Bondi Blue iMac before reaching the door to the room next to the lab. Locked. I grabbed for my lock picks and then looked a little closer at the door. It was a flimsy interior door with a push-button lock. I let go of the lock picks and pulled my ID from my wallet, slid it into the crack between the door and the jamb, and pulled it down, pushing the latch into the door. I opened it and stepped into the room. The framed photo of

Mom and Dad and Misha and Carleson, B. hanging on the lab side of the door clapped against the thin wood as I shut it behind me.

I stashed the USB drive, then turned around and found a pen. The printer drawer provided a blank piece of paper, and I rolled a stool up to a long table. My shoulders fell as I rested my arms on the table, trying to slow my breathing and relax enough to sell having been here the whole time.

I sketched a glass tube pouring liquid into a beaker.

My parents had kept me out of the other physicists' way, Dad with his logic puzzles and Mom with her descriptions of teleportation, like flying through the air at some fraction of the speed of light, faster than The Flash. I paid more attention to the superpower narrative than the technicalities, at least while my age was in the single digits.

I doodled a superhero in a lab coat in the sky with one arm in front of her and one leg bent for extra power. I started drawing speed lines behind her when the intercom clicked on again.

"All visitors, please report to the lobby immediately." The pleasantly threatening announcement sent a shock through my body and my pen jerked in my hand, making my superhero look like she was flying in a wonky zigzag instead of a nice, straight line.

That would be me, if I were a superhero. Unconventional, but still flying. I idly wondered who got to record the announcement. Was she ETC, or some voice model? My head pounded where I'd hit it with the door. I bent forward, angling my head so that the sore part rested on the table. The cool metal felt nice for a second before the pressure added to the throbbing, but I had to be able to explain the redness somehow. I rested my right arm on the drawing, letting the pencil fall from my hand, and allowed a little saliva to ooze its way out of the corner of my mouth.

As I closed my eyes, the lab door burst open, and Manuel's voice called out to the hallway. "See, she's right here where I told you to look in the first place."

Someone plodded into the lab. I startled awake for them, blinking and wiping my cheek. "Oh, man, I must have—"

"Come with me," said a short ETC security goon with a long bowl cut. "We're clearing non-essential personnel and visitors for security purposes."

Manuel had already left again.

"Oh! Wow, what happened? I guess I'd better turn these back on." I pretended to fiddle with the toggle switches on the back of my hearing aids, hoping the guard would believe I hadn't heard the announcement.

The security guy waved toward the elevators. "This way, please." He motioned for me to get on and then stepped in behind me, his terrible haircut flapping against his ears. Did he not have anyone in his life who cared enough to point out that it made him look like something video game characters ate to power up?

I tried some innocent chatter. "Exciting day today, for a guard, I guess, yeah? Not your average boring shift."

"Sorry, what?" he asked.

"What?" I asked back, then looked at the wall, regretting my choice to speak. Thankfully, the elevator doors opened into the gleaming lobby.

I followed the young guard to the front desk, where Dr. Clarke was talking to my sister.

". . . the face of this company. I'm so glad I found this position for you. I took care of you, and you've been a perfect employee for four years, taking care of us here. I understand your sister wanting to spend time where your parents spent theirs."

"Thank you, sir."

Dr. Clarke spoke to Nadia in a calm, even voice, which annoyed me. It made it hard to tell what he was fishing for.

"But you have to do your job and stay aware of the time visitors spend in the building, even if it's someone you trust. While you were out with Manuel, there was unusual activity on our internal networks, and we can't afford that kind of breach."

"Yes, sir," Nadia said to the floor. "You know Alyona would never—"

"Even if it's the Head of Security who convinces you to leave your post while visitors are running around, you know better. Might be time to put you two on a more staggered schedule."

"Oh, Manny was just—"

Dr. Clarke heard me coming and turned around. He shot me a bright smile. "Of course I know Alyona wouldn't tamper with FutureMove files. I am merely using her as an example. Best practices. Treat all visitors the same way, and you won't be socially engineered to let the bad guys in.

"And in case someone inside the building is after something, we need to be more strict about protocol. No unsupervised lab visits. I couldn't live with myself if I let anything happen to you two. That is, after all, where your parents—"

"Got it," I said. A jolt of pain spiked through the sore spot on my forehead. I couldn't stand people talking about my parents' death in everyday conversational tones, proving how they were past it enough to work it into normal conversations. The only way I could mention their death in a casual manner was the occasional sarcastic thought, bound to the confines of my mind.

Dr. Clarke beckoned to the security guy. "Gary? Wand, please." Dr. Clarke took the metal detector wand and stepped closer to Nadia. "I'd like you to take Alyona home, Nadia. Have the day. You can both leave as soon as I'm sure nothing has been planted on either of you."

My stomach dropped. I mentally raced through everything I knew about metal detectors and how much they could pick out through clothing. My eyes darted toward the revolving door. Could I feign a nervous breakdown and book it out of there before my turn with the quite unmagical wand?

Nadia stood two inches taller than Dr. Clarke in her business pumps, and he scanned slowly up and down both sides of her body, tracing her curves.

"You pass, Nadia, thank you. Alyona?"

"Oh, I didn't go near people, I was in the lab—"

"Sleeping. I heard over the guards' coms. Anyone could have bugged you or planted something they will steal from you later. Can't be too careful."

Awesome. He found a way to use my plan against me. Not that he knew that. I shuffled toward the front doors. "It's fine, I wasn't out for long. I'm not worried. I can even head home myself. You don't have to be without a receptionist."

Dr. Clarke pointed the wand at me and then curved it toward himself. "Stop, Alyona. Come on back, it'll only take a few seconds."

I came back. What else could I do?

Dr. Clarke waved the wand briskly over my torso, hovering at my pockets.

The beeping began, and I pulled out a couple of bobby pins, a napkin, and my lock picks.

Dr. Clarke picked up the lock picks and checked in the case.

Nadia stepped forward. "She always carries those. Every day. I think it's ridiculous, I tell her she's asking for trouble, because of situations exactly like this. Really, how does this look, Alyona?"

It might have sounded to Dr. Clarke like she was throwing me under the bus, but I knew she was exaggerating a small misbehavior to distract from anyone suspecting me in the larger breach. She had my back in the most annoying big sister way possible.

Dr. Clarke forced a chuckle. "We all know our Alyona. One more pass, little rascal, and you're off." He waved the wand past the same pocket again, not buying my red herring.

It beeped again.

I lifted a USB drive out of my pocket and held it up to Dr. Clarke. "Oh, this is mine from home. Nothing scary."

He plucked it out of my hand. "I'll do a check to make sure it didn't end up with anything on it you didn't intend to take; you were sleeping for a while, and through the intercom announcement. You can pick it up tomorrow at the front desk."

Nadia's lips parted and her eyebrows arched. She was going to give me away.

"I can scan it at home, don't worry about that," I said in one last effort to keep my drive.

"It's no problem, thanks for your cooperation. Off you go." He turned to scary-hair Gary and handed him my drive. "Take this to my vault."

I spun around and stomped toward the exit, heat rising in my face. His personal vault used to be *their* personal vault, my parents and his. It was *the* vault, where they kept top-secret prototypes and backups—or the only copies in some cases—of the most sensitive data. Not *his* vault. He'd probably filled it with backups of backups—he was as orderly as Mom and twice as paranoid. I hadn't been allowed in since they'd been gone.

"Alyona—" Nadia called.

"Let's go," I said, flapping my arm at her behind me and forcing myself to think of my parents instead of my current situation, worried I might crack. I had to get out of there before they found anything.

I had to look angry and upset, because I was about to laugh and blow everything.

I didn't care about Dr. Clarke finding Nadia's mortifying collection of before-and-after makeup selfies I'd copied from her phone last night to the USB drive he'd confiscated. But I had to make them suspicious and focused on the decoy. I didn't need anyone checking the ASF's drive I currently had pinched between my toes.

CHAPTER TWELVE

A Poppycock Chinwag and Bugger-All

I ALMOST RAN INTO Nadia when she stopped inside our apartment door, blocking my way to the living room. She spun around, arms outstretched like a point guard. "Shoes, and *then* couch. You are not tracking your filth all over our home."

"What? It's not wet out, and I need to sit on the couch to take my shoes off." My contraband poked my foot.

"Shoes. Then. Couch." Nadia slipped off her pumps and tucked her feet into fuzzy white house shoes. Only Nadia could make size ten look dainty.

I dropped dramatically to the floor and heaved a gigantic sigh to make sure she knew I was inconvenienced. I pulled off my shoes, crawled over to the couch and pulled myself up beside her.

She put her arm around me and shifted from warden mode to caring big sister. "So what do we do now, Alyon? What are they going to find on that USB drive? Do we need to pack, get out of the state? I have a friend in Arizona—"

"Well I'm glad my shoes are off. I mean, priorities. We can

worry about the life-altering state of affairs in which we find ourselves entangled after I do some dishes."

She shoved me. "Come on, seriously. This could be bad for both of us."

"I don't know, Nadia. You might not be ready. Are you ready?"

"Ready for what?"

"Ready for this!" I shot my sweaty sock foot into her face and wiggled my encumbered toes. I may have been a little slap-happy after my big win. She shoved me harder, and I tilted over and slid off the couch onto my butt, holding my leg up stiff like a fainting goat. I yanked off my sock and declared a triumphant *Vot*! *Behold*! I picked the drive from between my toes and held it up.

"Gross!" Nadia recoiled and scrunched her nose.

"Grossly underestimated, you mean. You totally thought I'd been caught."

Nadia relaxed her face. "You're right, this is impressive. Is it everything you need to get Jaxon back? What are you doing sitting here on the floor, go get him!"

"Everything I need and more. I have to sort it out, then I'll be off."

She reached out to give me a hand up, pointing to my other, not-holding-a-sweaty-toe-drive hand. She'd let me rot on the floor before touching my toe jam.

"So wait, then what was on the other thumb drive that Dr. Clarke took?"

"You don't want to know."

"I'm sure I do."

"The important thing is that the decoy worked. Everyone played their parts beautifully."

"Everyone who?"

Blin. I'd let the rush of victory override my common

sense. This was still a precarious situation, and I had to keep straight who knew what. "I mean, I was a total pro, and Manuel—well, you did a great job keeping him out of the building for a while."

"You're welcome, I suppose. I'm just happy he's not involved."

I frowned. I hadn't had time to consider what Nadia should know about how involved Manuel was. I hated having to balance and calculate what I said around Nadia. I hated that Manuel and the ASF had put me in this position and thought they could use people however they wanted. But I believed he thought he was doing the best thing for the right reasons, and I had to figure out whether he was good for Nadia, or a charismatic scumbag. I replied with a simple, "Sure."

Nadia pulled me into a delicate, cherry-blossom-scented hug. I sank into her soft sweater and let her stroke my tangled hair. "Everything will be okay, alright? Have faith."

Mama Nadia was always there when I needed her, but she couldn't possibly know how everything would turn out. She didn't even know her current boyfriend. Water welled in my eyes, and I took a slow, shaky breath, tamping down the misdirected frustration. I didn't want to be mad at her. *She should be mad at me.* I shouldn't have looked up the video files to check on Jaxon. I'd spent too long there out of selfish curiosity, and I almost got caught. I could have put her job at risk. And I would likely have to hide even more from her before this was over.

Exhaustion filled the vacuum my brief elation had left behind. "Will everything be all right? I'm not so sure, Nad." I let my pooling tears seep into Nadia's sweater and told her about Jaxon's fake foot, the broccoli, the horrible plain white socks. "And Manuel, he's alright. You can keep him for now." It was the nicest thing I'd ever said about any of my sister's boyfriends, and though she was clearly mortified by his involvement with the foot thing, when she pulled away from the hug, I could have sworn I saw hearts in her eyes.

Manuel did what he had to. It was the ASF ruining my peace and manipulating me for some stupid manifesto or another. Porting within Denver was already free if you used the port card. Some places required massive fees or subscriptions to port, and some countries didn't allow porting at all. The ASF should have been happy with the freedom they had. I was with Manuel on this one. I was no lover of power monopolies, but I didn't trust the ASF to be better stewards.

Nadia opened her mouth, but I spoke first. "I'm going to get this drive ready for the drop, I'll be back down in a bit."

After a brief detour to the kitchen for a handful of cereal out of the box and then a swig of milk from the carton while Nadia wasn't looking, I took two stairs at a time up to my room and started a file transfer from the USB to my laptop. I couldn't help browsing files while they transferred, even though I knew it would slow the process down. I opened the R&D folder and browsed some of the document titles. "Seismic Testing," "School Porting Needs Assessment," "CDC-pathogen-densities-list."

Interesting. I could have gone down a new rabbit hole for each title, and questions crowded my mind. Could the booths target a specific density and move only that? Could they pinpoint a deadly virus, and port it out of the body without pulling anything else out? We'd probably have to target other properties besides density or integrate AI to identify and port a certain selection. Could we port our trash to the sun? Remove grass stains I put in Nadia's white slacks? Send any spiders in the house straight to hell?

One of the folders wouldn't open when I clicked—it

was password protected. I could have found a work-around, but I took the opportunity to check in on my cyber-buddy, N031.

> *AuGurl: Hey, N, you there?*
>
> *N031: Yes. Researching. Did you know that FutureMove could make gold objects able to teleport, but instead they want everyone to give them phones to collect gold and palladium? They will melt all metal down and make currency for when they take over world governments.*
>
> *AuGurl: Nope, hadn't heard that one. And, dude, they'd probably make more money off the copper in there, there's more of it and it's worth a ton. And, like, platinum, right?*

I had no idea what ratio the metals were, nor did I know the value of copper vs gold. But N031 was always spouting one conspiracy theory or another.

> *N031: Yes, they take this too.*
>
> *AuGurl: Can you crack another hash for me?*
>
> *N031: Send it.*
>
> *AuGurl: Done. How's the squirrel?*
>
> *N031: Squirrel is very smart. More smart than many humans, but he will need training.*
>
> *AuGurl: Go on . . .*
>
> *N031: I train him to notify me if someone is coming to my property. I give him small reward, very tasty nuts. Very expensive nuts. It works well, until he finds where I hide nuts. Not important where I hide them, he smells them, he finds them, he eats them. All. I am selling some of my satellite equipment so that I can pay for nuts.*

> AuGurl: Send me your address, I will send you nuts.
>
> N031: Nice try.
>
> AuGurl: So what else can he do? I hope I get to see this someday.

Manuel had better not find out about this guy training squirrels while he was here trying to resensitize them to fear humans. He might get a clip board and start a petition.

> N031: Next I will teach him to wear his harness, for record video. He hates it too much for now. If I try to put it onto him, he falls down as if dead. He won't move again until I take it off. Not even for nuts. Oh, password is «KaRt0f3l»
>
> AuGurl: You're not missing one of your squirrels, are you?
>
> N031: One moment
>
> N031: They do not come for roll call, but I think not. Hard to say. Does he respond to commands in Russian?

Silly me, I hadn't thought to give the squirrel an order to test its language preferences. Rookie mistake. But N031 had also just screwed up and told me he was close enough to Denver for a lost squirrel to potentially be his, meaning not Siberia after all—if the whole thing wasn't a weird joke, that is.

> AuGurl: ⁻_(☐)_/⁻ I don't usually talk to squirrels. But thank you for the password!
>
> N031: Any time.

I opened the folder with the password and found something the ASF would have appreciated. Alongside the documentation about GPS porting, the Z axis, sea-level vs. ground-level measurements, and airspace maps, was a folder called ukaz_punkt-pribyt which was a shortened version of "indicate arrival point." Inside, I recognized the code as commands and configurations for the port units. They may have gotten rid of my parents' research about porting dense materials, but, knowingly or not, they hadn't destroyed the research on porting to a location outside a booth.

Manuel was right, though, no need to give the ASF more than they asked for. I took the relevant files for coding a standard port unit and a few interesting papers and copied them onto the USB they left me. I protected them with the password the ASF had used before, RoX+R0LZ. I copied some other even more interesting code onto my phone for future personal use and sent a text to Kendi.

```
Alyona: I got it. Where do I pick up
Jaxon?
```

When she didn't answer right away despite my concentrated stare at the messaging app, I pulled up the news feed. A click-bait article about celebrities with private port booths and clubs you could only get to with secret rolling port codes distracted me long enough for Kendi to get with it and text me back.

```
Kendi: Go to these coordinates.
You'll find a pill bottle wrapped
in camouflage tape with a port code
inside. Leave the USB and give us one
hour. Once we verify its contents,
we'll deliver Jaxon to the port code
location.
```

I'd expected to pick him up at the ETC, but I'd accept free delivery.

```
Kendi: And Alyona, thank you.
```

Whatever. Like I needed gratitude from a kidnapping

terrorist. But they were smart to use what sounded like an unregistered geocache as a drop location. AppyTrip put the coordinates smack dab in the middle of a private golf course in a fancy schmancy neighborhood.

I tapped on the course's business listing and read some of the description. "The Elk River Golf Club is pleased to provide traditional tungsten-weighted golf clubs for use by our members, and complimentary storage for personal equipment." People who could afford this place could probably afford the sky-high vehicle registration prices and bring their own clubs by car, but Elk River spared no luxury. I couldn't go waltzing around there with my ratty backpack and naturally distressed jeans, so I walked to the top of the stairs and shouted down to the expert.

"Nadia, what do fancy people wear?"

"Come down here, I can't hear you when you yell."

I plodded down the stairs and stood in front of her with my arms outstretched.

She looked at me like a pampered cat looks at dry food. "They definitely don't wear that."

"I need to roam around a country club's golf course without looking out of place."

"For Jaxon, I presume?"

"Would I ask for any lesser reason?"

"I'll lend you a skirt if you promise not to rip it. Or sit on . . . anything." I could almost see the light bulb flash above her head as she sucked in a gasp and sat straight up in her seat. "And you know what else fancy people do?" Where the hearts had been earlier, stars appeared in her emoji eyes. "They curl their hair."

I'd let her curl my hair three times in my life, most of them before she became my guardian. Any semblance of a put-together lifestyle died with my parents. Getting all gussied up and presenting myself as anything other than the real-life mess I was felt hypocritical.

"It's already curly, Nadia."

"That's not curl, that's the beginning of several forgotten crochet projects, my dear. And we're going to create a work of art. It's for the job. To save Jaxon."

She was right. So I let her curl it for a fourth time, for the job. I didn't want to mess up my chances of getting Jaxon back, and if I had to subject myself to Nadia's hair tomfoolery, then so be it.

After seventeen repetitions of "hold still" and twelve of "you're going to burn me," she was done... with my hair. I thought she'd turned around to grab a mirror, but she came back with a makeup sponge.

"Oh no you don't—"

"Alyonushka," she purred. "You can't have hair like that and not get a face to match. At least let me do something about the bruise on your forehead."

"But I—"

She shushed me and dabbed cold goop onto my chin. "Don't talk, you'll mess it up."

Nadia held the opposite opinion from mine on how to best present oneself. She'd aced every welfare checkup from Social Services. She made everything perfect before they came, from the angle of the toaster to the fresh topcoat on her nails. She looked completely put-together, even when she didn't feel that way—and I know she didn't always feel that way. Our walls were thin, and her nose blows were surprisingly loud for her delicate face.

I let her do her thing. She put four different colors of eye shadow over my eyes, all of them brown. She even put makeup on my nose. What kind of makeup would a nose need? Then, she had me make a ridiculous shape with my mouth while she slathered on three different lipsticks or glosses or whatever. I was going to look like I headbutted a sepia rainbow and then it punched me in the mouth.

"Finished," she finally said. She fit in a quick happy clap before she grabbed the mirror and held it up to me.

Some kind of vampire version of myself stared back at me with her jaw hanging open. Not the gross, blood-dripping kind of vampires who wouldn't show up in the mirror, but the glamorous kind, who became seductively gorgeous when they turned immortal. Nadia was a true master. It was still me, and the browns looked like natural tints and tones, and somehow, for the first time, she made me want to take a selfie. This hot vampire wouldn't have any problem walking onto a fancy golf course.

"Well?" Nadia asked.

"Okay, nice." I said. Her tutorials had paid off. All her beauty stuff had its place, I guess, and she was good at it. But I didn't want her thinking she could do this to me whenever she wanted. "I have to get this file over to the drop ASAP."

"Everything's going to be okay." Nadia squeezed my forearm as I stood from her stool. "I know it." She couldn't know that for sure, but I had to hope she was right. This was almost over.

⇢

I stepped out of the port booth facing a modern rustic clubhouse on a path lined with perfectly manicured bushes and those little bunches of wheat or whatever grass landscaper people thought looked nice. A well-dressed elderly couple left the building and passed by, giving me pleasant nods and smiles. I turned to make sure they meant to smile at me and not someone behind me, and by the time I turned back it was too late to return the gesture.

Confidence, Alyona. I had to seem like I belonged there to get to the cache out on the grass. Or, the field, or whatever they called it, which was separated from the path by a decorative fence on both sides of the clubhouse. I could easily jump it, but I didn't want to draw attention or flash unsuspecting golfers in Nadia's short skirt.

A clean-cut guy around Nadia's age greeted me as I pulled open the front door to the clubhouse.

"Welcome to Elk River, what can I do for you?"

I panicked and put on a vaguely British accent. "Oh, hullo. I'd like a quick peek at the court, er, course if you wouldn't mind terribly."

"I'd be happy to give you the grand tour. Are you new in the area? Visiting?"

I looked around the desk trying to conjure a town name. "Yes, My father and I quite recently moved here from Bell . . . ingdale . . . shire. We call it Belngdersher, a wee village, really, my father doesn't much care for city life." Okay, no. I needed to move on from this stupid town name.

The front desk man smiled. "I'm guessing that's in the UK?"

Beats me. My accent sounded like a cross between an Australian YouTuber I followed and Peppa Pig.

"North Wales." I cursed myself for making this harder than it needed to be. Keep moving past the desk, out to the grass. "Wondering if I might walk the course, give it the ol' looky loo and get my morning constitutional in. I won't sneak in any game time—no clubs, after all. Righty-o, we'll see you in a jiff." I apologized internally to the entire UK and then literally skipped straight out the back to the course. It was weird, for sure, but the guy watched me and didn't follow, so it seemed to have worked.

I kept skipping past the group of golfers at the first tee, wondering to myself who I was and why I thought a frolicking caricature of a not-Welsh posh country girl was a good, inconspicuous move. When I'd trotted my ridiculous self far enough away from the normal humans, I dug my phone out of my sister's fancy clutch and pulled up the pinned location I'd saved on AppyTrip. I was still twelve hundred meters away and, thankfully, it was deeper into the course.

I dropped the frolic and settled into a slow jog. My quads and calves rejoiced, their capabilities having been largely ignored since softball season. The longest I regularly walked was the distance between port booths—about a half a kilometer—and more booths popped up every day. I held my phone flat out in front of me as I ran along a cement pathway. My heart beat faster as the distance ticked down, partly from the abundance of exercise, but mostly because I couldn't wait to get Jaxon back and be done with this rigmarole.

When the distance had shrunk to ten meters, I slowed to a walk and continued toward a small stand of junipers to the left of the wide paved path and away from the part with the short-mowed grass . . . the pitch? I stepped up to the biggest of the stumpy trees and heard the whine of an approaching golf cart. I plucked a fragrant blue juniper berry, turned around and sniffed it as the cart zoomed by. I hoped they'd see I was simply smelling junipers—a totally normal pastime—and keep rolling by. My compass was jumping all over, so I knew I was close, if not right on top of it. I sent a text to Kendi telling her I'd made the drop. I hadn't yet, but I figured I could give them a head start and cut some of the hour they said it would take to retrieve and verify the files if I told her now.

I checked for crevices in the base of the trunk, looked for canisters dangling in the branches, and peeked under a protruding section of a rock about the size of a softball glove.

Nothing. I checked around the other junipers and around the stone border of the outcropping. I looked for fake sprinkler heads and checked the light pole nearby for false face plates but nothing there either. Geocaches are supposed to be visible, at least from a close angle. My hands trembled as I checked the time on my phone. It had already been fifteen minutes, and I didn't want to mess up by being here when the ASF came to collect.

I squatted down on my feet to think, then stood again when I remembered I was in a skirt. What was I missing with this cache? Except this wasn't a geocache.

It was a criminal drop.

I doubled back to the largest tree, grabbed the edge of the softball-glove rock, and tugged, and there it was, nestled into an indentation in the dirt beneath. I heaved the rock to the side and plucked the pill bottle out of the ground, pulled out a note, tossed in the USB, and covered it back up again. The note said to meet at the Elk River trailhead and gave the coordinates. Still breathing heavily from my jog, or from the adrenaline, I ran toward the trailhead.

Fancy neighborhoods like this didn't have port booths. It was the same with rural towns who didn't rely on tourism. Public transportation supposedly raised crime stats due to ease of movement, so they relegated porting to the outskirts and set up private shuttle services, drove golf carts, or built high-end parking garages outside their gated communities. The nearest booth on this side of the course was a mile away. I found a trail running along the back of the golf course, and several minutes later, gasping for breath, I collapsed onto a bench in the trailhead parking lot.

Apparently, I could have entered the golf course from the back side, completely unnoticed and in my regular clothes. My face tingled a little bit when I realized that Jaxon would see me in this getup. Maybe I'd have time to change while they sorted out his release. I didn't want him thinking I got made up for him, but I supposed it wasn't the worst way to present myself. The tingling in my face grew warm, like I was short circuiting.

The ASF had said to give them an hour to verify the contents of the file. I took about fifteen minutes after I sent the text to find the cache, ten minutes to get here, and another five or so to catch my breath. Still just under thirty minutes to wait.

Maybe they'd be early. I spotted the port booth at the end of the parking lot and watched the door, in case Jaxon came out sooner. I nervous-scrolled my news feed for a few minutes, stopping on an article highlighting the Ten Best Beaches in the World. I'd take any of them. I caught flashing red from the booth in my peripheral vision. Out stepped a middle-aged serious hiker-man, the kind with moisture-wicking shorts and water bottles strapped to his waist. Jaxon had a set of those for bicycling. A younger version of the hiker walked out after him. They came toward me and both gave friendly nods, the younger dude's exaggerated nod accompanied by a "Hi."

I gave him a small flap of my hand without taking my eyes off the booth. Goodbye, not-Jaxon. I picked up my phone to check the time. It had to be any second now. The phone buzzed in my hand with an incoming text.

> PRIVATE NUMBER: We asked for everything you could get. You failed to follow directions. Try again tomorrow.

The phone slipped to my lap and then fell to the gravel parking lot as I stood and roared in frustration. I grabbed my phone and a couple of rocks with it. I hurled the rocks at the trailhead sign, and they pinged and bounced off in what should have been a satisfying hit. It wasn't enough.

Somehow, my body produced even more tear water and it blurred my view of the booth. I sprinted towards it. I saw the younger hiker dude jog back out from the trail before I tugged the door closed, probably to see whether I was okay. I most certainly was not.

And the ASF wouldn't be either, once I'd found them.

CHAPTER THIRTEEN

Liar, Liar, Pants in the Wind

I THREW OUR FRONT door shut behind me so hard that it closed all the way on the first try.

"Liars!" I yelled to the apartment, but really so Nadia would come down and commiserate. "I can't believe I thought it would be that simple."

Silence.

I shouted up the stairs. "Nadia!"

She wasn't here. I was starving, and I had hoped she'd been here anxiety-baking while she waited in suspense for me to rescue Jaxon in my fancy getup. I plopped down in a kitchen chair and laid my head on the table. I was being selfish again and projecting my rage in unhealthy directions. I needed food in my body. I looked for the bread bag on the counter by the toaster, but it had been pushed away. The toaster was on its side. Nadia must have been in a hurry; she yells at me when I don't line the thing up with the oven the right way.

But that wasn't the only item askew. Three cupboards and a drawer hung open. I turned around to take in the living room. The lid to the storage ottoman wasn't exactly square, and the old Satari gaming console was pulled out from the TV stand. Either Nadia and Manuel had quite the romp, or something even more disturbing had transpired—someone had searched our apartment while I was gone and possibly taken my sister.

I sent her a text before I allowed full-on panic to set in.

She sent me one back. "Yeah, I'm fine, on my way home. Why?"

I dropped to a chair and let out my breath. Okay. We didn't have any cash or jewelry, and they didn't take the electronics from the living room. The most valuable items we had were my trade pieces, but an average cat burglar wouldn't care about what looked like assorted odds and ends. The one thing I treasured in this apartment besides Nadia was . . .

Please, no. I took three stairs at a time and bolted into my room. It was an absolute disaster area, but that was normal. Everything looked how I'd tossed it into piles, except for one area that was terrifyingly clean.

My desk was a vacant, hollow desert of nothingness where my laptop should have been. My fingertips grew frigid. *Breathe.* Maybe I'd stuck it in my backpack, which was still on the floor leaning up against the desk.

Not in there.

I'd maybe tucked it away in the keyboard drawer. Nope, same random crap in there, only it had been moved to one side as if someone had searched through it. This wasn't a well-hidden geocache, and I wasn't about to find any PEZ dispensers. Someone had stolen my most precious and most incriminating possession.

Someone had been in my apartment, searched my cupboards, sat at my desk in my bedroom. My stomach squeezed like a warm cinnamon roll through cold fingers, and I ran to the toilet to dry heave. Then I stuck my head into Nadia's room to see what they'd taken of hers. Nothing, apparently. Her old maroon netbook sat on her pillow where she'd left it after watching hair or makeup tutorials to relax. There was one other computer in the house, but it was living its best afterlife as a marble-filled beach sculpture, and the thief wasn't after antiques. My best guess was that the ASF or the ETC, who both knew I'd be gone, came to see whether I had anything else useful for them.

They'd never get into my laptop. My drive was encrypted, and I had a twenty-four-digit password of random characters.

But now I didn't have anything more to trade for Jaxon, let alone anything to trade for a new computer at the market when I needed one. Thanks to all that was holy, I still had my phone. I called Nadia. The ASF had known I'd be out, but the only person who could reliably get Nadia out of the house was her dear beau.

I relaxed somewhat when she answered brightly, unharmed. "Hey, how did it go? You know, the event you attended?" She was as bad an actor as I was.

"Not well. Put Manuel on. Please."

"Okay, he's right here, I'll be home soon. It'll be all right."

I heard a shuffling sound, and then, "Alyona?"

I spoke in a low, but furious tone. I didn't want to worry Nadia yet. "Did you do this?"

"Yes, I will do whatever I can to help you." Manuel must have pulled the phone away from his face because I heard him tell Nadia, "Alyona says there's been a break-in. Not much taken." I yelled and tightened my grip on the phone. He'd done it, and now he was playing the hero.

"Listen," he said into the phone, "I'll explain later. You will thank me, I promise." I highly doubted that, and I couldn't respond through my gritted teeth. "Don't go anywhere, I'm going to send Nadia home to be with you, and I'm going to stop by work for some tools. I promised Nadia I'd get Jaxon's bike; she was worried about it sitting out at the mall. So I'll ride it there and be over soon."

I wanted to throw my phone, but it was my only connection to the outside world. I gave Manuel the bike lock combination so he wouldn't damage Jaxon's lock and then hung up. I'd change the code later.

I tried to calm down. Manuel hadn't raided my apartment himself, but he knew who had—otherwise, he'd never have sent Nadia home without him. His infatuation with her was the only thing I believed about him.

Two minutes later, my phone rang with an unknown number.

"Who is this," I demanded.

Manuel spoke fast. "Alyona, don't hang up. Nadia will be there any second."

"Talk."

"After you left, Dr. Clarke called me into his office. He suspected you had more than what he found on your USB. He made me search your apartment, and I knew you'd be gone. I had to bring him something. I figured you would back up anything important, and you're not the kind to leave sensitive data out in the open, so—"

"It wasn't out in the open! It was in my home, in my bedroom! And I don't need more than one copy of evidence that I stole data."

"All right, I get it. I'll talk to the ASF now and get Jaxon released as soon as possible. But in the meantime, if you did find anything valuable that you don't want the ASF to find, your hard drive is obviously safer in the vault—where it'll stay except for the few minutes it'll take for the security team to realize none of them is good enough to bypass your encryption. What if it had been my ASF contacts and not Dr. Clarke who had asked me to raid your place for information? There is lots to juggle right now. It's crucial I maintain Dr. Clarke's trust."

"More crucial than maintaining the trust of your girlfriend or her sister? I see where your priorities lie." I could see his reasoning, but I couldn't stand feeling like his pawn.

Manuel's tone lowered to match mine. "I'm tired of you second-guessing my feelings for Nadia. It's not something I appreciate you taking so lightly."

"Well, neither is my personal space and belongings."

I heard the door swing open and wedge closed, and I ended the call. I told Nadia someone, probably the ASF, had broken in and stolen my computer. I said I needed some time alone. Truthfully, I didn't want to look at Manuel when he showed up, for fear I'd shake him and demand he take me to Jaxon that instant.

I stomped up to my room and sat at my empty desk out of habit. I rested my elbows on its desolate surface and pulled out my phone to talk to the only other friend I could think of.

```
AuGurl: Hey, you up?

N031: Always. Did you hear the news?
Scientists Discover New Sound in Deep
Space, Unlocking the Powers of the
Human Brain?

AuGurl: Did you copy paste a click-
bait headline?

N031: It is very interesting. I will
reconfigure my satellites.
```

I didn't have the energy for his conspiracy theories tonight.

```
AuGurl: I had a crap day. Cheer me
up.
```

> N031: You cheer me up. I also had a crap day.
>
> AuGurl: Squirrels got your nuts again?
>
> N031: Always! See?

N031 sent a five-second video from his point of view: him awkwardly holding up a blue bag of mixed nuts for two seconds before outstretched paws sprang into view, quickly followed by the rest of the body and a violent chattering. The squirrel's eyes shone with fury and its tongue flailed to the side of its gaping maw topped with two little buck teeth. It was the stuff of adorable nightmares, and I literally LOLed.

Nadia came up and stopped at my bedroom doorway. "Hey, you okay? *Oh!* Squirrel! Did you know the ETC has one? Manuel let me pet him once."

I snorted. "I bet he did."

"Anyway," she huffed, "he fixed the door so it shuts right, and added a latch. And he checked our window locks. He's a handy person to have around." She left without waiting for a reply and closed my door behind her.

> AuGurl: OMG I can't stop watching this. Thank you.
>
> N031: No problem. 800[) /\/18#7!

Was he trying to say good night in 1337, aka leetspeak? Leet was an old-school computer nerd language. People used it in handles and fun words like h4x0r and p0wn, but not many people went all-out anymore. Plus he was wrong, which was weird.

> AuGurl: Usually g=6, FYI.
>
> N031: Ah, so I should be N031fin6r.
>
> AuGurl: Sure.

He could change his handle to $ail0rUranu$ for all I

cared. But what would that new spelling make his name? No Elf-inger? Not an improvement. I leaned back in my chair and said it out loud. Noelfinger.

Holy crap.

"Nadia!" I called. I stood and paced my room.

I sat back down and stared at my phone. "Nadi—"

"What?" She leaned in through my doorway.

"I don't know." Calling her was a natural reflex.

She sighed and pushed away from the door.

"Wait, help me remember that Christmas spelling joke Dad used to tell."

She stepped inside. "How it used to be spelled Chirstlmas, but now there's—"

"No-el," I said with her. No L finger. I watched the squirrel video again, this time in slow-motion. Nadia laughed at the soaring buck teeth, and I verified that N031 *was* holding the bag of nuts weirdly. He was missing the finger used for the L key, his right ring finger. Was it possible he'd lost the finger on his way to the woods after fleeing my parents' company? Porting across the world was unlikely, but I'd already guessed it was possible he lived relatively nearby.

My thumbs flew across my phone.

> AuGurl: Who are you really? Tell me, now.
>
> AuGurl: You worked for my parents.
>
> N031: Finally. I wasn't allowed to tell you. But I can't help it if you guess.

I slumped in my chair. Not N031, too. Was everyone in my life a secret spy?

> AuGurl: This isn't a game. What's going on?
>
> N031: It's not a game to me, either.

> I am wanted man, and I'm tired of hiding, waiting. I hoped you would want to help, but the rest of ASF don't want to put you in dangerous situation. They doubt your ability to remain collected and discreet.

My ears grew hot. Manuel had said I acted without thinking as well. Yes, my mood could shift quickly. I wasn't a machine—I was a teenager. I reacted. What were they so afraid of? They trusted me enough to steal data without tipping anyone off, so what did they know that I didn't?

Nadia stepped farther into my room. "What happened? What is it?"

"I found Misha."

She pulled out the photo of our parents with their assistants from behind her phone case. "Is that why you borrowed this? Were you looking for them?" She handed me the photo.

"Kind of. Misha owes our dentist some money." For the first time, I examined the other assistant as well. She wasn't in sharp focus like my parents. Her lab coat sat loose on her slender shoulders. Her hair was secured by a medical cap, except for one unruly spiral peeking through. She sat behind the device, slender fingers poised with a small soldering iron. I imagined those fingers were steady and skilled enough to maneuver a rigged arcade claw into the perfect position to win a disgustingly adorable unicorn plushie. I hadn't paid her any mind before today, but there was no mistaking her now.

My eyes watered as I pointed at the photo. "It's him. N031 is this guy, Misha." And freakin' Kendi was the other one. I'd been either hanging out online or in direct contact with both of the ETC's most wanted fugitives. Maybe Dr. Clarke was right to be worried about what I might be carrying around on me.

Nadia took the photo and held it up to her face. "He's who? What's this about?" I did a quick internet news search. I found both assistants' names: Kolodetsky, M. and Carleson, B. Maybe she was filling in for B Carleson that day, or she went by another name. But it was definitely Kendi in the photo.

> AuGurl: Kolodetsky, Misha, right? What does the ASF want from the ETC, if not the porting code? Why do you still have Jaxon? Why did you run after my parents died? Please, be honest with me.
>
> N031: I can't say, but once we have what we need, you'll know everything. This is good for you also, trust me.

Trust? What an idiotic appeal to end on, considering everything that came before. The phone felt heavy in my hands. So many secrets. None of these people seemed to be on the same page with what they wanted from me, and how much they thought they should reveal.

> AuGurl: If you want me to trust you, tell me what's going on. Where are you, we can meet in person.
>
> N031: I'm in USA. I am still under investigation, but it is lies. Part of what we need is proof of our innocence. I can't tell you much, but I can tell you to think. Your parents, they invented teleportation. Why do you live in old apartment and make no money from big FutureMove deals?
>
> AuGurl: Money? That's what this is about? My parents dreamed of saving up for a country house, but they weren't in it for the money.
>
> N031: Not all about money. It's also about who controls FutureMove.

Nadia startled me with a reply to N031's—Misha's—question right next to my ear. "I don't know, doesn't the ETC control FutureMove? Or Dr. Clarke?" Apparently, she'd been reading the conversation over my shoulder.

> AuGurl: Okay, so it's about control, and money. Makes sense, seeing as how you can't even pay your dental bills.
>
> N031: Ask Dr. Clarke why you haven't heard anything about your shares. You will see he's not who you think.

Nadia shook her head and stood straight. "No. They would have had to tell us if we'd inherited anything. We got a little insurance payout, but that's it. *On voobshye s uma soshyol.*"

> AuGurl: My sister says you're out of your mind. They'd have to inform us if we had anything coming.
>
> N031: Not if what you had coming was in silent trust that its custodian wants to restructure. And especially not if that custodian fired and threatened his company lawyer. Ask Dr. Clarke, bring it up in casual way, so he does not suspect you know too much. You will see.

Sure. Act natural. Like, *hey dude, have you been keeping untold riches from us to secure them for yourself?* I threw my phone onto my bed and rested my forehead in my hands. I was tired, too, and I didn't want to hear yet another traitor talk about my family. He wouldn't answer any of my next questions anyway. Like, why was he under investigation, what did he do, what did he want out of this, what I am going to ruin if I let on that I've been talking to ASF rebels and former employees to Dr. Clarke. And the question I hated to acknowledge but had been pinging the back of my brain for four years: could something have contributed to my parents' accident other than overconfidence and an unlucky glitch?

Nadia stood behind me and kneaded my shoulders. "Faith, Alyon. Everything is going to be okay. We're going to get through whatever this is."

There she was again with the empty promises. I'm sure our parents thought everything would be peachy, too. They were very wrong.

Nadia smiled down at me in her motherly way when I didn't answer. "Why don't I make dinner?" She was even starting to look like Mom. I couldn't tell if it was because she was getting older, or if my brain was merging their images.

Nadia left, and my phone buzzed with an incoming call. I rolled my desk chair over some clothes on the floor to where the phone had landed on my bed. It was a number I hadn't saved, which I would normally ignore. Today wasn't normal.

"Yeah?"

"Alyona, don't hang up."

Manuel, yuck.

"I negotiated an easy way to get Jaxon out."

I said nothing.

"So listen, the ETC thinks I have him on suspicion of ASF involvement, right? So I told Dr. Clarke there was no way he had time for that if you guys spend as much time on the phone together as Nadia says you do."

Wow, thanks Nadia. "And?"

"Dr. Clarke has Jaxon's phone already, but he said if they could corroborate his story with your phone and text logs, they could be assured Jaxon wasn't fraternizing with anyone else, and they'd be able to make sure you hadn't been in contact, either. Win-win, and Jaxon goes free."

Uh, no. "This is stupid. They can get phone records from the carrier if they really want that. I'm not leaving him my phone."

"It might be ridiculous, but it's the simplest thing. To get phone records, we'd have to formally charge Jaxon and take the time to go through proper channels. But if we don't charge him, Dr. Clarke has ETC authority to approve my recommendation to release him. He doesn't know you're getting advanced warning before he goes through your calls and texts. See that there isn't anything interesting to find."

"There's nothing to find." There was plenty, but he had no right to snoop through my private texts. And where would I put the data, anyway? They took my computer.

"Come by early tomorrow. Nothing will get pushed through on a Sunday, and this gives you the night to clear your phone out. Jaxon will be thrilled."

I hung up on Manuel. His deal might satisfy Dr. Clarke, but the ASF still wanted more. Besides, I couldn't handle the loss of my phone right after losing my laptop.

I hadn't felt so naked since the time I'd agreed to be on Jaxon's team for a bike riding relay race in the mountains. I'd started out fully clothed, wearing the matching team shirt and bike leggings and everything. He gave me a mostly downhill stretch at the beginning, but I still managed to snag my pant leg in the chain. My leggings ripped up the inside seam all the way past the crotch, and when I kicked to free my pants from the gears, the whole right side flapped in the wind behind me, like a butt cape for a misfit superhero reject.

Jaxon had waited at the next section of the course. I showed up with watering eyes and sporty skivvies on display, he laughed so hard he cried more than I had. But then, he told me to look away while he took down his pants and wrapped them around his squishy parts like a diaper. I wrapped mine accordingly and passed him the flag. He squeezed my hand, said, "This is how we roll now," and took off. My hand tingled from his touch the whole way down to the bottom of the race, where the entire team of five had their pants tied up like bulky bikini bottoms. He had made me look like I fit in, despite my penchant for awkward mistakes.

When he was around, I felt like I was a part of something amazing. If he could diaper up for me, I could do whatever it took to set him free.

CHAPTER FOURTEEN

Early Bird Gets Confrontational

For the second time since my parents' accident, I voluntarily woke up before 8:00 a.m. Nadia and I stepped out of the port booth facing FutureMove's tall, white and gold pillars. She rushed inside past a group of protesters who'd lost jobs to teleportation and sprang up afresh after every accident. They waved signs and chanted slogans like, "One Limb Short, We Won't Port," and "Get There Safe with RideShareApp." I ignored them, anxious and light-headed due to both the excitement of freeing Jaxon and the dread of handing over my phone.

Manuel grabbed Nadia's hand as soon as she met him near her desk and attached himself to her face like one of his endangered amphibians fighting for survival.

"Hello, there," I shouted. "Let's get going on this, shall we?"

Manuel and my sister broke apart. He faced me with a grin so wide it made his mustache goatee thing look like a big clown smile. "Good morning, Alyona. I brought down the paperwork we need you to sign to clear Jaxon."

I looked on the tall desk for the papers and saw a clear

plastic evidence bag labeled *A. Zolotova cell phone*. I clutched my phone in my pocket. I was not at all excited about handing over my beefed-up phone to this circus. They couldn't even figure out how to have me e-sign the documents—they apparently had to print them on paper.

"So, what all do you need? Can I send you the call logs and texts?"

"Thanks for coming in last minute," said Manuel. "I'm excited to get Jaxon released, like I told you several minutes ago on the phone." He'd told me the plan the day before, of course, but he had to keep up pretenses for the lobby cameras. "We'll have the IT guys check your phone to prove he couldn't have associated with the ASF, and you should have it back by the end of the day. I can give it to Nadia."

I picked up a pen and clicked it open and closed a few times. End of the day? How slow were these so-called IT guys? "And girls," I said.

Manuel had already distracted himself smiling at my sister, and she was smiling back as if they were passing secrets between their twitterpated minds.

"Hmm?" he said.

"IT guys, and *girls*."

"Well, that could be, but they're all guys here."

"I guess that's something else I can talk to Dr. Clarke about, then. He might have a position for me as I work my way up."

Manuel snapped back to reality. "Talk to Dr. Clarke? Alyona, this isn't a big deal. There's no need—"

"Well I think it *is* a big deal and I'm going to talk to him. Now." I started toward the elevator and Manuel ran in front of me, blocking the way.

"Alyona," he said in a low, barely calm voice. "Please don't complicate things."

"They're already complicated. Now what?"

"You can't get to his office without a code, you know that."

"I have his cell phone number." I brandished my soon-to-be-contraband phone, skirting around him and mashing the elevator button.

Nadia came out from behind her desk. "Alyona? Are you okay?"

Manuel softened his stance. "I'm helping her get where she needs to be."

The elevator door opened, and I got in. Manuel leaned in and scowled at me where Nadia couldn't see. He swiped his badge and hit the top-floor button, and then stepped back into the lobby. "Stay calm, and don't make things difficult."

"Thank you," I sang, and then I may have made a rude face at him and held it while the doors slid closed. It was immature, but he was already treating me like a baby, so why not?

As the elevator lifted, I dropped my raised lip and eyebrow and lost all pretense of confidence. I never used to need anyone to badge me up to the top level, where my parents' offices were next to Dr. Clarke's. I'd been free to come and go. The entire place had always felt exciting and grand, yet homey, like I was the princess of teleportation in a castle of science for nerd knights in lab coats.

It was easy to work myself up and act defiant. FutureMove had turned from palace to prison. Today, the pillars out front were cell bars behind which Jaxon sat starving for want of anything but disgusting, soggy broccoli. I was princess of nothing, a holdover from the old regime, and the previous court wanted my help taking back the kingdom while they hid behind screens and pseudonyms. I had two more floors to figure out what I wanted to say before the doors opened and I confronted the actual head of FutureMove and liaison to the ETC, Shane Clarke, Doctor of Business Administration.

What if there was some truth to what the traitor Misha hinted at? Questions popped up all over my mind like advertisement windows I couldn't close fast enough. Had our parents left us a part of their company? Was it possible we could afford more than day-old pumpernickel? I had no more concept of how our living situation worked now than I did at thirteen, and eighteen-year-old Nadia had absolute trust in Dr. Clarke to guide her through the transition from sister to guardian. Even if she hadn't, she wouldn't have known which questions to ask. But why would Dr. Clarke keep that from us? He was plenty well off on his own.

And more importantly than the prospect of a full pantry: Why did Misha need proof he was innocent? Could my parents' accident have been a result of one of their assistants' mistakes, and not their own errors or a fault in the advancements they'd made? The investigations hadn't turned up any evidence of tampering, but it had never sat right with me that they would have made such a catastrophic error.

What was I going to start with? "Excuse me, sir? Are you actually a power-grubbing bourgeois douche keeping us in the dark about our parent's legacy and the facts surrounding their death?" I'd freaked out about my phone, and now I was seconds away from telling off Dr. Clarke with no actual plan and only the word of someone who'd been pretending to be my friend.

I could be, perhaps, prone to emotion-based reactions sometimes.

I should probably have gone back downstairs, signed whatever crap they wanted me to sign, picked up Jaxon, and then come up with an actual plan. But the elevator chimed, and the doors opened to reveal Dr. Clarke himself, waiting to greet me. *Speak of the devil...*

"Alyona, please come in." He swept his arm away from the elevators like a butler. "How nice to see you all the way up here."

"Manuel let me up," I said, as if blaming him for my rash insistence on being here.

"Yes, he called to let me know you were on your way. Good kid, that Manny. He came highly recommended. He's done a great job, other than spending excessive time around reception." I thought I detected an edge in his voice at the end, like a fatherly instinct kicking in when it came to Nadia.

I didn't really want Manuel to take the flack for me. I still believed he thought he was helping. "Yeah, he tried to tell me not to disturb you during the workday, but I insisted he let me come."

Dr. Clarke led me down the hall to his enormous office as we talked. After the accident, Dr. Clarke couldn't bear to see anyone else in the other offices and had remodeled the floor, making one large office and a swanky conference room. Combined, they were bigger than our apartment's main floor.

"You know you're welcome to see me any time. How can I help you?" He motioned to one of the overstuffed leather chairs in front of his desk and lowered into his ergonomic boss man swivel throne.

I took a breath and started with the obvious. "So, you know my friend Jaxon."

"I do. And I know he's being held. I'm so sorry, Alyona. It seems to have been a misunderstanding, and you know from his first infraction I can't play favorites. We have to go through the motions."

"I understand, but he's been here for a couple days. Can

we get him out? I don't feel comfortable handing over my private information and photos on my phone to a whole team of male IT geeks." I was paranoid I'd missed something they might flag. And I needed my phone. It was pretty much all I had left.

Dr. Clarke leaned back into his chair. "Alyona, this is for your safety as well as his, so let's make it quick, shall we? I'm sure you have nothing to hide."

I didn't know whether to laugh or stand up and yell in his disingenuous face.

"You're right about me not having anything to hide, but I think *you* might."

Dr. Clarke sat up, his soft smile gone. "Now, Alyona, you can't expect to simply change the subject and get out of—"

"Actually this is why I came today, not to hand over my private property when I've done nothing wrong." At least as far as he knew. I tried to think of some formal language to sound authoritative through my nervous energy. I couldn't afford to waver for the rest of the conversation. "I have recently concerned myself with the subject of inheritance, and I have reason to believe my parents left us with more than a run-down apartment and this outdated cell phone you're so obsessed with." *Nailed it.* My turn to smirk.

Dr. Clarke let his shoulders drop slightly, and pulled his chair forward so he could lean his arms on the polished mahogany desk. "Of course they did, dear."

His condescending nonchalance wiped my win away like a magnet to a hard drive. My hands hovered weirdly above my lap, and I let them drop. "So, we, my sister and I, we have shares or whatever?" *Ugh. Fail.*

"Absolutely. You and Nadia are slated to take your parents' shares and votes as soon as we work out the legal complications."

Keep it professional. "Such as?"

Dr. Clarke narrowed his eyes and leaned into his chair. "I can see that I've kept you out of the loop for too long. I suppose it's time I explained."

He pulled a legal pad and a shiny black pen out of a desk drawer. "You girls collectively own a majority share of the company. Sixty percent, to be exact." He drew shapes and lines and arrows as he spoke, like an animated explainer video for an exciting real estate investment opportunity. "These shares are in a silent trust, meaning that you're not to be told about them until you're both legal adults. So, I made sure you two had your basic needs met until the day I could surprise you with the happy news."

He drew an arrow from where he'd written 1/31, my birthday, to the number eighteen.

My heartbeat picked up and I straightened in my seat. That was less than four months away. Same-day pumpernickel, here we come.

"Now, don't get dollar signs in your eyes quite yet. Your shares are valuable, but they're not liquid, meaning you can't spend them. We're trying to separate the votes from the shares, and then transfer the votes to me so that you can cash out whatever you need and not worry about our majority vote going to someone outside of our circle."

"And what if we *want* to vote? Maybe I want a say—"

Dr. Clarke waved to stop me. "You really don't. It's nothing glamorous. It's a stuffy board room full of even stuffier voting members. More than that, it makes you targets for people who want a slice of our success. If demands from powerful people aren't expertly negotiated, the imbalance can lead to manipulation, or even threats of violence." He drew multiple arrows coming from all directions converging into a small circle. "You have no idea what I shield you two from daily;

everyone from the local school board to international political leaders lobby for our attention."

If I had thought my invitations to join the ASF had been annoying, I couldn't imagine the nightmare of so many constant suiters for my votes. Maybe he *did* know what he was doing, and Misha had it all wrong. I had no more words, authoritative or otherwise, just a lot to think about.

Dr. Clarke rested his chin on his knuckle and leaned closer. "Now, I'd like to know why this is suddenly an issue for you. If anyone has put this bug in your ear, it's in your best interest to tell me. They may be some of those who are trying to weasel away your inheritance."

I tried to lean back into my own chair to maintain the distance between us, but the chair, which had appeared shiny and inviting, was so overstuffed it didn't give at all when I sat. It trapped me upright, with nowhere to sink away to. "No, sir. Who would even know enough to claim something like that?"

Dr. Clarke took a deep breath, let it out, and took another quick breath in as if he had to warm up his lungs before spilling any more of his guts to me, like the cartoon emu spinning his legs for a while before he zips away from the dingo. "That's more of those legal complications I'm working on. You know the two assistants who are under investigation for the accident that took your parents from us? Carleson and Kolodetsky?"

My face flushed, broadcasting the fact that yes, I did know them. I hoped Dr. Clarke attributed the change in my face color to the mention of my parents, and wouldn't suspect I'd been chummy with those people for some time now and hadn't even realized who they were.

Dr. Clarke reached around behind him to a lighted beverage fridge and pulled out a glass water bottle. He held it out over the desk. "Have some water."

It sounded more like an order than a suggestion, but I was parched. "Thanks."

"They weren't mere assistants. They were apprenticing for your parents' jobs; we wanted them to run the lab someday. Both of them are incredibly intelligent, and if they're contacting you, if they're asking you for intel or data or anything at all, please know they have ulterior motives. Namely their current shares and voting rights. They're a fraction of yours, but we can't redistribute their shares until we prove their involvement, so I've suspended their rights until we can remove them."

"Or reinstate them," I said. I'd been looking for a way to stop associating Dr. Clarke with my feelings about the accident, and it would be easy to shift my focus to Kendi and Misha. I was already livid with Misha for deceiving me. But he seemed to think I could help him find proof of his innocence. And Kendi seemed in earnest, even if she annoyed me. She wasn't the one calling the shots. As for Dr. Clarke, it was clear the past couple of days that he knew or suspected more than he let on in words. I had reasons to distrust both sides.

"Yes, of course we hope it was only an accident. But something isn't right. Your parents should have followed protocol, but they were too smart to make fatal mistakes. Investigations haven't turned up any fault in the hardware or glitch in the software that could have accounted for what happened, so who does that leave? Perhaps, the ones who hid away rather than stay and help? I respect your parents too much to let this go, and we all want closure."

Closure. I wasn't even sure what that meant. Like once I knew what happened I could move on and forget it ever occurred? I didn't want closure, and I wasn't sure I wanted the company shares and the drama that apparently came with them. What I wanted eventually was to work in a lab and have access to the tools and materials and minds I could use to improve the booths. And right now, I just wanted my phone, my computer, and Jaxon.

I took a gulp of cold water. "So is that why you really want my phone? Was it you who had my computer taken, also? You want to find whatever you can on those assistants?"

"You misunderstand," Dr. Clarke said with a chuckle, raising his hands to face level. "I asked Manuel to secure your computer, yes. You weren't home when he arrived to retrieve it, so he found it inside."

Another unexpected admission. I sipped more water, unsure how to proceed. That wasn't how Manuel had told it. Either Kendi, Misha, and Manuel were all lying, or Dr. Clarke was the liar, and the others were simply misinformed and desperate.

He got up and hefted the second overstuffed leather chair around, so it faced me, and not the desk.

I pressed my back into the unforgiving leather.

"I worry about you, Alyona. You've been acting strangely lately. I had to know whether you had any information on the fugitives for your own safety."

I stared at the ground to avoid locking eyes with him sitting so close.

Dr. Clarke sighed. "You recall the woman in the news who lost her hand Saturday morning?"

I nodded.

"Her name is Melanie Moreno. The assistants scared her away from researching gaps in the records by planting that gold bracelet on her. She was a lab employee, and we still don't know where she is. She could be in hiding or being held against her will. The assistants put that fake foot in the teleportation booth to scare you, manipulate you into doing their will. Why else would they take credit for taking Jaxon into custody? While he's here, it's my call what happens to him, and he's safer here with us than out there, vulnerable to further attacks."

I took an indelicate swig from my bottle. Kendi had told me that Melanie was a friend, and that she'd *wanted* her to investigate. More proof that one of them was lying, which meant there really was something serious going on, something the offending party found worth concealing in this tangled web of lies.

"But why couldn't you have asked me to bring my computer by, like with my phone?"

"Taking your computer by force means you're not caught in the crosshairs. It's better for you and your sister's safety for the assistants to think you're unwilling participants with the ETC."

He reached out and laid his hand on my arm. "I miss your parents, too. I will do what it takes to protect you from the ASF."

I couldn't press any harder against the back of the chair without tipping over, and I resisted the urge to yank my arm away until he finally removed his hand. It wasn't necessarily him I wanted to escape, but I rarely enjoyed being touched and needed space to think. It did sound like he was trying to help me. Kendi had conveniently left out the part about them having financial stakes at play. First they said they wanted to be able to build their own booths. Then they wanted documents that helped prove their innocence. Now it sounds like they want their piece of the pie. What else weren't they telling me?

I wasn't sure how to respond. "It's been four years..." There were too many ways to finish my thought, and Dr. Clarke must have sensed my unsurety.

"Look, Alyona, let's seal the deal."

I made a what-the-crap face and he hurried to explain.

"Everything I do here is for your benefit. You and Nadia. Alyona, I am an open book. You know I loved your parents. Your father was my best friend and we joked freely about my obvious crush on your brilliant mother. Nothing I do is a secret, but I've failed to recognize that you're old enough to be more informed, and for that, I apologize."

My stomach roiled at his mention of Mom.

The chair's leather squeaked as Dr. Clarke stood. "I'd like to be more open with you. Come with me to the vault. You can have free access to all my inner workings. I can't let you copy any data, but I want you to know I'm not withholding anything. I could even release your laptop from there when you're done."

The mention of his inner workings was a bit much, but getting inside that vault was too tempting. I stood. "Great."

Dr. Clarke led the way out of his office and down the hall to what used to be my parents' vault.

CHAPTER FIFTEEN

Not Eggsactly Forthright

SECURITY WASN'T AS LAX on this level. It was only accessible through the badge-restricted stairwell door or the elevator. Entry to the front of the building was monitored via Nadia's reception station, and guards kept their eyes on the working labs. But the top floor had a few extras. Opposite the office was another door with a badge reader. I spotted a bubble camera in the middle of the open hallway area, another in the conference room, and a directional camera over the vault door.

As was my habit with any secure area, I paid close attention as Dr. Clarke led me into the vault. He tapped his badge to the blank digital pin pad hanging on the wall by the vault door, and the numbers populated on the screen. He angled his body in front of me as he typed in the code, but I could tell zero was the first number because his hand was too low for any other. I heard four beeps after that one, and from the way his elbow inched out again at the end, I guessed the last number might be zero as well. The smooth surface of that type of pin pad tended to collect fingerprints. If I could get a look at the keypad at an angle, I might be able to figure out the remaining three numbers. The door swung outward. Dr. Clarke stepped forward toward a second door and I suddenly had an uncontrollable itch on my right ankle.

I leaned over and attacked the "itch" with my left hand. "These new socks are too tight, I'm getting those sock lines, you know?"

Dr. Clarke looked around the floor and patted his pockets, as if he worried he might have dropped something I was trying to retrieve. But I wasn't taking anything physical today. From the ankle-itching angle, the overhead light reflected across the glossy number pad, and while the numbers had faded back into digital oblivion, a slight, oily residue remained in four places where the numbers eight, six, one, and zero used to be. I repeated the numbers in my head until Dr. Clarke spoke.

"Here we are," he announced like a ventriloquist, holding as still as possible for the iris scan. Once the scan completed with a low-pitched beep, Dr. Clarke worked on the last barrier—an old-school dial. I'd practiced cracking the dial's code as a child. If I turned my hearing aids to max volume, I could figure it out by the clicking sounds.

Dr. Clarke made one final turn of the dial, and I wanted a smooth female voice to say "Welcome, Dr. Clarke," like in sci-fi movies, but there was just a big ka-chunk and then a whirring sound as the lock disengaged and the door slid away.

The walls were thick concrete, and I could see the smoothed edges of a wire mesh layer—probably tungsten—to make the room port-proof. The oval-shaped room glowed bright white inside, like a giant Swedish goose laid an egg-shaped modern office showroom. It looked nothing like how my parents had kept it. Where the open shelves now held neatly arranged file boxes, Dad had stored bins of valuable or proprietary components, which Mom kept labeled and inventoried. It smelled sharp, like cleaning chemicals. The heavy table with the bowl full of dinner mints had been replaced by a semicircle desk with a big, curved monitor on it and a wired keyboard and mouse, everything lined up and centered. Dr. Clarke might not be a tech guy, but I would have upgraded to wireless before I picked out new, sleek furniture. I followed the wall around to the side we'd come in on, and there in a glass case lay several neat stacks of flat metal bars, each about the size of a thin thumb drive. The tallest stacks looked like copper, then there were two silver stacks, one of them probably platinum. The last was clearly gold. I took a couple of steps closer to see the mint marks.

"Lovely, aren't they," said Dr. Clarke, stepping inside the vault behind me. "I had them minted from the outdated tech coming into our recycling center from the exchange program."

A laugh bubbled up. One of Misha's conspiracy theories had been at least partly correct. He'd accused the ETC of doing exactly that with the phones they took to port-proof.

I leaned in closer.

"Go ahead, you can hold one."

I opened the unlocked case and picked up a gold piece, cold and smooth, except for the indented FutureMove logo: a maps-to symbol—a right arrow coming from a vertical bar—superimposed by the letters FM. I barely made out the tiny words underneath, "In memory of T. & N. Zolotov." My eyes blurred and I tilted my face upwards to keep the tears from spilling over. They seemed to be welling up more in the past day than they had in my lifetime. I held the gold bar high, pretending to get a better look at the inscription to my parents. They'd been the map to my entire world. I wished more than anything that they could point me in the right direction now.

"It was going to be a surprise," said Dr. Clarke. "For once we finally got to the bottom of all the investigations. I want you to decide the charities to which we'll donate these."

Again, I couldn't speak. I didn't know what to believe, let alone what words to put together.

I handed Dr. Clarke the gold bar and he took a few seconds to arrange it precisely, then put his hand on my back and gently guided me toward the clear acrylic chair.

"You take a look, open whatever files might help restore your faith in me. I'll return your laptop, no strings attached. I realize I may have overstepped allowing Manuel to enter your home, even if your home is company-owned and it was done with your safety in mind."

I whispered my thanks, and he headed to the shelves. I wiggled the mouse to bring the computer out of hibernation. The screen glowed in my blurry eyes, and I quickly wiped them while Dr. Clarke's back was turned. I silently chided him for not having a screen lock while I clicked around dragging selection rectangles on the home screen with the mouse, trying to clear my thoughts. I found a folder called "Spreadsheets," which, given the tidiness of the vault under Dr. Clarke's care, was likely to contain spreadsheets, precisely, and nothing more.

I heard the crinkle of plastic as Dr. Clarke retrieved my laptop from an evidence bag. "I know this might feel awkward with me in the room. I've got a call soon and a meeting to prepare for." He strode over to the door and pointed outside. "I won't close it, so take your time, and I'll make sure everything's locked up when you leave."

"Okay, thank you. I won't be too long."

A monitor hung on the wall to the left of the door showing the hallway outside, and I spotted a camera above it. Still, he trusted me enough to leave me in here alone, to let me go through his computer—something I would never willingly reciprocate. I'd come looking for evidence of secrets, but now I hoped to find proof he was really on our side. That he wasn't as bad as the ASF made him out to be. Maybe they were the ones out to take whatever I had left for themselves.

I double-clicked the Spreadsheets folder and, to my relief, found quarterly compensation diagnostics, net gains, profitability projections, and other combinations of boring business words. I closed that folder and checked the one next to it, Pictures. The most recent uploads were the ridiculous number of Nadia's selfies I'd copied to the decoy thumb drive during my first escapade through FutureMove's data. Dr. Clarke had probably opened the drive at this computer. But why copy these onto his own hard drive? The only evidence they provided was a record of her practice with YouTube makeup artist tutorials.

I clicked through her looks from different decades and occasions, from casual-natural on up to stenciled mermaid scales and glitter lashes. Scrolling down, I found other pictures of Nadia at work functions, waving from her desk, at lunch. Some pictures of me in there, and some with my parents. One of him with his arm around my mom, Nadia on the other side of her. I had a similar photo on my laptop, but in my version, Dr. Clarke had his other arm around my dad, with me standing in front of him.

I wanted to take some of the work photos of my parents; there were shots I hadn't seen before in here. But I stupidly didn't have a USB drive in these pants. I took a few pictures of the screen with my phone, but they came out lined due to the monitor's refresh rate. I had a lot to sort through, so I resolved to ask Dr. Clarke for the pictures later.

I opened a terminal.

```
>    search--keywords     'Tatiana'
```

```
'Nikolai'  'Alyona'  'Kolodetsky'
'Carleson'--fullscan

[+] Scanning  full  filesystem  for
matches . . .
```

The result was way too much boring for me to sort out, in part because Dr. Clarke, like Mom, kept at least two backups of everything. Tech projects they'd started and debates about which ones should continue, and which department heads should manage which pieces. Discussions and projections about partnerships they were working on with FedFastMail, pharmaceutical companies, Emergency Services, blah blah.

I found a folder for updates on the evidence against and whereabouts of the fugitives. They knew Carleson, B. lived with the company's former counsel, Athena Carleson, but didn't have enough to bring her in yet, and there was a carefully worded warning about the damage they could do to the company if brought in prematurely. "Ms. Carleson's allegations and the documents of which she claims to be in possession require delicacy," one document read. "Security agent Manuel Ourives will provide periodic reports on the movement and activity of both Carlesons."

If Kendi was Carleson, B., and she'd caught Manuel's scent, it was no wonder she was wary of him. It was literally his job to snitch on her to the ETC. They thought Misha Kolodetsky had possibly fled the country. I had thought he was somewhere in Siberia, but he'd admitted he was here in the US.

My name came up in some long legal documents about the board and the shares and voting and whatever else. I read enough to confirm that Nadia and I would indeed inherit our parents' combined 60% share in the company when I turned eighteen in a few short months. I hadn't entirely understood what Dr. Clarke was saying in his office about uncoupling the shares from the voting. If we cashed out some shares, we'd be rich—or at least able to buy a few extras and pay for more than one college class at a time. But why would Dr. Clarke assume I didn't want to vote on the company's direction? I'd have to ask him more about that when I asked for the photos of my parents. The documentation was too dry and wordy to mean anything to me.

I dropped my elbows to my knees and cradled my chin in my palms. I couldn't believe an unfettered foray into the heart of the ETC had proved so exhaustingly boring. Maybe even unnaturally boring? Dr. Clarke could be hiding the interesting bits somewhere else. This could be nothing more than a play for my confidence. I rubbed my temples, staring at the pulsing lights of the bay of external hard drives under the desk.

The pulsing appeared chaotic at first, like sparkling blue Christmas lights, the seven hard drives glowing and dimming in random order. But after a moment, they synced into a sort of rhythm. It looked as if they might line up and form a perfect wave of lights if I gave them a few seconds to hit the right timing.

I jolted upward as Dr. Clarke's voice crackled through the intercom. The monitor on the wall next to the door lit up, and there was Dr. Clarke's smiling face. I leaned toward the monitor and smiled back, in case it was a two-way video chat situation.

"I'm going to go ahead and have Jaxon sign his exit paperwork and bring him around to the front with your laptop, trusting you'll sign the affidavits and release your phone. You can head to reception once you're finished here, and we'll get everything squared away."

I wasn't sure whether he could hear a reply, but I told him, "Okay, thank you, I'll be right there." The monitor flicked to black again.

The hard drive lights caught my eye as I sat straight again. I watched them for a few seconds longer in hopes of catching the strangely satisfying effect of the lights lining up and pulsing one after another. I didn't want to keep Jaxon waiting, but it was so close . . . almost there . . . and . . . *now! But, wait.* The wave had hitched. Like nails on my mental chalkboard, the lights started the wave and then skipped a beat; one of the hard drives wasn't lit at all.

It could be an innocent hot-swappable setup with an extra drive, but Dr. Clarke wasn't tech savvy. It would have been easy for him to come in here and simply disconnect one of the drives from the bay, maybe the one with the top-secret info, before letting me in here. But it was also possible I was overreacting.

I pretended to lose my balance on the chair, in case he was watching, and fell to my knees. One of the drives leaned slightly to the left, which meant it wasn't seated fully into the bay connecting it to power and the computer. Strange, when Dr. Clarke was such a neat freak. It could mean nothing, or it could mean Dr. Clarke had deliberately kept the drive offline.

I picked up the drive, noting its size in my hand. Then I sat on my backside and eyed the front of my loose cargo pants. It wouldn't fit in the pocket, but I could hide it in the front part somewhere. Would it fall down a pant leg and clatter out before I could get it into my backpack? Hoping Dr. Clarke couldn't see under the table, I picked up the drive and tucked it halfway into my pants, but it stuck out at my waist.

So much for that idea. I couldn't sneak it out, but . . . I could plug it in.

I had no way to tell whether I was being surveilled at any given second, so I risked it. I'd tell him I'd noticed it was unplugged and wanted to do him a favor. I seated the drive snuggly into the bay and scooted out from under the table.

I sat and jiggled the mouse until I saw a new drive show up in the file directory. I clicked the first folder I got my pointer on to see whatever I could before Dr. Clarke caught on. I clicked successively through folders. *Investigation. Communications. Law Enforcement.* That folder opened to a list of documents which must have been arranged alphabetically. I opened *Areawide Alert,* skipped the heading and salutation, and read, "Alert posted at all metro-area hospitals to be pushed statewide if subject Melanie Moreno is not found after twelve hours, at which time reimplantation will no longer be possible. Ms. Moreno's hand is being cared for at Central General Hospital . . ."

I clicked back to the Communications folder and searched for Melanie's name. Several hits came up in the folder labeled *Internal*, and I clicked on one of the first documents. My ears felt warm and tingly. Dr. Clarke could stop me any second. My eyes flew across the page. "It has come to our attention . . . Ms. Moreno's inquiries . . . due to the sensitive nature . . . she must be made to cease and desist immediately. Non-compliance will result in appropriate measures . . ."

I scanned down to Dr. Clarke's reply below the memo.

". . . will be dealt with internally. No additional action will be required on your—"

Dr. Clarke's voice blared into the vault, and I hit my knee on the underside of the desk. I slapped the keyboard with a command to close all the windows and hoped he hadn't seen what I'd been researching. My ears were on fire and my hairline felt tight.

"We're ready for you now. I'll come escort you down. Jaxon is ready to go home."

My heart pounded behind my eyes. Had I just read that

Dr. Clarke promised to put a stop to Melanie's investigation? Hadn't he said it was the ASF who didn't want her investigating and caused her to lose her hand? What if her accident was his way of having her "dealt with?" Or was I reading into things and hunting witches? The first document seemed to prove they were trying to find Melanie and save her hand. Maybe her inquiries had to do with the faulty booths, and this was some kind of public relations deal. I wish I'd found a name to whom Dr. Clarke had been writing. I wasn't sure whether I wanted them to find Melanie.

I had a lot of thinking and digging to do before I'd know how to figure out what to believe about any of this. But I knew one thing. Jaxon was leaving with me, and we could solve anything together.

Spreadsheets_Q3-30

CHAPTER SIXTEEN

Friends in Cramped Places

THE ELEVATOR DOORS GLIDED open, and I shot a glare at Galileo, who stared smugly back at me from his frame, thinking, "I wouldst verily like to see thou wriggle thine posterior out of this one." *Up yours, dude.* The real Galileo had to have been nicer than this painting version.

Jaxon was almost free, and everything would be fine. I'd eventually figure out the company stuff and decide whether I could trust anyone from FutureMove, the ETC or the ASF. These were top-floor questions, problems I'd left back in the vault with the gold and the reseated external drive and all the other conspiracy theories. For later. Or for never. I could move to whatever island was in my dream where I could sip chilled drinks on the beach with Jaxon. I'd try to convince myself that surf and sand and sticky bun bras were better than a potential say in FutureMove and sorting the lies from reality. No one would threaten or manipulate me for personal gain.

If only.

Dr. Clarke waited for me at the reception desk with Nadia and the paperwork. My laptop sat in its evidence bag, and next to it lay a smaller bag—a little suffocating plastic prison for my phone. My chest tightened and I felt like the plastic bag was about to go over my head, choking off my communication with the outside world.

My fingers tingled and I pulled my phone out of my back pocket. Dizziness crept up my chest and into my head. My phone buzzed with a text, and from the preview I could see it was from the collection agency, letting me know they had more summons.

They couldn't take my phone; I needed it for my job. Would that excuse work?

"You know, I'm realizing it's probably a HIPAA violation to hand over images containing personally identifiable information from my job. I can sign the documents and have you check out my call logs while we're here."

Dr. Clarke pushed the first affidavit my way and handed me a pen. "It's not as painful as you might think, Alyona," he said with another gentle smile. "We'll match up geolocations with where Jaxon claimed to be with you and analyze texts between you and him, check for deleted messages in your thread with him, and compare it with the data from the phone he was found with. We're not interested in any other information."

The slim pen was too skinny to hold properly. Stylish, but useless. Like Dr. Clarke. He'd had the power to let Jaxon go any time, but no, he had to "go through the motions." They'd find plenty of deleted texts if they knew how to do that. And not much geolocation data. The holes I left in my phone's data were more likely to bring up ground-floor questions than do anything to clear Jaxon's name.

I nodded at him and scanned through the first paragraph. Then I put the pen down, ducked around the counter and pulled my backpack out of the top right cubby where Nadia always kept it. I put the straps around my arms and picked the pen back up. At least I'd have the security blanket warmth of the pack when I'd given up everything else.

Dr. Clarke folded his arms. "We've already removed Jaxon's anklet in good faith, and I'm having Manuel bring him up to say hello. He'll be released as soon as we verify the data."

I clenched the slippery pen in my fist. First the ASF stalled Jaxon's release with a demand for more information, and now the ETC wouldn't let him go. "I was under the impression he was coming with me right away in exchange for my signatures and phone data."

"I'm sorry you misunderstood, but you won't have to wait long. I'd expect, with your cooperation, he'll be out for a celebratory dinner."

Even if they didn't find more to incriminate us both by then, dinner wasn't good enough. I couldn't wait any longer. It was Saturday when they took him, and it was what now, Monday? *Oh, crap, Jaxon's work-study interview!* "Dinner won't work at all. He's got a job interview." I couldn't believe I'd forgotten. Not only was I losing my mind with him in custody, but now he might miss his interview and lose his shot at becoming a professional peruser of dusty documents. All of it would be my fault. The signature line at the bottom of the affidavit waved in my vision.

Jaxon's familiar voice bounced off the reception area's polished surfaces from the hallway beyond the elevators. I looked up and dropped the pen as Manuel and Jaxon rounded the corner. There he was, with his jacket draped over his arm, standing tall in generic shoes I didn't recognize—probably loaners from Manuel. A slow smile spread across his face as if the fact that I'd come for him washed over him gradually. His jet-black hair stuck out at random angles, but that was normal for my hilarious, thoughtful, sock-loving, triathlete history nerd. My best and possibly only friend, complete with all limbs. When his dark eyes met mine, a tidal wave of emotion drowned any lingering logic and knocked me into action. Fight or flight, or both, whatever it took to get him away from here. How hard would I have to shove Manuel to get both of us past him and out the front doors?

I ran into Jaxon with my arms spread wide, hugging him tightly and not stopping my forward momentum. I walked him backward into the elevator as it was closing, before anyone could think to protest.

The door closed, and I slammed a few floor buttons and hoped the elevator would engage before Manuel pushed the button on his side. As soon as I felt the car begin to lift, I hit the door-open button twice and the close button again three times in rapid succession. After the beeping sound, I punched in the three-digit code Manuel had inadvertently shown me.

Jaxon started to say, "What are you do—" and then the flash, the float, and we were in the utility elevator outside the evidence room.

"How did you do that? There's a port booth system within FutureMove? Incredible." Jaxon asked and answered his own question, so I answered his next one, and asked one of my own.

"We're in the evidence room. I need a couple of things. I'm so happy to see you!" I hugged him again, and this time I didn't shove him anywhere, despite my heartbeat pushing madly against my sternum, and the nagging feeling we had limited time before they figured out where we'd gone. "Are you okay?"

"Happy to be out of the holding cell." He stretched his leg out to the side. "I'm ready for a long bike ride."

"Well, we may be going on a long run, so to speak."

"Yeah, what's your plan here, Aly? I'm thinking if I

were actually free we wouldn't be scampering around this basement."

"I'm looking for a fancy wrench, I saw one here somewhere."

"This?" Jaxon pulled what looked like a hex key with a rubber handle off the crate nearest the elevator.

"Yes! You're amazing." I started a quick step over to the shelf with some interesting looking electronics when the elevator door rattled.

"Crapsicles. Let's get out of here." I waved Jaxon over to the back corner of the room and the door that led outside. Jaxon ascended first, blinking in the bright sun. The elevator doors slid open, and I heard another rattle, this one coming from the cage opposite the outside door. Poor squirrely. He didn't deserve to rot here, either. My logic hadn't made its full comeback, and I sprinted to the cage and opened the door.

The squirrel shot up my arm and clung to my shoulder. I ran back to the door as Manuel stepped out of the elevator. "Alyona, what do you think you're doing? You're going to ruin—wait!"

Jaxon held the door, and we bolted through, then ran toward the gaslight-blue booth closest to the basement exit. Jaxon was a stronger runner than I, and when he realized where we were going, he shot ahead and got the booth open.

Manuel was faster than I'd imagined. He had almost caught up. "Alyona, wait! This is a bad idea!"

My head spun and I tripped, but Jaxon caught my arm before I face planted on the sidewalk. Manuel was right. This was a bad idea. It wasn't an idea at all, really. I'd simply reacted, and now I had to come up with a plan to make this work out. My throat tightened and I could barely breathe. The three of us—two humans and one scared squirrel—crammed into the booth and I typed in the location code, which locked the door. I heard Manuel curse and slam his fist against the side. "They'll find you. Come on, Alyona!"

Accursed tears made it difficult to read my phone screen, but I managed to pay the booth toll so they couldn't track the card data in my ring. I held Jaxon's arm and closed my eyes. Manuel's fist hit the door twice more before the bright flash. For a brief moment, one of my problems floated away. But as I felt the ground beneath my feet, Jaxon's fugitive arm in mine, and a squirrel's claws digging into my shoulder, it was obvious I'd created several new ones.

The door opened to a wide street that once was dangerously packed with automobiles. Three people waited in line as I pulled Jaxon by the arm out of the booth and up a few meters to the street corner, the squirrel still clinging on for dear life. The traffic lights moved through their cycles, but I didn't have the time to wait for the one car I could make out in the distance. I reached around behind Jaxon and mashed the pedestrian button to cross the street, just for fun. If the car was law enforcement, they'd have to stop or turn on a siren, and we'd be long gone. But it was more likely someone doing a big grocery run, or a tourist too nervous to port.

Jaxon leaned his head away from my shoulder as the squirrel reached out its neck and sniffed him. "Where are you taking me?"

I tugged his arm again. "First, campus. You need that job."

Jaxon resisted my pull. "Alyona, no, we can't go there."

"You have to, Jax. You need—" a sob burst out of my throat and fresh tears spilled down my cheeks. How was I going to fix this?

Jaxon pulled the arm I'd been tugging and gently guided my head to rest on his shoulder. "Hey, you're okay, Aly. I'm okay. I'm just happy to be here with you."

Every nerve ending in my body tingled and buzzed with his nearness, and probably with my dropping adrenaline levels. I breathed in his scent and made a sound of acknowledgment.

"The ETC knows about my interview. I asked last night if I'd be released in time to get there. They said that was up to you. That's the first place they'd look for us."

I pressed my face into his shoulder to muffle my desperate yell. I picked my head up. "Those manipulative, bureaucratic . . . gah!" I rubbed my eyes. "I'm so sorry Jax. I thought I could help, and I made a bigger mess."

"You got me out of there." Jaxon kept one arm around me in a tight side hug. "It's fine, I can major in Accounting. It's business, and better than Marketing, like my parents wanted most. Think of the spreadsheets I'll get to create." He kept his voice light, but I knew this was a huge deal to him, and he had to be more upset than he was letting on.

"I know you love a good data set. But don't give up yet. You have a week before you have to declare majors; we can figure something out."

"Sure, maybe. It'll be fine as long as we aren't arrested again in the meantime." I could feel him holding back the sarcasm he'd normally use to rib me. He treaded lightly due to my obviously delicate emotional state. I didn't deserve his consideration when I'd never learned to think before I acted. He gave me a side-eye. "How much trouble are we in?"

"I'm not sure, but I think we need to stay out of sight for a minute and figure it out. I know a place. This way." I ran back down the other side of the street until we reached Exhibit A Beauty.

Jaxon followed, and I pushed open the salon door. The squirrel leaped from my shoulder to the top of the sign above. I suppose it didn't want to be indoors again so soon.

I waved my hand. "Happy Birthday, Jaxon! I got you a mani-pedi!"

Jaxon put his hand to his heart and looked overly bashful. It wasn't his birthday, of course, but I always missed the actual day on account of never keeping track of the date. I got him random gifts throughout the year to make up for it. This wasn't exactly a present, but it was the first place that came to mind where I might have space to think.

The door closed behind me, and everything stopped for a brief, beautiful moment—the running, the pounding in my chest and the ringing in my ears—as if the universe took a deep breath before diving into the next round of chaos.

"Well, hello there, darlin'," said Atty McNair. She gave me the smile the universe knew I needed and made her way up toward the front of the salon. She must have seen the panic in my face and asked, "You good, sweetie?"

"Not really, no. You know how you said if I ever needed anything—I'm sorry, this is so—anyway, I think some people might come looking for me—"

Atty put her hands up to cut me off. "This way, you two. Quickly, now."

I followed her, and Jaxon followed me, too confused to ask questions. He was far more trusting than I.

Atty opened a door at the back of the salon and motioned inside. "In here. Stay hidden until I sort this out."

She had such an air of command about her, I believed she probably *could* sort this out. I poked my head inside the room and saw two tanning beds separated by a thin privacy screen.

Atty leaned into the room and grabbed something off the table inside. "And take a pair of these, unless you want golden-baked retinas. The beds shouldn't turn on unless they've been preset, but just in case!" She held out a couple pairs of little eye shields.

Jaxon and I each took a set and then chose beds, lifted the lids, and lay down. I pulled my backpack around to my stomach and shut my lid slowly, hoping it covered enough of me to hide who I was, and the fact that I was fully clothed, if anyone were to look in.

Atty left and closed the door. Now I could say I'd been in bed with Jaxon. In beds, technically. It was a jokey thought, but I let my mind present a scenario in which we were laying closer, in the same bed. We were still fully clothed in this scene, but the bed was softer. A chill ran up my side where mental-scenario Jaxon would be.

Jaxon's whisper broke the silence. "Alyona?"

My face flushed. So glad he couldn't see into my thoughts. "Yeah?" I whispered back.

"I think I preferred the holding cell. At least in there I could move my legs."

"Yeah, sorry, Jax. I know this has been sudden and weird."

"I mean, so are most of your ideas."

"You're a good sport."

"So, where are we? And why?"

"It's kind of a long story, but basically, the ASF says they nabbed you because they want to make porting open-source, or at least they want to make an alternate port grid. They also want to prove that the ETC is hiding evidence and that the ASF—who in part, if not wholly, consists of my parents' former assistants—shouldn't be investigated. Dr. Clarke says they're after their own shares of the company and they're willing to hurt people to get them. And I'm an heiress, or something."

"Okay . . ."

"I'm not explaining it well, but I was tired of trying to play by everyone else's manipulative rules and I panicked and pulled you deeper into my mess."

I realized we were no longer whispering. I lifted the bed lid and peeked into the room, like a timid turtle, right as someone walked by, their shadow breaking the line of light shining in under the door. I shushed Jaxon, even though I was doing most of the talking, and pulled the lid back down.

We lay in silence, breathing in the coconut lotion air for another few minutes. I squeezed my eyes shut, hoping I'd made the right move relying on a random nail salon for personal security. She did say she'd help, but why? Had she known who I was? My toes tingled and I willed myself to picture floating in a tranquil sea under a wide, open sky. The room was blissfully quiet. Even with my hearing aids working, I could only hear the occasional spike of Atty's wild laughter.

I wasn't sure how long we were supposed to wait, but the glass was hard under my elbows, and I'd begun to worry I'd taken another misstep in my attempt to fix the last one.

Jax and I used to watch a show where the injured bad guys would get into a sarcophagus to heal themselves, and I tried to imagine I would come out revived, and stronger than ever. I made a noise like a reanimated corpse and swung the lid back open, sitting up stiffly and doing a zombie shuffle toward the door of the room again.

"Alyona?" Jaxon's restrained voice carried past the room divider.

I blushed, realizing he had heard my zombie noises. "Yeah?"

"You okay?"

"Yeah, I'm getting a bit stiff in there, you know? I am going to take a peek out the door."

"No, Alyona!" he whispered at me. "Wait until we know for sure it's clear."

"But, how will we know if we don't look—"

"Alyona! Shhh."

I would lie back down in thirty seconds. I cracked open the door and started to inch my head sideways through it when the bells on the front door gave a violent shake. A man in a black windbreaker had forced the door open so fast that I felt a quick draft of cold air before I eased the door shut and crept back into my tanning tomb.

A brisk, unfamiliar voice announced they were canvassing the area for a fugitive. I closed my eyes again, turned up my hearing aid volume, and tried to hold as still as possible. Two or three people's heavy boots stomped into the salon and around the corner down the hallway to the massage rooms. Someone knocked roughly and a door squeaked open. More footsteps.

"Excuse me, sirs! I don't believe y'all are invited back there." Atty said the polite words in quite the opposite tone, the way only a Southern woman could. "You can't willy-nilly pop open doors and cut on the lights when our clients might not be decent!"

"Step aside, ma'am." The boot stomping came back from the hallway, and I saw their shadows stop in front of our door. I stared up at the glass above me, concentrating on the fog forming from my agonizingly slow breath, which blurred my faint reflection. This was it. I would be taken and never heard from again, blurred out until no one remembered I ever existed. What had I done? How could I leave Nadia—

"Enough!" Atty's strong, feminine voice rang from outside the hallway, where she'd followed the intruders. "That will do, officers. You may leave. Now."

"Ma'am, we're here on behalf of the ETC. Have you seen—"

"I have seen nothing but a clear violation of my arrangement with your boss, young man. Y'all go back to work now and tell Shane I have stayed out of his business, and he would do well to stay out of mine."

Atty McNair, aesthetician extraordinaire, knew Dr. Shane Clarke? What did her salon have to do with him? I couldn't imagine he'd come here for the weekly manicure special, but then, I might not know him the way I thought I did. If the former assistants were telling the truth despite their ill-advised methods, then Dr. Clarke had been lying to me—or omitting some huge truths—for years.

The windbreaker man spoke again. "Ma'am, we—"

"To be clear, I meant for you to leave immediately, young man. And don't you *Ma'am* me one more time."

The boots made their way back out to the street and the click of fancy shoes came back to our door. The door swung open, and a tastefully manicured hand lifted the lid of the tanning bed to save me from my sarcophagal doom.

Atty held out her hand to me and said, "Come to my office, Alyona. We need to talk."

CHAPTER SEVENTEEN

A Fired Friend's Friendly Fire

Despite the feathery softness of the white chairs in front of Atty's green desk, Jaxon and I sat rigid in the small office. The walls were lined with shelves full of pictures and several framed certificates.

Our benefactor pulled up her pink chair and tapped a pen on her desk calendar. "Well, did somebody finally get sick of waiting and fill you in? Or did you figure it out by yourself?"

I looked at Jaxon and he looked back at me and lifted his chin as if he had asked the same question.

"I'm so sorry," I said. "I'm not sure what you're referring to."

The woman put the pen down and stared at it, letting out a deep sigh. "So much for staying under the radar."

"I only came here because you invited me, and I remembered the port code. The first four numbers are on the area grid system, and the last four are 1892, the year they invented the escalator."

Jaxon shifted in his chair to admire me. "I'm impressed you remembered."

"Numbers stick in my head."

"Yeah," said Jaxon, turning to the woman as if she were interested. "We were talking about how long it took to get from the wheel to airships and escalators, and only in the last hundred years or so, how quickly we upgraded to planes and rockets and now teleportation." And here Jaxon and I were, zipping through the air at impossible speeds, on the run from the law.

"Well things are certainly moving fast now," Atty said, echoing my thoughts. "The summons you served here wasn't real. I hadn't sent it to you, so I figured it must have been Misha. It's something he'd do. I took it as a signal of his impatience to put you in a more active role."

"Wait, you're saying you are the one who's been sending me summons to serve?" And had Misha given me the fake summons? If so, where? At Kim's Corner while I was waiting for Nadia? Was he the one who'd bumped into me?

Atty smiled and nodded. "That is correct. We go to the same dentist, so I had you hired through them. It worked out, gave me something to do in the legal field, and allowed me to help y'all out from a distance."

I looked back at Jaxon again and he gave me a tiny shrug, and then nodded toward the certificates on the shelves. They looked to be from law schools and bar associations. I didn't know much about salons, but I didn't think they usually kept in-house legal counsel.

I'd been sloppy sending pictures to and getting paid by the dentist. I hadn't thought about who prepared and filed the summons and then sent them to me.

Atty sighed and pulled a pair of reading glasses out of the mug on her desk. She put them on, picked her pen back up, and tapped it against the desk calendar, probably composing her thoughts concerning whatever news bomb she was about to drop.

The familiarity I'd sensed last time we met returned. I concentrated, and remembered seeing Atty around the building at FutureMove, but only in meetings or on the phone. More conservative suits, no teal hair, and no wild laughter.

I asked her an easy question to break the nervous silence, "So, are you a lawyer?"

She kept her eyes down, tilted her head to the side and said, "I was. Still am, technically, but not practicing outside the summons filing." She took another deep breath and then looked up at me. "My name is Athena Carleson. I used to be legal counsel for FutureMove. I was a friend of your dear parents, and after the tragedy I was . . . let go."

A friend of my parents. Blood drained from my face and burned in my fingertips. I wanted to cry and hug her and ask her a million questions, and I also wanted to do none of that and port away to anywhere else. I couldn't respond right away, and Jaxon picked up my slack, standing and offering his hand to Atty.

"Ms. Carleson, hi, I'm Jaxon Jeong."

Atty shook his hand. "Yes, hello Jaxon. We've met before, though you may not remember. Call me Atty." She motioned for him to sit back down. "I worked with your father, as well. He was our entire marketing department when we first started. As I recall, he also headed the strategic growth team. How is he faring?"

"He's great; he and Mom took a publicist gig in Seoul; they are there for probably a few more months. I'd prefer not to worry them with whatever is going on here, if you don't mind. But have you heard anything from Misha? He's the one who got me into bicycling back in the day, since he thought teleportation might scramble his brain."

"Just an obscure message here and there."

"Oh," I said, retrieving the Michael Wells envelope and

handing it to her. "Did you know you prepped a summons for him? He used an alias. Or was sending me this his doing, too?"

Atty inspected the envelope and the summons inside. "You're not supposed to open these, I'm sure you're aware." She paused to scold me with her piercing glare. "But this is one of mine. Makes sense, most of us used that dentist, and he couldn't port away with gold fillings. He must have been extremely spooked to finally take the leap. I'll double the pay for this one if you can find him discreetly. He can afford this bill—he has at least one rental property somewhere that I know of. A safe house might come in handy if mine is ever compromised."

Compromised? Was she wanted, too? *Like Carleson, B.?*

I gripped the arms of the chair and sat forward. "Wait, Carleson? Are you related to my parents' assistant?"

Jaxon put his hand on my knee and the blood in my fingertips rushed into my leg. His touch tingled and I twitched. He pulled his hand away. *Good going, Alyona.* Jaxon only wanted to comfort me. Why couldn't I relax and let him? My heart picked up to about three beats per shallow breath.

"Barbara is my niece. We were a small company at first, like a family. Your parents, Jaxon's dad, a few techs, including Misha and Barbara. And Shane." She spat his name as if it were a swear.

"But you said you didn't know a Kendall. Isn't—"

"Barbara's trying to avoid the drama that sometimes crops up when people recognize her name from the news. Changing her name feels like letting Shane win to me, and I'm not ready to give up on the name she's had for twenty-six years just because he's trying to label her something she's not."

Like a family, she said, but willing to keep so many secrets and kidnap their own? I bit my tongue so she'd continue.

Atty shook her head and stood. She stared at her bar certificate. "After the accident, I pulled all the logs and information I could about what exactly had happened. I knew I was up against the biggest legal mess of my life, whether the cause was a glitch or a miscalculation or a mistake by a technician. I wanted to honor your parents' work, but I also wanted justice for them."

I breathed in slowly so that my voice wouldn't crack when I spoke. "By justice, do you mean getting to the bottom of whatever mistake happened, or do you think someone might have tampered . . ."

Atty turned to the shelf behind her and pulled a tiny globe out from behind one of the framed documents. It bore the FutureMove logo on the base.

"I didn't suspect tampering at first. But we had to find the error. Shane wanted me to hold off, wait for PR to advise before we went any further. He thought someone like Mr. Jeong could work his magic and rebuild public confidence in our company. I pushed on—I reckoned the company was gone anyway if we couldn't tell the public what went awry. Trust in the safety of our products would plummet. The only way to save the company was to find out what had happened to them.

"Shane disagreed. He forbade my involvement. He fired the techs on the project—to save face, he said. Clearly, they had screwed up, right? He couldn't keep local law enforcement out, but he made sure I kept my distance."

I stood and paced behind the chairs. "I understand wanting to protect the company he founded, but why wouldn't he let you come back once the investigation was over? Didn't you want back in?" I considered asking whether she had any shares in the company, or if that was only her niece, but I remembered Manuel's advice not to reveal my cards. She didn't need to know how much I knew.

"We tried, but that's when things took a turn. Shane planted rumors that we'd left out of guilt or shame, like we had some conspiracy going. I wanted to give him the benefit of the doubt. He was grieving, looking for something to blame."

I stopped pacing and nodded. That made sense. I'd done the same to him.

Atty sighed and sat back down. "But that's when the threats began. He all but told us that he found the problem, and it wouldn't look good for us if we came back and started digging around again. He had some vague story about his top ETC superiors and how he'd keep everyone else safe if we kept our distance."

She looked at me, and I joined her at the desk. "But why would he lie? If it was a glitch, why push you all away?"

"Power. Greed. The age-old banes of mankind. He's already got our votes and shares, and he's got new legal counsel trying to consolidate anything remaining."

"He told me about the trust."

"Did he tell you he's trying to edge you out of your rights within your own parents' company?"

What she called edging me out, he called trying to shield me from manipulation and stuffy board rooms.

"Shane's not messing around. He knows where I live, and he knows Barbie lives with me. If I don't tangle with him or FutureMove, he doesn't tangle with Barbie or me, so we're careful to investigate quietly, without tipping him off. If I know him, he'll have a paper trail to cover his own hide. Finding the test logs and communication between Shane and his alleged higher-ups is our best chance to clear our names."

Atty folded her arms. "Even if he isn't motivated by power, his treachery could be simple self-preservation. He's elbows-deep in something foul and spinning hard to make it smell like altruism."

I let my gaze fall to the table. I didn't know what to think.

Atty held her pen out to me and pointed at the salon's name. "I'd been coming here weekly, and the owner was looking to retire. I bought this place with my severance package—aka my hush money. It's helped me to explore my less reserved side and prove to Shane I've moved on."

Atty handed me the pen. I took it and spun it in my hand. "Which, you haven't, of course."

"And I never will now that you're with us." Atty smiled broadly and hope shone from her eyes.

My chest ached with a dull stabbing. I wasn't *with* anyone but Jax, just yet. I'd shown up here when I needed help, but I hadn't understood who she was. I hadn't meant to lead anyone on.

I held the pen back out to her. "I'm . . . I need to process before I pledge any allegiance."

Atty waved her refusal of my returning the pen. "I understand it's a whole heap of news to sort through. Let's get you fed and give you a moment to think at my place, where it'll be safer to chat. Barbie should be the one to tell the rest, anyway."

The rest? I was dying for time to think, but was it insane to follow this woman to her home? I looked to Jaxon for an assist.

He shrugged. "You can't exactly go home at this point. Might as well hear her out."

I clicked the pen while I considered. I hadn't even had time to realize everything I'd risked by stealing Jaxon away. His freedom. Nadia's job, our apartment . . . I didn't know what recourse the ETC had for someone who escaped custody. Kendi implied her friend Melanie's lost hand was a consequence of her meddling. Was Dr. Clarke capable of that?

"Alright, then, lead the way." I stood, relieved to move and shake out some of my jitters. Too many skeletons had escaped their closets for one day. I felt like the closet skeletons were dancing directly behind my eyes, and I tripped over the door frame exiting the salon. Jaxon caught me. I willed myself not to flinch this time and let him lead me toward the nearest port booth.

"Are you alright, Aly? I can take you somewhere else quiet, we can make a list of what we know—"

Jaxon bringing up spreadsheets was a sure sign he was feeling out of his depth. He liked to see a situation laid out in writing and analyze pros and cons. I was terrible under pressure, so planning was inevitable. But this time, I didn't want to see all the contradicting claims displayed in neat columns, proving nothing but the fact that, until I found evidence, my decision about who to throw in with would come down to a gut feeling.

"No, I'm fine. Just a headache." I put my hands in front of my face as if to block the sun in case the ETC booth cameras were monitored, and all three of us squeezed inside.

Atty yelped when a squirrel darted past her as she was pulling the door closed.

"It's okay," I said. "He's with us."

She shook her head. "Young people today." She entered an eight-digit code.

The four of us floated toward our next piece of the puzzle.

Atty lived in a gorgeous little Victorian brick house not far from downtown. It had its own walled-in yard and everything. We sat in her kitchen sipping chicken soup she'd warmed up for us, perfect for a chilly fall day. I hadn't realized how hungry I was and could feel the frustrated fog lifting from my mind.

The squirrel found a wide oak tree to explore in the back of the yard. I put out some water and a small bowl of peanuts Atty offered for him—or her—I couldn't tell.

The digital lock on the front door beeped. Atty smiled. "That's Barbara. She'll be ecstatic you're finally working with us."

The door opened, and in walked our very own Barbie with a full head of tight, dark-brown coils, some of them dyed purple on the ends, free from its cat-eared beanie. She pulled off her jacket and hung it on the rack next to the door. "Hey, Aunt Atty, that smells del—" Kendi turned to face us, and her jaw dropped.

I stood with a start, almost knocking my chair over. I caught it without looking away from her. "Kendi." I frowned but tried to turn my mouth up. She may have left pieces out of her communications with me, but she wasn't to blame for this mess. Or she was. She was either a greedy liar guilty of fatal negligence, or she was as much a victim of the situation as I was. I wasn't sold, but so far I didn't get the manslaughter vibe from her, or from Atty.

Jaxon stood, too. "You!" He grabbed me by the arm and dragged me out the side door. "We need to talk, now."

I came willingly, and he shut the sliding door behind us.

He leaned in and lowered his voice. "That's the girl from the market. She told me you were in trouble. She led me to the booths, but Manuel had been tracking her and got to me first. He accused me of associating with the ASF, took my ankle bracelet off and ported me away. She's a liar. We can't trust anything she says. How do you know we're not their hostages—insurance against the ETC, or that they don't want to remove us as obstacles to the votes and power they say Dr. Clarke is after?"

I shook my head. "We don't. But they could have hurt—or

removed—us already, if they'd wanted to. Kendi, or Barbie or whatever her name is, I know she's acted shady, but I'm really starting to believe she thinks she is doing right. She said they'd planned on taking you only as a last resort to get my attention. Maybe she's desperate to get her share of the company or make a second port grid, but I don't think that's it. You should have seen her when she thought they'd hurt you. Did you know the lady who lost her hand was a friend of hers? She doesn't think that was an accident."

Jaxon shifted his weight and shook his head. "That's not a good enough excuse. Everyone in history thought they were doing the right thing. The worst villains you can think of justified their actions. We're all the heroes of our own stories."

I nodded. "That's true, but she doesn't seem malicious to me. She seems fed up, exhausted, and scared."

"And scared, desperate people are more likely to lie and manipulate."

A cold breeze ruffled my hair. "You said it yourself. Might as well hear them out. Dr. Clarke says he's protecting me and Nadia from outside pressures, and that my parents' assistants are to blame for their accident. Let's hear what they have to say and then we can decide together."

Jaxon blew some air between his teeth and his lip. "Wouldn't that be nice."

My stomach clenched. Jax was frequently sarcastic with me, but the ribbing was usually accompanied by his adorable smile.

He dropped his tight shoulders. "I'm sorry. I'm grateful for you getting me out of that cell. They wouldn't listen when I swore I hadn't been chatting up the ASF. But we both know you're going to do what you're going to do, no matter what I say. Sometimes I don't think you realize that your actions affect the lives around you."

I stared at the mostly dead grass. He placed a hand lightly on my upper arm. "When you say we can decide, I want you to mean we, together, decide our story, not you alone." His hand slipped from my arm down to my wrist, stopping short of taking me by the hand.

I took a sharp breath in, and my cheeks warmed despite the chill air.

Jaxon looked into my eyes. "You chose to launch this adventure on the lam, so I guess I'm asking you to let me help decide how we continue."

My face flushed deeper. I focused for too many seconds on the words, "our story" and, "together." I batted away my second instinct—offense that he didn't like the way I got him out of the holding cell. But he was right. He'd never seemed to mind following me around, but he had clearly reached his limits. I'd pulled him out of one prison and into another. He deserved to have a say.

Did I dare believe that he still wanted anything more than friendship? If I could ever work up the courage to open my scarred heart to anyone, it would be Jaxon. Scratch that. It already *was* Jaxon. I'd fooled myself into thinking that by keeping things platonic, I'd kept myself invulnerable. What an idiot I was, letting our relationship stagnate until he was annoyed enough with me to call me out.

I looked up, and he dropped my wrist. I crossed my heart. "I hereby promise I will not drag you through one more port booth without your consent."

"It's a start."

"And, I'll try to let you in on the planning more, but you might not want that once you get a good look into my mind. It's kind of a dumpster fire."

He pulled his lips into a half-grin. "I'll be the judge of that. And speaking of dangerous messes, do you really want to reenter the ASF lair and see what they have to say for themselves? Are we *sure* we don't want to spreadsheet this?"

I was absolutely sure, but I couldn't insist on my way right after agreeing to consider his opinion. I gave him what I thought were puppy-dog eyes to plead my case.

He gave me a look best described as the face-palm emoji. "You look like a pigeon dropped a gift on your forehead."

I followed him inside. We sat back down at the kitchen table across from Kendi, who now had her own bowl of soup. She stirred, smiling.

"So," I said, "Atty tells us you have a story."

She met my eyes. "First, I have to thank you," she said, eyes shining. "It's been so long since I've felt optimistic." She looked back down at her soup. "Thank you for believing in us."

I squirmed in my chair. I wasn't sure how everything fit together yet, and, though I understood why she'd done it, I hadn't forgiven her for using Jax, let alone taken up her cause.

"My being here wasn't wholly intentional. I saw Jaxon and freaked out. But I suppose we're with you for now."

"Tentatively," added Jaxon. "Ms. Carleson promised Alyona time to think before we make any decisions."

Kendi nodded and lifted her spoon. "So, how much of it do you know so far?" She looked at me.

"Of your side or both, because Dr. Clark paints a pretty convincing picture of you as the bad guys, the cause of the accident, only caring about getting your shares back . . . You said you want me to help break the port network free of the monopoly, but you really want me to find evidence that you had nothing to do with my parents' accident, and that Melanie's wasn't an accident at all, but you think it's dangerous for me to know what's really going on, or dangerous for Dr. Clarke to know that I know."

Kendi put the spoon back down.

Atty came in from the kitchen. "I think it's time to risk letting her in on the rest. If she positions herself against Shane, she should understand the danger."

"Agreed," I said, and then looked to Jax. "Right?"

He took a second and then nodded. "But let's at least finish lunch before we blaze ahead."

Atty stepped toward the front door and pulled her jacket off a coat rack. "I've got to get back to the salon, but you're welcome to stay as long as you want, even overnight. They won't bother you here. Alyona, your sister is invited as well, if she prefers to be with you. Fill me in on whatever plan you come up with." She walked out and closed the door behind her.

Jaxon and I kept quiet until our soup bowls were empty.

I took a few more minutes of peace before I looked up at Kendi. "Okay, let's have it."

Kendi filled her lungs and started. "Well, I guess what I want you to believe most is that we, Misha and I, had nothing to do with . . ."

Her gaze dropped and her breath hitched, and when she looked back up at me her eyes shone with unshed tears. As hard as it was for me to listen to her side of the story, maybe it was just as hard for her to tell it. I hadn't really considered that the assistants might have anything to do with the accident before Dr. Clarke implied something along those lines. I'd assumed my parents hadn't accounted for some variable, or that they'd been overconfident, or something had malfunctioned, and it wasn't anyone's fault. If Kendi was innocent, why had she run away instead of facing reality like I had to and trying to figure out the glitch?

"Kendi, tell me what you want me to know. We want to hear you out."

Jaxon pushed his bowl aside and scooted closer. He rested his arm along the back of my chair.

Kendi dabbed her eyes with her soup napkin. "I wouldn't, I couldn't have. I didn't change any settings; I was only there observing. It wasn't their first test porting dense materials, just the first human trial. Everything was fine, and then . . ." She sobbed once and squeezed her eyes closed.

I followed with a question before I could think about what she had witnessed. "So why is Dr. Clarke so hell-bent on blaming you? Why were you all so scared of me knowing too much and reacting in front of him? Why does Atty think I'm safer with you than with the man who made sure Nadia and I were taken care of?"

Kendi kept her eyes closed until the lines between her eyebrows smoothed and her breathing evened out. She opened her eyes and spoke softly. "My mom died ten years ago. I was a year younger than you are now. Ovarian cancer. My dad is a long-haul truck driver, and he avoids staying home too long. I'm not sure what his excuse will be when his loads are ported, and they don't need him anymore."

She was older than I'd assumed on Saturday, before I recognized her. When I was little, I lumped her into the "adult" category, because anyone over eighteen was ancient-of-days. But she was still only twenty-six, maybe twenty-seven. I didn't know how this parent talk was related, but I let her speak.

"I graduated early and worked part-time for your parents through my integrated Master's and Doctoral program, and my wildest dreams came true when they took me on full-time. Your parents were my idols. They were the parents I always wanted and the mentors I wanted to grow into. I hoped to work for them forever, and they saw so much potential in me that they put me on their most exciting projects. I can't even express how they've influenced my life for the better. Misha, too. We would never have done anything to hurt them, and there is no way we made that huge a mistake."

Either she was a really good actress, or she really *had* loved my parents, and I leaned further and further into believing what she said. But she was implying someone else would have done something to hurt them, namely Dr. Clarke, and as much as I wanted to know the truth, I didn't want to believe this man my parents regarded as family could betray them so completely.

"Let's assume I believe you." At least that the accident wasn't her fault. I'd believed my whole life that Dr. Clarke loved my parents, too. I'd chalked up the unease I felt around him to the fact that he'd lived on when they hadn't, and I was trying to redirect that.

"Then believe I need your help. Please, if you found anything you didn't give up earlier, or if you can look for other data storage, anything—"

"Yeah, you need my help. But you want me out sneaking around while you're in here sipping soup. Before I hear any more, I need you to prove you're willing to take some risk."

Kendi fingered a charm she had dangling from a chain around her wrist. "What can I do?"

"You can find your sturdiest knife, preferably a small electric oscillating saw. And a crowbar."

Jaxon raised an eyebrow at me. "I get a say here, remember? And I say this already sounds like a terrible idea."

A spark of annoyance zinged through my head at his interference. But he'd reminded me that he was his own person, not my sidekick. I'd taken him for granted. If I wanted him to be *my* person, I had to do better.

"We're going to steal a teleporter. Sorry. I mean, will you please help me steal a port unit off its booth wall? And Kendi, you'll be the lookout, and the first one the ETC captures if we're caught, and you'll stall them until we can escape."

"I'm in, if this is what it takes to prove myself." Kendi said. "I'll get some tools."

Jaxon sat back in his chair. "But why?"

"Because we're already on the run, so we'll need to be extra slippery. I don't want to be tethered to the booth grid. If we're going to do this—"

"Which we haven't decided yet," Jaxon said.

"A portable unit could make all the difference. Right? We're all on board? Grab your jacket, and Kendi, don't forget the knife. We can talk as we work."

The booth's door unlocked, and Kendi pushed it open. She glanced out to see where I'd ported us, and then pulled the door closed again. "Are you nuts?" she whisper-shouted, her slouchy cat-eared hat uncomfortably close to my face. "They're surely looking for you here."

I knew it was a risk showing up so close to my apartment, but Slaughterbox's port unit was the obvious choice to steal. It wasn't likely to be missed since the neighborhood residents rarely used it, and I'd already set it up to work with my Gooseberry remote once I installed a pairing chip. "It's the best option. The ETC might be watching the apartment, but no local will choose this booth to port out from and interrupt us while we're working."

I reached past her and pushed the door back open. "Use your knife to slice through the housing for the cable around back and unplug it. We don't want anyone porting in, either."

Kendi stepped out.

"Jaxon, you keep . . . I mean, can you keep watch while she's occupied? I'll call you in when I need muscle." And, I didn't quite trust that Kendi wouldn't take off if she spotted trouble.

"Fine. But I'm taking the crowbar."

I pulled it out of my pack and handed it to him as if I believed he were capable of violence.

Jaxon left, and a few seconds later, the flashing red lights around the doorway went dark. Kendi stepped back inside. "We're powered off. But wouldn't the booth stop someone from trying to land in here while it's occupied?"

"Yeah, it's supposed to send queued users to the next open booth in the row, but I'd rather play it safe while we're removing the unit." I almost sent her back out to keep watch so I could keep Jaxon inside with me, but I discovered a small hitch in my plan. I leaned my head out the door. "Hey, Jax, it'll be easier to talk to Kendi if she stays in here with me. But at the first sign of trouble, you jump in, and I'll kick her out to fend it off."

Jaxon grunted in reply.

"Wow, thanks," Kendi muttered.

I pushed my backpack into the doorway, blocking the door from fully closing. I eyeballed the unit, hoping it would fit in the pack when we pulled it free. With its card reader, screen, speaker, and housing, it was about the size of two loaves of half-flattened sandwich bread sitting side-by-side.

I dug out the proprietary wrench I'd taken from the evidence room and started on the plentiful small bolts attaching it to the wall. "So Kendi, if Atty has enough to keep Dr. Clarke at bay, why doesn't she go to the police?"

"A couple of reasons. First, the case was turned over to the feds early on. Dr. Clarke has been in constant contact with his federal overseers ever since he took on his role as liaison to the ETC, and he was never taken in for questioning, so there's obviously some kind of deal going on."

The first bolt fell into my hands, but the second wouldn't budge. Kendi grunted as she added her surprising strength to my efforts. "We'd do better going to one of the news channels, but the evidence would have to be overwhelming."

I started on the third bolt of about six million and wished I'd grabbed another wrench. "And the other reason?"

"The evidence is underwhelming. Hence your quest. Aunt Atty told them a friend of Misha's overseas would release everything she has if anything happens to us. But we have precious little more than unsubstantiated threats and a few emails to the legal team about what would happen to company shares and votes in a variety of outcomes with the case. She's bluffing."

"What kind of threats? Like, you might not keep your shares?"

Kendi planted her foot against the purple wall for leverage.

"You okay in there?" called Jaxon.

"Mostly," I said.

Kendi finally twisted the third bolt free. "No, actually. Nothing is okay." She pushed my shoulder around so I was facing her.

"Hey—"

"Hey yourself, Alyona. I've tried to be patient with you and I'm sorry we resorted to taking Jaxon. I was desperate. I wouldn't have signed off on the foot thing; that was too far. But I'm still desperate, and patience is not my strong suit. As smart as you are, you're not getting it." She lifted her wrist with the chain wrapped around it and held the charm up to my face. "Do you recognize this?"

"No, why would I rec—" and suddenly, I *did* recognize it. It was a delicate gold-colored symbol from a cartoon show that was popular when I was little. The same symbol the detective held up to the light in my news feed after it took a woman's hand off.

"Your friend, Melanie, right? She had the same charm."

"They're our Best Friends bracelets. We've had them for more than a decade."

Kendi had ported here with hers on. "And your hand is still here."

"It's a crappy alloy we got from a vendor at Pop Culture Con." Kendi's eyes filled again, and her tears spilled over when she blinked up at me. "She was digging into the testing logs. Dr. Clarke had asked her for some theoretical settings to give the group working on the booth safety locks. But then she found that not only had that group never received the settings, they'd never even asked for anything. She never found where they'd been sent, and the internal emails between her and Dr. Clarke about them were gone from her account. There were holes in the testing logs, too—data entered and then deleted, strange access codes created and removed later.

"She didn't want to put me at risk by telling me anything more. I should have told her to stop, stay out of danger, but I was so tired of living with the anxiety that someday Dr. Clarke would figure out how to get us locked away and take everything . . ." Kendi's sob cut off her words.

Dr. Clarke had said the same—that Melanie had been researching holes in the data, but that the ASF had stopped her. Kendy wouldn't have dismembered her BFF, so that had to be a lie. But could Dr. Clarke go so far as to cut off a hand? I didn't want to believe so. He'd helped us. Looked after us, in his own way.

I sorted my thoughts aloud. "So Dr. Clarke was the one who didn't want her investigation to continue, and he lied to me about it. But that doesn't mean he caused her to lose her hand. Someone else, maybe one of his dangerous bosses, could have done it and blamed it on the ASF." Except, I'd found the memo where he told those bosses in no uncertain terms that he'd deal with her snooping, and that they wouldn't need to take action. Nausea bubbled in the pit of my stomach.

Kendi shook her head. "Shane saw Melanie as a big enough threat to silence her permanently. There was no glitch with your parents' demonstration, either. Someone tampered with the settings, and the only people with admin access were your parents, Misha, me, and Shane Clarke."

I picked up the wrench and spun a bolt from the port unit at cyclone speed, grasping for explanations. "But even if someone caused Melanie's booth accident, they probably just meant to scare her. It's a bracelet. Misha lost his finger, maybe he's bitter—"

"No!" Kendi shouted, and I jumped, the wrench slipping off the bolt. She unwrapped the bracelet from her wrist. "It's a necklace. We moved them to our wrists a few days ago when she sunburned her neck skiing. Shane or someone loyal to him must have switched out her chain with a real gold one to make it look like an accident." Kendi wiped her eyes. "I haven't heard from her since."

I tackled the last bolt in the casing holding the port unit to the booth wall, twisting furiously. I pulled the bolt out, but the port unit was still somehow attached to the wall. I had to set it free. I grasped it by the sides and tugged hard. Everyone else knew things I didn't, had power I didn't. This port unit would give me an advantage I could use to make all of this go away, one way or another.

Kendi pulled out her knife and wedged it behind the unit. Seeing anyone but myself with a deadly weapon made me nervous, so I took over.

Kendi continued. "It's why we kept you in the dark as much as possible. We didn't want him to silence you too."

My own eyes pooled with liquid as her words penetrated. I shoved the knife in further and yanked. My thumb slipped, and the knife opened an inch-long cut on the skin at the base of my thumb. It stung, and blood trickled down my hand, but it was nothing compared to the stabbing in my chest. I dug my fingers into the gap I'd created behind the top of the port unit and yanked, roaring with the effort. It clung stubbornly to the wall. I grabbed the top of the unit's housing so I wouldn't damage anything hard to fix, then propped my foot up against the wall and tugged with my body weight. My grip slipped, and I fell back into the opposite wall.

Jaxon yanked open the booth door and helped me to my feet.

The skeletons dancing behind my eyes were full-on moshing now, and my vision darkened. I let go of Jaxon's hand and finally met Kendi's glare. If she was right, I had no excuse to be angry with my parents anymore, and my trust in them hadn't been foolish or naive.

They weren't reckless, and their invention wasn't flawed.

It wasn't their fault.

Tears streamed freely. I shoved the knife back behind the port unit. Everything in me screamed that Kendi's version corroborated what I'd always felt but had tried to justify and ignore.

Now that I was on her team, I braced myself for some heavy friendly fire.

Kendi's voice was steady and sure. "Alyona, Shane Clarke murdered your parents."

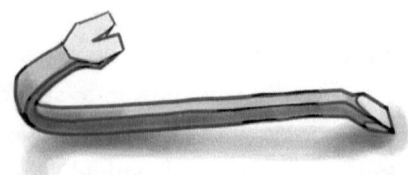

CHAPTER EIGHTEEN

A Walk in the Park

Adrenaline pulsed through my arms, and I cried out like the last survivor of the zombie apocalypse running headlong into the horde. I pulled the port unit with all my might, shaking the whole booth. Kendi grabbed the crowbar out of Jaxon's hand and wedged it into the gap between the unit and the wall, and together, we freed the unit with a loud snap of broken plastic. Two metal clips had anchored the backplate, and they were still embedded into the chunk of wall we'd taken with the unit.

I stumbled again and Jaxon caught me, a warm, solid presence at my back. He held me up, turning his head and pressing his cheek onto my tangled hair. I set the port unit at my feet, turned into him, and sank into a hug around his torso. I bawled into his chest. I never envisioned myself as a damsel in distress, but I wasn't a dystopian warrior, either. Nor was I the logic-based, emotionless machine I wanted to be. I was a human dealing with everything I'd tried so hard to avoid since a chunk of my soul snapped off four years ago, and I couldn't imagine getting through it without this human, my Jaxon, by my side.

I heard the sound of tearing cloth and saw Kendi standing outside the booth, blocking the door from closing and attacking the silk lining of her hat, ripping it into a wide ribbon. She reached past Jaxon and grabbed my arm, and before I could wonder why she was taking out her frustrations on her clothing, she had my hand bandaged tightly. I noticed the blood from my cut had traveled down my arm and dripped from my elbow. Jaxon wore a navy-blue shirt, so it was hard to see the blood on his clothes.

"Sorry for bleeding on you."

He lifted a foot where my blood had dropped onto his sock. "It's okay. Makes these basic socks a little interesting" He pulled me into his chest again and kissed the top of my head, sending shivers down my back. I thanked Kendi with a nod, and she backed out of the cramped booth. She was another fellow human I'd have to rely on if I wanted to take down the man who had ruined our lives.

I could have stayed wrapped in Jaxon's arms forever, living in the tiny world between us where everything made sense. But we'd been too close to home for too long. I turned and picked up the port unit with my good hand. Now that I wasn't in danger of passing out, I saw how simple it should have been to remove the port unit once the screws were out. I pulled a narrow screwdriver from my pack and pressed it into the sides of the clips attaching the unit to the backplate. The broken piece of bruise-purple plastic thudded to the floor, where I saw our squirrel friend curled up in the remains of Kendi's hat. He must have followed us into the booth.

Jax and I left the purple booth and headed into the gaslight-blue booth next in the row. Kendi followed, carrying the squirrel in her hat like a feral purse dog.

"So, now what?" Kendi said, petting the squirrel's head.

Now, I'd plan a magnificent data heist to get every byte

FutureMove and the ETC had about the accident. If there was any way Dr. Clarke was innocent, I would find it through whatever last-ditch effort I could. If not, I would prove Kendi and Misha's innocence and take Dr. Clarke down.

"Step One is to see what I can do with this port unit. I already found the code to program a destination outside of a port booth in the ETC servers, which will be essential to our other objective of stealing more data and staying on the more spacious side of the ETC's cell bars. This baby gives us the freedom to port without risking a run-in with guards who might be stalking the port booths. We can fly under the ETC's radar."

Kendi pulled the blue booth's door closed after Jaxon stepped fully inside. My arm blazed with heat where his pressed against me.

"And Step One-Point-Five is to consult with your wise and rational co-fugitive Jaxon, right?" he said.

He kept his tone airy, probably out of respect for my current emotional state. But how many chances would he give me to start including him more in my plans—our plans—before he finally gave up and made plans with someone else?

I turned my head to the side and caught his eyes already following mine. I wasn't sure hearts could actually skip beats, but mine seemed to throw an extra one in. "Of course, Jax," I said. "You're Step Zero-Point Five."

Jaxon smiled, and I wished that, instead of calling him zero, I'd told him he was my *real* Step One and I'd try harder to show him.

Kendi spoke before I could correct myself. "And what can I do in the meantime?"

I was too exhausted and overwhelmed to articulate anything clearly, let alone the fledgling ideas that would become my brilliant plan.

The squirrel wriggled free of Kendi's hat and hopped onto her shoulders. Apparently, Manuel's tactic for resensitizing the squirrel to people hadn't worked, and Kendi was already part of its inner circle.

"It would be amazing if you could head home and make sure the squirrel stays clear of my experimentation. I wouldn't want it to lose tail fluff or anything. And it's probably hungry."

Kendi put a hand on her hip and slid her head to the side. "You want me to squirrel-sit? Are you serious right now?"

"Um . . . yes?" I gave her a toothy grin. I probably looked completely unhinged with my face blotchy and my eyes bloodshot and watery.

She backed down. "Fine. Yeah. Don't worry about Tater Tot here. I'll take care of him."

"Tater Tot?" I guess if she was going to take care of it, she could name it.

"Yeah, that's what I have at home to feed him. I'll take the yellow booth." She stepped toward the door to exit the blue booth, and I reached out and grabbed her arm. "Thank you. And . . . I'm sorry, too."

"No need—"

"No, Kendi," I dropped her arm and my own arms felt heavy. I folded them in front of me, and then unfolded them, thinking I might look closed off when I was trying to be real. I let them hang awkwardly at my sides. None of this was comfortable, but it was necessary. "I need to tell you that I'm sorry for misjudging you. I'm sorry for calling you names and acting so superior."

Kendi pulled Tater Tot from her shoulder into her arms, the sparkling charm dangling from her wrist.

"And I'm sorry for your friend. For Melanie. I hope she's okay."

Kendi didn't smile, but her brow relaxed. "Be safe," she said as she left for the pustule-mustard booth, the last one in the row.

Jaxon squeezed my elbow. "Where did you have in mind to go work on this?"

I wiped my eyes again. "Oh, somewhere with some open space, where we can have a little privacy. What do you think?"

"City Park is probably a good, open place to test configurations, right?"

"Good call." I turned to the input screen on the booth wall, but before I punched in the code, I gave him a tight squeeze around the waist again. He leaned back and raised his eyebrows. I wasn't normally the touchy-feely type, but I couldn't help showing him how much his presence meant, for the past four years as much as the past several minutes of life-altering revelation.

"I'm glad to have you back, and safe," I said.

"Yeah, me too." He smiled at me, and the air in the booth grew warm, despite the autumn chill.

Jaxon held up a *gimme* hand between us. "Let me hold the port unit, just in case."

"Why? There aren't any dense metals in it. It'll be fine."

Jaxon took the backpack off my arm, some of the port unit's wiring sticking out the top. "I want to be useful."

He wanted to protect me without saying he wanted to protect me. I let him. I transferred my pitiful summons funds into an AppyBucks account registered to a burner number, paid the booth fee, and pushed *go*.

⋯➤

I stepped out of the booth and right into a flying disk.

"Aaouch!" I rubbed the side of my head where I'd been bludgeoned and bent over to pick up the disk.

Jaxon came out behind me and surveyed the scene. "Did that hit you? Let me see."

I cocked the injured side of my head toward Jaxon, and he brushed the area surrounding the impending bruise with light fingertips. "Does this hurt?"

Hurt? No. Make the hairs raise up on my arms, to say nothing of my deepening blush? Yep.

While he'd been gone, my thoughts about Jaxon focused on finding him and getting out. Plenty of anxiety with a backdrop of rage at his kidnappers. Since I'd sprung him from the ETC cell, his slightest touch sent my head whirring like a processor fan. Maybe the fact that he'd been taken from me helped me realize I never wanted to be without him.

I still had to respond to his question. "Nah, it's fine. Thanks."

One of the shorts-and-hoodie locals came jogging up with his mouth an aghast grimace. "I am so sorry! Are you hurt?"

I looked at him for a second, still holding his plastic projectile, and said in monotone, "No way, I love being bashed upside the head. It's so on-theme for today."

He appeared unsure whether I was joking. "Well, sorry again. I guess it really got away from me."

I wound my pitching arm into my side and flung the disk back in the direction the hoodie guy had come. A shot of pain reminded me I'd cut my thumb. Worth it. The disk soared well past where he'd been and far away from where I wanted to go experiment with Jaxon in peace. Er, experiment with the teleporter, with Jaxon helping.

Hoodie guy's gaze followed the disk's flight until it entered the trees across the field, and then he looked wide-eyed back at me. I was into softball before the accident, but I'd only attempted to participate for one season since.

I frowned at him. "Oh, no. I guess it really got away from me, too." I made a shooing motion with my hands.

Hoodie guy's eyes eased back to normal-sized, and he shifted his weight to his heels. "Fair enough," he said as he turned to jog away.

Jaxon looked at me with raised eyebrows.

"Don't say it," I warned. Jaxon would have told hoodie guy it was all good, and no harm done, and whatever other nice, forgiving words suited his gentle demeanor. Really, I was grateful to disc dude for giving me a small release. It felt good to be able to physically throw something that had caused me pain as hard and as far away as I could.

Jaxon shrugged. "What? I was impressed by your range." He wiggled his eyebrows up and down as he gave my limp noodle bicep a squeeze.

I jerked my arm away and smirked. "Oh, shut it already."

"No, really! Maybe after things settle down you can start up softball again. That guy was probably about to ask you to join his Ultimate Frisbee league before you shut him down."

I punched Jaxon's arm and then jogged ahead of him to a patch of grass surrounded on three sides by trees. It seemed like a good place to avoid anyone who might notice us porting away. We'd detached the cord from the power grid when we pulled the unit out of the booth, but it had internal backup batteries that should last at least a full day. Jaxon pulled my backpack open enough to tap the screen of the port unit. Sure enough, it glowed to life, though it was dim against the afternoon sun. He tapped several times, alternating between the top and bottom right corners, the way I showed him how to access the basic settings. "Uh oh," he said, showing me the display. "I got us locked out."

"I told you, six taps," I said, taking the unit from him. "But I'm not worried. I'll get in."

I walked further down the open field toward the trees and glanced around our small corner of the vast, three-hundred-acre park. No one hung out nearby or headed our direction, and the only camera was pointed down the paved path ahead of us. I sat on the grass and motioned for Jaxon to come closer. "Give me some shade," I said.

"Oh, okay wait, how's this?" Jaxon bobbed his hands out in front of him like a bad parody of a rap artist and threw down his best insults. "Girl, you're pushy and you're rude, and you're bad at ice skating. You don't even know what year Colorado became a state . . . ing."

I fell over sideways in the grass, groaning in mock agony. "Oh my gosh, Jaxon, you insufferable nerd. Not that kind of shade." I grabbed at his leg and pulled him closer. "Get over here and block the sun. I can't see the screen."

Jaxon shuffled over until his shadow crossed the port unit screen. I twisted my torso around and looked up at him. "And, are you for real? State history insults? Is that the best you can do?"

"Come on, it's like, the one area where I'm smarter than you are. And the ice-skating line was a sick burn."

"Yes to the first part." It was obvious he was trying hard to stay his silly self for me. I appreciated his efforts. It wasn't his fault the pulsing behind my eyes had only slightly lessened since Kendi chucked a Molotov into the dumpster fire in my brain. I briefly looked away from the screen to give him a smile of appreciation.

Jaxon rested his hands on my shoulders and squatted down to see the screen, his cheek only about a thumb drive's length away from mine.

I stared back at the screen and tapped the corners to access the system settings.

"For instance," he said, his breath smelling of grape gum in a way that made me crave some, "I have no idea what any of this means." He wiggled his fingers across the screen, blocking my view and messing up the access pattern I was attempting to enter. "Oh, shoot, let me help you with that." He hollered directions into my ear, which did nothing to help me remember the pattern.

"Up up, down down, left right, left right, B, A, start!"

I laughed, recognizing the video game cheat code, and adored him for keeping me from breaking down.

I rocked backward into his legs, and he toppled over, grunting and laughing. Then I stood and held out my hand to help him up. "Come on, let's get closer to the trees. They're better at shade than you. Even the insult kind, and they can't talk."

Jaxon reached up and grabbed my hand and when he stood, I wasn't ready to let go. I held on and dragged him toward the line of trees so he wouldn't know I was trying to keep his sturdy, triathlete hands in my soft squishy keyboard palms for as long as possible.

I hung my backpack on a low branch and sat under vivid red and orange foliage. Jaxon scooted back out into the sun and laid on the lawn, eyes closed, hands behind his head, and his knees in the air. I leaned further into the shade and concentrated on the screen, now bright in the dim light. I accessed the system' settings as I had done a hundred times working on my remote testing device.

"Mmmm." Jaxon's groan obliterated my focus. "I thought I'd never feel the sunlight on my face again." I ran my eyes along the curve of his lips as he lay soaking in the sun vitamins.

I blinked, trying to focus. "Okay, now I need to add the code to detect destination elevation. It already detects current elevation so the booth techs can relocate a booth or set up a new one."

Jaxon nodded his head. I wanted to chuck the port unit and cuddle up next to him.

I pulled up the code I'd transferred to my phone and found the access token and commands to activate the booth-free destination beta program settings. "This looks like it calls back to the destination GPS marker and calculates a safe landing elevation, instead of only being able to check starting elevation at initial install. It'll have to be precise if we'd like to avoid premature burial or an impromptu intro to free-falling."

Jaxon stopped nodding and shook his head. "No, let's not do that. I'm not interested in skydiving *with* a parachute, let alone without one."

"For sure. We don't need any more mangled limbs."

"Uh, yeah, I'd like to keep my hands and everything else intact."

As excited as I was to try this out myself, I knew enough to test the new settings on something less alive. I input my code.

```
>enable_features beta.gps_teleport
--auth.token '06%29&07JS+TM'
[!] Authorized testing only. May
cause serious injury or death.
>Proceed? [y/N]:
```

I glanced back at Jaxon, glad he couldn't see the screen. He lay there, completely trusting in my hacker magic.

```
>Proceed? [y/N]: y
[+] beta.gps_targeting enabled
>beta.gps_targeting --booth_require-
ment false
```

I entered a few test destinations to make sure the new scripts were calling up the correct data, cross-checking with a couple different map programs. And because my parents were geniuses, it seemed to be working perfectly.

I flicked a twig at Jaxon's relaxed face. "No more sleeping on the job, lazy. Time to run some tests, and then where should we go? Downtown? La Jolla Beach? Seoul to interrupt your parents' business trip?"

Jaxon leaned up on his elbow. "You got it?"

I grinned and bobbed the port unit in my hands as if it were dancing in triumph.

"Nice, Aly! How about we start with moving across the park?"

"Boring. But sensible. And, if we're successful, then where?"

"Won't we have to run back here and pick up the unit?"

"No, I can have it include itself in the port. Not a setting accessible for the average user, but I'm me so . . ." I gave him a falsely demure grin.

"Well then, we'll port back here instead of running."

"Dude, where's your sense of adventure?"

"Hiding behind my sense of *I'd like to stay in one piece.*"

I laughed and searched the grass around me for a good test subject. "What should we test first?"

Jax lifted his torso and wiggled a pinball-sized rock out of the grass. "Will this work? It's been digging into my ribs."

I stepped over and took the stone from him. Flecks of mica sparked against reddish brown. Nothing in regular rocks came close to the density limit. "Perfect!" I moved away from Jaxon a few paces and set the rock on the grass. I dropped an AppyTrip location pin about five meters away from us to find the coordinates. Next, I double-checked that the unit pulled from sea-level elevation data and not ground-level data and adjusted a few settings to help it know what to port.

```
>beta.gps_targeting  --mode radius_
scan --radius_cm 5
>beta.gps_targeting  --targeting
auto_detect
>beta.gps_targeting  --self-carry
false
```

I looked up. "Alright, I think that's it! I guess we'll see how well the algorithm detects what ports and what's part of the surrounding environment."

Jaxon started to crawl closer.

"Maybe hang back for this first test. I told it to only scan a softball-sized area, but just in case."

He sat back and watched from a kneeling position.

"Oh, hold on. Let's tell it not to make us pay or use a booth card." I saved the scan configurations and wound my way back to the system settings.

```
>usage_token null
```

I set up the port and faced the unit toward the rock. "Ready? Three, Two, One..." I reached my finger over the top of the unit and tapped the screen where *go* would be.

The rock disappeared, and I jogged over to where I estimated my destination pin to be. It didn't take long to find the rock on the short-clipped lawn, sparkling triumphantly in the afternoon sun.

I grabbed it out of the grass and hollered. "We did it! Yes!"

Jaxon hopped to his feet. "Alright, Aly!"

Something tickled my hand, and I rolled the rock over. A two-centimeter section of earthworm stuck to the side of the rock, slowly wiggling. Must've been checking the rock out when we blew his little wormy mind. I grimaced and shook it off.

Jax jogged over. "You okay?"

"I am, but I can't say the same for the late worm with his head too far out of the dirt."

"Uh oh."

"But hey, now he's two worms, right?"

"I don't think that's how it works."

"Anyway . . . let's try something bigger." Something that I'd feel worse about chopping in two. I looked up and spotted my backpack where it hung. My heart skipped a beat when I pictured the trusty pack split down the middle, but if I was afraid to test an inanimate object, how would I ever port myself or Jaxon?

"Here we go," I said, leading the way back to the tree. I changed a couple of settings while I walked.

```
>beta.gps_targeting --radius_cm 30
--radius_elevation_cm '+150'
```

"OK Jax, stand behind me. And three, two . . ." I pointed the port unit at my backpack where it hung on the low tree branch and closed my eyes, then opened one long enough to position my finger over the *go* button. "One, go!"

I heard a cracking sound. "I can't look, did it—" *Oof.*

Jaxon tackled me a meter to the side, and I opened my eyes in time to see a tree-full of bright autumn leaves land in the grass where I'd been standing. My stomach sank deep into my bowels. The tree's trunk sank flatter to the ground as the once-tall branches snapped.

I swore and covered my mouth.

Jaxon stared at the tree. "Yup. We should probably get out of here."

I spun around to where the rock had landed during the last test, and there was my backpack with part of the branch and a curved section of tree trunk still attached. We'd taken a perfectly rounded bite out of the side of the tree.

The ground was intact, though, so now we knew the algorithm could detect the surrounding environment to some degree.

I pulled my backpack away from the detached tree limb. "As it turns out, the algorithm isn't perfect." The pack itself was untouched. So the ported radius was safe, but it was a crapshoot for the surrounding objects.

Jaxon's head whipped around to a sound my aids hadn't caught yet. I turned and heard the yelling as it got closer. A pointing boy and his barking dog jogged toward us from about 100 meters away, followed by two man-shaped figures in black windbreakers. Whether they were ETC out looking for us or park security in similar garb, we had to move fast. I picked up the port unit from where I'd dropped it during the tackle and stabbed at the screen.

```
>beta.gps_targeting --radius_cm 125
--radius_elevation_cm '+120'
>beta.gps_targeting --self-carry true
```

I only had a few seconds to spare after I'd configured the quickest out-of-reach destination and before the approaching windbreakers came into crapshoot range.

"Do you trust me?" I held my hand out to Jaxon.

"What?"

"Do you *trust* me?"

He took my hand. "Yes."

I pulled him close. "Then jump."

I pushed *go* as we both leaped into the air. The flash wasn't as bright through my eyelids as usual—the light wasn't bouncing off port booth walls. But the familiar floating feeling told me it had worked before I realized I was falling. Terror throttled my senses for a heartbeat until I landed, Jaxon still gripping my hand. He held fast as my leg buckled under me. I felt the cement roof under my hands and looked out over the park. I'd done it.

I couldn't hold in a loud, triumphant whoop.

Jaxon squeezed my hand in alarm, and then, seeing joy on my face, let go of me and joined in. "Yeah! Aly, you did it!" He looked past me and took in the view. "You flew us to the top of a building. We're like superheroes!"

I'd chosen the first structure I found on the map with a quickly estimable height—the one-story concrete restrooms on the other side of the park. I'd overestimated the height so that we wouldn't risk our feet fusing with the roof, and I figured we'd land better if we were already in the air.

It was the most free I'd ever felt. We were Queen and King of the hill. Sure, right now the hill we'd conquered was a literal pile of crap, and the thrones were porcelain. Or more likely, industrial metal that froze to your bare skin in winter. But I'd literally risen above my messed-up situation and come out stronger. I could fly. I was like, some kind of fecal phoenix. Only cooler, and not gross. I would leave the metaphors to Jaxon.

"Yeah we are," I said. "It's better than a magic carpet."

My phone vibrated with an incoming call, and I pulled it out of my back pocket. Dr. Clarke. My heart jumped and I swiped *Reject Call*. A text buzzed in.

```
Dr. Clarke: Alyona, we need to talk.
You're not in trouble, yet.
```

I deleted it, but not before my hands quivered.

"Hey, you okay?" Jaxon put his arm around me and looked down at my phone as another message came in.

```
Dr. Clarke: We can fix this. Please
come in. I don't want anything to
happen to you.
```

Was that a threat? Did he think he could intimidate me

into compliance? The phone rang again, and my heart sped. I had to show him I wouldn't be manipulated. I wouldn't play his way. I swiped *Accept Call*.

"Dr. C-Clarke," I started and hoped he didn't notice my nerves, "I know you've been lying, and I'm going to find out for sure how far your lies go. Don't try to contact me again."

"Wait. Don't hang up," Dr. Clarke shouted. He mellowed his tone again and continued. "I have cleared my schedule today. I have time for you. Please, ask me anything. I will tell you—"

"I have nothing to ask. I'll handle this internally. No need for any action on your part. Good—"

"No!" Dr. Clarke barked. "Please," he added softly. "I want to clear up any misunderstandings. Talk to me."

I didn't answer. He did seem intent on conversation. Maybe I could get something useful out of him.

Jaxon rubbed his hands together and paced the small roof. He fiddled with his pant leg, which had caught in his plain white loaner sock. Where Dr. Clarke had removed his tracking device.

Crap crap crap. I swiped End Call and dived back into the port unit's system settings.

```
>tracking false
```

Dr. Clarke wasn't eager to fix things. Unlike me, he hadn't forgotten about the port unit's internal tracking, and he'd been trying to keep me from moving before his cronies arrived. I checked AppyTrip again and looked for another open space where we could think.

"Aly, they've found us again already." Jaxon pointed in the direction of the two wretched windbreakers waving their arms at us as they ran.

"Yes, I stupidly let them track us. I fixed it, and now I'm reconfiguring—"

"They're almost here. Hurry!"

"Hurrying!"

"I wish you could add some kind of quick mode and not have to enter so much data. I somehow don't think this is the last time we'll need to make a quick getaway."

"That's actually really smart." I made a mental scribble to think about that one when we were more than ten seconds from capture.

"Thanks, I think." Jaxon said. "And we are *actually* out of time."

The security duo was hoisting one another up and shouting at us to come down, trying to find a way to the roof. One of them got an arm up and yelled at me. "It's over. Put the unit down and get your hands up."

"No can do, buckeroo," I said. I pulled Jaxon in and hit *go*.

CHAPTER NINETEEN

Something Old, Something New, Something Stolen

We landed inside a blue port booth downtown. I tilted my head away from the safety lights above the booth where any cameras would be, then tucked the port unit into my backpack as far as it would go and attempted a brisk, but inconspicuous pace.

Jaxon kept up easily with his springy road-biker's gait, shielding his face from surveillance with his hand. "Can't they track us through the booths?"

"I mean, maybe if someone notices a port into this booth without a specific origin. But it won't matter as much if we can put your quick mode idea into action. I even have a remote ready, I just need a pairing chip."

"Your DIY maintenance device!" he said.

"It's perfect. I'll be able to program shortcuts into physical buttons for self-carry, radius adjustments, or pre-programmed destinations that we could pop to without warning."

I stopped us in front of a large pawn-slash-vintage memorabilia shop.

Jaxon craned his neck up at the sign. "You think they might have a new pairing chip here?"

"It doesn't necessarily have to be new, just more powerful than the ones they install in phones. Go look around while I find what I need, I know you like old-timey junk."

"You mean historical artifacts?" He might have had more to say, but we entered the shop, and he immediately discovered the section for decrepit books. He beelined in their direction.

I approached the counter with my own sense of awe and respect for those who came before me. A breathtaking timeline of gaming history graced the gray metal shelves, from a twenty-year-old YBox-FullCircle, back through the first GameStation, and all the way to the collection's crown jewel: their own functioning Satari, complete with joystick and guns. I checked the price. *Holy sizzling circuits.* For one, brief second, I considered selling Dad's Satari and using the cash to pay for a month-long beach vacation rental, far away. But no vacation was worth losing any piece of my parents I had left.

I forced my attention on the assorted accessories and adapters along the counter and scanned for USB dongles, which used long-range pairing chips. I avoided eye contact with the surly dude behind the counter and his wild-west looking mustache so he wouldn't ask if I needed help, and I wouldn't hear myself say, "Please show me your dongles." Luckily for all parties, I found one on my own.

"Hey, how much are your . . . these?" I held up the dongle.

"Accessories can only be purchased with a vintage system that requires their use. Otherwise, you'll need to register as a new purchase."

Not happening. I shelved the dongle and scanned the

aisle signs. Gaming, Musical Instruments, Recreation, Automotive—*yes*. I passed the hanging fuzzy dice and a collection of seat covers, then hit the jackpot: a conversion kit to allow phones to connect with cars. I picked it up and found Jaxon staring down at a book as if he were about to propose.

"What did you fall in love with over here?"

Jaxon tore his gaze away from the gilding on its linen cover. "It's what pre-digital-age Homo Sapiens used to call a 'book.' They used to read these back when people wrote in letters instead of emojis."

I turned his hand with the book in it so I could read the title.

"*The Silmarillion*? Don't you read enough real history? I don't know why you want to read fake history, too." I flipped the book over to show the edge. "And besides, the gold won't let it port."

"I know." Jaxon sighed. "And even if it could port . . ." He tapped the price tag with his finger.

I sucked in a sharp breath. Who would pay two hundred and twenty-seven dollars for a faded copy of a boring book? "Maybe just read the e-book."

"It's not the same, and I don't have my phone. You pushed me right through with only the shirt on my back, remember?"

I tried not to picture him in only his shirt. "Hey, you have your jacket." I grinned and he raised an eyebrow at me. "Fine, I'm sorry. I'll get your phone back for you ASAP. Let's get out of here. Give me the book so you don't have to go through the pain of setting it back on the shelf." Also, I knew he'd put it back in the precise location it belonged, like a good citizen, where anyone could find it and buy it out from under him.

Jaxon lifted it up to stare at the cover again, and gently leafed through a few pages. "At least I got to hold it for a minute."

I took the book and set the conversion kit in his hand. "I'll meet you at the counter." He trudged away and I found a good stack of heavy encyclopedias. I tucked his book behind them, cover down, to give it the best chance of remaining in the store, in case we could ever afford the time and money to come back and get it.

We approached the surly associate and his mustache. He had his arms folded and head tilted to the side, chewing on a toothpick, like a sheriff about to tell me this town wasn't big enough for the both of us.

"Ready to check out?"

Jaxon placed the kit on the counter. "Yeah, we'll take this."

"You got a trade-in?"

I turned the kit to face the clerk. "This is vintage, right? So I don't need a trade-in."

"You got a car to put that in?"

"Uh, yeah. I own a car, don't you?"

The brusque man rolled his head to tilt the other way. "What kind?"

"It's a, like a black one, with the round logo . . ."

Jaxon attempted a save. "You know what, how much do you want for this?"

"With a trade-in or proof you're using it for a car and not for parts, it's twenty bucks. Without, it's illegal to sell."

I quickly checked my AppyBucks balance. "Would you take forty?" That would leave us with enough for another couple of incognito ports if we needed them.

"Why would I take forty?"

"Can you do me a solid? Please?"

"Nope. Too many fines for me if I get caught selling something you scrap. I'd say around a hundred bucks in fines. I couldn't sell for less than one-twenty, in the event that you get caught and point my direction." His mustache quirked up on one side.

This crook was trying to pull one over on me. "Dude, I have sixty bucks, that's it. Come on."

"Don't let the door hit you—"

Jaxon leaned into the counter. "Hey, friend, is there anything we can do? We both found several items we'd love to come back for, if we can come to an agreement."

Sheriff Shartface pulled out his toothpick. "Yeah, I agree to sell you whatever you want if you bring me the money I ask for. Otherwise, move along."

Part of me wanted him to finish his sentence with "little dogies" and the rest of me wanted to punch him in the 'stache. He tucked the kit behind the counter. I stormed out of the store, Jaxon in tow. I'd have to come back with the money. We'd had a close call at the salon and again at the park, and our luck wouldn't hold out forever. Getting the port unit to work with the remote and having a quick way to escape dodgy situations was still our best option.

I checked the block for ETC security types, and we jogged to a bench that used to be a bus stop, back when buses were a thing. It still had a cylindrical spinner that used to hold information on the bus route and schedule, but the city had replaced the bus schedule with a list of port codes—some nearby and a few major landmarks around the city. I sat and pulled the two remaining envelopes out of my backpack.

"Sixty bucks isn't enough to sustain us, even if we find a cheaper chip. Especially if Atty's place *is* ever compromised and we can't go back there. We need to serve a summons, and the sooner we do, the less likely the dentist will hear I'm being sought and cut me off."

Jaxon tugged the more battered envelope out of my hand.

Misha's. "If we get a minute, I can help look for this one." He tucked it back and held up the next one.

"Ah, yes, Doris should be easier," I said, "and we can get some essential practice in with this mobile port unit."

My phone buzzed with another incoming text. I whipped it out and checked it. Dr. Clarke.

> Dr. Clarke: We didn't get to finish our conversation about misunderstandings.

He sent another text: a picture of Nadia, frowning and staring at the entryway from her desk at the ETC.

> Dr. Clarke: Come in. She's waiting for you. And I'd hate for her to get caught in the crossfire of any more misunderstandings.

My fingers froze, and I somehow managed to stuff my phone back into my pocket without dropping it. I had to get everything in place, now. If I wasn't planning on playing by Dr. Clarke's rules, I'd better win.

Doris Boon's address was on the envelope. Her social media didn't reveal a job outside the home, and the AppyTrip street view didn't show a video doorbell. There was a good chance she'd be home on a Monday afternoon. I plugged in the GPS data, grabbed Jaxon's arm, and pushed *go*.

···➤

We fell about three feet and stumbled to the ground one house south of our target. It still felt safer to land high. AppyTrip wouldn't know if someone had piled up dirt or crates or boxes on recycling day, which it seemed to be in Doris's neighborhood.

"A little warning next time, yeah?" Jaxon rubbed his knee where it had touched down before we righted ourselves.

"I thought you said no more dragging me through port booths."

"Well, it wasn't technically a port booth," I countered.

Jaxon frowned.

"But you were on board with the summons serving, right?" I said. "You got out the envelope."

"Sure, but the last I heard, Michael Wells was hard to find, and then you're over there tappity tapping between your phone and the port screen, and the next thing I know, I'm crash-landing in some HOA-forsaken suburb."

"I'm sorry, I get in the zone, you know? I'll try to think out loud better."

"I can help you think. I need you to let me in."

My heart squeezed tight for a few beats, telling me I'd better try harder.

We walked past the yard where a squat, muscular dog sniffed around the trunk of the tree to which it was tethered with a long, worn rope. A wheelbarrow lay upside down in the dirt nearby, and a rusted metal swing set leaned away from the house as if trying to escape to a distant past where children swung and played without fear of tetanus. There was no way this collection would be paid, but all *I* had to do to get paid was get the summons into the addressee's hands.

"Okay. People are more likely to answer the door if it's a friend or a package. So maybe we grab a box from someone's recycling pile and carry it up the porch? What do you think?"

Jaxon's gorgeous smile returned. "I think you'll need someone to distract the dog while you do so."

"Love it." Doris's neighbor had a few boxes out. I found a small clean one and closed it up. If I'd had a scanner and a vest, I'd be in for sure.

We approached a gate in the low, chain-link fence surrounding the lot. I took a moment to set up the next port destination. "Here, you hold this." I handed Jaxon the port unit "I'll run straight back to you once I serve the summons, and then you hit *go*. Okay?"

"Got it. Good luck playing delivery driver." He reached up and pulled a piece of grass out of my ponytail, then tucked some escaped frizz behind my ear. "I'd say break a leg, but I'm afraid that rotting porch might take it literally." His nice gesture would have made the heat rush back to my cheeks if he'd paused any longer before giving me a goofy, oversized wink.

I pushed him toward the tree. The dog perked up, and Jaxon sprinted to hide behind the wheelbarrow, trying to lure the barking monster away from the cracked path to the door.

The dog stopped for a moment, whipping its head between the two of us. I backed away toward the sad swings.

Jaxon captured the dog's attention with a noise like an asthmatic dolphin and I made it to the house. I pulled gently on the creaky screen door, afraid it would fall off its hinges, and jumped like a lost cat when the front door flung open.

"Yeah? Who are you?" A roughly human shape appeared in a cloud of cigarette smoke.

"Hi, Um, Doris Boon?"

"I never met you. What do you want?"

Good enough. I shoved the envelope against her arm, and she reflexively took it in her hand. "You've been served." I clicked a picture of her and sent a quick text for payment while Doris gathered her wits.

I was halfway to Jaxon before I heard her try to respond, but the dog shot straight towards me. Jax desperately amped up the random tortured animal sounds to no avail. I arched wide in what I hoped was a radius outside the tied-up dog's reach. Apparently this was more excitement than it had seen in some time, because the rope frayed and then snapped. The dog came flying, saliva trailing behind flapping cheeks like exhaust spewing from an out-of-control woodchipper. I stumbled over an exposed tree root, barely catching my balance as Jaxon dashed toward me. I collided with his sturdy chest, grabbed his neck, and yelled, "Go!" as he pushed the button.

Back outside the pawn shop, Jaxon peeled my sweaty hands off of his neck. "What happened to 'Doris will be easy'?"

"Sorry, but those noises, Jax! Were you trying to summon the souls of mistreated pets to your aid?"

"I was doing squirrel noises. You know, like how they chatter when they're mad."

"You're the mad one. No animal ever sounded like that."

He did a dorky foot dance and said, "We're all mad, here."

I rolled my eyes at him as I shoved my way through the vintage store's doors, and then shoved the doors even harder on my way back out, one hundred twenty-seven dollars later. *Highway robbery.* My funds were nearly wiped out again, but I had what I needed.

Jaxon shifted his weight. "Is there a way you can use this kit without the remote you're working on? I don't feel good about going home, knowing the ETC is likely monitoring your apartment. Can't you send Nadia?"

"No! Dr. Clarke is watching her like a lion stalking a gazelle. And I'll need to use her curling wand to solder again, anyway. We'll be fine. I doubt they'll expect me to go home. Hopefully they assume I have some good sense about me."

"But, you're proving them wrong by actually going home, right?"

"Or I'm proving them wrong by using their assumptions

against them. Come on, we'll be quick." *Remember to give him a say,* "Okay?"

Jaxon put his forehead in his hand, sighed, and then did a lead-the-way motion with his other hand. I pulled out the port unit and left my good sense in my backpack while I dialed home.

CHAPTER TWENTY

Beaches and Flip-Flopping

I asked Jaxon to stick his head out of the booth and check for an ambush before we scooted out and sprinted to our apartment building. We wouldn't be able to port from inside because of the tungsten powder in the building's exterior paint. FutureMove wouldn't splurge for gold leaf to decorate the employee housing, but a kilo of tungsten powder only cost two summons payments. I hated how the tungsten powder gave our building its perpetual dingy, muted look. Like a jail. No escaping those walls. But as long as I could get outside the building before the ETC showed up to get me, we were fine.

I charged up the stairs and pushed the door open with a hard shove of my hip, then flew straight inside while the door banged against the wall. I sprawled on the worn laminate floor and slid into the side table like I was stealing second base, sacrificing my right elbow to keep the port unit from hitting the ground. I'd forgotten Manuel had fixed the door for us while he was over stealing my computer to keep his cover. A single blue Memory Marble fell from the side table and rolled toward me. I picked it up and cursed Manuel in my mind before admitting to myself that his handyman skills were impressive, and that having an inside man might work to my advantage. Maybe he was not a total waste of Nadia's time.

Jaxon offered me a hand, but he was laughing at me so hard I had no choice but to refuse his help. I loved his touch, but I had my dignity.

I rolled the cool marble around in my fingers and wished I had time to admire its swirling depths. "Are you sure you don't want to port to the beach? We could hide out in a thatched hut and eat clams or whatever beach people eat."

"I'm sure I *do*. Sounds amazing. But I don't have my beach socks! What would people think?"

I hoisted myself up. "Seriously," I said. "We could move. What happened in Denver could stay in Denver. We could get jobs in some new city far away, and they'd forget about us, and we'd be rid of this drama."

He chuckled. "If only it were that simple."

I put the marble in my pocket. Life was anything but simple at the moment.

I found the piece in the car conversion kit we bought that housed the pairing chip and added that to my shoebox of components, leaving the rest of the kit on the counter. Then I packed my disassembled Gooseberry phone into the shoebox. "Okay," I said, pointing at him with my broken-tipped knife, "but don't rule it out. We could be basking away in Bombay." I added the knife and the curling wand to the box.

"Mumbai."

"Fine. Is Mumbai near the beach, too? My mom told me about this epic trip to Bombay—"

"No, the name changed to Mumbai decades ago."

"Okay, nerd. A beach is a beach. What about Seoul with your parents? That's at least close-ish to the water, right?"

"My parents are working on a huge project right now.

They won't come up for air for at least another month. And you have to promise me they will never find out their son was arrested, *again*. They would freak. Forget forcing me to major in business; they'd probably make me come live with them and hook me up to one of those toddler backpacks with a leash to eliminate the possibility I'd embarrass them any further."

"You know I'm no snitch." I zipped my pack over the shoebox. "Let's blow this joint."

"Be sure you have everything. We can't come back until this is over."

I felt the marble in my front pocket. I'd meant to throw it back in with the other Memory Marbles, but I couldn't let it go. Though I was born thousands of miles from Denver, this was the only place I could remember living. The small apartment was as full of memories as the obsolete shell of a computer was full of trinkets. Memories of my family, back when it was whole.

"Yeah, I'm set," I said, but I didn't move. I had my components, my tools, and a piece of home to carry with me. I considered taking a set of my mom's backup drives, but no one knew they existed, and they didn't contain anything FutureMove didn't have on their servers. Still, I couldn't shake the feeling that I was forgetting something.

Jaxon placed a hand on my arm, sensing my hesitation. "We *will* come back. We'll figure this out."

I stared into the deep blue glass of the marbles. "Well, let's move, then, If you're sure we can't go hide on the bea—"

The nagging notion that had kept me rooted bubbled up. We couldn't hide on the beach. But something could hide *in* the beach. Something the ASF would absolutely covet, and the ETC feared and tried to destroy. I'd already searched the apartment for my mom's density project backup multiple times. That would have gone a long way to help me make the booths safe, but she'd never added it to the small drives hidden in the bookshelf or the lentil can, so I'd assumed she hadn't gotten around to creating a backup before it was too late. I'd never thought to check the Marbles. It wasn't a place where we hid things, it was a place we kept memories out in the open to avoid losing them. But this research would have been their crowning achievement, breaking the last barriers of teleportation—the most significant development the world had seen since the internet. So, maybe she'd keep it among her most meaningful memories.

I shoved my hand into the small sea of marbles and mementos, and they pushed over the little umbrella like a rising tide. I couldn't feel anything but marbles, so I scooped some out and set them on the side table, where they promptly rolled off the edge and onto the floor.

Jaxon rushed over and tried to catch some of the wayward marbles. "Aly? What are you doing? It's too loud! We've got to get out of here!"

"I have a hunch." I felt the rough motherboard and the boxy hard drive. My fingers brushed along smooth, wide ribbon cables, and then, finally, a small, loose object about the shape of a lighter.

I pulled it out and it was exactly what I was hoping for—a sleek, secret USB drive.

"Is that something your parents put there?" Jaxon said.

I tucked it into my shoe under the arch of my foot and excitement buzzed from my toes up to my fingertips, which were eager to get to a safe computer and find out what Mom had been keeping in the depths of that make-believe ocean. "I think it's their density project. Now what are you standing there for, let's go!"

Jaxon shook his head, stepped toward the door, and pulled it open.

Manuel's flushed, panting face approached the threshold.

I took a shaky step back and tried to stand sideways so he wouldn't notice the Satari-sized port unit under my arm. "What are you doing here?"

"I came," he panted, "to ask you that same question. You know the entire ETC is after you. Why would you come to your house?" His tone was somewhere between a scolding teacher and a disappointed parent. "Get out of here. There are three guards right behind me."

Jaxon grabbed my free arm and pulled me toward the door, but it was too late. Running footsteps echoed up the stairwell and three helmeted heads came bobbing up the stairs into my apartment.

The guards pushed their way through the door, and I backed further away, around the back of the couch toward the TV. They came toward me. Jaxon still held my arm. I moved further to the right, and the guards crept closer, looking ready to pounce if we tried to make a break for it. I saw Manuel step left toward the kitchen in my peripheral vision. I inched toward him, and the guards followed my lead.

Manuel took slow steps toward me across the kitchen vinyl. "You're too late. You can't leave now," Manuel said. His tone was sharper than it had been before the guards had arrived, but his hazel eyes pleaded for forgiveness.

I turned slowly to face Jaxon. I motioned with my eyes toward the stairs behind him, and he gave me a microscopic nod. I backed up a few more steps and then we bolted for the stairs.

Manuel sprang up behind Jaxon and grabbed the port unit out from beneath his arm.

I couldn't risk pausing to try to take it back. Jaxon and I lunged up the stairs, leaving behind a holy ruckus as guards slipped on the spilled marbles and tripped over one another.

That only left Manuel on our tail. The port unit slowed him slightly, and we made it into my parents room against the back of the building, locking the door behind us seconds before he started pounding on it.

"You won't get far," Manuel shouted through the door. "All of the port booths nearby are guarded. By the time you run to one that isn't, they'll be there."

I'd heaved the window open and climbed out onto the fire escape. I yelled back at Manuel. "Thanks, pal. Any other helpful hints?"

"Turn yourself in, Alyona. If I catch you, I'll lock you in the vault, same as this unit you stole, until we can undo whatever dangerous alterations you've made to it."

"Pass," I said on my way down the metal ladder.

Manuel said something else; I thought it was orders to the guards in the living room, but I didn't understand it from down the fire escape. He'd taken the port unit, but he'd also given us a good tip about the port booths, disguised as discouragement. I knew he had to maintain his position as head of security, but I wished he would pick a side. It was hard to trust him when he kept flip-flopping like a dying flounder.

I jumped from the end of the ladder to the cement below. "So, I guess we'd better run, then." I said to Jaxon as he dropped off the ladder behind me. He wasn't even breathing heavily yet and could surely outrun anyone chasing us. But me? I shoved down a wave of panic building in my chest as I jogged along the back of the building.

"Aly, stop, come this way."

He indicated the direction to the right of where I was headed, around the corner of the building. I'd forgotten to fill him in again. "Oh, sorry, I think we should head to Atty's house, okay?" I kept jogging.

"Alyona. Stop."

Now wasn't the time to scold me for my thoughtlessness. I had to do better, but right now, we had to escape. My heart pounded hard. I could sprint around a softball field, but I was no good over distances. I'd never escape them.

I stopped, like he asked. "Jaxon, you take this." I pulled the pack off my back and shoved it toward him. "Make a plan with Atty and Kendi. It's my turn to take one for the team."

"Aly, no—"

I shoved the backpack into his chest and shouted. "Go! I'll stall them."

"Will you listen—"

"Tell Kendi about my remote. She can probably fix it. I'll see what I can do from ETC custody. We can still—"

Jaxon growled as he hoisted my pack and ran away.

I'd wanted him to go, but it still cut like a broken paring knife to the chest as he sprinted full-speed ahead and disappeared around the corner. My vision blurred as if I'd already been running too long. Manuel turned everything we'd done to get ahead into a waste of time. Shouts echoed behind me, and I pivoted to see Manuel rounding the opposite corner of the building trailed by the three guards. He must have and led them out the front door to chase me down. He'd bought me time, going back for the other guards and coming around the long way, and I would buy Jaxon a little more. My head spun, and I steadied myself against the wall. *Get a hold of yourself.* I couldn't stall the guards if I passed out before they got to me.

I stood tall, took a deep breath from my gut and shouted, as much to rile myself up as to slow them down. "Hey, you big herd of—"

"Aly!"

I whirled around. "J-Jaxon? What—"

"Shut up and get on the bike." He patted the cargo rack over his back tire. "You're going to put your aggravating butt right there, and you're going to hold your feet up as best you can. Do *not* get your toe caught in the spokes. Hold tight around my waist. Understand?"

I threw my leg over the back tire and sat as instructed. I wrapped my arms around him and opened and closed my fists. I couldn't reach my hands together and had no idea what to do with them.

"Stop! Hold it right there!" Manuel and the guards called as they drew dangerously near.

"Feet up!" Jaxon shouted, and he pushed off. We picked up a surprising amount of speed in just a few seconds. I didn't dare look back, but I was sure the guards had fallen far behind us.

I should have kept the backpack. I pressed the side of my face into what felt like my shoebox, and I wasn't sure how to hold onto his torso. My still-bandaged left hand throbbed, but I kept my arms wrapped around him like a human slap bracelet.

"You can kindly stop tickling my ribs now."

My face burned and I pressed my palms flat against his shirt. "I'm just trying to get a good hold. Are you sure this cargo rack will take my weight?"

"The owner's manual gives it a maximum capacity of two hundred and fifty pounds. It could hold two of you."

"Who reads the manual? Nerd." I owed him and his sturdy cargo rack, though, and I appreciated his underestimation of my weight.

Jaxon's balancing prowess and his port-restricted time getting to know bike routes around the city came in handy as he pushed forward through the alleyways. Porting made for a convenient traverse, but it made my broader vision of the city's layout a little hazy. I didn't need to know where we were on the map when I could port from booth to booth. After about ten minutes, I got a feel for the bike's rhythm and eased my death grip. My legs burned, so I found a bolt to rest them on, careful not to rotate my toe or heel into the spokes.

Tears flowed as the chaos subsided and my emotions found their way to the surface. "You came to get me. Again." He hadn't let me leave town four years ago, and he wasn't leaving me behind now.

"You came to get me, too." Jaxon was finally breathing heavily, panting every few words. "I couldn't let you even out the score."

"But what if they'd caught—"

"Hush, woman. Let me drive, okay? This isn't easy, you know."

I sat quietly, teardrops dripping from my chin into the wind.

"And it wasn't like I made some heroic choice to return, Aly. I left to get the bike, like I was trying to tell you. It would've saved some time if you'd listened to me." He paused to breathe. "I would never leave you."

His tone was annoyed, strained, exhausted. But his words were everything. I'd come face-to-face with some of my worst fears, and Jaxon's promise fulfilled my deepest wish. I closed my eyes and leaned into his back, cursing the shoebox separating us. He made some terrifying twists and turns, and I was completely lost, but I trusted in his navigational skills and held out hope that we'd arrive wherever Jaxon thought best without an armed welcome party.

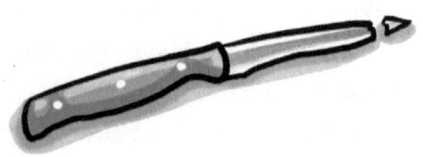

CHAPTER TWENTY-ONE

All's Well That Ends Wells

Jaxon practically had to shake me off of him when he finally stopped his bike in front of Athena Carleson's house. I tried her front door. Locked. Good for her. Most residential homes used one of three major lock brands, and I was sure homeowners would be shocked to see how quickly they could be bumped open with each brand's generic bump key. But Athena had an electronic combination lock, so no picking the deadbolt. I tried a couple of incorrect combinations and peered through the decorative glass in the door. No movement inside.

"You could try knocking," Jaxon said. "Like a normal person."

"In what universe am I considered normal?"

Jaxon pulled the bike around to the side of the house and I followed him. Athena's house had an attached garage around the side, which was rare for this area of the city. More importantly, her attached garage had a back door with a top-three-brand deadbolt on it.

"Hey, Jax, come here. Do you have a hammer? Or a mallet?"

Jaxon laid the bike against the garage wall next to the door. "Yeah, right here in my pocket with my phone. Oh, wait."

Usually, his jabs were accompanied by a grin or his ridiculous wink. Now, he let his comments drop like tungsten paperweights. I wanted to believe he was simply tired from the ride, but he was more likely at his wits end with me.

"The sarcasm is strong with you, my padawan. We need a stick."

Jaxon bent over, picked up a twig and presented it to me with a small bow like a fancy waiter showcasing a vintage wine. Still, no smile.

"Hmm, I think maybe something more substantial." I jogged over to the tree in the back corner of the yard and couldn't find anything bigger than Jaxon's sad excuse for a stick. But I did find a circle of baseball-sized rocks ringing the tree. I grabbed one with a smooth side and came back to the door. I grabbed Jaxon's hand, flipped it palm up, and placed the rock in it.

"I'm not breaking any windows," he said.

"Good, and I also need you to refrain from breaking my fingers, if you would be so kind."

Jaxon shook his head. "No promises."

I pulled my lockpick set out of my cargo pocket. I always carried a rake pick, a diamond pick and a short hook pick, as well as two different sized tension wrenches, an elevator key, a handcuff key, and bump keys for the top three brands. I pulled the bump key that matched the deadbolt in front of us and pushed it into the lock.

"Okay, when I say, you hit the key with this rock."

He shook his head and sighed. "Alright, like, a little love tap? Or Hulk smash?"

I pulled the key out a few millimeters until it caught on

the lock, then I held rotational tension on it in the direction it would open. "Somewhere in the middle. And don't slip."

I nodded to Jaxon, and he bumped the key with the rock. The bump sent the lock's pins up into the barrel, and my key turned, sliding the deadbolt open.

I grinned up at Jaxon. "I'm in." I never tired of saying that cheesy phrase.

"That was disturbingly easy," he said.

"Yeah, most security measures exist to keep honest people honest and lazy people moving on to the next one."

And that was when I noticed the alarm system control panel mounted just inside. I hoped Atty had set the police alert to at least thirty seconds, so I had time to turn it off. I sent a text to "Lawyer" in my contacts, since I hadn't updated her name.

> Me: Hey, what's your security system code?
>
> Lawyer: 020505 I'm glad it's you breaking into my house.
>
> Me: Okay, disarmed.
>
> Lawyer: You could just as easily have asked me for the front door code.
>
> Me: Where's the fun in that?
>
> Lawyer: It's Meatball Monday tonight. In the meantime, help yourself to whatever you can find. I want an update when we get home.
>
> Me: K. TY. Oh, and what's your computer login?
>
> Lawyer: Use the one in the kitchen nook, it's not locked.

I shook my head at her lack of security best practices. "Atty says eat whatever you want."

"Sweet." Jaxon set off to browse the cupboards, and I sat

at the kitchen computer, taking a minute to watch him. Jaxon didn't think himself heroic, but he'd saved me from Manny and his goons in the nick of time. And I'd blown another chance to listen to what he had to say, thinking there was no time to discuss the matter. He'd risked more time back in a cell to haul my infuriating self onto his trusty steed and rescue us both. He was my knight in reflective safety tape.

I squatted down to retrieve Mom's USB backup out of my shoe. There wasn't anything I could do about the port unit Manuel had taken, other than make up for lost time. We still had the Gooseberry remote. I could code another booth to pair with it, and in the meantime, if I found my parents' research about programming the booths to port anything of any density and had time for testing, there would be no stopping us. I could port right into the building, grab the evidence that would free us from this nightmare, and port right out again. I lifted the kitchen laptop's lid and jiggled the mouse next to it.

Jaxon pulled up a chair and watched me plug in the drive. I could smell him, a mix of his outdoorsy deodorant and the sweat he'd worked up on the ride here, rescuing me. I breathed him in, and while my mind reeled, my heartbeat settled into a calm, steady cadence.

I clicked open the folder and several other folders populated on the screen. I couldn't read the folder names, because every time Jaxon took a bite of the chips he'd found, a little waft of pine and musk blurred my senses.

"Kale chips, Jaxon? How much kale do you need in your life?"

"They're actually amazing, try them." He held the bag out to me and gave it a little shake.

"Get that abomination out of here." I unlocked my phone and held it out to him. "Here, check your email or something.

Over there, where you can crunch as loudly as you like." It pained me to send him away, but I needed to concentrate.

Jaxon took my phone and headed toward the living room couch. He flashed a thumbs up, but I could see in his weak smile that he was still annoyed at me. The banter came naturally for both of us. The real talk didn't. At least not for me.

"Hey, Jax?"

He looked up from my phone. "Yeah?"

"Thanks for saving me, and I'm sorry I didn't give you a chance to tell me your plan. I know I'm failing you, and . . ." I hadn't scripted out my little speech, and I didn't want to say sorry again, but there weren't any readily available words that fit how I felt. My cheeks burned in frustration and embarrassment.

Jaxon waited for a couple of heartbeats, and then looked back down at my phone.

I couldn't let him give up on me. I stood and joined him on the couch. "I wish," I started.

He put the phone on the end table and gazed into my face, his eyes shining with what surely must be his last shred of patience for my antics. My thoughts and plans jumbled and crashed into my worries and anxieties. My lower lip quivered.

I closed my eyes, took a deep breath, held it, and then let it out slowly. If I could be real with Kendi, I could open up to Jaxon. I tried again, keeping my eyes closed. "I wish I could write a program that would sync my intentions with my actions. Something to override the firewall."

I could feel Jaxon watching me, but no movement. No change in his stiff posture.

This was scarier than Manuel's trio of guards chasing me down, but it felt like the most important fear to face, and I didn't want to leave room for misinterpretation. I opened my eyes and rubbed the dampness out of my palms with my thumbs, then looked into Jaxon's deep brown eyes. "Jax, I—"

Pounding at the door startled us and we jumped apart. "ETC, open up!"

I sank to my hands and knees and motioned for Jaxon to follow.

More banging on the door. "Alyona Zolotova and Jaxon Jeong, if you're inside, come out immediately."

Yeah, no. Jax and I crawled to the bathroom and locked the door. I wrote a text to Dr. Clarke.

```
Me: Call off your hounds or I'll tell
Athena you've breached contract and
she'll release everything.

Dr. Clarke: . . .

Dr. Clarke: Our understanding doesn't
pertain to you. But think, Alyona.
If I'd played the part she accuses
me of, and she had proof, she would
have released it. She's grasping at
whatever she can because she knows I
have something on her. Is this who
you want to affiliate with?
```

No help there. I sent one to Atty.

```
Me: Help. ETC is at your house look-
ing for me.

Lawyer: Have they seen you?

Me: No

Lawyer: Stay out of sight. I'm almost
home.
```

I heard muffled conversation between the guards.
"Can you tell what they're saying?" I whispered.
Jax shook his head.
I gently unlocked the bathroom window, nudged it up a crack, and turned up my hearing aids.

Radio static clicked on and off. "Sir? Yes, seeking authorization to force entry. Yes, Sir. Standing by."

"I'll check other points of entry," the short windbreaker with a bowl cut said to the tall windbreaker with frosted tips. I wondered which section in the ETC guard training manual banned decent hairstyles as they walked past the porch along the side of the house.

"Hold it right there, son." Atty's winded voice bounced closer. She must have run from the nearby booth. "Get back 'round the front of the house. I do not consent to a search, and you will get off my property."

"Ma'am, we're here to bring in—"

"Ain't nobody home, boys. Didn't you knock?"

"Yes, ma'am, but no one—"

"No one *answered*, because no one is *home*. Good Lord, Gary. First you interrupt me at work, and then you come snooping around looking into my house like a pervert."

"But ma'am—"

The frosted tips windbreaker spoke up. "It's fine, we aren't supposed to engage Ms. Carleson yet."

"Yet? What is that supposed to mean, Billy?"

"I go by Will now."

Atty stepped back and looked down her nose at Will. "Look at you, all grown up and disrespecting your elders. Neither of you has even offered to help an aging auntie with her groceries. Your mommas taught you better than that. And Willy, tell yours I still need her potato casserole recipe."

"It's just Will, not—"

"You kids all think you can up and try new names on like tee shirts. Go on home now, and stop embarrassing yourselves."

I wished I could see their faces after that lashing. They didn't reply, but they must have left. Beeping sounded at the front door and the lock disengaged. We crawled out of the bathroom and stood when we were sure it was Atty coming in.

I went in for a high five. "That was epic."

Atty shot down my high five with a sharp glance. "I can handle those boys. But Shane's getting persnickety."

"He sent me a text," I added. "He's casting doubt on your blackmail abilities."

"High time we found Misha and made his place an alternate base of operations, should we need it. Now, one of you, take these grocery totes."

Jaxon and I each took some groceries and set them on the kitchen counter.

"Supper in about an hour, once the meatballs are ready."

"Perfect," I said. "I brought a drive I want to sort through, I'm hoping it'll help with our plans."

"Good luck, Alyona. One of you can help Kendi with the salad when she gets here, but for now, you get to scheming."

"Yes, ma'am," I said, mimicking Willy's low voice. "But I go by Aly-Bo-Bally now."

Atty sent me another glare, but her mouth quirked up.

Jaxon held up my phone. "I'll keep researching to find Misha."

Atty scuttled about the kitchen organizing her purchases and preheating, and I sat at the kitchen laptop. I opened the only folder, labeled "Density Project-main." I loved how straightforward Mom was—a perfect counterpart to Dad's puzzle-driven, whimsical ways. If I were the star of a cartoon, the laptop would have shone a golden light across my face. It felt like I'd opened a treasure chest filled with the secrets of the universe. I clicked and scanned and scanned and clicked, speed-reading to absorb as much as I could. Research, trials, mathematical formulas, all annotated and organized, and quite far over my head.

"Hey," Jaxon called after about thirty minutes.

"Can I help you?" I said, failing to keep a straight face while feigning annoyance in an exaggerated tone that would have gotten me fired from even the most lenient customer service job.

"I'm trying to help *you*, you ingrate," he laughed.

I smiled at him, relieved we could fall back into our natural rhythm without weirdness. Or, with the appropriate level of weirdness. I knew we'd need to revisit our truncated conversation, but not with a potential audience. "Proceed."

"Misha is proving difficult to track down. Have you ever found any other hints?"

"Nilch. Best of luck." If I hadn't found him yet, I wasn't holding out hope for Jaxon finding him. This was a living person, not a historical figure.

We worked for another fifteen or twenty minutes before Kendi came home with a gigantic smile on her face and a squirrel on her shoulder, its bushy tail draped around her neck.

"Everyone, check out what Tater Tot can do," Kendi squealed. Atty emerged from the hallway, and we all joined Kendi near the kitchen table. She held her hand out, palm up, and Tater Tot jumped from her shoulder to her hand. She bobbed her hand up and flipped it over, and Tater Tot jumped and landed on the back of her hand. She flipped back and forth, Tater Tot jumping and landing a few more times, and then Kendi made a brief chittering sound and the squirrel returned to her shoulder.

Kendi cooed with pride and pulled him into her hands, scratching between his large ears. "Who is the cleverest little squirrely in the whole world? You are! That's right!" She giggled, and I noticed a dimple she'd never smiled enough to reveal before.

Atty's matching smile revealed their family resemblance. She'd been watching her niece more than the squirrel. "It's good to see you enjoying yourself, but let's get busy with supper, y'all."

Kendi turned toward the fridge.

Atty clicked her tongue. "No animals in my kitchen."

Kendi lifted the sliding door bar lock and opened it to the yard. She knelt to let Tater Tot hop away. "Not too far, mind," she told him.

Atty handed me a glass bowl with two whole tomatoes and a head of red-speckled lettuce. "How's your hand? Can you chop veggies?"

I pulled a knife from a wooden block on the counter. "It's sore, but okay. Thanks. But salad is Jaxon's thing." Jax wouldn't need the knife. He always tore his lettuce. Something about the cells and torn lettuce staying fresh longer. "I'll cut the tomatoes."

"Any progress today?" Atty asked as we ate our team-made meal.

I shifted in the tall wooden kitchen chair, not ready to share everything I'd discovered. If we could get it working, the density information could make simple work of acquiring the files she and Kendi needed to prove their innocence. But implementing the full density functionality would require stealing and programming another port unit, and I hadn't worked that all out yet. I still wasn't sure I could translate the research and documentation into specific booth settings. They'd documented the tests and written out the formulas and subsequent adjustments. It was probably simple for them to glance at the latest formulas and adjust the port unit settings as needed. But I wasn't the physicist they were, and I'd have to run a lot of tests before I used it on another human, even if the initial accident *was* due to nefarious interference.

I deferred to Jaxon. "Should we tell them what we accomplished at the park?"

He smiled at me. "Alyona found some code in the FutureMove files, and now she can port without a destination booth."

"And without the landing issues we had with the mice, I assume from the fact that you're both alive and well," Kendi said.

Atty stabbed some lettuce. "There's a reason porting outside a booth is illegal. I hope you two are smart about this."

"Yep! Still working out a few kinks,"—like not taking trees down with us—"but it's looking good."

Jaxon nodded. "Not much else exciting enough to share."

I agreed with his cue to keep anything else I may have found on the drive to myself. I took a talking break to finish my food. Porting to any point on the map was a big enough headache for security. Porting with no density restrictions would mean the end of secure spaces altogether. It was dangerous, powerful information. It really was the singularity Dad had spoken about, and, though I wanted to find the truth once and for all and help these ASF members clear their names, I didn't know anything about the organization as a whole—whether there were others, how many, or what their end game looked like. Manuel and Dr. Clarke had spoken of leaders up the hierarchy. I wouldn't hand over this kind of power and trade one brand of tyranny for another.

I stood with my empty plate and held out my hand for Kendi's.

She handed me the plate with her fingers flat due to her long, bright yellow fingernails, and recoiled as I took it. "Don't touch any clean dishes with those nasty fingers."

"Barbara." Atty cocked an eyebrow at her niece.

"What? I did not work all day beautifying hands to come home to this." She waved circular motions around my hand. "Girl, let me help you. Drop off those dishes and then sit back down."

I looked at my nails. They were clean from washing before dinner, but they were a ragged, torn up mess. I hadn't realized Kendi was a nail tech at the salon. It seemed an odd transition for a gifted hardware engineer and physicist, but it also made some sense. She probably wouldn't have felt safe out of Atty's sight for long. Plus, she could probably make some cool designs with her steady hands. I heard myself agree, not sure whether I acquiesced because I felt bad for what she'd been through, or because I suddenly remembered grabbing Jaxon's hand in the park and hoped he hadn't noticed how unkempt my poor nails were.

I rinsed the plates and sat back down at the table. Kendi came in with a few colors of nail polish and an array of metal tools that could have belonged to a KGB operative seeking international secrets.

"Hand," she said. She grabbed my thumb and attacked my cuticles with a tiny spinning file attached to a small electric rotary tool.

I flinched. "Calm down there, you don't need to skin my whole finger."

Kendi gripped my finger harder. "*You* calm down, and trust me."

I blew out a breath and looked over at Jaxon to distract myself. "Did you find anything else about Misha?"

Jaxon passed me my phone. "Unlock it, and I'll pull up some screenshots."

I tried to swipe my unlock pattern with my left hand while keeping my right hand still. "Why is Misha so scared?

Isn't he the one who set up the supposed data release, in case Dr. Clarke tries anything?"

Kendi nodded. "I think he's scared *because* he's the one with the means to release the data. Take him out, and none of us have any leverage. And he's always felt some responsibility, like he could have done more to stop the tragedy or something. We couldn't talk sense into him after it happened."

Atty shook her head. "Not like we could talk much sense into him before, either. He and your father always loved turning everything into a puzzle challenge. But I don't think that boy's pudding ever fully set up, bless his heart."

I chuckled. Misha—and his online alter-ego N031—certainly had some kind of metaphorical connector undone. He was smart, for sure, but obsessed with conspiracies. And squirrels.

"Stop jerking around, or I will cut you," Kendi warned . . . or threatened.

"I thought you said I could trust you," I quipped.

"Right, but you need to at least try to do your part. Help me help you."

Story of my life lately. I passed the unlocked phone back to Jaxon.

He tapped and swiped around for a few minutes, adding a few screenshots to the ones he'd taken this afternoon. "So, I didn't find anything definitive—there are a ton of Wells families out there. I searched property records from Douglas County up to Larimer, like I sometimes do for genealogical research. I found a Michael Wells who owns a rental in Fort Collins," he showed me the screenshot from the County Assessor's website, "and another one who owns a townhouse in Castle Rock." He swiped over and showed me the next one. "Here, take a look."

He set the phone down in front of me and I carefully

swiped back to the other screenshot, and then forward through the rest of the pictures. Along with a few promising address records, Jaxon had gifted me with several selfies. The first was his signature open-mouthed wink, then a raised eyebrow model pose—I'd be keeping that one—and then another open mouth, this time filled with chewed up chips.

"Oh, gross!" I shoved the phone away from me.

Kendi threw down her nail file. "I guess I'm done shaping. Don't make me duct tape your hand to the table for painting."

"Not a bad idea, though," I said.

She glared at me while she shook the bejeebers out of a bottle of polish in a metallic blue color I didn't find repulsive.

Jax took the phone back. "I narrowed down the results to right around the date of his summons. I figured maybe he sold the rental property Atty mentioned if he was planning on staying away from town. I changed it to M. Wells in case it didn't list the whole name, and I found a property out in the boonies purchased in the same month by a Mikhail Wellson. Gotta be the same guy."

"You know," I said, "You could probably make more money finding people and serving summons than you do as a history tutor." I should have asked him for help a long time ago, but I was beginning to understand that past me was, apparently, a moron.

"So did you get an address?" Kendi asked.

"Not quite. It's listed as unimproved land with only the county road for an address, which is miles and miles long."

"Maybe Nadia knows something." She was past due for a check-in, anyway. I had to tell her I was okay, and make sure Dr. Clarke hadn't taken her into custody, or whatever he'd threatened. "She knows all the hot goss around the office, and he was still there when she first got the receptionist job, at least briefly. Maybe he mentioned his off-the-grid cabin in the woods?" I reached for my phone.

"Gaaah!" Kendi yelled as her nail polish brush streaked a long line crossing the back of my hand.

"Ah, sorry," I said to her. "But I have to call Nadia." I switched hands and dialed her number, tapping on her picture when it popped up.

"Hello? Alyona? *Vsyo horosho*? I've been so worried, but I didn't know when was a safe time to call—"

"Hi Nad, yeah, everything's fine, don't worry." I turned the video on for the call and set the phone up where Nadia could see I was perfectly unharmed.

Nadia frowned on the screen. "Are you . . . getting your nails done? You never let me—"

"Yeah, and you can see why." I held up my paint-streaked hand and half-done nails. "I hold still about as well as a toddler."

"Worse," Kendi cut in.

"She was about to tape my hand down."

Nadia rested her cheek in her palm and shook her head at me.

"So, you know Misha, the assistant?"

"What about him?"

"Did he ever mention buying a property? Like land in the mountains, or a county house?"

Nadia paused. "I don't think so. He didn't talk much, though."

"Dang, I was hoping he'd found you charming like everyone else and invited you for s'mores or something."

"No, sorry. But why? What do you need him for?"

"Well, we might invite *ourselves* over for s'mores if the plan goes south around here."

"Plan? What plan, Alyon? What are you up to?"

"We don't actually have a plan yet, I just mean if we can't

stay here for any reason, it would be nice to have a safe house. But nothing to worry about for now."

"Well let me know how I can help you, okay? And remember, nothing too stupid."

I gave her a Jaxon-esque wink, and then waved and hung up.

Jax took my phone back. "With more time, I could find the legal description of the property and research it on a plot map. For now, we can bet he's in this general area." He held out the phone and drew a circle in the air around a section of map in the mountains west of Denver.

Genius. I sat at a table with a sharp-as-a-tack lawyer, a nail-artist-by-day wunderkind physicist/engineer, and a history nerd walking knowledge database who could research like a champ. I also had a shifty guy-in-the-chair hacker hiding somewhere in the Colorado Rockies, and a double agent I could probably rely on, if only as far as my sister was involved. And I had Nadia herself, who gave up formal education to take care of me. Who knew what she could accomplish given the chance; she had my parents' genes, after all. I only needed a plan, and then faster than we took down dinner, we'd crush Dr. Clarke and the ETC, and restore our rightful places at FutureMove.

CHAPTER TWENTY-TWO

Misery Loves Co-Conspirators

My plan boiled and congealed and pulsed in my head like a semi-sentient amoeba as we cleared away dinner. "You guys," I said, slapping my palms down on the smooth wood of the now clean table. "We have a heist to discuss."

Atty put a stop to my momentum. "We most certainly do not. Not tonight. Every one of us has had a long day. Y'all are going to bed. This plan is too important to force on a tired mind. Jaxon, you take the couch and the main-floor shower. Alyona, you can use Kendi's trundle bed and upstairs shower."

There was no way I'd be able to sleep now, with the heist of Dr. Clarke's drive taking shape in my mind and my Mom's backup drive calling to me from the laptop. After everyone turned in, I'd have space to think.

Atty found me a plush, blue towel and a pair of Kendi's pajamas, and I took a long shower. I didn't fancy staying up to pillow fight with Kendi, or whatever girls did at sleepovers, so I stalled, hoping Kendi would be asleep when I got to the room. The tea tree bath gel sharpened my excited but drained senses, and I reminded myself that adults might paint each other's nails, but they didn't pillow fight. She still had a trundle bed because this was her teenage bedroom, and not somewhere permanent the Adult Kendall would live if she'd had a choice. It was probably safe to come out. I dressed in her pajamas, the pant legs landing just below my knees, and ventured out.

I pushed her bedroom door open at a sloth's pace, expecting it to creak like every door in my apartment. It fell open, smooth and silent, revealing what looked like a glitter-obsessed middle schooler's fever dream. She'd probably stayed here often while her mom was sick and her dad was away. It looked like the bed, dresser, side table and vanity had once been a matching set in ballet pink. She had covered everything in rainbow glitter paint at one point, and then added holographic stickers and permanent marker doodles with math equations on top of that.

The walls, too, displayed a layered history—drawings of G-rated cartoon characters barely visible under TV14+ anime posters, with a periodic table over the top.

I stifled a laugh at the hodge-podge, but then my eyes found her head, asleep in a nest of fluffy pillows, hair wrapped in silk and colorful makeup gone. She looked older without it. Wiser.

If her decor was any indication, she had a strong sentimental streak, or maybe it was loyalty. She'd never let go of anything she cared about. Knowing her friend Melanie was hurt and in trouble and not being able to do anything about it must have rocked her to her foundation. She'd lost her mom, like me, and never really had a dad. Yet still, she didn't shut herself away. She relied on Atty to keep her safe. She believed in me, that I'd come through for her. She even opened her heart to a rodent. My demeanor would never entice woodland creatures looking for a friend, but maybe I could learn to include people who wanted to help me.

I padded over to the pulled-out trundle bed and tried to avoid too much creaking as I sat. I guess I hadn't considered that other people might have endured things. Like, really, really hard things. Because I *was* a moron.

Kendi and I were opposite in so many ways, but if I let myself, I could understand where she was coming from and why she was willing to do whatever it took to bring Dr. Clarke to justice.

On the outside bar of the trundle frame, she'd drawn an equation involving a couple of backward sixes, an 'H' with a roof, and what looked like two candelabras. I'd learned the symbol Psi represented wave functions, but we hadn't yet hit on quantum mechanics in my half-finished freshman-level physics class. The symbols reminded me of when Jaxon had tried to write Russian characters once and asked me what he wrote. I'd acted impressed and told him he'd written, "I'm a buffoon."

I reached up to the side table by my head and picked up the phone she had plugged into her charger. It was already fully charged, so I unplugged her phone and plugged in mine. I'd switch them back sometime in the night. I set my phone down next to hers, and it chirped with an incoming text, like a megaphone in the quiet room. The sound reminded me to pull out my hearing aids. I popped open the little doors to extend the battery life and set them on the bedside table, then grabbed my phone and turned down the notification volume. I checked the text.

```
Manuel: How dare you.
```

What could he possibly be mad at me for? Wasn't he the

one making my life difficult? I started to type an incredulous response, but he sent me another text.

> Manuel: You're going to do what you're going to do, but leave Nadia out of it. She told me you're planning something. You have no idea what you're messing with.
>
> Me: Then tell me what's going on, or butt your bun out of our business. This will be easier if you look the other way.
>
> Manuel: . . .

The three dots indicating he was typing kept pulsing for what seemed like several minutes. My heart beat too fast to lay down and I paced the room until the quick incoming-text vibration.

> Manuel: You are an absolutely selfish self-centered brat. You think you know everything, don't you? You may have finally put together some of the drama that's been stewing around you for years while you've been playing hacker. But there is more at play here than you or Kendi or Misha, or even Athena knows about. I can't tell you any more than you know now. You're impulsive and reckless. I can only beg you to keep Nadia out of your plans, if you even have any.

Talk about a buffoon. Of course I had a plan. I just had to fine-tune. Besides, saying selfish and self-centered was redundant.

My hands shook as I typed my reply, then deleted it. I took some deep breaths. He thought I was too impulsive? Too emotional? I could prove him wrong. But I had to talk to him in person. I could use his honest assessment of my plan, and I didn't want to have to guess what he was thinking. He would ask thorough questions, and I could make a decision about whether I could trust him with the assignment I was considering giving him in my plan. He could make or break this whole thing. But I needed a little time, and I couldn't face him without every detail worked out. I needed to sound a thousand percent confident.

> Me: We need to talk in person. I will tell you when and where. It will be soon. Tomorrow. Be ready.

I turned my phone on silent and put it back on the nightstand face-down so I wouldn't see any reply he might send. Schemes and ideas swam around my brain, adding themselves to the amoebic plan as I snuck downstairs to the kitchen laptop. In the most ambitious version, I'd also figured out how to use my parents' research. But my parents were ambitious too, and look where they ended up.

I unplugged Atty's laptop and carried it over to the love seat next to the couch where Jaxon slept, still and peaceful. I lost a few minutes watching him until I realized I was being a creepy weirdo and turned my attention to the laptop screen. I lost many more minutes reading through research diagrams and notes, then adding some of my own.

Mom's notes were all in Ukrainian—probably an added measure of protection against prying eyes. I tried to read them, but my Ukrainian skills were practically nonexistent. Even my Russian was spotty sometimes. I had to use an online translator in incognito mode for the phrases I didn't know.

According to Mom's notes, once the port booths were up and running, my parents worked for years on porting denser and denser matter. But when they got close to being able to port every material, regardless of density, the project was officially shut down.

"We are permitted to develop the density detection

mechanism for the port units," Mom had typed, "and because we're working on density-related problems, it's not difficult to further that task and continue our forbidden research covertly at the same time. The following equations represent successful density calculations which have been tested and replicated in several instances, which are more thoroughly documented below.

"Shane has been dismissive of our repeated proposals for peer-analyzed testing and refuses to seek funding for further development. He claims his hands are bound by ETC regulations concerning the danger posed by the testing, and strongly encourages immediate termination of any further density-related research and development. I am of the opinion that the technology is safe, and I have organized an official proof-of-concept test as described in the following documentation. Once the opposition to the research on the basis of safety is eliminated, we will acquire the funding to develop safeguards against its potential unintended uses."

The no-nonsense tone of my mom's writing reminded me of how she used to read fairy tales to us at night, and I had to wipe my eyes to continue. She would remove the adjectives and adverbs and let us know the facts of the situation, then have us brainstorm ways in which science could replicate the magic. Another kid might have felt like she was stripping any fun from the stories, but for me, it made the magic real. It meant that anything was possible if I could find a way.

I skipped down to what I thought were most likely the actual equations I would need to input into a port unit to move matter of any density. I might not have time to figure it out and run tests before the heist, but there was no version of me in any universe that could set this all aside and sleep. This wasn't just about a potential backup plan. Kendi claimed she'd seen the tech work, but the research and logs had been destroyed. If *I* could make it work, I'd have the proof-of-concept my Mom wanted. Her life's work would be reanimated, and her murderer's methods would be unveiled.

I scrolled through math until my eyes blurred. So. Many. Symbols. I stood, stuck my head under the kitchen faucet and sucked down some water. I scooped up the water that had dribbled down the side of my cheek and rubbed it over my face. I checked the time on the microwave clock. One thirty. Still time to discover more in Mom's notes that might help.

I sank back into the loveseat and looked for patterns, reading the notes with a keen, yet still-slightly-blurry eye. I didn't have to understand what they meant. I only had to figure out why each piece fit where it did, and what I needed to change to up the portable density levels. It was like when I taught myself different coding languages by reverse-engineering finished code.

A couple of hours later, I was almost sure I knew which pieces I could change without rendering the whole equation useless—or deadly. Kendi probably didn't plan to wake up for at least another four hours, but I couldn't wait, and this was for her, too. I tiptoed to her room and pushed the door open.

"Hey, you awake?"

Kendi made a low noise with her mouth and eyes still closed.

"Oh, good. I have a question for you."

Kendi groaned and lifted her head enough to face-plant into her pillow.

I took her up on her cordial invitation and tried to avoid her legs as I sat myself down on her bed. "It's quick, I promise."

Kendi sat up and tucked a stray coil into her silk bonnet.

She grabbed her phone to check the time and grunted. "What."

I pointed to the fancy equation in black marker on her trundle frame. "What is that? It's something to do with teleportation, right?"

She leaned over to see. "Yeah, it's a foundational piece. It's the Schrödinger Equation."

I nodded, as if that were a given.

"It's kind of like F=ma for quantum systems."

I did know that force was equal to mass multiplied by acceleration. I didn't understand how it applied, but that didn't matter. I only had to know she knew enough to answer my actual question.

"So, you need that in order to get anywhere in teleportation," I said.

Kendi leaned up on her elbow, her eyes brightening. "Exactly. Like, you know how an electron is basically a cloud of probability density? Imagine—"

"Better yet, let's look at some actual equations." I was too anxious right now to hear out her explanation, and I knew she'd be excited to see some of what I'd found. I pulled up the laptop and highlighted two equations. "I need you to look at the difference between these equations. One is the programming for the current units, and the second one is the part I think I need to override. I think I've changed the second one to account for a higher density, but I don't want to write over anything essential. Did I do okay?"

Kendi stared at the screen for a few seconds, and then stared at me and sat completely upright. "Where did you get this? Is this . . . is it what I think it is?"

Kendi's hand moved to the laptop's trackpad, and I slapped it away. "Yeah, it's my mom's. And I promise I'll let you see it after all this is over, but for now, I just need a little help. She didn't include the full program for a port booth unit. I need to make sure I added and subtracted the right formulas."

"Right, well, the answer is yes, sort of. May I?" She gestured toward the keyboard, keeping her hands a safe distance away until I slid the laptop onto her legs. She annotated more equations and formulas, muttering about electron density versus mass density and not forgetting to account for the effects of temperature. I wasn't listening well, but I watched like a hawk. A smart hawk who loved math. I might not have been on Kendi's level with quantum physics, but I was boss-level at deciphering patterns. I compared her mumbo-jumbo with Mom's long string of gobbledygook, and I was ninety-nine percent sure I knew what to add to the settings to replicate her success.

Kendi stopped typing and looked at me, pointing to the screen. "See? Like that."

I hugged her. I was a little shocked that my arms did that, but I couldn't contain them. "Kendall Carleson, you're my favorite mad scientist in the whole wide world. Thank you."

Kendi bent her arm up under my bear hug and patted me lightly on the shoulder. "Great, thank you. Don't try this at home, or anywhere, until I have a chance to look at it again. I'm going to try to sleep some more now."

"Don't worry, I'm not stupid enough to try it without some serious testing."

I released Kendi and took the laptop back into the living room, sighing as I sank into the loveseat. My parents had done it. They'd found a way to make magic. I let myself relax and closed my eyes to give them a rest.

The next time I opened them, the sky had brightened just enough to see into the dining area. My eyes watered from lack of sleep, but the teary sensation suited my emotional state.

Jaxon shifted a quarter-turn on the couch.

"Oh, you're awake, too," I whispered, swiping the salty tear leakage away from my cheeks.

"No, I'm not," came a voice muffled by a tasseled throw pillow.

"They did it, Jax."

Jaxon turned his body back my way and made another sound.

"They could teleport anything."

"Mm great." He hadn't opened his eyes.

"Let's go. We need to try it. There's a booth down the—"

"What? No." Jaxon sat up on his elbows and wiped his palm across his face.

"Yeah, there's an old light bulb in the oven. I looked. It's incandescent. We can use it to test. I need to get to a port unit and program in the code to talk to my remote—"

"Aly, no. Do you know what time it is?"

"It's the dawn of a new day, of course. Time to take matters into our own—"

"It's not even dawn yet. It's nautical twilight at best. This is a bad idea on so many levels."

"Nautical twilight? Is that one of those Tiny Pony Friends?"

"No, it's from back when sailors... You know what? It doesn't matter. We narrowly escaped your last plot to use a port unit in a new-fangled way, and now you're talking about doing it again, only amping up the danger level. Go to sleep. You can still get an hour in. We'll come up with an actual plan tomorrow. Today."

"But, Jax, this is huge. We would be unstoppable."

"*You* could, but not me. I'm not like you."

Ouch. I didn't know what he meant, but I wanted him to think of us as a team, at the very least. I hesitated.

He turned away to stare out the window. Then he said

what sounded like, "Aly, I done ink it earth it." I couldn't hear him as well, having left my hearing aids in Kendi's room.

I paused for a moment, trying to work out what he had said.

He turned back to me. "It's not worth the risk. You agree, right?"

Ah, *I don't think it's worth it*. But I had too much mixed emotion buzzing through my veins to consider the cost-benefit with any accuracy.

Jaxon sat up straight and slid to the side of the couch until his knee pressed against mine. "You know I love you. You're a genius, you're hilarious, you're beautiful, and you inspire me to stretch myself. There's not another person like you in the entire world."

The skin on my face tightened and tingled, like shrink wrap under a heat gun. Beautiful? I lowered my head further behind the laptop screen, suddenly aware of the bags that must be sagging under my tired eyes. He loved me, as is. A surge of confidence welled up into my chest. His backing meant everything to me. But like, brotherly love? Or let's forget all this and run away to Fiji love?

"I am average-level everything, and I'm lucky you let me tag along on whatever adventure you're chasing any given day."

I shook my head. "No, you're above average."

Above average? I'd meant to say something more along the lines of the conversation I'd started yesterday. Fail.

"I don't want you to change or stop, but I am begging you to pause. Please rest. I have been through a lot these past few days, and I'm drop-dead exhausted. I can't have you endangering yourself when I'm not at the top of my game to help you. We will plan today. We'll succeed with a plan, and I'll be all-in, I promise. Right now, I am telling you, no, Aly, for the first time ever. Please respect that."

How could I push him any further? He'd put his foot down, and he was right. He'd almost *lost* a foot because of me, and I owed him. It was a step toward the trust I wanted so badly to become two-sided.

"You're right, Jax. I'm sorry I've put you through so much. I don't know exactly why you stick by me, but I want to be a better friend." *Or maybe more.* I gazed out at the nautical twilight, drowning in excess feelings and wishing the quickly fading stars would guide me into safe waters.

"If Nadia is my motherboard, you're my kernel Jax, the core of my system. She's my home, and you're my heart. You're both ... both, I guess." Not smooth, but honest. I looked down at my hands. "I'm afraid I'm taking too long to rewire my brain so that my actions prove my words. It's not because I don't want ..." My head swam. I closed my eyes again, afraid I'd pass out from nerves before I finished.

His knee slid further up the outside of my leg as he scooted to the edge of the couch. He reached up to smooth my bedraggled curls, which sent my pulse and any hope of forming sentences reeling into space. "I do want, Jax. This. Us."

Where I saw the tatters of his patience with me before, his eyes now shone as if he couldn't get enough. "I do too." He kept his hand at the side of my face, cupping my cheek.

I could barely breathe as he pressed his fingers gently into my hair, guiding me closer.

"I thought you wanted sleep," I whispered.

"I'm awake, now," he said, leaning slowly toward me. His lips curved in a gentle, heart-stopping smile, and every cell in my body woke up with anticipation.

The hallway light flickered on, and I startled so hard I ended up on the floor. Luckily, the laptop had slipped into the loveseat.

Jaxon sat wide-eyed and tried to rest against the couch,

but he'd scooted so far forward that he ended up leaning back at an awkward, forty-five-degree angle.

Kendi walked in from the hallway and took in the scene. "Good morning. Hope I didn't . . . wake you."

I wasn't sure whether it was better to say she had or hadn't. "Oh, it's okay, we were just planning our plans. Making them. Forming the plans for—"

"You're up early," Jaxon said.

"I like to run before work. I'll be out of your hair and then you can . . . plan."

My face felt hotter than the bright rays of sun peeking over the horizon. "Have a great run. Looks like a great day. What's after nautical twilight, Jax?"

"That would be 'civil twilight.'"

"Have a very civil run, Kendi." I gave her a little wave.

Kendi rolled her eyes, popped in some earbuds and left.

Jaxon struggled to right himself from his weird lean-sit. When he'd positioned himself like a normal person on a couch, he picked up one arm and draped it across the back, like he was trying to look casual. "Sun sure is rising out there."

"Sure is." I picked at the stripe of blue nail polish across the back of my hand.

"Too late for sleep now, or anything, I guess, right?"

I couldn't answer, because my immediate reaction was to shout no, it wasn't too late for *anything* and let's pick up where we left off. Instead, I said, "Day is early," and the awkwardness neared critical mass.

I pulled my hair to one side just for something to do with my hands. "Oh, I left my hearing aids on the nightstand." I jumped up and ran out of the room.

Safely behind Kendi's bedroom door, I collapsed on her

trundle. *Whoa.* That was huge. The almost-kiss ranked right up there with the life-changing heist I was—*we* were— about to pull off. I closed the battery doors and inserted my hearing aids. Locked and loaded. Bring on the dawn.

$$i\hbar\,(\partial\Psi/\partial t)=\hat{H}\Psi$$

CHAPTER TWENTY-THREE

Potential Energy

"Rise and shine, Jaxon Jeong!" It sounded like the title of a children's book for kids who love mornings. I'd never been an early bird, but civic twilight might have just become my new favorite time of day.

"I'm up, I couldn't sleep past that beautiful sunrise."

My heart squeezed a few extra beats into the second it took me to breathe. "Oh, good. I need your help polishing the plan to steal the data."

Atty came bouncing into the living room with a Kendi-like gait. "Good morning!" She checked her watch. "Kendi and I have about thirty minutes to hear what you've come up with so far and do some brainstorming before work. I will do whatever I can for you from my office. If it takes me leaving work to help you get the data we need to shut Dr. Clarke down and clear our names, I am at your beck and call.

"If I think of anything you can do, I'll let you know, but I think your main job will be to sort through files and find whatever will help the case best from a legal standpoint." I followed her into the kitchen. "Dr. Clarke let me into the vault, which makes it look like he was trying to convince me that a search for data was a dead end. It had the opposite effect. I know what drive the files are hidden on, but it will be tricky to get it out of the building. Is there any specific information I should be looking for? Anything you think he might have that would incriminate him and clear you?"

Atty started coffee. "Look for communications between him and the legal counsel, and anything from the ETC authorities in Washington. He's their liaison, so he's got a boss to report to. He'd have kept correspondence, not only due to his obsessive record-keeping, but to be used as blackmail, backup in case someone outed him. I'm not sure that's the right avenue, but anything you find on that drive you think he's keeping backed up, you grab."

I nodded. "Insurance, like whatever he thinks we already have on him."

"Exactly," Atty said.

My stomach rumbled at the smell of the coffee, but I was too excited to eat. Or delirious from minimal sleep, it was hard to tell. "Then we hand you the info, and you, what, call the press or something?"

"Or something," she said.

Kendi came in from running and walked straight to the coffeemaker.

"Alright," I said, "so first, I need to get into the building. Nadia can disguise me, but I'm a pretty hot commodity right now, so I don't know whether I'll make it in."

Kendi joined me at the table, blowing steam from her mug. "Did you get to program a booth last night with the new data? Could you simply port in?"

"I think we're on the right track there, and it'll probably be important to prove it worked once we have other evidence of tampering. But we're several trials away from humans still."

"I bet you could make it in with a disguise if you have a distraction," Jaxon said. "Like that art heist in Stockholm."

I nodded at him to explain further. "Yes?"

"You know, the one in like, 2000 or 2001? They set some cars on fire to distract the police, and then they broke into the royal palace and stole some paintings. A couple of Rembrandts, I think. I remembered it because their getaway vehicles were mopeds and I tried to picture how I'd ride my bike holding a big famous painting."

"And because you remember every historical event you hear about." I nudged him with my shoulder. "But yeah, that could work. Sans explosions—unless the legal council approves?" I flashed Atty a smile like a kid asking for quarters for the gumball machine.

She shook her head.

"I guess there aren't a lot of cars parked along the streets these days, anyway. So what could get Dr. Clarke out of his office?" I asked.

Kendi's hand shot up into the air. "I could create a distraction."

"Absolutely not." Atty clunked her mug on the side table. "You will not make yourself bait—"

"No, I won't be the distraction, I'll bring him."

I wanted to ask who, but Kendi was already halfway out the kitchen door.

"Tater Tot!" she called, and then made a fast-clicking sound with her tongue. "Here, boy!"

The squirrel jumped, seemingly out of nowhere, right onto her shoulder.

"See? Tater here's the smartest squirrel I've ever seen. I can come around the side of the building where the first-floor hardware lab is. There's a lady with a station near the window, and she almost always keeps it open. At least she did while I was there. Said she needed the fresh air. I'll boost Tater Tot through and let him loose. If she's not there, we'll find another way in."

"Is that enough to get Dr. Clarke to come down?" said Jaxon.

I pulled up my phone to make a note to myself. "It will be if the security guy tells him he should." I added that to the list of tasks I would give Manuel, as soon as I convinced him it was for Nadia's benefit.

Kendi scratched the squirrel's nose. "That won't be necessary. He may appear cute now, but he's like a wild wolverine when he's in attack mode. Aren't you, little guy? Yes, you are!"

Atty leaned away from her niece. "No wolverines in the kitchen. Get him outside."

Kendi stepped out the sliding door and I hurried to follow her out. She set Tater Tot on the ground and patted him on the bushy tail. "Scoot, little dude."

Tater Tot scurried out the kitchen door and off in the direction of the tree in the back corner of the yard.

"Hey," I whispered, catching Kendi before she went back inside. "Do you really think Tater will be enough?"

"I hope so."

"Yeah that's what I thought. You have a backup plan, and I need to know about it."

She kept her eyes on Tater Tot as she whispered back. "Are you sure you can get into the vault and back out again?"

"If you get Dr. Clarke off the top floor, I can get in and out."

"Then I'll make sure Shane gives you some space to work. It won't matter whether it's T.T. or me if you get what you need to condemn him and set us free."

I nodded, and raised my voice to a regular level as I stepped back inside. "Yeah, so between Manuel and Tater Tot, Dr. Clarke will come down from the top floor. From there into the vault, it's a badge swipe, a PIN at the door, an iris scan, and a dial lock. I have a plan for the badge and the iris scan, and I know the PIN from last time he let me in. He wasn't as secretive as he thought he was. And the dial might be the same combination it was before Dr. Clarke took it over, but either way, I can crack it." I glanced over at Jaxon. "I need to borrow your bike to get something from the apartment."

Jaxon shook his head. "No way. Nadia can grab it for you."

"I'll be quick."

"You'll be caught!"

"I will not. Nadia won't know what she's looking for."

"She's smart; she can handle it."

"I know she's smart, but she's as terrible as I am under pressure. I need to keep her out of it."

"Alyona. She can help you if you trust her. Even a little bit."

"Ugh, Jax. Maybe you're right—"

"Definitely I'm right."

"—but so far, teamwork sounds like a lot of you telling me no."

Jaxon smirked and said quietly, "There are some things I will always say yes to."

Game, set, match.

I'd let Nadia help, though Manuel would tear me a new one. I'd have to convince him that keeping me out of an ETC cell was the best way to keep Nadia safe.

I let out the breath I'd trapped in my throat. "Alright. I'll text her."

Atty stood. "Look at you two, working it out. You're going to make a lovely couple."

I flushed, and Jaxon sneezed.

"It's about time Barbara and I got to work, but I have two last pieces I'd like to see sorted first."

"Okay," I said. "Shoot."

"A: How are you getting out of the building once you've got the files copied, and B: What is your timeline?"

I sat up straighter and pushed phantom elevator buttons. "The elevators at FutureMove are port booths. They can't port me out, for obvious reasons." I squirmed at the idea of being cut to shreds in the fancy gold filigree decorating the outside of the building. "But I need to get to the elevator, punch in the code to activate the port, and then I'll end up in the evidence and supply room in the basement. If they've changed the code, I'll try my elevator key to put it in maintenance mode, or pick the lock leading in from the stairwell, the point being that I can get out the basement door and book it to the nearest booth, and I can come back here, or over to the salon, whichever you prefer." I didn't love either option, but I didn't know where else to go.

"Come to the salon. More witnesses around, in case anyone comes after you," Atty said.

"Okay. Kendi will leave as soon as she lets the squirrel go. And Nadia will be fine if she acts natural. I'll keep her out of the loop as much as possible so she doesn't endanger herself or the plan." Kind of like how Atty kept me from the truth so I wouldn't turn Dr. Clarke against me. "As far as when it'll happen . . ." I checked the time on my phone and thought for a few seconds. "I'd like to do it today, if I can get it set up. I'll text you guys."

"And me? What's my part?" Jaxon said.

"Oh, you've spent long enough in that place. You get to sit this out."

"I don't think so. I am helping."

"You told me yourself it took a toll on you. I can handle this one."

"Not a chance. I will not—"

"Well," said Kendi, standing and reaching for a backpack with a cartoon on it of a girl shooting water out her hands. "I'm out, before you kids get into it again." She tucked most of her curls into a blue beanie with a green lining. "Let me know when you need me and T.T."

She and Athena left, and I rested my head in my hands. I didn't want Jaxon to feel left out, or to think I didn't want him helping, but any job I could think up would sound patronizing at this point.

"Let's get out of here," I suggested. "I need a change of scenery."

"It isn't safe. We can't wander around town—we're wanted."

"It's not safe here, either. Our Attack Auntie's gone, and Willy the ETC Guard could be lurking around the bend."

"You have a point."

"We'll take your bike. You can pick the place."

"And we're going to talk about my role in this plot of yours?"

"Sure."

"Not 'sure.' I want to hear a commitment."

"Okay. Yes."

"The library."

"The library? That's—" I stopped myself from saying it was boring and smelly and worse than being trapped in Athena's living room, because this was the new, thoughtful, trusting, attractive Alyona. "That's an option. But, why?"

"It's quiet, it's public, it's got a million nooks and crannies where we can talk in private, and it's got public computers where we can upload files or whatever we need. It's only a couple blocks away from here. And I like it there."

I tilted my head to the side. He had me at private. "That makes sense. It might be a smart place to meet up with the drive when I get out. They'd be looking at the salon, and their relative truce might not hold up if Dr. Clarke realizes he's been robbed."

Jaxon stood, grinning. "Awesome. To the bike!"

"Yeah, right. I think I saw a bike in the garage I can borrow."

Jaxon's smile faltered. He probably thought I would mess up Atty's bike somehow. "Nah, it's close, you could ride on the cargo rack again."

I was not opposed to riding the same bike with him. "Uh, yeah, if you're okay with that." But I would wear the backpack this time instead of holding it between us.

We found his bike on the side of the garage where we left it. Jaxon ducked inside and came out with two helmets, one glitter purple and one sporty pink. Both of them were too small for our heads, to his disappointment and my relief. He moved the bike to the walkway and held it steady while I stepped over the cargo rack. He pulled my arms around his torso, then rested one of his hands on top of mine, holding my arm tight against his side. His heart beat against my forearm, even faster than mine. I propped my feet up on the rack bolts and he pushed off.

He held on for two or three houses, and only let go when he had to use both hands to steer us around the corner. Maybe he was afraid I'd make us fall. Or maybe he didn't mind riding close, either. I wasn't afraid of falling. Against my better judgment and the post-apocalyptic style helmet I'd secured around my heart, I had already fallen. Hard.

Now, I had to focus on not failing everyone I loved.

CHAPTER TWENTY-FOUR

Fool Me Twice, I'll Take You Down

I FOLLOWED JAXON AROUND the library, lagging a few keystrokes behind like an overloaded CPU. This was his turf, and I kept wondering whether every printed word in the building could fit on my phone's hard drive, or if I'd need two.

I rubbed my tailbone. Even without a tungsten ankle bracelet, Jaxon seemed to prefer biking to porting. He appreciated the longhand experience. I guess it was the same with books; he liked the physical presence, the fact that they took up space.

I couldn't cut him out of my plan; he wouldn't be happy hearing about it second-hand. And he wouldn't feel so strongly about being a part of my plan if he didn't feel strongly about me, right?

"Over here," he said. Jaxon had found a set of two cushioned stools at a small table between a couple bookshelves.

I'd walked right past, lost in my head. I spotted him over my shoulder and did a silly robot backward walk until I got back to the table and sat across from him. "So," I said, leaning over the table on my elbow. "Come here often?"

Jaxon leaned in, too, and I willed myself not to flinch away. "Not every day," he said in a husky, teasing voice. "Most Tuesdays and Thursdays during the school year and an occasional Saturday if extra... *research*... is required." He wagged his eyebrows.

"You're such a nerd that you're not even joking. That's your actual tutoring schedule." And by extra research, he literally meant looking up facts in old dusty books.

"But I'm a skilled nerd who can pedal two people on one bike with muscles to match my bulging brain." Jaxon playfully flexed a bicep, but his sculpted arm was no joke.

My hand came toward his muscle to give it an impressed squeeze, but I wasn't sure I'd be able to remove my skin from his if I touched him. So I gave him an awkward salute. "And I thank you for the lift, good sir." If only I could port myself into a deep, dark hole where there was a chance I wouldn't embarrass myself further.

Jaxon put his arm down and saluted me back.

"So, I think I have a job for you."

"You'd better. I can't believe you thought I would twiddle my thumbs while you have all the fun."

"Yeah, sorry, I'm not great at delegation. But I do need you."

He started to say something, but cleared his throat softly, and waited for me to continue.

"What I need Nadia to get from the apartment is a badge reader. I need her to get close enough to Dr. Clarke for the reader to copy his badge, and then I'll need the SD card it writes the badge information onto. It'll be a risk for either of us to approach her, but I'm a bigger target. They only wanted you so they could get to me. No offense."

"None taken."

"So I'll have Nadia pull the card out in the bathroom,

then leave it somewhere, like a geocache, and you can go pick it up and bring it to me. Could you do that?"

"I can do that like a boss. Like a boss of geocaches. A Master Cacher."

"Dork." I laughed and leaned back, forgetting the stool had no back.

Jaxon shot up and over the table, grabbing my arm before I toppled. "Klutz," he said. "Try not to injure yourself. You need to talk to Nadia, and I am going to catch up on some emails. If my phone's in that vault, please steal it back for me."

Jaxon chose a computer within my line of sight, and I pulled out my phone and sent Nadia a text telling her to take a break and call me. Two minutes later, her picture showed up on my phone with her incoming call.

"Hey, Nad."

"Shhh!" Some lady darted her head out of the next row of shelves and oh-so-politely reminded me where I was.

"Sorry."

"What did you do?" Nadia asked in a whisper. The slight echo told me she'd taken a bathroom break for the call.

"Nothing," I said in a hushed voice. "I need you to do something for me. A couple of things."

"Like?"

"I need makeup, to look bland and boring, like someone of no significance."

"That'll be hard. You're my sister, so you're gorgeous even though you try so hard not to be."

"Thank you?"

"Besides, isn't Kendall your stylist these days?"

I looked down at my half-finished nails. "Nad, if you could see these nails, you wouldn't be mad."

"Don't change the subject. Of course I'll help you. But what's your plan?"

"It's need-to-know. I want you to have plausible deniability and stuff. Plus, Manuel would murder me if I put you in danger."

"Manny," she sighed. "I really like him, he's so thoughtful. He has what it takes to protect me, you know?"

"Hmm." He'd better.

"But I need to know what you're thinking so I can get you the right look. Obviously, you're trying to sneak in undetected, right?"

"Yeah."

"So, you'll walk right into an institution you've already stolen from twice, and where they're looking for you specifically, to steal from them a third time? Is that what you're thinking?"

"Yeah. But I mean, there will be a distraction. And—"

"What distraction?"

"Um, a squirrel?"

Nadia sighed into the phone. "Okay, so you're going to walk in the front doors where they literally held your boyfriend prisoner, and it'll all work out, because you put on a bit of makeup and you brought a squirrel?"

"He's not my—and when you put it that way, it sounds—"

"Exactly like something you'd do. There is likely no amount of makeup that will fool Dr. Clarke. But if anyone can help you, I can. And with the right clothes it might be enough in passing, if he's thoroughly distracted."

"Nadia," I sighed. She still didn't know the scope of Dr. Clarke's betrayal. She had to know what was at stake for all of us, and she deserved to understand what had really happened to our parents. "You know that lady who lost her hand on the news?"

"So horrible!"

"Her name was Melanie. She worked at the ETC."

"Melanie Moreno? I know her. I thought she was out on leave. Dr. Clarke made it sound like she was somewhere tropical. That was her? Oh my gosh, is she in trouble?"

"She's a good friend of Kendi's, and she's missing."

"Oh no! You don't think the ETC had anything to do—"

"I know they did."

"Shhh!" spat the book lady from the next aisle. *Oh yeah. Library.* I had to be more careful. This was still a public space. I lowered my voice and walked toward the study rooms.

"Nad, I saw her name in a hidden file on Dr. Clarke's computer. Her disappearance, her hand—this was their doing. She was looking into our parents' . . ." I heard her shallow breath on the other end of the line.

We rarely discussed the accident—the murder—directly. We both had a healthy respect for the aftereffects of doing so. But I had to tell her.

I sat at the desk in an empty study room and shut the door, hating that I had to have this conversation over the phone. "Dr. Clarke told Melanie to leave it alone, but she didn't. He took action to cover up . . . he didn't want anyone to know what really happened . . ."

Nadia gasped into the phone. "Alyona, no."

"Mom and Dad, they didn't mess up, Nad. They knew what they were doing. It was all—"

"Alyon, stop. Just . . . wait." I heard a click as Nadia set her phone down. I heard the bathroom door close, and then I heard a muffled cry of frustration I'd only ever heard when she tried to open the most stubborn jars of low-sugar jam. I felt horrible for making her cry alone in a bathroom stall. She knew what I was trying to tell her, and it hurt her as much as it did me. Everything did, she was simply better at keeping it tucked neatly beneath the surface. I heard her tell-tale nose blow, and she came back on the phone.

"You don't have to say it," she said, her voice quivering.

Even now, she was trying to shield me as best she could. I let her. "Love you, Nad. I'm sorry."

"I love you, too. You know that. You and that squirrel are going to take down the ETC."

"You'd better believe it."

"With my help, you and squirrely might make it past the front doors. And let's say by some miracle you get all the way to where you're going undetected. What next? And how are you getting out of there?"

"This is where you come in. I need an iris scan and a badge from Dr. Clarke."

"No way. I am not going to steal a badge from my boss. I couldn't today, even if I tried. I'll be an emotional mess. We don't even know he's done anything—"

Some library person walked past my study room, and I turned away from the door.

"No, it's okay. You don't have to steal a badge. And you're right, he might only be covering up details until he can figure out what happened. Either way, what we're doing will help all innocent parties."

I heard her let out a fast breath. "All right, what do I need to do?"

"You just have to get close to him with a badge cloner. Do you ever carry, like, a big purse that holds binders or a laptop or anything? Like for presentations or whatever?" I couldn't remember what business purses were called.

"Well, I'll have a large attaché case full of paperwork today." That was it. Attaché. "We're having a new employee lunch. Dr. Clarke likes to take the new people out to make the paperwork and handbook rigamarole more bearable." Nadia's restrained voice broke on the last word. It must have been hard for her to accept that Dr. Clarke had done such horrible deeds when she'd only ever seen his friendly, supportive side.

It was hard for me, too. This whole situation was a lot to process. But we'd know after today. If he was guilty of the crimes Kendi and Misha claimed he was, he wasn't a good guy.

Nadia's voice softened. "Is this the right thing, Alyon? What if Dr. Clarke is innocent? What if it's Kendall and Misha who are the dangerous ones? What if it's some kind of trap?" Fair questions. "Or, what if Dr. Clarke is a puppet for some other boss?" An even better question.

If he was, then we truly were getting ourselves caught up in something we knew nothing about, and we could be making our lives much harder. Manuel had made it clear he was working for a third party and had to keep his cover. His panicked warnings to make sure Nadia stayed clear of it all would make sense if he knew we were crossing into some political kingpin's playing field. He seemed to be of the mind that the less we knew, the better. I thought my parents would have disagreed.

"You know, that might be the case. I don't feel like this is all him. But we need to know for sure." I wanted to know exactly what had happened to my parents with all of my soul. I also wanted to learn to trust again, and to know whom to trust. I knew I trusted Nadia more than anyone on the planet to do what was best for our little family. So I did something I had never done before—and deferred to her judgment.

I took a deep breath. "I think I can do this, and I think it could answer most of our questions. But I don't know, and I could be putting you and me both in danger. What do you think we should do, Nadia?"

The phone's speaker was quiet for several seconds, and then Nadia spoke, her voice cracking. "I know you can do this. I don't think we have any other choice."

Tears welled. "Thank you." I shook my head, trying to jiggle out the emotions before they swept over me. I had to keep a clear mind. "I need you to go home with your attaché and find my badge duplicator. It's a flat gray case the size of a bathroom scale. You'll need to get within about one foot of Dr. Clarke's badge with it. Then you'll take the SD card out and leave it at the restaurant. Tape it under a table. Someone will come get it after you leave."

"I can get close to him to take a selfie with the new hire, and I'll make sure it focuses on his face for the eye scan."

"Yes! Perfect. You can text me that picture."

"Be careful, yes?"

I was about to say "always," but I was rarely careful. I would try, for everyone counting on me. "I will. You, too. If Dr. Clarke senses something off about you today, tell him it's allergies. Or you have a migraine, but don't want to miss the lunch."

She promised she'd be fine, and I took a few steadying breaths before I left the study room.

I found Jaxon brains-deep in his computer station, and I poked him in the ribs.

He jumped and reflexively elbowed me in the gut. "Sorry, not sorry," he said. He moved his hand back to the mouse and closed the browser tab with his email on it.

I caught a few words before it disappeared. Tutoring, open position. interview. "Jax, what was that? Something about the job you missed?"

He pulled up another window with a map on it. "Nothing important."

"What do you mean? What was it?" Why did he feel like he had to hide it from me?

"Don't worry about—hey!"

I reached across him and typed in a keyboard shortcut

to reopen the closed tab. I read the email aloud. "'Due to our expansion of the tutoring program, we're approved to hire one more work-study position. Interested parties in the open position must register for interview slots via this form.' Jax! This is amazing! You have to sign up."

"All the slots are for today," he said, closing the tab again. "And I'm booked."

"No, Jaxon. You will not give that up for this stupid plan of mine. Do the interview. By the time they hire you and run a background check, I can have this fugitive thing handled. You have to—"

"Aly, shut your face for a minute. I get a say, remember? I get to choose my own future. I don't have to do anything, except to follow my passions."

"But—" My mind blanked when he said the word passions.

"We don't have time for this right now. Look, I found more info on Misha, and I think this is his place."

My brain promptly refilled with much more to say, but I forced myself to respect his authority over his own life. I nodded, and he zoomed in on a map of a wooded lot in the mountains with a rough cabin and some outbuildings, and what might have been an array of satellite dishes. *Yep, that could definitely be N031.*

"This is awesome, thank you! Looks like we have our safe-house if Atty's gets too hot."

"Yeah, sounds like he's always been so welcoming and open, I'm sure he'd love the whole crew dropping in unannounced."

"Exactly. We'll roast hot dogs and sing campfire songs. He and Kendi can compare squirrel notes. He'll be so excited."

I told Jaxon when and where to pick up the SD card. It would take some time to ride there, and he decided to go early to find somewhere a little ways off to park the bike where it wouldn't be noticed, and to find a vantage point where he could watch and see when it was safe to retrieve the data.

"I'll meet you back at Atty's," he said. "Are you sure you're okay walking there?"

"Yeah, I'll be fine."

"And you'll go straight there and not do anything stupid?"

I pushed his shoulder to spin him around, then nudged him toward the library's exit. "It's two blocks. Get out of here. I'll see you in a bit."

I might make a detour, but there was no point worrying him about it. I had one more huge serving of trust to dish out, and it would take every crumb I had left.

Jaxon turned back to me and looked like he wanted to protest, but then he saluted the way I had earlier and left.

I sat at his computer station and texted Atty and Kendi to let them know everything was in motion. This heist could work, but it wouldn't be easy. Breaking into the vault would be a grand old time. Trusting Manuel? Agony.

CHAPTER TWENTY-FIVE

Objects in Motion

IF I REALLY DID want to trust Manuel—and vice versa—meeting at his preferred location was the obvious choice.

> Me: Arcade. Ten minutes.

He'd been fine with siccing Kendi on me there, so it was unlikely to be crawling with ETC security. Plus, the people and gaming noises would mask our conversation. I sprinted to the nearest booth and used my burner account to port into the booth across from the twenty-four-hour arcade. The pins and needles from the port lingered with my nervous energy as I jogged up to the building.

I pulled the door open. The wave of sound and warm air, heavy with the essence of processed foods, made my stomach churn. Was this a huge mistake, relying on people who had been at the company when my parents died?

A villain-themed pinball game squawked out a tinny, maniacal cackle. I jumped and rushed toward the Skee-Ball machines at the back of the room, where I hoped to hear myself think. I picked up a ball someone had left behind and rolled it around in my hands, trying to force the tingles out.

Manuel took the lane next to me a minute later. A snug Captain USA shirt had replaced his usual security windbreaker and polo, and his shoulder-length hair fell loose. He seemed more approachable this way. He'd probably dressed all common-man for the express purpose of appearing safe, which annoyed me. And I was still upset by his texts from last night.

I wasn't here for small talk, so I didn't give him the chance to try any. "Quarters," I said, holding out a hand.

He glared at me, and then reached into his jeans pocket. To my surprise, he had a few and handed me three.

I snatched them up and plowed ahead. "I don't appreciate your scolding," I said, shoving a quarter into the machine. "How can you claim this high-ground crap when you're working for someone like Dr. Clarke? You pretend to help us, but you've only made it harder in the name of keeping some kind of cover." I lobbed the ball into the machine too hard, and it hit the back wall. "You're afraid to stand up for the truth."

He gently rolled his quarter into the slot. "You have no idea what you're talking about. You're in over your head, kid. I told you things are not as they seem. You are not the only one peeking behind Dr. Clarke's digital curtains. Think of your poor sister." Manuel let his ball roll in a straight line, but without enough power to get to the first ring. He'd been too careful.

"Nadia isn't a poor anything. She's amazing, and she'll kick you to the curb as soon as I tell her what a two-faced coward you are." My second ball scored twenty points. *Take that, Manuel.*

Manuel put his second ball down and turned to face me, his mouth flat and his jaw clenched. He wasn't being too careful; he was fighting for control.

He sighed, sandwiching the next ball between his hands. "I'm sorry for attacking. You're not some kid, and you're smart, if somewhat reckless. Nadia is the most amazing woman I've ever met. I love her. And she loves you, so I need to treat you better."

Manuel's jaw relaxed. His whole face kind of melted, and he hugged the ball to his chest. "I haven't said that out loud before. But it feels right. I love Nadia Zolotova." He gazed affectionately at the dull, battered ball and lobbed it into the small fifty-point ring, barely looking where he was throwing.

"Okay, weirdo. So prove it. Stay out of my way."

Manuel looked from his next ball back up to my face and some of the tension returned to his brow. "I want to help you. You called me here, and I came. You haven't even told me what you want yet, besides quarters. But before I hear you out, I need *you* to hear me."

I folded my arms and lifted an eyebrow at him.

Manuel picked his ball back up. "I want you to take one minute to consider Nadia's life from *her* perspective. She became mother to a teenager while a teen herself. She never got to pursue her interests. She wants to go to culinary school; did you even know that?" He met my eye. "She gave up her young adulthood to give you yours, without complaint."

An arcade attendant walked past us on his way to a door at the back wall, so we both rolled balls up the Skee-Ball ramp. I was glad for a reason to break Manuel's penetrating gaze and rub my itching eyes.

Manuel turned to me again, speaking loud enough to carry over the arcade noises, but without accusation. "You weren't the only Zolotov daughter to lose her parents, and when she did, she lost herself, too."

I didn't look back his way. I forced myself to pick up another ball. *Keep rolling.* My eyes blurred in the bright light of the scoreboard, and I couldn't see my point total. I'd thought I was beating Manuel, but now I wasn't sure. It hurt that I didn't know about culinary school. I squeezed my eyes shut and he guided my shoulder around to face him.

"Nadia cannot lose you," he said.

I took a sharp breath in and turned away, pretending to be distracted by something in the crusty ceiling tiles. I would not let Manny ManBun see me cry.

He picked up his next balls and sank several high pointers. He'd found his stride. "The best step for you right now is to turn yourself in, throw yourself at Dr. Clarke's mercy, and trust his day of reckoning will come. He won't hurt you. He's gone to great lengths to protect you and Nadia. You should at least try to protect her, too."

I frowned and grabbed another ball. After that parental lecture, cutting enough to make up for four years without a dad, I half expected him to finish with, "Now go to your room, young lady." I looked at his score; he'd gained an irritating lead. I ignored him for the moment, took a breath and rolled another notched ball up the ramp with more focus. It didn't clear the gap and plunked into the abyss.

I shook my arm and refocused. "Whatever you feel for her, multiply it by your whole life and add in all the love you have for your mother who raised you. That's how I feel about my sister. I will only ever do what is best for her. I *am* a brat, and technically still a kid. But what I think is best for my sister is to receive our inheritance and to live free from Dr. Clarke's manipulation. I am going ahead with my plan with or without your help." I couldn't let Dr. Clarke literally get away with murder. We had to get to the bottom of this, no matter what Manuel said. Nadia had agreed.

I lobbed a ball. *Ten points, yes!* "Finding and exposing the truth is the best way to protect Nadia and to give her something in return for the years she's given to me." Once Nadia got her share of FutureMove's assets, she could go to any school she wanted and start her own business doing whatever combination of makeup and meringues her heart desired.

I sent another ball up. *Thirty points!*

I shot a sideways peek at Manuel, who was staring at his hand and flipping a quarter around his fingers like a closet illusionist. I sent another ball. *Forty points.* I could not trust my safety to Dr. Clarke's whims, as Manuel suggested, but I was beginning to think I could trust Manuel to make tricky choices for Nadia's benefit. I could work with that.

"Hey, I'm only thirty points down now, sucker." I told Manuel.

"And one ball left," he pointed out. "I'm not giving you any more quarters."

I could go for the fifty-point ring at the top middle. If I didn't make it, I'd likely get forty or thirty and at least tie him. But I didn't want a tie, I played to win. I studied the rings with the highest scores. They were up in the corners and required looking at the whole game from a different angle. Like pinball, the best way to win wasn't always the most obvious. I hefted the ball and squatted down to choose the best route, then lined my ball up on a path other than the worn line up the center. I rolled it up at an angle and sank it like a Skee-Ball champion.

One hundred points.

"Nice shot, Zolotova," Manuel said. "Now tell me how you're going to dominate like that at the ETC."

I looked into his eyes, a shade or two lighter than Jaxon's and just as clear. I could do this, but not the way most people would, and not without his help.

"I know you have to keep your cover for your mysterious higher-ups. But is your cover more important than Nadia?"

"I'd choose my cover over *you*," he admitted. "But nothing is more important than Nadia."

"So I think we agree, protecting her means that whatever I tell you, it's for you, alone."

Manuel nodded. "Trust doesn't mean you have to tell everyone everything. It means that you trust they'll do the best they can with what they have."

I appreciated his definition, and it made me feel a little better about the off-center method I had in mind to ensure our success. I could trust Nadia without giving her undue informational burdens, just as the ASF had probably been right not to tell me right away what Dr. Clarke had done.

"Okay," I told him, and pointed my thumb at the score on the Skee-Ball machine. The unease in my stomach had transformed into hunger. "I win. You buy the nachos. We've got a plan to discuss."

⸻

I hadn't brought a jacket, but the morning chill felt amazing after the loud, stale arcade air. Planning session: complete. I wiped some nacho cheese off the corner of my mouth and covered my face as I entered the booth across the street. After a small errand across town, I ported near Atty's.

I ran the two blocks to her house, shopping bags bouncing in my hands. I pulled open Atty's front door, and Jaxon whirled around from where he'd been staring out the side window.

"Where have you been?"

"I had to pick up a couple of things. I didn't go near my apartment or the ETC building."

"Well the ETC came near here. I saw them exit the booth down the street on my ride back and had to make a detour and wait for them to leave again. By the time I got back here, I thought you'd be close. What was so important to pick up?"

"Supplies for the heist. Vittles. See?" I dug through one of the bags and tossed him a protein bar.

"Vittles? Did you bring some knapsacks and moonshine as well?"

"Dang it, forgot the moonshine. That would have made this much more fun." I ran past him into Kendi's room and rearranged my backpack. I returned with a small badge writer, my bootable Linux USB drive, and grabby hands. "You get the SD card?"

Jaxon nodded and reached two fingers into the coin pocket of his jeans. "Barely. I slipped in while they waited outside for Nadia, who'd said she'd gone to the bathroom. I saw her leave. She looked like she'd just biked around the city."

"Poor Nad! Maybe they'll let her take the rest of the day off if she blames it on the pie not sitting well."

"Let's hope." He pulled out the tiny card and held it between his first and second fingers. "I got it, but it wasn't easy. The Pie Plant is huge inside. I had to jog around looking for tables they hadn't fully cleared yet on a made-up quest to find the perfect bench seat, feeling the underside of each one." He grimaced. "You'd think a nice restaurant would have less gum."

"I'm sorry, and thank you!" I held the u sound as I raced over to Athena's laptop, turned it off and booted it from the USB. From there I had access to the drivers to code the badge number into my RFID ring. Goodbye booth card data, hello vault.

"What's next?" Jaxon leaned on the back of my chair.

A text came in from Nadia—a group selfie of her with Dr. Clarke and the new hire staring directly at the camera. She sent two, and I saved the one with the clearer image. She'd taken the photo in HD mode, bless her.

"Well," I said, "Nothing for you. Nadia sent me a picture for the iris scan and hid the card reader in the Pie Plant bathroom. I'm sure it made her nervous to carry that around. She's done, too. It's up to me and Kendi now. And Manuel."

"And who is picking up the card reader?"

"I'll get it once we're done."

"But what if someone finds and reports it before then? Did she wipe her fingerprints?"

"Probably not, but by the time anyone suspects anything or connects it to the ETC, this'll be over."

"Still, extra security would make it even harder for you, let alone Kendi, to get in or out, and you'd have to take Nadia with you. What if Dr. Clarke suspects her of being your mule for the card reader? I wouldn't risk leaving it there. I'll go get it."

"Okay, good point. Thanks, Jaxon. If you're sure you'll stay safe, it would be good to get the card reader out of the equation." And it would keep him away from the main action.

"I can do it." He peered into my eyes, and then grinned and blinked dark eyelashes, the length of which drove Nadia to jealousy.

"Well, well, a hidden talent!" I said. "I didn't know you could flutter your lashes. Lovely." I tried to do it, but probably looked as if I were trying to keep a contact lens from slipping around the back of my eyeball.

Jaxon laughed. "Okay, no. That'll be my thing. Your eyes don't need any help; they're beautiful as is."

Whoa, again with the beautiful. His statement was so blunt it hurt, but in a dull, achy way, like a massage therapist kneading deep tissue. The ache spread through my chest to my lips, yearning to close the distance we'd almost closed early this morning. I shut my eyes to clear my head.

I believed my plan would work; I'd come at it from several angles with Manuel. But here in real-time, the inherent risk shot through my mind like a flare gun, illuminating the ways I might get Jaxon locked up again.

"Don't do it," I said.

"What?"

"Don't go get my card reader. It's too dangerous."

"I thought we'd established that it wasn't."

"But, what if someone from the FutureMove lunch saw you pick up the SD card and is now watching for you? Or what if the restaurant staff stops you from going into the ladies' room due to your previous purchase-free bench testing? I'll get it later. Stay here. I'll share the vittles. Wait for me."

"It's fine, Aly, really."

"It might not be. If you want to take a risk, go do your interview, get your job. Stay away from here, where they know your also-beautiful-as-is face." There were a lot of variables to this plan, and I didn't want him to be one.

"Give me your phone."

I handed it to him. I saw him go to the university's website and click around. I let out the air I'd held captive in my anxious lungs.

He handed the phone back. "There. Now you can drop the interview topic."

"So what time did you get?"

"My own. I didn't sign up for an interview, but I did declare my major as Social Anthropology."

I opened my mouth, but he covered it softly with his warm hand. How would he afford the major he wanted without a work-study job or his parents' support?

"Hear me, please. I choose you, and I choose me. I do not choose to let you or my parents dictate what I do with my life." He moved his hand to my cheek. I was sure he could feel the heat radiating from my face. He half-grinned. "This is your fault, you know. You set your eyes on something, and you make it work. You only make a plan when it's absolutely necessary, and then you pull it off. No one can tell you what to do or how to be. I love that in you, and I want it for myself."

I took a breath, but it didn't feel like any of the air made its way inside my body.

I understood how Manuel could have lost his composure thinking about Nadia in danger. Jaxon was right about two things: he had definitely made his own choice, and if I failed and he got hurt, it would be my fault.

It was almost time for Nadia's break. She would video call to coach me through my makeup any minute. "Be careful. Don't trust anyone."

"Of course."

I tried another breath, but it hitched, and I coughed.

Jaxon rested his hands on my shoulders and gave a soft squeeze, which did not help my breathing in the slightest.

"Hey," he said. "You're going to be fine. I'm going to be fine. I'll bring the reader back here before we meet at the salon. Everything is going to be fine."

Famous last words.

Nadia's incoming video call startled me, and Jaxon let go. He mouthed the words, "I'll be back soon," and a tear slid down my right cheek. I'd set my plan in motion and there was no stopping now. I wiped it away before I answered the phone.

Nadia was speed-walking through the park—a regular break for her and an unsuspicious choice for a clandestine conversation. I saw the bare trees shrink away behind her as I carried the phone into Kendi's bathroom and snooped through her full gamut of beauty products, from soft pink blush to metallic green lipstick. I had to use her lightest concealer for my base, as her skin tone was several shades darker than mine, but Nadia guided me through a bold rouge in my cheeks and some fine lines in my forehead. She showed me how to make my lips look thinner and brow lower. I messed up the shading on my nose, but I wasn't going for vampire-level attractive this time.

Nadia slowed to a walk after a few more rounds of contouring. "Now step back and show me the mirror," she said.

I stepped back and held up the phone.

"You look amazing, you're welcome. But that's definitely still your hair," Nadia said.

I patted my voluminous curls.

"Can you find a scarf or something? Hurry, I've got to get back to work."

I traipsed to Kendi's bedroom. She had nothing in her closet suitable for a middle-aged woman. She didn't even have anything most people over fourteen would appreciate. I raided Atty's closet and put on a dark green pants suit. It looked like an unseasonable capri-pant on me, but it probably cost more than my entire wardrobe, so hopefully it would fly. I found a floral-patterned satin scarf, which I folded into a triangle and tied on to cover my unruly head. I jogged back to the bathroom and held up my phone for Nadia. I hardly believed the transformation. I looked at least thirty years older, but still more than presentable. Except for my botched nose job, I could only hope to age like the sophisticated woman in the mirror. I would definitely have to try this in my summons work.

"Tie the scarf in back, not under your chin like a babushka," Nadia said.

I tied two corners behind my head. "Now I look like a pirate. I think I prefer that people suspect I'm the type to carry hard candies, and not doubloons."

"Right, so keep the part covering your head, and twist the loose ends of the scarf into your hair and tuck it all up together like a low, loose bun. And stop grinning. Give me a pleasant neutral. Good, yes, fabulous. My job here is done."

I certainly hoped it was. She'd done a fantastic coaching job, and my whacked-out emotions threatened to ruin it with yet another round of tears. How could my body produce so much saltwater, and what was the point of making my face wet when I felt emotion? I had to get a handle on this, focus on the job.

"Very good," I told Nadia, shooting for emotionless professionalism to force away the feels. "Radio silence." I hung up. I transferred supplies—my phone, some snacks, lockpicks, et. cetera—from my backpack to a roomy, cross-body bag from Atty's room and walked to the nearest port booth. Thanks to my Doris Boon summons, I still had enough to port myself to FutureMove without a booth card.

I sent Kendi a quick text saying, "prepare to release the kraken," engaged the port booth door, squeezed the bag to my chest and pushed *go*.

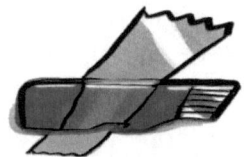

CHAPTER TWENTY-SIX

ManBun Strikes Again

I STEPPED OUT OF the port booth in front of the FutureMove building, blinking in the bright sun as if I'd tunneled my way out of a penitentiary. The sun burned brighter and hotter than was quite proper for an autumn day, and the gilding up the walls of the building shone reflections into my eyes.

I wasn't nervous; the gurgling in my stomach was the effect of forgetting to eat a protein bar. I lifted my chin, adjusted Atty's scarf, and pushed Kendi's biggest sunglasses up my nose. I took long, purposeful strides, attempting to carry myself the way Atty did. I hadn't considered how my gray sneakers clashed with the suit, and hoped the rest of my getup would convince people that it was a hip fashion choice.

I waited until I saw a group of employees heading into the building and caught up, matching my pace with theirs to tailgate in with the herd. I didn't even glance toward reception. Nadia would recognize me regardless. If I acted like I belonged and did this every day, the guard wouldn't ask me to register as a visitor. I walked past the front desk, avoided eye contact with that holier-than-thou Galileo, and social-engineered my way onto the elevator as someone else stepped off.

I sent a quick text to Kendi. "Now." *Come on, Tater Tot. Show us what you're made of.*

A hand appeared in the elevator, stopping the door from closing, just as I was considering what good timing I'd had. A whole gaggle of employees pushed into the elevator with me. Apparently these ones worked on another floor. Great. They were too busy gabbing at one another to notice me, but when the elevator stopped at the third-floor labs, I was caught in the herd and exited with them. I had a key in Atty's cross-body satchel with my lock picks that would put the elevator in maintenance mode and allow me to take it to the restricted top floor, but I couldn't very well sneak it out in a crowd.

I let the lab workers flow around me and shuffle out of the hallway, and then one of them returned to the elevator. *Stairs it is, then.* I jogged down to the stairwell door and heaved it open. How long would it take to get Dr. Clarke out of his office and down into the lab? I sat on a step and heard someone enter the stairwell from the floor above me. I held my phone to my ear and faced the wall, pretending to be in a riveting phone conversation.

"Mm-hmm. Yes, the upgrade."

Descending footfalls.

"The whole server, in the redundant racks."

A tap on my shoulder. "Alyona."

I let my phone drop and unclenched my other fist. "Manuel! You scared the crap out of me."

"I got the call; they've found a squirrel in the first-floor hardware lab."

"Great! So far, so—"

"Dr. Clarke told me to handle it, so it's still got to escalate. I'll see if I can get the squirrel riled up, but I am not happy we're using an innocent animal this way."

"Good luck," I said. "Maybe he'll remember the way you kept him in a dark cage all alone."

"For his rehab," he sighed as he pushed open the door and jogged out. I took the stairs up to the top floor, then waited a little longer in the stairwell to give Manuel some time. He would try to text when it was clear upstairs, but he might not have a covert moment.

Precious minutes ticked past without a word. I hoped Tater Tot went full wolverine soon so Dr. Clarke would leave his post.

I startled as the intercom came on, not with a pleasant announcement voice, but with Kendi's voice, angry and demanding. "Get down here, Shane Clarke." She had taken matters into her own bedazzled, yet unflinching hands. "I'm not going anywhere with this security lackey of yours. You're going to pay for what you did to Melanie, and everyone will know what happened to the Zolotovs." There was a furious chattering and then an "Ow!" from someone who sounded like Manuel, and the speaker clicked off.

I wiped a bead of sweat away from Atty's silk scarf on my head and leaned against the stairwell wall. I'd known Kendi was done playing around, and I was going to have to take her with me when I got out of here. She was trusting me with no less than her freedom and possibly her life, and whether or not I found enough to take Dr. Clarke down, I couldn't leave her here.

The intercom clicked on again. "All visitors, please report to the lobby immediately. Personnel, remain in place." Lockdown. I waited ten more seconds, then used my copy of Dr. Clarke's badge to unlock the door from the stairwell and dashed into the gleaming top-floor hallway. I crept toward Dr. Clarke's office and heard pacing, so I jumped into the conference room and hid behind the door. His muffled phone conversation seeped through the walls while he yelled things like, "—catch her yet?" and, "I'm coming," and "—not let her leave."

It sounded like he finally left his office after that, and I gave him plenty of time to get into the elevator before I sneaked back out into the hall. I was so close to getting what we needed. If Kendi got away, I could leave even faster. She'd have to lie low, but they wouldn't know I—or Nadia or Jaxon for that matter—had been involved in today's adventure until it was too late. I had to get into the vault, grab the drive, and get into the elevator before he returned.

I sped to the vault door down the hall, my sneakers slipping on the polished floor. I didn't bother hiding my face from the cameras. I'd be long gone before anyone checked the footage. The vault monitor on the wall above the pin pad was dark. Numbers appeared on the pin pad next to the door with a tap of Dr. Clarke's badge. I entered the first zero and ran the other numbers through my head: Eight, Six, and One. I knew it ended in zero, which left six possible combinations for the five-digit code. I should have come up with some plausible guesses before this moment, but I had at least a fifty-percent chance before it locked me out.

I searched my mind for something significant that might have happened in 2010, 1980, or 1960, since the vast majority of numerical pins were dates. Not anyone's birthday in my family, but Dr. Clark could have been born in 1980. I tried 01680. *Nothing.* Not a January baby, then. I typed in 06180. *Nope.* He wasn't born in September, either, even if he wrote the day first, like my parents.

I considered 2010. Twenty years ago. *FutureMove's founding date?* I thought of the picture of my parents and Dr. Clarke at the ribbon cutting for the building. Dr. Clarke wore a suit, but Mom and Dad were in short sleeves. I tried 06810. *Bam, success.*

I held up my phone for the iris scan, and Nadia's photo passed beautifully.

Last, I tackled the dial lock on the front of the door itself. Turning my hearing aids all the way up, I pressed my ear against the door and listened for the faint clicks and drops that indicated the correct positions on the dial. I'd practiced with this dial as a kid and not only knew its particular sounds, but I could feel the tiny differences in tension when I hit a winning number. After a few dragging minutes and four tries, I got the door open.

"Welcome, Dr. Clarke," I whispered under my breath in a robotic voice. The door slid back, and I stepped into the vault, which was lit up inside. Someone had taped a piece of black paper over the camera lens inside the vault, blocking the monitor that showed the hall outside. And someone had tied Jaxon to the clear plastic desk chair.

"Jax!" I rushed over to him and unwound the extension cord used to bind his hands behind him. "What happened? How are you here?"

"It was Manuel and a couple of his henchmen! I went back to get your badge reader—he betrayed us!"

I balled my fists. "I told you not to go. I—"

"Well, I went, and he caught me and ported me to FutureMove."

I pried my hands open and tried to slow my heartbeat. I reminded myself that I had a plan. "I'm so sorry. I tried to avoid this, but things don't seem to be going the easy way today. I can still get you out."

"I know you can. I have been sitting here for what feels like an hour, but was probably less, telling myself you can do this—that you were almost here, and I would be able to leave the same way you do. I'm so glad it was you coming through that door." Jaxon stood and wrapped his long arms around me, and then leaned away. "But what do you mean, you tried to avoid this?"

I let some air out between my teeth. "I thought you should stay at Atty's, stay low until I had the files. It would have been simpler."

"Again, I feel like you know something you're not telling me."

"You know me, I am full of creative solutions." Nothing wrong with that. It wasn't lying, and it wasn't that I didn't trust him, or Kendi, or Nadia. I had honestly hoped the squirrel would work, Kendi would be gone, no one would know I'd ever been here, and Jaxon would be waiting at the salon. But it hadn't worked out the easy way. Jaxon was here. Dr. Clarke knew something was going down, and if he found out what, Exhibit A Beauty would no longer be a good rendezvous option. "I love you all too much not to have a backup plan."

He stepped away, increasing the space between us. "And this backup plan involves us escaping with the data, correct?"

"Of course. It's going great. Don't worry." I was freaking out enough for the both of us on the inside. It was one thing to perform a daring escape as the hero of my own fantasy, but it was another to see it happening up close and personal with people to save and a dwindling margin of error.

I crossed over to the shelves and found Jaxon's phone. It was completely dead, but I ripped the plastic bag off and threw it back on the shelf, ruining Dr. Clarke's perfectly organized aesthetic. Then I squatted at the desk and pulled Atty's cross-body satchel to the front. I opened the satchel's flap and made a nest for the drive among the vittles I'd packed. I swept my gaze down the row of pulsing lights to find the unplugged drive, but all of them were lit. All six.

My stomach dropped and bounced on the floor, and I fought back a wave of nausea. *Oh, no.* Last time I'd stuck my snooping head under this desk, I'd counted seven drives. I inhaled through my teeth and eased my breath back out. I'd been wrong, that's all. I'd miscounted. There was no way I could have gone to all of this trouble, all of this risk, to fail now. The drive was the entire point of the heist.

"Got it?" said Jaxon, inching toward the open vault door.

"Just about," I said. I couldn't outrun any potential snags in our exit from the building carrying all six drives, but it would be quick enough to find the one I'd explored before. I wiggled the mouse and hovered over the chair, too tense to sit. The monitor came to life. I clicked down the tidy row of icons representing the numerically sequential drives. Drives one through four were a bust. The next drive was labeled Backup_Drive_6, followed by Backup_Drive_7.

"Nononononoooo," I whispered. Dr. Clarke had removed Backup_Drive_5 from the vault. My heart strained up toward my throat, threatening to cut off my air. I wrestled the panic back under control and clicked on drives six and seven for good measure, but I knew I wouldn't find the files we'd come for.

Jaxon hung a hand on the vault doorway, keeping a part of him free, and leaned toward the desk. "Is this something we can research more at home? Or at the library? We should probably—"

"It's not here."

"Wait, what? What do you—"

I accidentally knocked the chair over as I straightened and winced at the ruckus. "It's not here, Jax." I whirled toward the shelves and raked my eyes across every surface. But Dr. Clarke wouldn't have removed it from under the desk just to leave it in the vault. "His office. He most likely stashed it there." My throat constricted. *Please, please, please let it be there.* I'd make it be there, the way Nadia used to try to make good things happen for us during her "manifestation" phase.

Dark speckles had already begun to obscure my periphery, so I closed my eyes and visualized the drive hiding under a stack of papers in Dr. Clarke's desk drawer. I forced my lungs full and held the air inside for a count of five to steady my voice. "I'll text Kendi, make sure she got out. We'll run to the office, grab the drive, and port to the basement through the elevator."

I sent a text and eyed the stacks of gold and silver bars in the case by the desk. I couldn't bring them with me through the elevator port booth, but if we ended up leaving a different way, I'd take a souvenir.

Jaxon stepped closer. "Aly, breathe. We can figure out the drive later, right now we need to focus on getting—"

An incoming-text notification dinged from the hall outside the vault.

Jaxon grabbed my arm and pulled me to the side of the door, flattening himself along the curved inner egg-wall. A few sets of footsteps sounded in my hearing aids, headed straight toward us.

Manuel marched forward holding Kendi's arms behind her with one hand and towing a sobbing Nadia by the wrist with his other.

CHAPTER TWENTY-SEVEN

Powerless

Manuel dragged Kendi and Nadia into the vault and then plucked the service weapon off of his belt. His arm pointed the gun toward the floor in our direction, but his eyes stared blankly ahead. "I'm going to shut the vault door now and take executive control. You won't be able to open it from the inside."

"Manny, wait!" said Nadia, dabbing her eyes with the inside of her sweater sleeve. "There's still time. You could let us go. Let us get to the elevator and we'll leave."

I put my arm around her narrow torso and squeezed. "It's going to be okay, Nadia." She'd be okay, even if I wouldn't. I'd put all of us in this horrible situation and then completely bungled the thing. I might never trust myself again, but I wouldn't give up until Nadia, Jaxon, and Kendi were safe.

Manuel raised his gun to just over our heads and widened his stance.

I glared at him and side hugged Nadia. "He's got to do this. It's his job." I'd failed my part, but if he kept his cover, he could still help us find the data.

"But, why?" Nadia's head dropped into her hands and her

shoulders shook, and she forgot about being careful of her mascara.

Manuel waved us farther into the vault until we all cleared the doorway. Then he backed up to the control panel and didn't even look at us as he tapped the keypad and scanned his badge. The door slid shut between us.

Nadia ran over and tore the black piece of paper away from the camera and monitor. "Manny! Can you hear me? Why would you do this? I thought—" She sobbed again, despairing and heartbroken.

I had to turn away. I tried to focus on the shallow fact that as her mascara ran, she looked now more than ever like Baba Yaga, the forest witch. My heart hurt to see her that way, but she would understand soon.

The monitor showed Manuel looking down the hall, and then at his watch. His stony face hadn't faltered since he'd locked up the supposed love of his life. He was good. Or, he was really bad.

"Manuel," said Nadia. The voice was so soft, I had to look and make sure it was her. She asked for him like the caged leader of a besieged city asking for water. "Please."

Her plea blurred my vision, and I just stood there empty-handed, doubting everything. What was I thinking? How had I convinced anyone to go along with this? The information on that drive justified every risk I'd convinced everyone I loved to take. They had played their parts perfectly and trusted me to complete this one, simple piece. Pick up the drive and leave. But no.

I shrank away from the monitor. I was the weak link. Because of my overconfidence, Kendi was captured, Jaxon was scared, and my sister was hurting, all for nothing. What else had I overlooked?

Manuel's mouth stayed flat and still, but his eyes glistened in the hallway's fluorescent lights. Apparently there was a mic inside the vault with the camera and monitor, and he'd heard Nadia's message. He reached for his badge, tucked into the large shirt pocket over his heart on a retractable lanyard, and glanced again toward the elevators. He looked as if he were considering letting us out, calculating the risk.

Kendi noticed, too, and spoke up. "We could make it look like an ambush. There are four of us; it wouldn't be hard to believe. I can punch you hard enough to make it look real."

Nadia sobbed again.

Jaxon righted the chair and yanked open the top drawer of a low filing cabinet next to the desk, mumbling as he rifled through paperwork. "Got to be an owner's guide . . ."

If a user's guide to the vault existed, Dr. Clarke would have it highlighted and annotated in its own labeled manila folder. I hoped it did exist and had enough diagrams and appendices to keep Jaxon feeling optimistic.

Manuel tugged his badge halfway free. Dr. Clarke could arrive any second. It was now or never. I couldn't let Manuel fail, too.

"Manuel," I said, demanding his attention. "Think about what you're doing."

"Where would you go?" he said in a flat, defeated tone. "The building is totally surrounded."

"I trusted you to think about what's best for Nadia."

Manuel set his jaw and pushed his badge back into his shirt pocket.

More footsteps sounded from the elevators, and Dr. Clarke came into view of the monitor. "All of them?" he asked, peering into the monitor on his side of the vault wall.

Manuel nodded. "Sir."

"Listen carefully," Dr. Clarke said. "I need you all to place your phones on the floor in front of the door, and then line up against the back wall. I will open the door, and Manuel will pick them up. We need to have a little discussion before I let this nonsense continue."

Everyone in the vault looked at me, as if I were a competent leader. Nadia and Kendi still thought I had the situation under control. My pulse thunked behind my sternum. I might not have what we came for, but they still needed me to get them out of here. I couldn't afford to let them down any further. I nodded to myself, and then again to my crew.

We placed our phones gently on the polished white floor and backed up. I hated to part from mine, but I wouldn't need it to escape. Jaxon went back to his paperwork, and I inched toward the left side of the room, where Manuel had stashed the port unit he'd confiscated from Jax and I.

The door slid open. Manuel scooped up the phones.

"And Alyona," said Dr. Clarke. "your purse, please."

I set Atty's satchel on the ground and stepped back. Manuel opened it and pulled out the Gooseberry.

"It's not a functional phone, it's just one of my tinkering projects."

Manuel flipped the Gooseberry over. The back of the phone case hadn't fit over my modifications, so the components were open to his view. He stuck his thumb nail under the edge of the flat battery and popped it out of place. "I'll hold on to the battery. This relic of a phone is useless without power." He dropped the rest of my remote device back into the satchel, set it down, and backed out of the vault.

There went my remote. Fine. I could still get us all safe once we could port, I'd just have to enter the settings into the unit itself.

None of us moved, but I shielded the unit from Dr. Clarke's view with my body.

Dr. Clarke glared at me. "I'm disappointed, Alyona.

Attempted robbery is poor repayment for my openness with you. I need to gather my thoughts, but I'm sure we'll come to an understanding, and then I can let you go, along with your sister and poor Jaxon, the innocents you've dragged into your misguided battle."

"And Kendi?"

"I have more to discuss with Ms. Carleson, which doesn't concern you."

"We're not leaving without her."

Dr. Clarke sighed and tapped the control pad outside the vault. The door slid closed. I heard Dr. Clarke's voice from the speakers inside the vault, but the outside mic wasn't picking up enough to hear much as he and Manuel walked away. "Be ready . . . ends today . . ."

Kendi kicked the wall and let out a hitching yell. She rounded on me, fists clenched. "What's your plan now, genius?"

I flinched but said nothing.

Nadia hugged herself and paced across the room, which felt much smaller with four people trapped inside.

Jaxon turned to face me. "She's got backup plans. Right, Aly?"

I couldn't meet his eye. I didn't know how to face the people I had told to trust me, then knowingly kept things from, and all for a heaping pile of nothing. I turned away from him and retrieved the port unit. The screen glowed to life after some tapping, and everyone crowded closer to watch.

The speaker squealed, and I startled, nearly dropping the unit.

Dr. Clarke barked into the microphone. "What is that unit doing in there? Hands off. Do not touch anything." The hallway still appeared vacant on the vault monitor, so he must have picked up the video feed in his office.

Kendi rushed to retrieve the black paper from where Nadia had tossed it. I looked into the camera and showed Dr. Clarke my middle finger before she taped it into place.

I proceeded deeper into the root settings of the port unit.

"Alyona, that unit is useless to you in there." Dr. Clarke didn't sound entirely convinced. "Put it down at once. I'm sending Manuel back to pick it up now, and if you give him any trouble, I'll have him move you to your own cell," Dr. Clarke warned.

"Jax," I said, "check the panel by the door. See if there's a lock button on the inside." I couldn't have anyone barging in and ruining another phase of my plan.

"Hold on." Jaxon flipped to the front of a thick booklet he'd found and ran his finger down the table of contents. "Mm-hmm." He licked a fingertip and leafed through a few pages in the middle, then tapped on a printed chart. Folding the booklet open, he carried it to the panel and punched in a series of numbers and arrow keys, and it made a low buzzing beep. "Safe Room Mode: Activated."

Manuel came jogging into the hallway.

"So, they're locked out?"

Jaxon nodded. "We can't override his lockdown command, but the Safe Room feature means he can't override our internal locks either." He leaned into the chair, lifting his chin and one eyebrow. "And *that's* why you read the manual."

I relaxed my shoulders. I had time to think and do this part right. No more failures. I could have kissed Jaxon, self-righteous nerdiness and all.

Dr. Clarke blared over the speaker. "Please, Alyona. Between the tungsten inside the walls and the gold on the outside, you'll be ripped to shreds if you attempt to port. After all I've done to protect you girls, please don't make the same mistake as your parents."

My vision darkened and the unit shook in my hands. He probably wouldn't mind at all if I left that way. Though maybe seeing Nadia go like Mom might give him pause.

Kendi came close again. "You know that's true, right? You can't port out of this vault." She leaned in and whispered, "Unless you figured out the density settings, but even if you did, you told me yourself it would take some serious testing before you did anything that stupid."

Dr. Clarke came on again. "Alyona, listen to your poorly chosen company. There's no way out until I say so. My superiors trust me to keep you in check. You're not doing yourself any favors by undermining my attempts."

I ignored him.

"I'm coming down there. Don't try anything. I'm begging you."

Everyone stared at me again. I could feel them willing me to reveal my brilliant plan to save us all.

I ignored them, too. I'd get them out, but my plan lost its brilliance when I'd botched the main objective. I patted the satchel still hanging across my body, jostling the vittles—gifts I'd brought to add celebratory flair to my big finale. Maybe I could still hand them out as consolation prizes.

I pulled Atty's satchel to my front and opened the flap. "Bad news first. The drive's gone. We'll have to find another way to prove Kendi's innocence and Dr. Clarke's involvement."

Kendi shook her head and opened her mouth to respond, but I cut her off.

"The good news," I said, frowning, "is that I have a present for each of you." I pulled out a tube of cotton candy lip gloss and handed it to Nadia. "Your favorite flavor. You might need it for the dry air." I retrieved a pack of Ichi Ban Chewies and tossed it to Kendi. I'd seen the wrappers in her room. "For the trip," I said, my tone flatter than the lap of an overworked mall Santa.

Kendi stared at me like I had failed a third-grade math quiz. "Really? You get us caught, locked up with nothing to show for it, and you're doling out gifts like you're executing your last will? You have got to be—"

"And," I shouted over her, closing my eyes to keep the panic at bay, "Jaxon, this is for you." I pulled out the geektastic book from the pawn shop. The one with the gilded pages.

Jaxon took the book from my hand and his lips parted. He turned it over and ran his finger along the gold-embossed spine. "How did you get this? And when?"

"It was essential vittles. I'd hidden it in the pawn shop before we left so no one would buy it, and I returned and . . . acquired it. I know you like books more than food." I shrugged.

Jaxon met my eye and his face filled with a broad smile. He'd guessed what the book meant, besides my ever-growing affection for him.

I had ported gold.

His smile vanished when he realized it also meant that I'd been conducting experiments behind his back. "I thought we agreed it was dangerous to gallivant around town."

All four of us jumped when Dr. Clarke's voice shouted through the speakers. "Jaxon Jeong, if you care for Alyona at all, you will open this door, now," he said through gritted teeth. "What would your parents think? What will your new school's admissions office think of the criminal record you'll have if you don't cooperate?"

Jaxon lowered his voice and leaned in close, paying no mind to Dr. Clarke. "You could have been caught," he whisper-yelled, like a referee with tonsillitis. "How long did it take you, standing there in an ETC booth, to configure a new port unit with such complicated settings?" He was still more concerned with my safety than the fact that I'd given us a way out.

"Not much time at all, just long enough to program the port unit to connect with my Gooseberry remote. Your idea by the way. More or less."

Manuel joined Dr. Clarke in the monitor's field of view.

"Manuel, call up a few guards. Once we get this door open, we'll need to get a firm handle on all of them." Beeping from the number pad on the outside wall sounded through the speakers.

"Sir, what about the port unit? If they do find an unorthodox or highly classified use for it, is that something you're willing to have my guys witness?"

Dr. Clarke closed his eyes and pinched the bridge of his nose. "Fine. Yes. We just need to get *inside*." The vault wall shuddered with a muffled thud, probably Dr. Clarke's patent leather dress shoe connecting with the door.

"Anyway," I said, turning back to Jaxon, "I configured the rest through my remote, and luckily for your limited-edition hardcover, the book ported safely from the booth to Atty's doorstep." I wasn't whispering anymore. I didn't care what Dr. Clarke heard. I may have underestimated him by failing to consider that he might move the drive, but he couldn't stop me like he stopped my parents.

Kendi looked at the book, and then the port unit. "You ported gold?"

Nadia gasped. "Alyona! You did it? You beautiful little mess."

Dr. Clarke paced in front of the monitor. "Manuel, we have a reciprocating saw in the basement. Bring it here as quickly as you can."

"I don't recall—"

"Now!"

Kendi watched as Manuel ran to the elevator, then she looked at me. "So, why not simply port in and out of the vault yourself and grab what you need?"

"Because, as you reminded me, I'm not stupid enough to try that without significant testing. My tests so far consist of one book. And if I'd survived testing it on myself like that first, Jaxon would have killed me anyway."

Jaxon nodded in agreement.

"Sure," I said, "a gilded book is impressive, but it's not human." Books couldn't die an excruciating death at the hand of someone they trusted. I shook my head. "It wasn't worth the risk if I could make this work any other way."

Dr. Clark pounded on the door. "Please," he said, voice wavering, more desperate than threatening now. "You must believe me. Everything I do is for you and Nadia. My superiors wanted your father stopped. He was about to release dangerous technology to the world at large, unleashing chaos in the name of science."

I glared at the monitor. "You leave my dad—"

"He wouldn't listen, Alyona, and they were going to make him. They would have used Nadia to make their point, and—"

"*Stop!*" I yelled. "You're a liar and a murderer. My dad wasn't releasing anything, just testing it. And besides, you can't stop the progression of science just because you like the status quo. The ETC overseers might be annoying, but they aren't the Mafia."

"And you're overconfident. If you were as smart as you think you are, you'd have escaped by now. Your plan failed. Mine, too. I couldn't keep the Zolotovs under control. But we can still salvage this for both of us. Give me the unit. Never speak of this tech again. We can draft a non-disclosure agreement, and all of this can just go away. I will drop all investigations into everyone involved. We can all go about our business in peace."

I smiled at his pathetic attempt to bargain, and then confirmed the final port unit settings with a few taps. *Done.* The last step was to program a destination. Good thing I had a head for memorizing numbers. "Nah. I think we'll just head out now."

Manuel jogged into view holding out a hand saw. "I couldn't find any power saws."

Dr. Clark pulled the saw from Manuel's grip and flung it against the wall. "Worthless." He dived at Manuel and yanked the service pistol from his holster.

"Sir, no—"

Dr. Clarke aimed the pistol at the control panel and squeezed the trigger. The monitor showed static, but we heard the gunshot through the wall, which was still wholly intact.

The door didn't budge.

I turned my attention back to the port unit and tapped the screen, but this time, it stayed dark. *No!* I tapped some more, but nothing.

Jaxon and I couldn't have used all of the backup power while we'd been testing earlier, but the unit was dead. I stopped breathing.

"Power," I said to the room. "Find me power."

Jaxon scooted his chair out and pointed under the desk. "Here!"

I crawled underneath and jerked the power cable away from the drives' docking station. "Kendi, I need—"

The speakers crackled as Dr. Clarke's voice thundered out. "It's too late for Kendi. You made your choice for all of them." He must have made it back to his office to try more vault settings from there. "You weren't smart or sneaky when you used to steal power from the ETC, and you're not smart or sneaky now. I too can steal power. I hate to do it, but for all of our sakes, I cannot let you leave with that port unit."

The microphone picked up Manuel's voice in the background. "Turning off power in the vault will trigger the vault's fire suppression system. They'll be stuck inside while—"

Dr. Clarke's voice came back, calm and monotone, and dead as the port unit's unresponsive screen. "While the vault's externally powered vacuum system removes the oxygen. They'll suffocate. Wonderful fire protection, tragic for the would-be thieves trapped inside. The police won't have a hard time believing we'd found you too late. We hadn't expected a break-in, after all."

"You can't do this," Manuel protested.

"All they have to do is agree to let this power trip go. I'm making the choice simple. Unlock the door, leave the unit behind, and let's end this nonsense for good."

Kendi growled toward the speakers. "My aunt will hunt you down if you lay a finger on us. Your bosses will be the least of your trouble. She will destroy you."

"There's something about the vacuum in here somewhere," Jaxon muttered to himself, picking up the owner's guide.

Nadia glared into the camera. "You wouldn't, Dr. Clarke. You said we were family."

"You *are* family, so stop your sister. She's making a deadly mistake. If she doesn't kill you all with untested tech, my superiors will."

I pushed the power cable into the unit's charging port and the screen waxed bright again, then flickered. I needed steady hands to hold the cord in place. "Help me attach this cable," I said, nodding at Kendi. "Squeeze in, everyone." I would set the port radius wide enough to pick up all of us, but I didn't trust the AI enough to risk taking too much of the ceiling and have it crush us when we landed. A chill ran up the back of my neck, despite the three warm bodies huddled close to mine.

What if I was wrong?

What if I *was* about to kill us all with my overconfidence? What if I felled us like trees, or sliced us like that poor earthworm? Dr. Clarke had known about my power-stealing, but he hadn't stopped me. Maybe he *had* been trying to protect me. Maybe I should listen to him now. He said he'd tried to stop my parents, and here he was, trying to stop me.

Nadia put her arm around my shoulders.

I blew out a quick breath. *No.* I couldn't let Dr. Clarke freak me out. No one in the room trusted the deal he was trying to force us into. I tapped my way into the port unit's destination settings.

"You—" Dr. Clarke's voice caught, and he stuttered over the speaker. As if he had even one byte of feeling. "You've left me no choice."

With a loud click, the port unit's small screen snuffed out, along with every light in the vault.

CHAPTER TWENTY-EIGHT

Between Tungsten and Gold

A SLOW HISSING BROKE the brief silence, amplified by the absolute darkness of the windowless, powerless vault. Probably the vacuum, already sucking our life-breath out of the small oval room.

"Power," I said again. But I was powerless. Powerless to achieve the basic objective of this whole scheme. Powerless to start the unit, powerless to save my friends.

Nadia whimpered and shuffled until I felt her hand on my arm. She felt for my elbow and wove her arm into mine.

Secretly stealing power was something I'd always thought I was so good at, but Dr. Clarke had known all along. He was right. I wasn't smart or sneaky. I was pathetic. "Maybe we should think about doing what he—," I said, more to myself than to Nadia.

"We *will* find power," Jaxon said. Loyal to the end. "We have time, I think. I was looking up the suppression system when the lights cut, but I'm pretty sure they'd design it to leave enough oxygen for human life."

Pretty sure? Even if he was right, would there be enough

air for all four of us? And for how long? I was *pretty sure* I wouldn't kill him by teleporting through dense metals, but since when was that good enough? It wasn't, and it had taken complete darkness for me to finally see that.

Kendi wasn't so quick to jump on board. "For all your planning, you didn't consider this possibility?"

Nadia squeezed my arm. None of them wanted to believe I had failed them so miserably. But their trust in me had been unfounded from the start. I tried to sound confident, but my voice wavered. "I thought about power, but the unit's emergency bank should have lasted at least a couple of days. And again, this wasn't my ideal scenario for the day, but once plan A derailed with you throwing yourself into Dr. Clarke's crosshairs, the easy, incognito plan flew out the window. Getting all of us caught together was the only way to get all of us *out* together." I swayed, strangely dizzy without any visual frame of reference. Nadia took my hand and lowered us both to sit on the floor.

I sat for a beat in silence, and then someone's shoe squeaked. Kendi took a sharp breath in. "So, what you're telling me is that you kept a gigantic secret plan from us. You told us one version—used our strengths to get what you needed, and then you shifted plans and tricked us into getting caught. You got us locked in this death trap together on purpose."

I felt sick and tried to swallow. I did not want to barf in the dark.

Jaxon and Nadia came to my defense at the same time, Jaxon with justifications and Nadia trying to tell Kendi I'd never do that.

"But she would," Kendi said, "and she did. And it's genius." Her voice lifted and lightened. Probably laughing so she wouldn't cry.

"I *did* tell Jaxon to stay home. I thought maybe he could

meet us at the salon if everything worked out simply. I hoped you and Tater Tot would get away, and if Manuel hadn't brought Nadia up, I'd have told her to go home sick. Jax could have run if all else failed."

I turned to where I imagined Jaxon still sat at the desk. "But Jax, some FutureMove busybody spotted you at the Pie Plant. Manuel had no choice but to bring you in. I wanted to beg him to let you escape and get far away, but I wanted even more to respect your will. You chose to go get the card reader, and I figured you'd choose to be with me, whether or not we got out. So I had Manuel bring you here."

My pulse felt like it paused for a long moment in the silent darkness.

Jaxon's voice came thick with emotion. "Thank you, Ali. I'm glad you finally understand my priorities."

My heartbeat resumed and warmth rushed through my veins. I'd choose to run to him over running to safety every time, and I knew now that he'd choose me, too.

"T.T. made it back out the window," Kendi said, "but Shane wouldn't have let Nadia leave during a lockdown. I'm glad Jaxon didn't listen when you told him to stay home. This is the best way. The only way." I heard her patting her hands along the shelves. "If we had known your plan, we might have given something away. We had to react genuinely to being caught and thrown into the vault." She rifled through crinkling plastic bags and pushed papers around. "None of us are as terrible as you under pressure, but we're not actors, and an unconvincing performance would have tipped Shane off. It had to be like this. And we need to find you some power."

I breathed as slowly as I could, partially for fear of the low air supply, but mostly so no one would hear the emotion clogging my throat. Tears fell down my face. Could people with good ears hear them drip onto the floor? Kendi knew the truth, and she didn't hate me, not even for a second. She trusted my judgment.

Someone's clothing rustled. "At the apartment, Manuel took the port unit," Jaxon said. "Was that staged? Was it just part of your plan? I was really worried."

"No, Jax, I was scared, too." So much for hiding how choked up I was. I wanted to touch his arm, but I was afraid to flap my hand around and possibly poke him in the eye. "But when Manuel told me where he was going to store it, I knew he was on our side. And I knew where I needed to end up."

Nadia spoke next. "So, he was in on this? He was pretending?" She squeaked as she sucked in some of our limited air. "Is he going to be okay?" She dropped her voice to a whisper. "Can Dr. Clarke still hear us? Why couldn't you get Manny locked in here with us, too?"

Typical Nadia to immediately forgive and start worrying about him. "There's no power to the vault," I said. "So there's no audio, unless it's wired in from a separate circuit." With a possible electrical current I could use. I scooted along the floor until I felt the legs of the case holding the FutureMove metal bars, and then felt my way up the wall to where the mic was, looking for seams or bolts as I answered Nadia. "He and Dr. Clarke both have ETC bosses, but they're clearly on opposite sides of the moral spectrum. He chose to keep his cover and stay in the fight." Nothing helpful along the wall. I didn't have Kendi's sturdy knife or my crowbar, so even in the unlikely chance that the mic was hot, there was no way to get to the power.

"Power, you guys. Let's go." Kendi made more sorting noises along the shelves. "Sometimes there can be residual power in the supplies for something like the desktop, or the drives plugged in underneath," she said.

Nadia brushed my arm with her fingertips, and then grabbed on. "Will that work, Alyon?"

"No." The port unit didn't need a lot of power, but it would need more than the phantom charge left in a disconnected power brick. "That won't be enough." I didn't have the power I thought I did. I wasn't enough. I was a mere ghost of my parents' brilliance, lacking the true substance I needed to pull this off.

I tried to take a calming breath, but the air didn't seem to make it down my throat. I doubted Jaxon's theory about the vacuum system leaving sufficient oxygen. We had to calm down and stop breathing so heavily. Maybe Manuel could figure out a way to free us and still keep his cover.

"Everyone, just sit down and breathe slowly. We can wait this out." I sat on the floor and put my head in my hands.

"We'll find power," Jaxon said.

"No giving up at this point," Kendi said. "You said you ported gold, and I believe you. Check the mouse and keyboard."

My heart sank the short distance to the cold floor. I'd really done a number on my friends for them to still have faith in me. "They're wired," I sobbed. No point in hiding my weakness at this point. The overwhelming darkness illuminated my impotence. "How could I forget to account for something so fundamental as electricity? The drive isn't even *here*! Who knows what else I've missed. I could be wrong about everything."

"You're not wrong," said Nadia. She pulled me into her and rubbed my back. "And neither were Mom and Dad. You are every bit as smart as they are. It will all be okay."

"How can you say that? You're always saying things will work out, but you can't possibly know. We're a little past hollow promises."

"You told me everything would be okay when the love of my life had a gun pointed in my direction."

"Yeah, because I had a plan. I *knew* things would be okay with Manuel."

"And are they?"

I stopped. I didn't know anymore. My plan lay in shambles. "Probably not, or he'd be getting us out of this tomb. I guess my promise was empty, too."

"It wasn't empty. You believed it would work out, and that belief allowed you to move forward. It's not empty now, either. And I don't make hollow promises. I choose to believe, and that choice gives me the power to keep going. Faith is always a choice, even when you think you know what you're doing. We can never know the future, but you can choose faith now."

I knew she meant faith in Mom and Dad.

I attempted another deep breath, tried to clear my mind and force myself to come up with a different solution. Either the air was already too thin, or the task I faced made me dizzy.

I thought trusting Manuel would be the hardest task today. But that was before every piece of my careful plan had blown up in my face. If we found a way to power the port unit, I'd have to trust one more time, I'd have to open myself up to the worst pain I'd ever felt. I'd have to put my life, and the lives of everyone in the vault, everyone I loved, into the absent hands of my parents, the two people whose loss had sliced gashes into my soul.

It was easier to be bitter, to harbor anger for my parents after they left me, to build a dam out of heavy blocks of blame. If their technology had always worked, there was nothing holding back the reservoir of deep despair. It would spill over, and what would happen to me? I could drown in four years of bottled sadness.

And if it didn't work, we would all die, either by suffocation or the same way my parents had, our bodies ripped to pieces. Another teardrop slid down my cheek. Nadia felt for my hand and opened my fingers, placing a small metal bar inside. I ran my finger along the inscription which I knew said, "In Memory of T. & N. Zolotov."

Nadia threw her arms around me, and then helped me to my feet. "Let their work help you save us."

Jaxon's hand found my shoulder and he ran it down my arm until it reached my elbow. He squeezed my arm gently and his voice came from somewhere exhilaratingly close. "'For of us is required a blind trust, and a hope without assurance, knowing not what lies before us in a little while.' It's from the book you ported. You know I'll follow you anywhere, Aly. So let's go."

He started to let me go, then inhaled sharply. "Wait," he said, and pulled me closer. He ran his hand up my arm. I stopped breathing altogether as he slid his fingers upward along my neck. "That's it," he said.

"What?" I choked out.

"Your batteries."

With the low oxygen in the room and Jaxon's hand on my neck, his words meant nothing to me.

But Kendi gasped. "Batteries, Alyona! That day at the market swap, it was the first thing you bought."

It was my turn to gasp. Jaxon's fingers had found my ears. I brought my hands to his and tapped the back of my hearing aids, checking to make sure the brand-name batteries I'd bought hadn't failed me. I'd never heard such a glorious sound as the scratchy, staticky feedback that proved they had power. If I used both batteries together, they should have enough to jump start our journey.

"Can I take them out?" Jaxon asked.

He felt me nod and pulled the hearing aids from my ears. All the faint noises disappeared, including the incessant, hissing reminder that our air was nearly gone. I allowed myself a slow, shallow breath. It wouldn't be long before the ringing started in my ears—my brain doing its best to make up for the sound it was missing.

I crouched and ran my hands along the floor until I felt the port unit, still plugged in to the wall.

"Kendi! Come here, I need your talons."

Kendi shuffled over. "My what?"

"I'm going to hand you a cord. I need you to slice through the plastic with your nails so I can access the wires."

"Um, no."

"Please. We need—"

"I'm not going to chip my polish when I have a pocketknife with a wire stripper blade in my pocket."

And why wouldn't she carry a knife? I carried lock picks, so someone good with wires could carry wire strippers.

"And," Kendi said, "I'll wire it."

"Yes. Good." Of course she should do it. I was still getting used to relying on others. But she and her unicorn-winning fingers were better at circuitry than I was. If anyone could do this in pitch blackness, it was her.

I held the wire out, groping for her like the undead.

She took the wire. I heard nothing of her task without my hearing aids, but she made quick work of it.

"Batteries," Kendi said.

"Jaxon?" I held my hand out for him, and he found me. He placed the aides in my hand with the metal bar I still held and closed my fingers around them. I resisted a strong urge to cup my other hand around his and keep him from breaking our touch.

I opened the battery doors and tipped them into my hand. "Here," I said, and then felt for Kendi.

Our hands collided, and I squeezed my fist closed, hoping I hadn't dropped them. I placed my hand in her palm and slowly opened my fingers, feeling for the squat, cylindrical batteries with my other hand. *One . . . and two!* I rolled them into her hand.

Kendi probably made some more noises, but the only ones I could hear were a low grunt, and then, "Right, let's try this." Half a minute later, a flicker of precious light cut through the dark. "I got it. I'll hold them in place."

I held my breath. If she were to drop the wires or lose the connection halfway through . . . I cradled the unit in my left hand. "You got it? You're sure?"

"Yeah, I'm good." She *sounded* sure. If she could trust me, I could trust her.

"Okay. Don't let go. Everyone, get close," I said.

Nadia and Jaxon hadn't gone far, and I felt their hands on my arms. I slid my thumb along the rounded corner of the metal bar in my hand and wondered how much gold leaf decorated and, until now, protected the walls of this building. I thought of the dull, tungsten-dusted paint covering the dreary walls of the apartment building where my parents raised me. We would never be trapped between tungsten and gold again. And, between tungsten and gold, I'd take the gold, thank you. And the silver, and the copper. And everything else in the programmed six-foot radius.

"Can we all scoot over a few feet?" I said. "I want to make sure we get the hard drives. Might as well." And, of course, the precious metals. I grabbed Kendi's arm to help her hold the wires in place and penguin-walked the group over toward the stand.

I tapped the screen, and it came ablaze with light and

hope. "Are you sure?" I hesitated, the question directed at myself as much as at my small, but growing family, holding one another in a tight huddle.

Jaxon answered first. "Never a doubt."

Kendi sighed. "Let's move, already. My arm's getting tired."

"It's your choice," Nadia said. "I believe in you."

"Then I choose faith," I said. I leaned into Jaxon, squeezed my eyes shut and pushed *go*.

CHAPTER TWENTY-NINE

Not Out of the Woods Yet

NADIA SCREAMED, AND I whipped my head up, catching her jump for joy as she stumbled out of a snowdrift. We weren't ripped apart. We'd floated and fallen, but instead of landing on the plastic floor of a booth, we took a frigid plunge into three feet of snow. FutureMove-minted bars rained down around us, forming a cratered moonscape in the sparkling snow.

Kendi spun, taking in the surroundings—evergreen woods with no civilization in sight, just a roughly built cabin at the top of the hill. She bent over with her hands on her knees and cried softly, her shining cheeks curved in a bittersweet smile. "It worked. I wish they could have seen—ouch!"

A perfectly round disk of the vault's inner wall about the size of a manhole cover bumped into her leg and slid past, cruising downhill like a sled. Some of the metal bars and most of the stray paperwork slid over the top of the crusty snow with it. A final bar *tink*ed against a large rock and landed in a pile of debris downslope from us, and then the woods fell silent.

I closed my eyes and breathed in the freezing but

abundant mountain air. "We didn't d-die," I stammered, shivering as much from the ordeal I'd put us through as from the cold. "They really did it."

Jaxon had made his way through the snow to my side and pulled me into his arms. He kissed the side of my head and I turned to look at him, hoping he'd repeat the process on my face.

"My faith never wavered," he said, face inches from mine.

I'd barely begun to lean forward when he shoved me backwards. I caught my balance before I fell into the drift, and we both watched Dr. Clarke's heavy, curved monitor slide down the snow between us. *So no face kiss for me, then.*

"Heads up!" I called downhill to Kendi. I dug around and found Atty's satchel, depressingly empty except for my Gooseberry, which it had protected from the snow.

"Thanks for the save, Jax," I said.

"Thanks to you too, of course," he said, smiling and then sticking his nose in the air. "But I'm mad at you for literally and figuratively keeping me in the dark. You told me you had a backup plan, but maybe next time you can let me in on the finer points."

I didn't deserve thanks. We had escaped with our lives, but not much else. "Fair, but you'll be pleased to find out that I'm about to make it up to you right away. I need all of us to help figure out a plan to find that drive. Let's get up to the cabin."

I waded toward the edge of the snowdrift, and a fluffy squirrel hopped onto the rock and picked up a copper piece. "Tater Tot?"

"No way," Kendi called. "That one's bigger. And female."

"And it's stealing our loot," Nadia added.

The squirrel stuffed the small bar into its cheek and bounded uphill.

"At least it was copper, and not gol—oh no, the book!" Jaxon whipped his head around and dived upslope toward a rectangular hole in the snow. He thrust both arms in, pulled out the gilded tome, and gently brushed away a bit of crumbly ice.

Nadia swatted the dirty snow off her nice work slacks, and Kendi, pockets full of FutureMove metals, straightened and faced away from me, scanning the landscape, "Arab oob rot uh, anyway?"

That can't be right. Without batteries, my hearing aids blocked some of the sound I actually heard. "Sorry, what?"

Kendi faced me and enunciated louder. "Where have you brought us?"

"Mikhail Wellson's place, I'm guessing," Jaxon called back to us, using the name Misha had bought the property under.

"A.K.A. Misha Kolodetsky," I said. "A.K.A. N031, A.K.A.—Ah!"

Misha burst out from the cabin's door with a red-brown squirrel perched on one shoulder and a shotgun held steady against the other.

I shouted, ducking and throwing my hands in the air.

He halted and his mouth fell open. Then he spun and tore back into the cabin.

"You found him!" said Kendi. "Good. We need to have some *words*."

A tinge of fear shot through me for whatever Kendi would do to Misha. But I also wanted to know about his role in this. He might be able to help us salvage our situation.

Misha came running back out with a pile of tattered blankets and handed one to Jaxon, then wrapped one around me and passed one to Nadia. He was shorter than I'd pictured, and his hair was lighter brown than it looked in Nadia's photo.

It was strange to see the high cheekbones and oversized glasses in real life.

Kendi pushed through the snow up to where we stood and stared at Misha for what felt like an hour. His glasses looked as if they'd been bent not-quite back into place, and the eyes behind them were in urgent need of soothing drops. The blanket he offered her was as worn as his odd combination of flannel shirt and tracksuit bottoms.

Misha's squirrel, which I could now see was sporting a nylon harness, scurried up Kendi's leg and pushed its nose into the pocket of her joggers.

Kendi relaxed her stance and smiled at the squirrel. "Hey, fellah. Paws off my Ichi Ban Chews." She pulled the overgrown fuzzball off her leg and lifted it to her eye level. "You don't want tummy troubles, now, do you?" She nudged the squirrel up onto Misha's shoulder, accepted the blanket, and wrapped it around her shoulders. "Thank you, Misha."

Misha looked down at the frozen dirt. "It is good to see you."

Kendi wrapped her blanketed arms around him. "It's good to see you, too."

She let him go, and he pushed up his glasses to disguise a quick eye rub.

"Come inside," he said, rounding out the 'o' in his Northern Russian accent.

We followed him into the cabin.

"But how did you find me?"

My stomach grumbled. "I will tell you all of that eventually, but first, I'll give you a solid gold bar for a sandwich. Then, we counsel. We have to get that drive, if it still exists, and if it doesn't, we'll need to—"

"Copper," Kendi said. "He's not a gold-bar-level chef. And you need to slow down. You just revolutionized already-revolutionary technology. Take a minute to enjoy this, girl!"

Misha held the cabin door open and shut it behind us, securing four separate latches on the inside.

I couldn't deny the thrill pulsing through my body at what we'd just accomplished. None of those locks meant a thing, now, at least not to me and my parents' density breakthrough. But I didn't deserve to celebrate. Not yet. It wasn't enough that I was free. I still had to free Kendi, Misha, and Atty from Dr. Clarke's accusations and stop him from threatening Nadia and Jaxon to get to me.

I stepped further into the warm cabin. A creative sales brochure might have called it "open concept with an airy loft." A ladder leaned against a plywood platform, above which plastic paneling made up patches of the roof in pustule mustard, bruise purple, and gaslight blue. Below sat a cluttered desk complete with three monitors, an ergonomic keyboard and mouse, high-backed gaming chair, 3D printer, and a bunch of half-open drawers full of components it would have taken me months to hunt down at underground swap tents.

Jaxon stepped past me to take a closer look at the 3D printer. "I don't even see a bathroom or running water. How are you running all of this?"

Misha pointed through the wall behind the desk. "Solar array and generator out back. Next to outhouse."

I had to admire his priorities. "So it won't be a problem for you to power this?" I held up the port unit. I dug through the satchel and found the Gooseberry remote. "And this? I need them working ASAP." My fingers itched to program a route into Dr. Clarke's office, and then back out here, or somewhere far away from the official booth grid to sort through evidence in peace.

Misha held up a finger before he turned to fetch what I hoped was a secret cache of batteries.

"Impressive," I said when he returned with a brick-sized power bank and a flat phone battery that would work for the Gooseberry. "I can see why you like it out here." I walked over to the area one might call a kitchen. "Just tell me you have something to eat. A good sandwich, maybe, or a hearty stew."

"I have only soup of tomatoes," Misha said, walking to the carpet scrap next to his desk. He started to pull up the corner but glanced back at us, as if deciding whether to trust us with his stash location. He sighed in resignation, then revealed a loose rectangle of sub floor covering a plastic tub full of cans.

He squatted, then retrieved a can of generic tomato soup and tossed it to me.

I stared back at him with my eyebrow up.

He shrugged. "I do not keep all food in one place, of course. What if someone comes to steal? I will survive."

Fair. It couldn't hurt to have a paranoid survivalist on the team.

Misha clicked his tongue as he pulled a jar of cashews out of the tub. The harnessed squirrel hopped over from somewhere above us.

"I see he's not playing dead in the harness anymore," I said.

"Progress, yes. I was attempting to attach accessory for testing when you all fell from sky onto my property. Camera, USB clip, tracking device, anything useful." Misha showed the squirrel the jar of nuts and fished a button-sized video recorder from his pocket. He walked to the pallet table, set down the unopened jar, and tugged the squirrel's harness. The squirrel squirmed and wiggled and reached for the jar. Misha wagged his finger at it and held up the recorder.

"Best of luck," I said as the squirrel flicked its tail. I set the port unit on the rough wooden countertop and rummaged through the mismatched cupboards and drawers for a can opener. Kendi held up a crusty frying pan, shaking her head. Nadia found bread, and cheese in a lighted mini fridge that looked like it had been misappropriated from a FutureMove breakroom.

Jaxon hop-stepped past a low table made from old pallets to the patched couch and bent over, rubbing his ankle. "I think I landed weird on my foot when we got here. It's not feeling so great."

I grimaced, eyes snapping to his ankle. "I'm so sorry, Jax. I should have yelled for everyone to jump."

Nadia handed me what she must have decided was a can opener—a claw-like sickle on a wooden handle with a stirrup-shaped metal brace around the blade. It looked sharp and threatening enough that I could probably hold it near the can and ask it in a calm voice to open, and the can would pop its lid and tell me every secret it's ever heard. I took it with my soup and the port unit to the couch and gently pulled up Jaxon's pant leg. "Nad, if you find any plastic bags, would you mind filling one with snow for Jaxon's ankle?"

Nadia gave a thumbs up.

"A bit of swelling starting, looks like. But it could have been much worse," I said, recalling the smell of rotten jam from his fake severed foot. "Trust me."

"Yeah, maybe," Jaxon said, rolling his pant leg to keep it in place.

"So, guys," I said to the room. I channeled my nervous energy into the so-called can opener and attacked the soup. stabbing the sickle's point into the middle of the lid. I tried to slice a hole into the top, but the stirrup piece got in the way. "Thoughts on our next move?"

Nadia put down her knife and hurried to one of the chairs across from me. "What on earth are you doing to that poor can?"

Misha turned from his squirrel and snickered.

"We had one of these back in Russia, but I guess you were too young." Nadia took the can and the torture instrument. "You relax and help Jaxon. We'll all think more clearly with a break and something in our stomachs."

Maybe *she* could relax, but she hadn't just wasted the best shot at solving everyone's problems with her oversight. I couldn't—wouldn't relax until I fixed my gigantic mistake.

Nadia used the metal stirrup for leverage as she deftly pulled the blade in rocking motions along the rim of the soup. She folded the lid back and handed me the open can. "Careful, it's sharp."

I took a long swig of tepid soup. "Needs salt. But now that I've got something in my stomach, can we start the thinking, please? Make this a working lunch?"

Misha's squirrel wriggled free and skittered back and forth between the kitchen and the back of the couch, the camera dangling from its harness. "I vote yes," Misha said. "The more soon we have plan, the more soon I will have quiet again. You excite the squirrels."

Kendi's purple-tipped coiled hair swayed with her head as she marched toward Misha. "Well then, maybe you can help us instead of hiding in the woods. And your fake summons troll on Aunt Atty doesn't count. You made it clear you wanted something to happen, and now it has. So what's next, Mish?"

I guessed these were some of the words she'd had saved up for Misha. I came to his rescue. "Next, we break into Dr. Clarke's office. I do, that is. No need to involve everyone this time. But how can I be sure he won't be in there?"

Misha frowned and lowered his eyes. "In his office, you will look for what? What, exactly, do you need to bring the justice?"

"There's evidence saved on a hard drive that proves he had something to do with Melanie's accident, and that he conspired with his bosses or some outside force. There were a lot of interesting files I didn't have time to explore."

Jaxon picked up his leg and winced as he eased it over his knee. "Are you sure he took the drive to his office? And that it'll implicate him?"

"And are you sure he didn't chuck it into a trash compactor?" Kendi said.

"I mean, I thought I knew where it was before, and I was painfully mistaken. But I think his office is the most logical place to check next. And it shouldn't be hard with my Port Unit Two-Point-Oh here. Dr. Clarke would have kept a paper trail—something he could use to shift blame away from himself. The drive, along with testimony from Atty, Kendi, and Manuel, and Melanie, if we can reach her, should be plenty to prove his involvement with my parents' accident. Even if it doesn't contain the smoking gun."

Nadia stood and returned to the kitchen area. "He got chatty in the vault. What if we got him to talk, and admit he's been lying about everyone's part in the . . . in this whole mess?" She bent and pulled a plastic bag from the cupboard.

Misha's eyebrows pushed together. "If he admits his guilt, this is best outcome, yes? Maybe his smoking gun is not needed?"

I sat straighter. "Yeah, of course a confession would be great, but how would we make him talk?" I side-eyed the can opener on the table. *Maybe I bring a Soviet tool of persuasion.* I took a sip of soup and shifted my mental direction to a saner path. "Maybe Manuel could put him in Jaxon's old cell, and feed him only broccoli until he confesses?"

"Or Nadia could call him and beg him to explain why he did it," Kendi said. "He might be desperate enough for her to understand him that he'd spill. We could record the call."

Nadia shook her head. "He's too paranoid to say anything incriminating over the phone."

"So that idea's out, because I'm not sending you in person," I said.

"We could send squirrel," Misha offered. "This is what I train him for. Spy, record the secrets, return."

"But we'd still need someone to get him talking," Kendi said.

"Manuel," Nadia said, sliding a cheese sandwich onto a pan on the hot plate. "Dr. Clarke trusts Manny. He's been able to convince Dr. Clarke where his loyalties lie through his actions against us. And he probably has training in gathering intel. He's amazing, you guys; did you know that one time—"

"Nad," I said, "I've become somewhat of a fan of Manuel myself—he's been a huge part of this plan. But right now, we need to focus. And this squirrel idea might have merit," I said.

Misha clicked his tongue and called to the squirrel. "*Ko mne!*" Three squirrels bounced onto Misha's shoulders from who knows where, one still wearing the harness. "My furry friends need a test mission. We send one with message for Manuel, in case that his phone is not safe for communications, and when we hear back, we will know plan will be successful, and squirrels will be reliable. We can hit two rabbits with one shot."

"We say birds here. Two birds with one stone." I'd gotten used to helping The N031 side of Misha with English.

"Ah. But rabbit is more meat, bird is puny—and why with a stone? Very inefficient—"

"Anyway," Kendi said, "I think this could work. I hate the thought of putting the squirrels in danger, but they're amazing at keeping out of reach when they want to."

"This is very true." said Misha, who'd found two more harnesses. He eased a squirrel off his shoulder with one hand and attempted to secure a harness around its squirmy body with the other.

Kendi strode over with her hand out. "Hold on, let me help you!" She took the panicked squirrel in her arms and muttered to it. I couldn't quite catch what she said until she looked up again and addressed Misha. "Does she have a name?"

"That is Shest. She is very stubborn."

Kendi raised an eyebrow. "I know enough Russian to know s*hest* means six. I asked for her name, not her number." Kendi pet its ears, holding it in place, and motioned for Misha to put the harness over its head. "You're going to be called Shasta from now on, you brave girl." Kendi buckled the harness, and Misha attached the camera.

Nadia fiddled with the locks at the door until she had them all open. "I'm getting snow for Jaxon's foot, and then I want to help you name the others." She stepped out, shaking the bag open, and closed the door behind her with a soft thud.

BAM! Something heavy crashed onto the cabin's plastic roof.

Misha dropped flat to the ground. Kendi shouted. I startled mid-sip, splashing tomato soup into my face. *Did Nadia shake snow loose when she left?* I dropped the can onto the table and sprinted to the door.

WHAM! THUD! Several more objects landed on the roof and rolled toward the front of the house.

Nadia burst in as I reached the door, her eyes wide with

terror. "It's raining men!" She caught sight of my dripping face and screamed.

"It's just soup! Get in, hurry!" I would have laughed if there weren't actually men, uniformed, organized, and armed, falling from the sky. Four ETC guards formed a semicircle outside the front door. Two heartbeats later, Dr. Shane Clarke himself strolled into view behind them. Two more guards followed, pulling Manuel between them, bound and gagged.

"Manny!" Nadia cried. She rushed toward the guards.

I lunged for her and caught her shirt. Misha leaped up and helped me pull her back inside. I slammed the door and Misha closed the locks.

Jaxon rolled along the couch and knelt behind it, facing the door.

"Stay low, Jax," I said. "I would hate for you to jack up that ankle any worse than it is. Kendi, SquirrelCam! Misha, shotgun!"

"No firing pin," he said. I assumed that meant it was basically a useless prop.

Kendi was already switching on the two cameras they'd managed to attach to the harnesses. "And you, port unit," she said to me.

Something hard slammed against the outside wall.

"Stay clear from windows!" Misha shouted.

I ran to the couch and picked up the unit and my remote.

Kendi shooed the squirrels up to the rafters and ran to grab the non-working shotgun. Apparently, she had the same thought I did: get out of here, but first, the confession.

Another bang on the wall made me jump. "Everybody get close," I said. "We'll leave as soon as we get anything useful on camera."

Jaxon grunted as he crawled out from behind the couch.

"Oh, Jax, I'm sorry! Everyone, gather to Jaxon."

Nadia didn't move. "I'm not going anywhere without—"

The pointed end of a black metal bar popped through the thin wall next to the front door, and then plywood shards flew into the room as a guard kicked his way in, expanding the new hole. He came inside, unlatched Misha's locks and opened the door for Dr. Clarke and his hostage.

"Manny!" Nadia wailed.

Dr Clarke breathed a heavy sigh. "Friends. I'm tired, and I'm too old to be teleporting onto rickety cabins in the woods. Now, before you ask how I found you, just let me remind you that I did warn you. There's no place you can go that I don't know about. If you can find Mikhael's hovel, you'd better believe I already did. Or maybe you forgot my humble beginnings as a real estate mogul? I know my way around property records."

He paused to look around the room. Nadia stood nearest to him, dripping bag of snow in hand. Jax held the aggressive can opener in front of him. Kendi hefted the shotgun to her shoulder.

"Drop your weapon!" one of the four guards behind Dr. Clarke yelled as they all aimed their drawn pistols at her.

Misha started to rise from his crouch near the desk.

"Freeze!" Two of the guards shifted their aim to him, and he sunk back with his hands up. I glared at Dr. Clarke, red ooze dripping from the corners of my mouth down my chin and neck.

Dr. Clarke grimaced. "Alyona, you might need to get that looked at. And listen, we all need to calm down, there's no need for this hostility. I don't want anyone hurt. I simply need to take some of you in for questioning, and I'll need to recover all stolen FutureMove property."

I wiped my face with the back of my arm and turned to the two guards holding Manuel. I recognized them both: bowl cut and frosted tips, or Gary and Willy. The two Dr. Clarke had sent to Atty's house. He'd chosen the youngest, most malleable of the guards to keep closest and feed his lies to.

Nadia raised her hands to eye level, still holding the bag of melting snow. "I agree, of course. Please, everyone, let's be reasonable. I'm going to set this down in the kitchen basin, if that's okay, Dr. Clarke, and we can talk." I was impressed she was keeping her cool so well. She, like Kendi, was proceeding with the plan to get his confession, and she'd likely keep her distance from me so I wouldn't port us all away without Manuel. We had to get Dr. Clarke to talk, then free Manuel, then get close enough together and far enough from Dr. Clarke and his goons to port away without them.

Nadia took one step toward the kitchen, and one of the guards hollered, "Stop!"

Nadia jerked to a halt and dropped the bag as she lifted her hands above her head.

Manuel spit out his gag and dragged Gary and Willy a step before they regained control. "Kammeyer! Get that pistol out of her face!"

The guard covering Nadia flinched, but his firm stance and regulation buzz cut told me he wasn't as easily intimidated as the newer guys.

"I swear," Manuel growled. "If you hurt her, I will hunt you down."

Willy replaced and tightened Manuel's gag.

"Dr. Clarke, I want to help," Nadia said in a soft, soothing tone. "But it's hard to think with my arms up like this. And why is tying up Manuel necessary? He helped you lock us away."

Dr. Clarke glanced behind him at the four guards not guarding Manuel. "Manuel took things too far. I had him lock you in because you were trying to steal company tech and data, but when he realized what you'd accomplished, he took control of the vault and turned the power off. He would have let you all suffocate in there."

Manuel tried to yell through the gag, and Kendi shouted. "Lies. You're the only one here capable of such calloused—"

Kammeyer holstered his weapon and marched toward Kendi.

"Wait," she yelled, gripping the shotgun tight.

Kammeyer shook his head and grabbed the gun out of her hand. "Next time you want to threaten someone with an antique single-action hammer, try pulling the forend back first."

Kendi huffed in frustration as he checked the shotgun for shells and tossed it aside. I gritted my teeth. Hopefully Dr. Clarke would talk without the threat.

"I tried to warn Alyona," Dr. Clarke said. "People will do anything to get their hands on this technology once they know it works. Manuel is no exception."

Manuel strained against the guards.

"Gary, please keep Manuel restrained. Can I trust you with this or not?"

The newbie guard had probably never carried anything more potent than a taser around FutureMove. He held a service pistol now—Manuel's, judging by his empty holster.

"In fact, why don't you take Manuel outside. We don't need any of you here for this."

"Of course, sir," said Gary, tightening his grip on Manuel's arm as he and Willy pulled him out the front door, followed by the other four guards, leaving the door open.

Nadia watched Manuel disappear from view. "What can we do to resolve this?"

"It's simple, really. I've only ever tried to keep you safe. Give me the stolen port unit, so I can continue doing so."

"It's just . . ." Nadia sighed. "I want to trust you. I'm dying to. You're the closest thing to a parent I have."

Real tears pooled in her eyes. She'd always thought of him as family, so not all of this damsel-in-distress routine was fake. "Dr. Clarke. I know you loved my mother. I know you love me, too. I don't care about the port unit, and I'll give it to you, but please, I need someone to trust, someone to go to when I can't call Mama." The tears spilled down her cheek, and my nose tingled. "Please, help me understand why you would hurt my mother."

Dr. Clarke's stance softened, and his shoulders slumped. He closed his eyes and breathed in through his nose. "Nadia—" he began. He cleared his throat and turned to the guards outside the door. "You four, I think we're covered. Get back and prepare the holding cells. Gary, Willy, make sure Manual is secured, but stay close."

Kammeyer opened a hook-and-loop flap on his utility belt and pulled out a device the size of a hand-held radio. The other three gathered around him and they vanished.

"A portable unit," I said aloud. Maybe an early test model from before the project was shut down, or something Dr. Clarke had his techs put together after they snooped through my settings in our stolen unit? Except this one didn't take anything around them. Either way, it was smart of him to send away extraneous witnesses to whatever he was about to reveal to Nadia.

Dr. Clarke headed for the mismatched chairs at the pallet table.

"Here, let me." Nadia hurried to the chairs and pulled them closer to Dr. Clarke, keeping him away from the rest of us.

"Now, let's put this to rest and discuss where to go from here."

"Smyrna," Misha chirped.

"Pardon?" Dr. Clarke peered across the room.

Jaxon spoke up from behind the couch. "Smyrna, Greece? I don't think Dr. Clarke was literally asking for destinations."

I caught a flash of ruddy brown fur out of the corner of my eye. Not Smyrna, *smirno. Steady.* A command to the squirrels to be on alert. "Ignore them, Dr. Clarke," I said. "We're ready to hear what you have to say."

"Someone, get the girl a washcloth, for goodness sake. I can't talk to you like that."

Kendi poured some water from a jug onto a kitchen rag and tossed it to me. I scrubbed the crusty smear of tomato sauce from my face and arm.

"Now, Alyona, it's important you listen closely, because you never have grasped what this tech you've got in your arms means to the world. The most powerful players on Earth will all want a piece of this if they find out it actually works, and at that level, the lines between legitimate and criminal power structures can blur."

He turned back to Nadia, who wiped her eyes. "My superiors were willing to make sacrifices in order to keep this nation—and the world—secure. That meant stopping the density research, or at least keeping it secret." He leaned forward in his chair. "I'd asked your father to stop. When that failed, I begged him not to run tests, to keep the research theoretical."

Nadia sniffed.

"This will be difficult for you to hear, my dear Nadia, but you deserve to understand the choices I was forced to make. I had an ultimatum, you see. Control the Zolotovs, or someone else would step in. My superiors were ready to secure compliance by any means necessary."

He turned back to me. "They were willing to *kill* Nadia to

keep your father in check. Then they'd hold *you* as leverage once your parents knew they were serious."

Nadia stifled a sob, and I did my best not to react to the burning in my chest.

"I had to . . . I had to save her. I need you to believe me, I never meant for your mom . . ."

Nadia finally lost her long-suffering composure and wailed. She launched out of her chair toward Dr. Clarke and swung her fist at his face, connecting with a soft, unsatisfying slapping sound.

Dr. Clarke grabbed her wrist and pulled down as he stood, pinning her arms to her sides in a bear hug. Kendi jumped in and reached for his arm, but Nadia came to herself and stilled. "No, Kendi, it's okay. I'm just—I just don't know what to think. Please, Dr. Clarke," she said, turning her head to the side resting it on his shoulder, "go on." She closed her eyes and steadied her breathing.

Dr. Clarke reset his expression to neutral and loosened his hold but didn't let go. He stared past Nadia and resumed. "The glitch served two purposes. It stopped Nadia's death by removing the possibility that her father would reveal the density tech to the world. Second, it acted as proof to my superiors that the tech didn't work."

Surely, that was enough for our recording. I couldn't take any more. "So they used threats against your life, or at least Nadia's, to shut you up. Is that where you got the idea to do the same to Kendi and Atty? And Misha, and Melanie? And who, exactly, is *they*?"

Dr. Clarke's tone sharpened. "I saved you, you ungrateful brat. I sacrificed my best friend and the only woman I ever loved for you, and this is how you honor that? I've done everything I can do to protect you, and you're trotting around flaunting the working tech which their deaths served to keep hidden. If word gets out you've uncovered your parents' density research and it works, you'll be locked in a cage for the rest of your days, and they'll keep everyone you love under constant threat to keep you in line."

Dr. Clarke's arms tightened around Nadia as he spoke, and she pushed sideways and ducked, trying to slip through. Dr. Clarke caught her with one arm around the neck, the hug shifting into a chokehold. "It's time to hand it over, girls."

Bile rose in my throat. "Over my dead—"

"Wait," Jaxon said. "Maybe you should just give it to him."

I looked at Jaxon and slammed my mouth shut. His eyes told me to hear him out.

"Whoever his bosses are, they must be dangerous to force him to make such impossible choices," he said. "Maybe he was right to do what he had to do. Give him the unit, and he can get it away from here, take it to Greece, or there's a Smyrna, Texas, too. He can take it to Texas, like Santa Claus."

My eyes let him know I had no idea where this was going.

He tried again. "Sayn-tuh Clauwz," he repeated in a slow, Texan drawl. "Like in the movie."

I gasped. Jaxon and his documentaries. His pick for a Christmas movie last year was a historical reenactment of Texas bank robbers who took hostages but were attacked by an armed mob on their way out. A bandit dressed like Santa demanded some kid give up his car. The kid gave it to him and skedaddled, and the criminals loaded up their loot before they realized the kid had taken the car key with him. They had to leave everything behind and run, but they were all caught or killed.

Genius. Dr. Clarke could have the getaway car, but I'd keep the key.

"Okay, Jaxon's clearly delirious from pain, but I actually agree with him," I said. "Dr. Clarke is on our side. Let's give it to him, and he can keep his superiors happy. I can't let anything happen to anyone else I love. Nadia?" I held up the unit.

"But," Kendi said. "Alyona, are you sure?"

"It's for the best," I said. She narrowed her eyes and nodded at me, granting me trust I still didn't quite deserve.

Nadia pushed against Dr. Clarke's arm to stand straighter, then took the port unit. I programmed the Gooseberry in my pocket while Dr. Clarke's attention followed her.

She held the unit up to Dr. Clarke.

He gave her arm a squeeze with his free hand and nudged the port unit back to her. "You hold on to the unit, and I'll keep you safe with me until we have everyone else in holding cells." He pulled out his phone and used a voice command to send a text to the guards, then looked back at us. "They'll come as soon as they see that you and I have made it back."

I had to get her away from him before he ported them both. I needed an angry mob, quick. "Misha, squirrels. *All* of them."

Misha sprinted out the hole next to his front door and bellowed, "*Ko mne!*"

Dr. Clarke turned and pulled Nadia with him. "William, stop him!" he yelled out the door.

Misha pointed at Willy. "*Vo ataku!*" Through the hole in the wall I could see at least a half dozen squirrels attacking from all angles, nipping and scratching and chittering like mad. Willy dropped his taser, and Misha picked it up.

"*Ko mne!*" Misha stood with his arms out to the side.

Dr. Clarke reached under the back of his suit jacket and tugged a narrow handgun out of a concealed holster. "I really didn't want it to come to this." He strode out the door, Nadia stumbling beside him with her neck still clamped under his other arm. Kendi and I followed.

Manuel turned to Nadia as she tripped over the threshold.

His face turned the color of molten steel, and he tore his arm from Gary's grasp. Gary planted his feet, flicked his hair out of his eyes and raised Manuel's weapon.

"Move!" Manuel shouted at him through the gag, hands still tied behind his back. He gave the young guard a half-second to comply before knocking him out cold with a head-butt to the face. Then Manuel made a break for Nadia. Dr. Clarke trained the sleek gun on him.

Nadia screamed and yanked downwards on Dr. Clarke's arm around her neck, pulling his aim off.

Dr. Clarke tightened his hold on Nadia and shouted. "Everybody freeze, or I shoot Manuel."

Nadia whimpered and everyone stilled.

Silence.

I looked at Manuel, then Misha.

Misha stood before a backdrop of trees, arms outstretched and taser aloft with seven squirrels clinging to his person, like a criminally insane Snow White. "*Davay,*" he growled, ready to take out the huntsman. *Bring it on.*

I looked back at Manuel.

He nodded, and I readied my Gooseberry.

Manuel dived into a forward roll.

"*Vo ataku!*" Misha yelled, pointing at Dr. Clarke and Willy, and then zig-zagged toward the cabin.

Willy ran shrieking away from the attacking squirrels into the trees. Kendi sprinted after him, flinging bars of precious metal at him from her pockets like throwing stars.

Squirrels lunged toward Dr. Clarke, one of them landing on his gun hand.

He jerked and shook his hand, but the squirrel jumped and landed back in place. After three jumps, the squirrel chomped into his flesh. Dr. Clarke dropped the gun, screaming. He swatted the squirrel hard, and it landed a couple meters away in a patch of dirt. Nadia twisted out from under Dr. Clarke's arm and spun to face him.

With a frantic lunge forward, Dr. Clarke yanked the port unit away from Nadia. She scowled, then shifted her feet into a kickboxing stance, and with a "Ha-ya!" arched a powerful, crescent-shaped kick across his jaw before he could port away.

Dr. Clarke flew backward, sprawling onto the cold ground.

I added a final command to my remote.

```
>beta.gps_targeting  --self-carry false
```

Dr. Clarke reached and picked up the port unit from where it had landed next to him and glared at me.

I smirked and hit *go*.

The port unit thudded back onto the ground.

Dr. Clarke was gone.

CHAPTER THIRTY

A Little Squirrely

Nadia caught Manuel in a one-sided hug as he ran up to her, and then she pushed his shoulders around and worked at his bonds until they loosened enough for him to slip his hands free.

"You saved me," Manuel said, scooping Nadia into his arms. "My hero!"

She returned the hug, and I turned away as she went in for a kiss.

Kendi emerged from the trees dragging Willy by the ear—a maneuver she most certainly learned from her aunt. She dropped him when she spotted the limp, furry body on her way to the cabin.

"No," she breathed. She knelt and gathered it into the crook of her arm. "My sweet boy, what happened to you? How did you get here?"

I jogged to her side. "That isn't—"

"It's Tater Tot," she said, voice cracking. "He's alive. Just hurt."

"Misha!" I hollered.

He ran over and gaped at the sad creature. *"Blin, eto*

Chetyre!" He examined the squirrel's limbs and body. "I thought you ran away to squirrel circus. Am glad to see you again." He looked up at Kendi. "Bruised left forelimb. Possible fracture, but I can help him."

Kendi followed him toward the cabin. "Thank you. And he's called Tater Tot, not *Four*."

Twenty minutes later, Tater Tot lay splinted in Kendi's lap, Misha sat at his desk transferring video files to Atty, and Jaxon, Manuel, and Nadia took up most of the couch.

I eased a fresh bag of snow onto Jaxon's ankle.

Nadia pulled off her suede bootie and peeled her sock away. "I might need one of those ice packs, too." Bruising already appeared on the side of her foot where her impressive kick made contact with Dr. Clarke's jaw. I would never make fun of her cardio kickboxing videos again. I chuckled and fetched another bag. We'd started out with one fake foot injury and ended up with three real ones.

"Thanks, Alyona," Manuel said when I handed him the snow. "Are Gary and William still hanging out there rubbing a sore jaw and ear?"

"I made sure they'd heard enough to get their heads on straight and sent them to convince the others not to let Dr. Clarke out."

"Out of where? Where'd you send him?"

"I put him where he thought he could keep us—his vault. We took a piece of the inner wall with us when we left, so there's no seal. Probably still pretty dark in there, but he'll have air."

"Athena would like to speak to everyone now," Misha said, putting his phone on speaker as he walked over. "Okay, we all listen."

"Thank you, Mikhail. Now, first of all, my children," Atty said with a tone I could feel staring me down through the phone. "Explain to me why not *one* of you thought to call me until just now? I have been worried sick."

"Well, ma'am," Jaxon said. "Our phones actually—"

Kendi kicked his good leg and pulled her finger across her neck. "Absolutely right, ma'am, we should have called you."

"Apology accepted. One moment," she said, voice cracking on the last word. A few seconds later, she came back on the line. "I'm just glad you're all safe." She paused to clear her throat. "And now, to business. Nadia?"

"Here," she said.

Misha pointed the phone at her.

"Sweetheart, you did a spectacular job loosing that coward's tongue. We have motive and opportunity, but we're lacking the means. He was careful, even while baring his bereft soul. He never actually admitted to pulling the trigger."

My throat squeezed tight. "You mean it *still* might not be enough?" I croaked.

Atty said something her phone's mic didn't quite catch before addressing us again. "I've got associates coming to help me prepare next steps. My point is to tell you all I love you, and we'll do everything we can to put him away. What we have will be good enough, and once I send this out to my media contacts, it'll be safe to come home."

"Great," I said, forcing optimism into my voice. "I'm not sure Misha has enough blankets." And I could not imagine Nadia pooping outdoors.

"Y'all stay safe, now." She ended the call and Misha returned to his desk chair.

Kendi pet Tater Tot's tail. "I suppose it's up to her now. I hope it *is* good enough. I'm ready to be done with this mess."

I suddenly found it impossible to sit. I pushed away from the couch and paced past the hole in the wall. The room was much colder without warm bodies on both sides of me. I pulled a space heater from under a kitchen shelf and plugged it in while I rehashed the day's events in my mind. "I wish there was something else we could do. I can't stand the uncertainty. I just want to find the final nail for his coffin, you know?"

Jaxon started to stand, and his ankle reminded him that was a bad idea. "You've done more than any human has the right to accomplish in one day. You don't need to do anything besides maybe take a nap and wait to hear back from Atty. Now come back here; you left a cold spot."

No amount of nerves could keep me away from Jaxon's waiting arms. I nestled in next to him, and he rested his head lightly on mine. My heart rate relaxed, but I couldn't let go of the undercurrent of worry. His finger twitching against my arm told me that, despite his soothing words, he couldn't either.

The cabin fell silent, unless Misha's bouncing knee made a sound I couldn't hear. His eyes moved from Jaxon to me, to Kendi, and he stared at the sleepy squirrel in her lap. He looked at war with his thoughts.

Finally, his knee slowed and came to rest, and his expression smoothed. "*Good enough* isn't good enough for you, my friends. I can do better."

"You did awesome," Manuel said. "Your timing with my duck and roll could not have been more perfect. So don't think you need to go and do anything else—we need to lay low until we get the all clear."

"I don't need to go anywhere. I've got the smoking gun right here." He opened his top drawer and reached inside.

Manuel shifted. "Whoa, wait—"

Misha held up a USB drive, and Manuel relaxed.

I raised an eyebrow. "That's a thumb drive, pal."

Misha shook his head. "No. You must listen to me. Dr. Clarke gave it to me, and told me it was ETC safety measure, no need to bother Zolotovy about this. They wouldn't like ETC interference. I didn't trust the way teleportation worked, with the waving through of all my atoms. So I was happy to make safer the experiment."

Kendi stood up. "What are you saying, Misha?"

Misha sank into his gaming chair and clamped his eyes shut. "I didn't verify; we didn't have time before the test. Like good little worker, I uploaded settings." He fought to keep his voice steady. "It is all my fault."

Nadia leaned forward. "Misha, you can't—"

"I tried to find proof he gave this to me, but the settings were cleared after the test. The logs were sanitized. I couldn't share without implicating myself. Then Melanie began searching for last person to enter changes, and Dr. Clarke turned against us, and I ran."

Misha rolled the drive between his palms like he was praying to the gods of technology to protect him. "I don't ask forgiveness, but I hope this will help." He tossed the drive to me.

Kendi slowly transferred Tater Tot to Nadia's lap and then stood and crossed the room to Misha. She spun his chair around to face her. "Stand up."

Misha stood a head taller than her, eyes to the patchwork floor.

"Look at me," Kendi said.

Misha looked.

Kendi balled her fist, reared back and decked him in the nose. Misha crashed back into his chair, and Kendi said between her teeth, "That's for Melanie, and for being a coward."

Misha rubbed his face. "I deserve more. I am sorry."

Kendi nodded. "I know. But that'll do. You can stop wallowing now and help us."

Misha faced the wall and wiped his eyes.

I was tempted to take a swing at Misha myself for keeping something like this back until now. Or at N031, for hiding behind three monitors in a remote cabin while we looked for answers with our boots on the ground. But I'd hidden the truth about my plan from my closest friends and family, and they'd given me their forgiveness, and their trust.

I picked up Atty's once-lovely satchel and walked over to squat in front of Misha's chair. I didn't make him look at me. "We could not have brought Dr. Clarke into custody without you. I know my parents would be proud. They wouldn't blame you, so it's disrespectful to them for you to blame yourself."

His lip quivered. He pulled his glasses off and rubbed the lenses with his scrubby shirt and steadied his breathing.

"And you can do more to bring them justice, if you're willing."

"What can I do?"

"You can testify in court, if it comes to that. You'll have to sacrifice your anonymity, but you can publicize what Dr. Clarke told you. Tell everyone exactly what happened. You'll be okay. And if you're not, there's no prison that can hold any of us if we stick together and trust one another." It was more than a cute metaphor—we could literally pass through walls. And it would take all of us to figure out even part of what that meant for our future and for the future of the world.

Misha looked up at me after a long moment and nodded. "Okay. I will testify." One tear escaped from under his glasses. I reached past him and plugged in his USB drive. He started another transfer to Atty.

I reached into the satchel. "And here, Atty and I have a present for you."

"Okay?"

Misha waited as I pulled out a battered envelope.

I handed it to him, grabbed his phone, and snapped a photo. I'd forgiven him, but he could still make me some spending money. "Or, for Michael Wells, at least. You've been served."

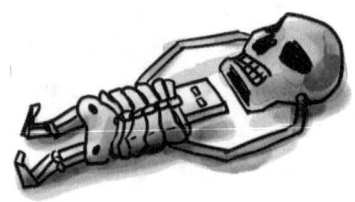

CHAPTER THIRTY-ONE

A Few Footnotes

THE FOLLOWING DAY AT Atty's house was as chaotic as a cabin full of attack squirrels. We recounted our experiences for police reports, detective questions, and a few media interviews. Of course, we'd all agreed to keep the small detail concerning the density breakthrough to ourselves and had to come up with a plausible story to explain our escape. We stuck as close to the truth as possible, saying we'd used a tool we found in the vault to punch through the inner wall for air. From there, we reasoned, we'd been able to manipulate the door from inside the wall and free ourselves.

Law enforcement kept our phones for processing, but Atty bought us cheap prepaids and registered them to us so we'd be able to keep in contact.

Jaxon limped into the loveseat next to me. I pulled his leg onto my lap and massaged his upper calf through his soft athletic joggers.

He pulled up his news feed. "Check it out," he said, facing his phone to me, and then tilting it in Kendi's direction.

Kendi leaned over and read part of the top story. "Blah blah ... okay, 'According to sources close to the case, the

CEO's charges may soon include murder of former partners, lead scientists Nikolai and Tatiana Zolotov, with possible ties to the mutilation and disappearance of Melanie Moreno, a FutureMove theoretical physicist. Clarke is being held without bond on multiple secondary charges, including kidnapping and attempted murder, and has declined comment.'"

"I guess news travels fast when you go straight to the media," I said.

Kendi sat on the couch and sighed. "It's a start."

Manuel held two plates of buttered toast and cut fruit. "I'm relieved they haven't reported on the new porting capabilities," he said. "There will be no escaping attention if anyone finds out. We would never be safe." He shook his head and carried the plates out the sliding side door.

We'd need to be careful to keep the knowledge contained. Once the legal detangling of the whole thing with the shares and power over the company was complete, and I turned eighteen, Nadia and I could assign a think tank to come up with ways to counteract or limit the ultimate freedom of movement my altered port unit provided. Until we found a way to temper its power, we had to keep it hidden.

Atty looked up from the kitchen computer. She'd recruited several lawyer-type friends to the high-profile case, and they'd been on and off video conference calls building their arguments. "Whoever wanted that technology to stay a secret before certainly wants to keep it secret now. Shane may have gone rogue in the end, but my team believes he was telling the truth—at least about having direction from a powerful source."

"Manuel mentioned a boss on the less corrupt and self-serving side. Maybe he can help," I said.

"We'll talk to him, absolutely. But—Oh! Barbara, come here. Sorry, Kendi, if you prefer."

Kendi beamed and came to look at Atty's monitor.

"Look! Word must have reached Melanie. She sent me a very brief email."

Kendi gasped. "She's all right?"

Atty leaned to the side so Kendi could see.

"'Congratulations. Glad you're all safe, I am too. Can't chat yet, I'm in deep. Tell Kendi I'll be a bionic woman once my stub heals. I need her to get my necklace charm now that she has access to the FutureMove building. Love you all, will update soon.'" She'd attached a picture of a prosthetic hand, sleek and state-of-the-art.

Kendi's eyes ran back over the words a few times.

"Aaaah!" Nadia let out a squeal from outside that made me regret replacing my batteries. "Everybody, get out here to the yard!"

I helped Jaxon up. The security officer stationed out front jogged through the side yard past the screen door toward the screaming out back. I didn't recognize her; Gary must have taken some time off.

Atty stopped the guard and waved her away. "Never you mind," she said. "Get back out front and keep watch."

Jax and I rounded the corner from the side yard into the back and saw Manuel, shoulder-length wavy hair freed from its bun, and his security jacket traded for a suit coat. Admittedly, I could see the appeal, but I preferred whatever unruly, grown-out crew cut Jaxon had going on.

Manuel held both of Nadia's hands in his own and his knee began to bend.

"Wait!" Nadia yelled in our direction. "Who is recording this?"

I pulled out my temporary phone, started a video, and held it up for her to see.

Nadia turned back to Manuel, who tugged a tiny black box out of his pocket and lifted the hinged lid. I pushed forward to get a good shot of the ring. Nadia would kill me if I missed it. The greenish stone in the center encircled by small diamonds must have been alexandrite. It was her favorite, with the way it changed from blue-green when outside to pinky purple in indoor lighting.

When Nadia had finished screaming, and the security officer had once again come to check out the ruckus and been sent back to her post out front, Manuel spoke.

"Nadia, like this precious gem, I've seen you change and blossom over these past months. You adapt depending on where you find yourself and the duties you take on. But every single facet shines with a beauty I can't begin to describe. I love every single side I've seen, and I want to ask you to take on one more role: my forever partner. I can't imagine life without the light and color you bring into it."

Manuel settled on his knee and gazed at my sister. "Nadia Nikolayevna Zolotova, will you marry me?"

More screaming. I winced, but I didn't blame her. Manuel had really pulled it off. It didn't even come across as cheesy. If I had tried to say any of that, I would have been internet meme fodder for sure.

I cleared my throat of the lump forming there and pretended to be distracted by Tater Tot hopping back and forth between the limbs above the happy couple so I wouldn't leak any tears. It worked for a minute. Nadia cried her acceptance, and Manuel lifted her into a bear hug and twirled her around like a princess at a ball.

Nadia rested both arms around his shoulders, and he held her gently around the waist. They kissed, no wandering hands or sucky slug stuff, just a promise that Nadia wouldn't have to keep taking everything on herself. They'd make a good coupling, like when a bead of molten solder jumps into the gap between two heated wires, melding both together to make something stronger. And I was an adult now, or close enough. Mama Nadia could finally retire, and I'd get Team Siblings back, new and expanded. She deserved a partner who could complete her circuit.

I didn't say any of that, of course.

I said, "Gross, let's get out of here," and I tugged Jaxon back toward the house. He half-smiled at me. He'd seen the eye wetness I hadn't been able to contain sneaking down my cheeks. I guess I was an almost-adult *and* a crier now.

I turned back to my sister. "I'm kidding, you two are the cutest. Congrats, guys."

Jaxon winced as I pulled him forward to join our group hug.

"Is your ankle still hurting that much?" I asked him.

"The ankle's actually a lot better, but the pain has moved down into my foot. I kinda wish I could chop the thing off for a while."

I stared at him and crossed my arms. I wanted to slap him, and I wanted to kiss his ridiculous mouth. "Too soon, Jax. Too soon."

"What? I wouldn't want it gone forever—I was joking. Were you planning on removing it later?"

I wouldn't have been opposed to removing things later, but not feet. It occurred to me that I'd never told him what the ASF, aka my current companions, had led me to believe about his foot. He had no idea.

"No foot removal, promise," I said. "But maybe better socks and more supportive shoes would help."

"Yeah, I thought it was odd I had to remove my shoes *and* my socks before porting. I guess they were too amazing to give back."

Amazingly covered in moldy jam. "Actually," I said, "you stay right here. I'm taking you on a field trip."

Jax raised an eyebrow. "Oh, really?"

"Don't worry, we'll be safe. You trust me, right?"

"Always have, always will," he said.

I ran inside and picked up the teleporter, and after making some GPS calculations, I programmed in our destination with my remote.

"Tell me you're finally taking us to the beach," Jaxon said.

I tapped the leg with his hurt foot and told him to land on his good side, in case we came in high. "We'll save the beach for when you're healed," I said. "For now, this will have to tide us over." I giggled at my own pun and pushed *go*.

We landed in a large gift and souvenir shop between two racks, and I kicked one of them over as we came down.

A store associate came jogging over. "Are you alright? You scared me, I didn't see you come in."

Thank the maker.

"Yeah," Jaxon said. "We're good. Sorry for the mess, we'll pick it up." He motioned to his wrapped ankle and took the blame.

The associate pulled her radio off her belt loop. "I'll call someone to—"

"No, no," I said. "It's fine. We came to shop for these anyway, this is perfect."

"If you're sure," the store lady said as she walked back over to the registers.

The floor before us was spread with a dizzying assortment of novelty socks. I'd found the shop during one of my market swaps, and it boasted a whole section of the quirkiest, tackiest foot covers I'd ever seen.

I helped him to the floor where he could sit and sort through his terrible options. He explored several pairs covered with the obligatory pickles, bacon, tacos, and cats. I also spied a set that resembled an eel eating your leg, and some where the toes sported actors' faces from popular movies. I'd never pry him away from this hoard.

He looked up from the assortment piled over his legs. "They're so beautiful, Aly. How did you ever find this place?"

"Happy birthday, Jax." It still wasn't. "I'm rolling in dough from the summons I served to Misha, which I couldn't have done without you. So go wild. Get two, even *three* pairs." We sat side-by-side, where the store lady couldn't watch or listen to our conversation. "Thank you for trusting me. I've been holding out for a special occasion to bring you here."

"Well, you messed that one up. Should have come the day you saved our lives. Today is Nadia and Manuel's big day." Jaxon held a purple Denver Mustangs ankle sock in one hand and picked up an orange Colorado Apex knee sock in the other.

"The day's not over yet," I said. I followed my urge to rest my hand on his leg. The nerves in my arm shouted excited pulses up to my brain, as if celebrating my bravery. "We can still make it special for us, too."

Jaxon's hands froze, and he stared at the socks unblinking, as if he were a sock factory shift leader inspecting the seam work.

"Unless you're too enraptured by the sports-ball socks." I turned ninety degrees toward him, took his arms in my hands, and shook the socks loose. I wasn't sure what to do next with his forearms. When we were younger, I would have flopped his hand into his face and told him to quit hitting himself. I knew what I wanted to have happen instead, but not by manipulating his limbs like a weird puppet master.

Jaxon came back to his senses, slowly looking up from the space where the socks had been. I loosened my grip on his arms. He slid one arm around my back and touched his hand to the side of my face. He held it there, testing the waters, daring me to tip our friendship into the well we'd been filling together. I leaned in, dancing along the precipice, when he moved his hand. He wiped between my eyes, laughing as he showed me the makeup on his thumb.

The disguise. I'd fallen asleep without a shower last night and forgotten all about it. "Oh my gosh, do I still look like an old lady?" My cheeks flushed.

He leaned in to inspect my burning face. "Most of it's gone, there are just a couple of lines here and there. You've looked a little bit angry all day."

I swallowed my mortification and kept my face close to his, not budging a millimeter.

He dabbed gently at the makeup between my eyebrows and then let his thumb slide down my cheek, the pressure easing to feather-light at my chin.

Goosebumps spread from my neck down my arms. He'd said he would follow me anywhere, but I wanted him to take the lead on this one. We'd defeated Dr. Clarke, and we had a long road ahead of us. It had to be his choice to walk it with me. I watched his lips and leaned closer, then met his eyes.

He dived in, pressing his full lips to mine, pushing his hand into my hair and pulling me in tight. My entire body tingled, and flashing light having nothing to do with the port unit danced beneath my closed eyelids.

The pins and needles intensified as his mouth moved against mine, teleporting me somewhere I didn't know I could go, but never wanted to leave. He pulled away before I lost myself completely and his eyes searched mine. I hoped he found what he wanted. I had.

I heard footsteps coming our way—probably the store lady coming to check on us. I pulled a silver bar out of my pocket and set it on a low shelf next to me without breaking eye contact. I estimated it was more than enough to pay for the several pairs of random socks I gathered onto my lap, and I scooted us away from the shelving so it wouldn't be caught in the port radius. I scooped the teleporter onto my legs while Jaxon's deep brown eyes drew near again.

"Hey, you two, that's enough—" the store lady started before moving into view.

Wrong. I'd never get enough of Jaxon, and I wouldn't let her ruin this. I tapped the port unit screen with practiced motions. I closed the distance between my lips and his and pushed *go*.

END

Acknowledgements

Before I knew how this book would end, I knew my first acknowledgement would recognize Kara Reynolds. Her writing sparked my curiosity, and she took me to the Storymakers writing conference in 2017. Jennifer Nielsen spoke about finding our climbing team on the multi-summit mountain of our writing journey, and Ally Condie taught us to forge our paths with boldness and heart. Kara's been my pathfinder through every peak and valley, even when I bury her in text avalanches of stream-of-consciousness overthink. When I'm feeling less-than-bold, she sends the best GIFs and hands me my climbing gear. Kara, this couldn't have happened without your powerful influence for good in my life.

Thanks to the hundreds of people contributing endless hours at Storymakers and LTUE, These phenomenal conferences are hosted by beautiful creative communities where I'm honored to have volunteered and presented over the years. I won my first edit for this manuscript in the Storymakers first chapter contest from the brilliant Laura Baumgarten, whose insights elevated my story and my craft to the next level.

I'm rich with inspiration and support from friends inside and outside writing circles, and I wish I could name them all. If you're a friend or writing colleague who has encouraged or humored me in writing endeavors, I'm talking to you. You helped me finally realize what I want to be when I grow up. I sincerely thank you for every listening ear and every kind word.

The Missing Link Writers Group has been party to the untimely demise of more than a few darlings for over a decade. Figurative murder aside, I couldn't ask for a more uplifting squad. Thank you to current participants Kara, Elisa, Brandon, Em, Jacob, Kasey, Leisha, Rusty, Kim, Sara, and Jessica, and to all past participants!

Thanks to my book club, cleverly named "Book Club," and the wonderful ladies therein, whose warm reception of another manuscript convinced me to keep writing, and who tolerate me when I prattle on about all things writerly.

Thank you to my parents, who taught by example that the pursuit of creative whims is like drinking water—unspectacular, inherent, and life-giving. Thanks to my brother Jordan and the other two-thirds of the sister trifecta, Kasey and Kimberlee. It's easy to take family for granted, but I want you to know that I appreciate you deeply and love you fiercely. Also, I was born first, so I'll always have been your fan for longer than you've been mine. So there.

Reader, yes, it's cliche, but I thank you for spending time with my characters and story. You just made my dreams come true. And if you're still here, you'll be glad to know I have only two more shoutouts to make.

Splinter Press. I accumulated plenty of letters saying, "great writing, but...." After so many buts, seeing four faces over a video call chatting excitedly about my manuscript was a peak moment in my life. Thank you for not being "buts" and taking a chance on me. I truly believe this novel found its perfect home, and you made it gleam like burnished gold, inside and out.

Finally, I'll attempt to convey the depth of my gratitude for my husband. John Skipper is not only my hacking Subject Matter Expert and tech advisor for this project, but he is first to celebrate my wins and swear vengeance for my losses. No one puts up with more of my ridiculous nonsense than he, yet he continues to insist that I follow my passions. Skipper, you're the Jaxon to my Alyona, the Manny to my Nadia, the Misha to my scurry of half-trained attack squirrels. My ground zero, my refuge, and my endless love, I thank you.

TARYN SKIPPER studied languages, philosophy, and international relations, but she didn't know what she wanted to be when she grew up until she wrote her first manuscript. Taryn writes and illustrates for children and adults and enjoys teaching and volunteering at writing events. Her publications include picture books, poetry, and short stories. When she's not working on indoor projects, she loves to hike the Colorado mountains with her family.

www.ingramcontent.com/pod-product-compliance
Lightning Source LLC
LaVergne TN
LVHW040037080526
838202LV00045B/3374